Crew Chief

KEITH MYERS

ISBN: 1496145550
ISBN-13: 978-1496145550

Special Thanks

TI, TM, MA, CL, JH, FM, LT & the Secretary of the Air Force
Office of Public Affairs National Media Engagement

Foreword

THE BASE

It's the summer of 1989. Located a few miles southeast of the city of Dover is Dover Air Force Base. The base is one of a handful of bases in the Air Force's Military Airlift Command and is home to the 436th Military Airlift Wing. Dover Air Force Base's primary mission is to provide the strategic airlift of cargo and passengers in support of operations around the world. The base is home to 38 massive C-5A and B model cargo aircraft and is the major C-5 base on the east coast.

Every year, thousands of people drive past the base and never realize it's there. They are on their way to and from the beach or just driving the coastal route between Philadelphia and Norfolk, Virginia. They might see the base or signs leading to it and never really give it a second thought. The majority of the structures on the base are large aircraft hangars, warehouses and dorms. They are light blue, tan, or grey in color and are all dull, flat and faded. There are hardly any trees on the base. It truly has the look and feel of an industrial complex. Hidden on the other side of all those aircraft hangars, warehouses and dorms is the flightline.

THE FLIGHTLINE

Dover's flightline is a mile and a half long and 750 feet wide. It has 25 C-5 parking spots on it. The parking spots or rows are in a straight line paralleling the hangars. They are labeled using the military phonetic alphabet system and run from E through Z, AA, BB and CC. A large grassy area between Whiskey row and X-Ray row disrupts the huge expanse of concrete and asphalt that makes up flightline. Due to their weight, all the planes are parked on 200 by 180 square feet concrete pads. From X-Ray row to Charlie-Charlie row the entire flightline is concrete.

The planes face the hangars and are parked wingtip to wingtip with about 25 feet clearance in between each plane. Behind and in front of the parking spots are two asphalt taxiways. The planes enter the parking spots from the back taxiway and leave through the front. There are many connecting yellow taxi lines painted on the flightline. The taxi lines guide the planes up and down the front and back taxiways and on and off the parking spots.

Between the flightline and the hangars is a long wall constructed with three-foot-tall Jersey barriers. The wall runs the length of the flightline. There are openings or entry control points in the wall where people and vehicles can enter and exit the flightline. The first entry control point is by Lima row next to the wash rack hanger. The second is at Whiskey row and the third is down by Zebra row. At each entry control point is a cop shack. A cop shack is a small booth about four times bigger than a phone booth. They are there so the security police that guard the flightline can get out of any inclement weather. The wall also has six other large openings so planes can be moved on and off the flightline and parked in and around the hangars. These opening are blocked with large orange metal anti vehicle barriers.

On the hangar side of the wall there is a two lane service road that runs the distance of the wall. At night the flightline is well lit from large stadium style lights that are on top of 100-foot metal poles. The light poles sit between the service road and the hangars. There is a light pole every 300 feet and they run the length of the flightline. They are needed because Dover's flightline never sleeps.

THE OPERATIONS TEMPO

Operations on Dover's flightline go on 24 hours a day-7 days a week-365 days a year. Words like holiday and weekend are never used on the flightline. There is not a time on the clock that people look forward to. There is no light at the end of the tunnel. Weather doesn't even halt operations. Snow, rain, hot and cold do not matter. There is one exception though, and that is lightning. If there is lightning within five miles people are ordered to cease operations and seek shelter but more often than not they stay on the planes to keep operations moving.

The base's 38 C-5s come and go on a regular basis. Additionally, there are another 85 C-5s that belong to other bases. These planes constantly stop at the base for any number of reasons. They may need to refuel, pick up or drop off cargo or have urgent maintenance issues that must be taken care of. The planes often stay for at least 24 hours to give the aircrews time to rest.

The C-5s on Dover's flightline are constantly on the move. They are shuffled on and off the flightline for many different reasons such as washes, fuel cell maintenance, special inspections, refurbishment and cannibalization. It never ends because FRED, the plane's nickname, is always in demand.

THE PLANE

The C-5 is the United States Air Force's largest aircraft and one of the largest aircraft in the world. It measures 247 feet long and has a wing span of 222 feet. The tail reaches to a height of 65 feet. It's slightly bigger than a Boeing 747 Jumbo Jet. The top of the fuselage stands as tall as a three story building and its tail reaches to the sixth floor.

The first thing that makes the C-5 unique is the ability of its landing gear to kneel thus lowering the aircraft. The second thing that makes it unique is that the nose or visor of the aircraft opens. Kneeling makes the loading and unloading of the aircraft much easier and the forward and aft ramps allow the aircraft to be loaded simultaneously from either end. Both ramps have two configurations, drive-in and truck bed. In the drive-in mode the ramp rests on the ground and allows vehicles and equipment to be driven on and off the aircraft. In truck bed the ramp becomes a loading dock where palletized cargo can be on and off loaded. A roller and rail system is built into the cargo compartment floor as well as both ramps. The floor can be configured to accommodate any type of cargo. The cargo compartment is 13.5 feet tall and 19 feet wide. If you include the loading space on both ramps the cargo compartment floor is 143 feet long.

The C-5 also has an upper deck with two separate sections. This is where the crew and passengers stay while the aircraft is flying. The primary entrance to the forward part of the upper deck is the flight station ladder. It's located in the front of the cargo compartment. The flight station ladder leads into the large and roomy flight deck. The flight deck consists of the pilot's and copilot's positions up front. There is a vast array of instruments and components in front of them. There is also a center console and an overhead center panel with numerous components and switches on them. Behind the pilot and copilot seats is an instructor pilot seat. It is on a track and can be slid side to side and positioned where it's needed. On the left side of the flight deck is the navigator's station. It consists of a deep table and a seat. There are a few instruments at this position that still work but the aircraft does not require a navigator. Modern technology has made the navigator's role nonexistent. On the right side of the flight deck is the engineer's station. It has a small table and two seats. The second seat is considered the scanner's seat. The engineer's station has an overwhelming assortment of instruments, gages, components and switches.

Behind the flight deck is a narrow hallway that leads to the crew rest area. As you walk back there are two bunk rooms on the left. Each room has three beds in it. On the right side of the hallway there are two rooms or avionics bays that house the plane avionics, communication and autopilot equipment. At the end of the hallway is the crew rest area.

On the right side of the crew rest area is the crew chief table. There are four airline style seats, two each facing each other at the table. Crew chiefs work from this table and it is also used as the plane's dining room table. On the left side of the aisle is an additional three airline style seats. Further back on the left side is a latrine. It's two or three times as large as a latrine on a commercial airliner. Behind it and still on the left is the galley. It is equipped with a small refrigerator, oven and a coffee maker. Just behind the galley the area opens up and forms the courier compartment. This area has eight additional airline style seats and extra storage areas.

The aft part of the upper deck is called the troop compartment. The troop compartment is accessed primarily by using a ladder which is located in the back of the cargo compartment. The troop compartment is spacious and has 75 airline style seats. Two of the seats are for crew members and the other 73 are for passengers. In the very back of the troop compartment is a galley. It's twice the size of the crew's galley. In the forward section of the troop compartment there are two latrines. These latrines are slightly larger than a commercial airliner's latrines. The C-5's ability and size is something to behold.

THE TRUTH

With such a big plane there must inherently be big problems. FRED is an acronym that stands for Fucking Ridiculous Economic Disaster. To put it lightly, the C-5 is a maintenance nightmare. Seventy seven C-5A models were built between 1966 and 1970. Additionally, there was 50 C-5B models built between 1983 and 1987. The B models had a hand full of upgrades but for the most part they were built with 1960s era technology.

Think about it. There are five separate landing gears with 28 tires. Each landing gear not only retracts and extends but also kneels. Also there are large and numerous flight control surfaces such as flaps, slats, ailerons, spoilers, rudders, and elevators that maneuver the plane inflight. In addition, there are forward and aft loading complexes with their ramps, ramp extension, cargo doors and visor. There are four enormous engines that in total produce over 160,000 pounds of thrust. There are two auxiliary power units. The plane has 12 fuel tanks that hold 51,000 gallons of fuel. There is a liquid nitrogen system that is used to inert fuel tanks. It is also used for fighting fires. There are four independent 3,000 psi hydraulic systems. Two oxygen converters hold 100 liters of liquid oxygen for emergencies. There are miles of wires that snake throughout the plane. There are a vast amount of autopilot computers, flight instruments, navigational aids, and communication devices on the plane. All of these systems have emergency backups and overrides. Also, the C-5 is littered with warning lights, gages and switches. The amount of sheet metal and rubber seals alone is staggering. What could possibly go wrong? The answer…everything!

THE CREW CHIEF

The people who take on the daunting task of maintaining these aircraft and keeping them flying are crew chiefs. Not only are crew chiefs responsible for fixing the planes, they also manage and coordinate all the maintenance on the C-5s at Dover Air Force Base. They are a jack of all trades and the master of the C-5. Crew chiefs are one of the hardest working people in the Air Force and their job is one of the most challenging of any career field.

Not only are C-5 crew chiefs expected to know their own job extremely well, they are expected to know and perform maintenance in nine other career fields; engines, hydraulics, electronics, communications, navigation, autopilot, instruments, fuels and sheet metal.

To keep the planes flying and accomplish their mission crew chiefs work around the clock and are often on 12 hour shifts. A crew chief's uniform is always covered in fuel, oil and hydraulic fluid. Their knuckles are busted and their hands are greasy. They deal with power hungry, overzealous leaders above them and angry wives and girlfriends at home. They put up with less than eager flight crew personnel and pampered specialists. Crew chiefs are foulmouthed, forward thinking, multitasking innovators. Their office is the plane and their job is on the flightline.

C-5 crew chiefs are a tough group of maintainers that have been hardened by the plane, the overwhelming work load and the sometimes brutal elements. Their dedication is second to none. Their spouse will leave them, they'll lose their home or their car and still show up to work on time and bust their ass. The death of a family member takes a crew chief away but soon after the funeral they are right back to work. Sacrifice is a word that fits crew chiefs well. Dover's C-5 crew chiefs are a rare breed.

THE BOOK

Crew Chief was originally written as a movie screenplay. The story takes place between July 1989 and June 1990. During this time frame thousands of C-5s were launched and recovered and tens of thousands of maintenance actions were completed or managed by crew chiefs. Two major operations Dover C-5s supported during this time were the invasion of Panama and Hurricane Hugo disaster relief. A crew chief's job, the flightline and the overall mission of the Air Force is a very serious matter.

This book is intended to give you a unique glimpse into the lighter and funnier side of a handful of Dover's C-5 crew chiefs. Crew chiefs work hard but they also have a reputation for playing and partying hard. They like to have fun. Nothing gets by them. Everything and everybody is fair game. Remember the movie Stripes starring Bill Murray? In the movie there was a scene where they were all sitting around introducing themselves to each other and telling a little something about themselves. Then it came around to Bill Murray he said, "Chicks dig me, because I rarely wear underwear and when I do it's usually something unusual. But now I know why I have always lost women to guys like you. I mean, it's not just the uniform. It's the stories that you tell. So much fun and imagination." This book tells many such stories. It shows the wild and at times unbelievable side of a group of C-5 crew chiefs both on and off duty.

CREW CHIEF

CHAPTER 1

----------March 1987----------

Kyle Mansfield is a senior airman and is twenty-seven years old. He entered the Air Force at the age of twenty-four which is considered late. He is a proud flightline crew chief. He started his career on grave shift. This was a blessing in disguise as he was able to learn his job twice as fast as he would have on any other shift. He read a lot of technical manuals and listened to the experienced people around him. Kyle loves the mission and fixing planes, but he also likes playing jokes on the other guys at work. He despises the politics of day shift and has little patience for those who have taken advantage of the system. Kyle always changes into his coveralls at work because of the amount of oil, hydraulic fluid and grease he gets on him.

Kyle's father was in the Air Force, which enabled Kyle to move around the world to different locations throughout his life. He is fun loving and always looking for adventure. He loves women, especially tall, thin model types and is always in search for "the one". Even though he came into the military from a small town in Alabama, he craves the big city life. His favorite place is New York City. He goes up as often as his budget will allow. Kyle is a very good athlete. He plays every sport and is often one of the best players on the team.

Kyle is six weeks into his first training course at Sheppard Air Force Base in Wichita Falls, Texas. The course is called Aircraft Maintenance Specialist for Airlift Aircraft. It's a seven-week course that gives an individual basic knowledge of maintenance procedures on aircraft. He's very excited! He's about to complete the first hurdle in becoming a crew chief and has received orders to Dover Air Force Base in Dover, Delaware. Travel arrangements have been made and Kyle can't wait to get to his first assignment. He'll fly from Dallas to Philadelphia and take a limousine from Philadelphia to Dover. When the travel agent told him this, he couldn't believe it - a limo! For the entire next week Kyle has been on a high. He is going to be chauffeured to his new assignment in the back of a limousine.

Kyle wanted to know more about his new assignment, so he went to the library to see where Dover, Delaware was located. He knew it was in the northeast, but wanted to know exactly where it was. Kyle found an atlas, grabbed it off the shelf and flipped it open to a map of the United States. There it is - Dover, Delaware - just as he imagined. It's a city in the northeast and the capital of Delaware. Dover is surrounded by Washington D.C., Baltimore, and Philadelphia, and not far from New York City. Kyle slides the atlas back on the shelf. Now he is even more excited.

A long week passes and Kyle finally graduates. He thought the day would never arrive. He returns to his room and packs his bags. He is all set. All Kyle needs to do is go to sleep and the next morning he will be off. He decides to check and make sure his reservations are still on. Kyle doesn't want anything to go wrong. He grabs some change, his travel itinerary and walks out to the pay phone in the hallway. He calls the reservations line. The woman on the other end of the phone is nice. Kyle gives her his reservation number and she is more than willing to assist him. A slight pause has Kyle worried for a second, but then she locates the reservation. She informs him that everything was still a go. Kyle follows his itinerary as she reads through it. Dallas to Philadelphia departs at this time, arrives at this time and then J&G Limousine service from Philadelphia to Dover.

The airline information was pretty straightforward. Kyle has flown many times in his life. The limousine service information was not as clear. Kyle has never been in a limo before. He'd seen them on television and in the movies. Did it work like that? Will there be a man in a black suit and a hat holding a sign with my name on it? He didn't want to ask because he wouldn't sound very worldly, but he had to know.

Kyle asked, "Ma'am, the limo, how do I find it?"

She replies very politely and the last part of what she said was in slow motion. Well, at least that is the way Kyle heard it.

She said, "Grab your bags, head out to the curb and look for the lime…green…van."

Kyle was devastated. His first class limousine service in reality was just a coach-class shuttle van. He quickly pulls himself together, thanked the woman and hangs up. All was not lost.

The next day Kyle arrives in Philadelphia. His excitement is still there. He retrieves his bags from baggage claim and heads outside. The airport is busy. There are a lot of people coming and going. Kyle looks to the left, and then to the right. He sees a sign about fifty yards away that says "Shuttle Service Pick Up." He starts walking towards it. He can see the skyline of Philadelphia in the distance. Kyle stops at the sign and waits a few minutes with several other people. He looks over at the skyline. He can't wait to get to Dover. He turns back just as the lime green J&G van pulls up. His limo has arrived. Kyle and five other people help the driver load their bags in the back of the van and then they all pile in. Kyle is the last one in the van. He's sitting in the first row of seats on the right side of the van. The van pulls off. In a little over an hour Kyle will be in Dover!

Sometime during the drive Kyle falls asleep. The driver hits the brakes a little hard and changes in the van's momentum. It wakes up Kyle. It's dark outside now. Kyle looks around at the other people in the van and they are all asleep.

He leans up between the seats and ask the driver, "Where are we?"

"We are on the outskirts of Dover," said the driver.

Kyle starts to come alive again. He's almost there. His head is on a swivel. He's taking in everything around him as the van starts passing through traffic lights.

As streetlights start to appear, Kyle asks the driver, "What is that over there?"

He replies, "The Dover Mall."

Kyle thinks to himself, "If that's a large mall, the city must be close!"

Kyle search from side to side for the city's skyline, but he can't find it. He leans up again and asks the driver, "Where is the city?"

The driver points forward and off to the right, "It's over there."

Kyle continues to look off to the right as the van passes through even more traffic lights. There are a lot of single story restaurants and businesses on both sides of the highway. He can't find the skyline. Ahead, the highway splits and the van veer off to the left. The sign above says "Highway 113 South, Dover A.F.B., Milford and Beaches." The van stops at the intersection as the traffic light turns red.

Once again Kyle leans up and asks the driver, "Where is the city?"

He turns and points back off Kyle's right shoulder. "Do you see that small white tower just above the tree line that looks like a church steeple? That's the capital building. It's right in the middle of the city."

Kyle is in shock. He sits back and doesn't know what to think. This can't be true. He's in the Northeast, in the capital city of a state, and the tallest thing in sight is a church steeple? The traffic light turns green and they continue down the highway.

The further the van goes down the highway, the more infrequent the traffic lights become, and the streetlights become nonexistent. It appears that the van is heading out into the country.

Kyle thinks to himself, "What's next? My limousine turned into a lime green van and my big Northeastern city has only one six-story building that is barely taller than the trees."

The excitement Kyle had a week ago was almost completely gone.

The driver turns back towards Kyle and gets his attention. He points out in front of the van and off to the left. "There it is - Dover Air Force Base."

Kyle leans forward and looks out the front windshield. In the distance, he can't make out anything on the base except for the tails of the planes that are lit up by large stadium style lights.

CHAPTER 2

----------July 1989----------

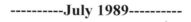

Fast forward two years. It's just after midnight on the flightline. It's a warm summer's night. There is a lot of activity on the front taxiway. Vehicles are constantly on the move like they are at any civilian airport. They are all following the yellow centerline on the front taxiway as if it's the centerline of a highway. Some are turning on and off the flightline and others are turning to park in front of the planes. All are following the yellow taxi lines that enter and exit all the parking spots.

The normal flightline noises are heard in the distance with power units running, a plane with its engines at idle and an APU running. The never-ending chatter between crew chiefs, the Maintenance Operations Control Center, or MOCC, and truck drivers can be heard on the radio. The team of Kyle, Buckner and Boner are waiting for Joker row for C-5 9027 to land off of its mission.

Bo Buckner is a buck sergeant in his mid-20's. Bo is somewhat of a Vermont redneck. He starts most of his sentences with the word "chief". He always has a dip in his mouth and is constantly spitting tobacco juice on the ground or in a cup. Bo hardly ever wears his uniform to work and is always in green coveralls. Bo is a great worker, but he never follows the book. He has a shortcut to every task on the plane. He likes to play cards, mostly hearts or spades. He has a little green book to keep his card game stats in, kind of like the NASCAR points system. He loves

Dale Earnhardt. He is married and in financial debt. He is always coming to Kyle and proposing different schemes.

Sam "Boner" Canterbury is an airman first class and is in his early 20's. He is from Connecticut. Boner is a smart ass. Whatever he thinks comes right out of his mouth. He has no filter. He is good at finding people's weaknesses and picking on them. Boner dips tobacco and smokes cigarettes.

Kyle and Buckner both have on faded olive green coveralls and white reflective belts to make them more visible at night. They are both wearing black steel-toed boots. They both have a pencil and a red pen sticking out of their left breast pocket. Crew chiefs are never without their writing utensils. They are needed to fill in the aircraft forms.

Kyle and Buckner are standing next to a neon green fire bottle at the front corner of an empty aircraft parking spot. A fire bottle is a large, 150-pound fire extinguisher mounted on a frame. It has two wheels and a tow ring so they can be moved from spot to spot. There is a fire bottle at the wingtip of every plane and one at the nose. Fire bottles also serve as message boards, guest registers and painter's canvases. Crew chiefs are constantly writing and drawing on top of them. They put down their innermost thoughts and feelings. They'll use the fire bottles to showcase their artistic abilities, or to simply say they were there.

There is a plane on both sides of the empty spot that Kyle and Boner are standing at. Boner can be seen in the distance out by the wall, smoking a cigarette. He has on his uniform. There is no smoking in the vicinity of the planes, so the rule is you have to be at least at, or beyond, the centerline of the front taxiway. Some people will stand at the line and smoke, but most choose to walk the extra 150 feet so they can sit on the Jersey barrier wall that separates the flightline from a service road.

On the ground next to Kyle and Buckner is a red toolbox, a marshalling kit, two backpacks and a helmet bag. There is also a thin, black, rubber engine mat used for engine inspections. It is rolled up and secured with bungee cord and has a "remove before flight" streamer tethered to the corner. Along with the mat is a white bunny suit, which is a pair of coveralls with no pockets. It is always worn when entering the engine inlet for inspections or maintenance. Ten feet away from the guys are eight, 24-inch yellow, wooden, aircraft chocks. The chocks are divided into two stacks of four. The chocks are worn and the ropes are dirty and frayed from the weather and all the various liquids that have seeped from the plane or spilled from various support vehicles. Twenty five feet behind them is a power unit. A power unit is large, mobile generator on four wheels. It supplies external electrical power to the planes when they are parked.

As Kyle and Buckner talk, various support vehicles start to pull up and park out by the wall in front of Joker row. The maintenance debrief truck has also arrived on the scene. Boner is walking back from the wall. Kyle is stretching as if he is getting ready to play in a game of basketball.

Buckner pulls out a can of Copenhagen, pops it against his thumb, and takes a dip. "Chief-chief, what do you want to do tonight?"

"Knock this bitch out before it starts raining," said Kyle. "It's supposed to be in good shape."

Buckner sticks the can back in his pocket. "Ok, I'll take the outside. You debrief and get the inside and we'll stick Boner with checking engine oil and inspecting the I's and E's."

I's and E's are the engine's inlet and exhaust areas.

Boner walks up beside Kyle and Buckner. "Did I hear my name?"

"Yea," said Kyle. "You have oil and I's and E's."

Boner tries to protests. "What the fuck! Who decided that?"

Buckner spits. "Son, shut the hell up and put that mangy bunny suit on."

"We voted and you lost," Kyle said. "So man up and quit your crying."

Boner knows he is stuck with the job. "You guys are dicks. I didn't even get a say in this."

"Chief, next time, speak up when we are trying to figure this stuff out," said Buckner.

Kyle starts snickering. "I picked out the nicest bunny suit CTK had. It was the best one on the shelf."

The Consolidated Tool Kit, or CTK, is where crew chiefs sign out tools and equipment. It is located inside the same building where roll call is held, building 585.

Kyle continues to stretch as Buckner moves and stands beside him. Even though Kyle is consumed in the conversation, Buckner constantly taps Kyle on the arm as if he isn't paying attention. Buckner spits regularly as they talk and laugh amongst themselves.

The plane, whose engines have been idling, revs up and starts coming down the front taxiway to their right. At first the plane cannot be seen, only heard. Kyle reaches in his helmet bag, pulls out his black headsets and puts them on his head. They are a communication type headset use for interphone and radio transmissions on the plane. The other guys do the same. The plane appears and passes in front of the guys. They all pause for a moment and watch it go by. They are not in awe of the plane. They've seen hundreds go by every year. Though they'll never admit it, they are proud that their shift has launched another plane. They are also scanning for things that might be wrong; leaks, a dragging tire or a loose panel. If they spot something, the plane can be stopped before it takes off.

The plane passes out of sight on its way to takeoff. All the guys take their headsets off and hang them on the fire bottle. Boner takes his uniform top off and lays it on top of his backpack. He picks up the nasty bunny suit and holds it up. The bunny suit is filthy and covered in grease and oil. The arms and legs of the bunt suit are frayed from constant use. Boner starts putting on the bunny suit as the expediter truck, Sierra 6, approaches.

There are four main expediter trucks or step vans that directly support the crew chiefs on the flightline. They are Sierra 6, 7, 8 and 9. Sierra 6 and 7 are considered the "Blue side", and Sierra 8 and 9 are the "Red side". The trucks are the expediter's office. They live, eat, drink and conduct the bulk of their work in them. There are always papers and food wrappers on the dash, cans or cups in the center console, backpacks and helmet bags on the floor and a clipboard lying around. During day shift and swing shift, all the trucks are used to support people working for each of the four sections. On grave shift, only two trucks are used, Sierra 6 and 8.

The Sierra 6 truck pulls up. Rob "Hangar Nose" Heidelmann is driving the truck and Aaron, his team member, is riding shotgun. Aaron is laid back in the seat with his right foot on the dash. He is dipping tobacco and is spitting it into an empty Coke can. No one else is in the truck.

Rob "Hangar Nose" Heidelmann is a technical sergeant and is in his early 30's. He just started the job as the grave shift expediter, or Sierra 6 driver. Rob has a big nose, thus the name "Hangar Nose". Rob never seems to have money or cigarettes on him, even though he out ranks most of the guys. Rob tries to do a good job but most people don't take him seriously. One reason is because Rob likes to joke around as much as the next guy and will screw off at any chance he gets.

Aaron Leake is a senior airman in his early 20's. Aaron is from North Carolina and seems to always have a dip in his mouth. He also smokes now and then. He is Rob Heidelmann's sidekick and gopher on grave shift. He is always in the truck with Rob and is a bit on the lazy side. Aaron's humor is very sarcastic and he always tries to keep a straight face no matter what is going on.

As the truck pulls up, Rob tries to get the truck mirror close enough to just miss the fire bottle tow ring. He misses badly and the mirror slams against the fire bottle, folding the mirror in, but not breaking it. Rob has an "oh shit" look on his face and everyone else is laughing. Kyle, Buckner and Boner step to the window of the truck. Kyle grabs the mirror and pulls it back in place.

"Chief, that's how Earnhardt brings her into the pits, four tires, gas, in and out," said Buckner.

Kyle looks in the truck at the center console. Sitting there are two, large white styrofoam cups of coffee. It's obvious that Rob and Aaron have made a coffee run to the passenger terminal.

"I see how it is Rob," said Kyle. "Your first week in the truck and you make a coffee run and don't ask anyone if they want something."

"I know driving this truck is way over your head. So why didn't your bitch over there coordinate that for you?" asked Boner.

Aaron can't help but notice Boner has on a bunny suit. "Nice bunny suit! It sucks to be you right now assholes."

Boner ignores Aaron's comment and stays on Rob. "Rob, did you say something?"

Kyle joins in. "I thought I heard Aaron, but it was kind of muffled."

Kyle moves Buckner and Boner back a little with his arm, steps over and opens the door of the truck. He grabs Rob by the arm. "Rob, get up! Is Aaron stuck up your ass again? He might need some fresh air."

They all laugh.

"Aaron, you should have been out here earlier," said Buckner. "You could have smoked out at the wall with Boner and kept him company."

Aaron takes his foot off the dash and turns. "I'm trying to quit smoking cigarettes."

Kyle jumps right on Aaron's comment. "What are you switching over to, smoking dicks?"

Aaron gives Kyle a mean look and spits in his can.

Boner is still focused on Rob. "Rob, what are you doing driving the truck anyway? You fucked up on that DOPP inspection and let that engine thrust reverser panel blow off on takeoff."

"Anyone could have missed that," said Kyle. "The panel is only 3' x 6' and has 150 screws holding it on."

They all laugh. It was determined after the incident that the panel only had four of its 150 screws installed.

"Yea, I kind of did a Stevie Wonder DOPP that night," said Rob.

Buckner spits and wipes his lower lip with his hand. "Chief, you fuck up and you move up. That's the way it is."

A radio call comes in to Sierra 6 from MOCC. With all distractions around them, everyone hears it. They are always tuned into the radio for their call sign or aircraft tail number. Everybody leans in and listens.

"Sierra 6 and 9027, MOCC."

Rob answers the radio. "Go ahead MOCC, this is Sierra 6."

"Your inbound is a few minutes out. It's Alpha-2 for minors."

"Sierra 6 copies. I'm here on the spot with the crew. I'll let them know."

"You faggots will probably take all night on this," said Aaron.

Buckner, who isn't a big fan of Aaron, responds. "Keep it up and I'll break your scrawny ass in half."

Rob points over to the power unit. "Hook me up to the power unit. I'll pull it in for you guys when the plane gets on the spot."

Boner takes a last shot at Rob. "Are you sure you can do that for us? You don't need to run back to the terminal for breakfast, do you?"

Everyone steps away from the truck and Boner kicks the door closed. Rob puts the truck in reverse, cuts the wheel to the left and starts backing up towards the power unit. Kyle walks over to the power unit and kicks off the brake with his right foot. He grabs the power unit's tow bar with his right hand and releases the brake with his right foot. Kyle lowers the tow bar to give Rob something to aim for. Rob has turned in his seat and is looking out the back doors of the truck. He has a good view of the power unit, the tow bar and Kyle. Kyle is guiding him back with his left hand. As Rob gets closer he slows a little, but not enough. He slams the truck's pintle hook or tow hitch into the tow bar. Bam! The power unit is knocked back a few inches. Kyle has to act quickly. He jumps back to avoid getting hit by the rear bumper of the truck.

"Whooooah!" yelled Kyle.

Rob hits the breaks and stops the truck just after the impact. The tow bar is jammed in the pintle hook and will not close. Kyle stands on the tow bar. His weight forces the power unit backwards and the tow bar ring slides into the pintle hook. Kyle closes the pintle hook and inserts the cotter pin. Kyle looks up towards the front of the truck through the cargo net where Rob and Aaron are sitting. They are both looking back at Kyle and smiling like kids. Kyle ignores them and walks from between the truck and the power unit. He hits the side of the truck twice with his right hand to let Rob know he is clear. Rob, with the power unit in tow, pulls away and heads out towards the wall.

Kyle walks over to the fire bottle where the marshalling vest and wands are lying out on the ground. The marshalling vest is orange in color and slips on over your head, secured by two straps around your waist. The wands are basic grey flashlights, with eight-inch translucent cones attached to them. Kyle puts the vest on and picks up two wands. He tests them to see if they work and turns them off again. He puts a wand in each front pocket. Buckner and Boner also have a set of wands. Kyle grabs his headset and starts walking towards the front of the parking spot. Boner, with the engine mat slung over his shoulder, heads to the other side of the parking spot.

Kyle is standing on the centerline of the forward taxiway. He is facing the empty parking spot. Buckner is still next to fire bottle off to Kyle's left. Off to Kyle's right, Boner can be seen pulling a B-2 stand out of the way and over to the next parking spot. There is also a B-5 stand next to Boner.

A B-2 and a B-5 stand are large maintenance platforms. Both stands are used quite frequently on C-5s.

There are a lot of support vehicles waiting on the plane to arrive. They all have their lights off and flashers on. Kyle puts his headsets on properly and pulls the wands out of his pockets. The plane can be seen coming down the back taxiway to Kyle's right. Kyle turns on his wands but one does not come on. He puts the good wand in his front pocket and bangs the bad wand against the palm of his hand. It comes on. He pulls the other wand out of his pocket. He straightens his arms and holds the wands above his head so the pilot can see him.

The plane emerges. The engines are very noisy and the plane has all its landing, taxi and navigation lights on. It's an overwhelming mixture of size, noise and lights. Kyle starts to marshal the plane. He is supposed to be standing at attention and making crisp movements. Instead, he is standing nonchalantly, with his arms are lower than they should be and most of his movements are with his wrists.

All of a sudden the plane's landing and taxi light turn off.

Kyle says to himself, "Thanks."

Kyle, Buckner and Boner marshal the plane onto the spot. The plane stops suddenly and rocks back and forth. Kyle drops his wands to his side and then raises his right one to signal the pilot that he is finished. Kyle turns his wands off and starts to walk towards Buckner. All the vehicles that have gathered for the plane's arrival hold their ground.

On the forward left side of the plane the crew entry door opens and the ladder slides down. The flight engineer comes down the ladder. He has the scanners interphone cord in his left hand and uses his right hand to hold the rail. The flying crew chief positions the excess scanners cord over the rail of the ladder and throws down two grounding wires. The engineer scans the area and the plane. He calls upstairs and lets the pilot know that it is clear to shut down the engines. The engines shut down...number four, three, two, and then one. As each engine shuts down, it dumps excess fuel from the bottom of the engine cowling. It's blown backward by the fan exhaust. Now, the plane's APUs becomes the dominant noise.

Buckner drags both sets of chocks to the right aft main landing gear. He positions four of the chocks under the tires and heads around the back of the plane to the number three main landing gear to position the remaining four chocks. Boner is on the left side of the plane. He is underneath the B-5 stand pushing it towards the number one engine. With his vest still on and his wands in his front pockets, Kyle pushes the fire bottle in towards the front of the plane. He positions it 15 feet directly in front of the nose. As he walks over to the right side of the plane he looks back to make sure Buckner has finished chocking the tires on the left side.

The Sierra 6 truck, which is the only vehicle that has moved away from the wall, pulls the power unit to the right side of the plane. Kyle marshals him in and lines up the power unit on its designated spot. Kyle is thinking about getting Rob back for slamming the truck into the power unit's tow bar. Normally, Kyle's first step would be to unhook the truck from the power unit. Instead, he walks past the back bumper to the left side of the power unit and starts it. The exhaust from the power unit shoots into the back of the Sierra 6 truck. Rob is stuck because the power unit is still attached. Kyle revs up the power unit from idle to on speed, which pumps even more exhaust into the truck. Buckner pulls the long cord off the power unit and hooks it to the plane. Kyle walks to the back bumper of the truck, unhooks the tow bar and looks up at Rob and Aaron. The truck is full of the smelly diesel exhaust. Rob and Aaron have pulled their t-shirts over their noses and are looking back for Kyle to give them the sign that it's ok to pull away. Kyle is laughing as he gives them a thumbs-up. Rob and Aaron turn around and the Sierra 6 truck pulls away.

Kyle walks up to the fire bottle at the nose of the plane. He pulls the wands out of his front pockets, turns them on and signals to everyone in the trucks that it is clear to come to the plane. All the vehicles that have been waiting start moving slowly toward the plane. They pull in, one by one, into the designated parking areas in front of the plane.

Kyle and Buckner walk back over to where their tools and bags are. They gather the marshaling equipment and put it away. They grab the toolbox, their bags and walk back over to the plane and set everything under the nose. Buckner takes off and starts his inspection as Kyle heads for the debrief truck.

Kyle takes the strap off the door and steps into the back of the debrief truck. The debrief truck is the same style truck as Sierra 6. In the back of the truck is a large picnic table with attached benches on each side. This is the debriefer's desk. The truck is much cleaner than the Sierra 6 truck because it's only used to debrief aircrews. The debriefer, who is in his full uniform, is already sitting at the table on the right side of the truck. He is filling out some papers.

"What's up man?" asked Kyle.

Kyle slides into the picnic bench. He sits on the left side of the truck across from the debriefer.

"Not much," said the debriefer. "I want to get this knocked out. It's my last plane of the night."

"Yea, Alpha-2 should be a piece of cake." said Kyle.

The debriefer stops writing. "Nice game tonight. I can't believe the catcher dropped the ball."

Kyle chuckles. "In team sports there's always a weak link, and in softball the weak link is always put at catcher."

"That was a hell of a throw. Where did you get that arm?" asked the debriefer.

Kyle holds his right arm up and looks at it. "I signed it out from the armory."

They both laugh.

"Thanks," said Kyle. "I dabbled a bit in baseball but nothing ever came of it."

Another person entering the truck interrupts the two. It's the FCC Duncan. Kyle's expression changes from jovial to serious. Kyle stares at Duncan and gives him a dirty look.

Rudy Duncan is a buck sergeant and in his mid-20's. Rudy's main objective in life is himself. He is a terrible mechanic but a great ass kisser. He gets out of work all the time by constantly having appointments or going to school. Kyle and most of the other crew chiefs on the flightline despise Duncan. No one respects Duncan but it doesn't seem to bother him at all.

Duncan is in a flight suit. The flight suit has a patch on each shoulder and one on each side of the chest. There is an additional patch above his nametag. It's the Military Airlift Command Flying Crew Chief patch. FCC stands for flying crew chief. One flying crew chief is sent out with the plane every time it goes on a mission. Duncan is carrying the aircraft forms, which are in a medium blue plastic binder. He is also carrying some papers, his helmet bag. Duncan sits down next to the debriefer. He sets his helmet bag on the bench next to him and puts the aircraft forms and the papers on the table. The debriefer takes the papers. Kyle reaches over and slides the forms across the table and starts reviewing them...flipping through the pages. Kyle looks at his watch to check the date.

"How's the plane look?" asked the debriefer.

Duncan gives a less than convincing answer. "Ok, I guess…"

"What is your man number?" asked Kyle.

"02421," said Duncan.

Kyle continues to flip through the forms reading each discrepancy carefully. The deeper Kyle gets into the forms the more emphasis he puts on turning the pages. Finally, Kyle looks up and pushes the forms a few inches out in front of him. He exhales deeply. "How many days were you out?"

"Five or six," said Duncan.

"I don't see your name or man number anywhere in these forms. What the fuck did you do all trip?" asked Kyle.

Duncan has a stunned look on his face. He doesn't have a good answer. Kyle flips back to the front of the forms to the 781H.

The 781H form is used to track and record inspections, exceptional releases, flight times, takeoffs and landings and all servicing information.

Kyle points at the forms. "Here are two H's and your name isn't on either of them for the servicing or the inspections. And the pre-flight runs out in two hours."

Duncan is clueless. "Really, I didn't know that."

Kyle responds sarcastically. "Well, what the fuck do you know?"

Kyle flips the forms to the 781A's and starts looking through them again.

The 781A forms are where crew chiefs record maintenance discrepancies. Each 781A has three blocks for discrepancies. The longer the plane stays on its mission the more discrepancies it gathers. Planes usually return home with 20 or 30 pages of 781As. It's not unusual to see a set of forms with over 50 pages of 781As. Now and then a plane will return with over 100 pages of 781As.

Kyle stops at the last page of the 781As. "Look at this shit. Where are the symbols and the work unit codes?"

Duncan plays dumb. "What? I didn't know the crew put those write-ups in there. The crew should have put symbols and work unit codes in there."

"No dumb ass, that's your job. What, did you just wake up?" asked Kyle.

Buckner sticks his head in the truck. He sees Duncan and gives him a dirty look. He then looks at Kyle. "Chief, what type of inspection are we looking at?"

"Take a guess, pre-flight," said Kyle.

Buckner spits on the ground. "Call for the tire trailer and a tire change kit. 2A1 and 4C2 tires are worn slap out."

"Got it," said Kyle.

Buckner leaves after giving Duncan another dirty look.

Kyle sits back in disbelief. "I don't understand why they let you fly. The forms are a God damn mess and you don't have a fucking clue about what is going on."

Duncan tries to defend himself. "I busted my ass all trip. I can't be on the jet 24 hours a day. I have to get my crew rest. I know what the regulations say."

Kyle fires back! "Crew rest! Regulations! You need crew rest for exactly what? Did you have to help the pilot fly the plane? You are a God damn crew chief! You don't get crew rest! And as far as regulations go, quit hiding behind them! As a matter of fact, take those regulations and stick them up your ass. You know the only thing keeping me from kicking your ass right now is this uniform!"

Two aircrew members entering the truck save Duncan from more of Kyle's tongue lashing. One is a captain and the other is an enlisted flight engineer. They are also in flight suits, but have different patches that reflect their squadron. They remain standing.

"How was your trip, captain?" asked the debriefer.

"Not bad," said the captain. "Ramstein and Incirlik maintenance kept us going."

Ramstein Air Base is located in Germany, and Incirlik Air Base is located in Turkey.

The debriefer slides a paper across the table to the captain. "Sir, can you sign here please."

The captain signs the paper. "Do you guys have any questions for us?"

Kyle has gone through the forms several times. There are no real mysteries. "No captain. I've figured everything out. Everything is pretty cut and dry."

"Thanks guys," said the captain. "Have a good night!"

The captain exits the truck.

The engineer turns towards Duncan. "Your shit is on the ground by the ladder."

The flight engineer exits the truck. Kyle turns 180° in his seat and looks out the side window of the truck. At the foot of the crew entry door ladder sets luggage, two cases of beer and a large rug wrapped in tan paper. In the background, the B-5 stand that Boner is using is at number two engine. Boner has come down the ladder and is walking towards the truck. Kyle turns back at Duncan.
"Busting you ass huh?" said Kyle. "Looks like you had a rough time shopping."

Duncan doesn't respond and sits quietly. He knows that saying anything else will only inflame Kyle.

Kyle lets Duncan have it! "Duncan, you are fucked, these forms are fucked and I'm guessing the plane is fucked!"

Boner comes to the door of the truck and sticks his head in. "I just serviced 18 quarts of oil in number one and number two engines. How many hours did this thing fly?"

"I guess I was right," said Kyle.

Kyle flips the forms to latest 781H and finds the most recent oil servicing information for the engines. He answers Boner. "The last leg was a six hours flight from Lajes. Prior to that flight, it flew five hours from Ramstein. The last time the oil was serviced was in Ramstein by a T. Polk, 00108."

Kyle turns back to Duncan. "It says here you checked the oil in Lajes with zeros across the board and 36 for totals."

"Yea, I checked it in Lajes," said Duncan. "They all had oil in them."

Boner lives up to his name. "Did you use the dip stick, dip shit?"

Duncan is squirming like a criminal in an interrogation room. "No, I usually just look down in there and if I can see oil, I call it good."

Kyle gives Duncan both barrels. "What the fuck! Are you serious? How stupid are you?"

Boner adds a parting thought. "Your daddy should have pulled out."

"You want me to fix these forms?" asked the debriefer.

Kyle shuts the forms and picks them up. He slides to the end of the bench and stands up. "No brother, I'll do it. It's my job. Thanks for offering."

Boner steps back as Kyle exits the truck with the forms. Duncan and the debriefer work their way out of the picnic bench and stand up.

"Hey, will you give me a hand with my stuff?" asked Duncan.

The debriefer climbs back in between the two front seats and sitting down in the driver's seat. "No, get your own shit."

Twenty minutes later Kyle is standing in front of the plane at the fire bottle. Lightning can be seen in the distance. Kyle is holding the forms and the radio. Most of the vehicles have departed from in front of the plane. The Sierra 6 truck pulls in and parks. Kyle walks around the back of the truck to the side door. He unhooks the strap and enters the truck. He pulls the butt can out from between the two front seats and sits on it. Rob is in the truck by himself.

"How's she look?" asked Rob.

Kyle hands Rob the debrief sheet. On it is all the discrepancies and the plane's vitals, which is the servicing data.

"I'd say AFU!" said Kyle.

AFU stands for all fucked up.

"Alpha-2 my ass!" said Kyle. "Duncan didn't even know what was in the forms. Who does that guys blow to be able to keep flying?"

"They love him up top," said Rob. "All he does is volunteers for shit and go to school."

"What about his job?" asked Kyle.

"I guess that doesn't matter to them," said Rob. "He looks good on paper."

Rob looks at the debrief sheet that Kyle handed him. Rob can't believe what he is seeing. "Holy crap!"

Kyle agrees. "Yea right! More like Alpha-3…broke dick."

Rob starts transferring the information from the debrief sheet to his clipboard.

Kyle starts talking on the radio. "Sierra 18, 9027."

Sierra 18 is a small bobtail truck. It's a beefed up, modified Jeep that is used to tow stands, powered and non-powered Aerospace Ground Equipment, or AGE.

Sierra 18 answers Kyle. "Go ahead."

"Yea, can you bring me the tire trailer and a nitrogen cart?" asked Kyle.

Sierra 18 answers again. "Got it."

"Can you drop it on the right side?" asked Kyle.

"No problem," said Sierra 18.

Kyle calls over the radio again. "Sierra 19, 9027."

The Sierra 19 truck is a mobile parts truck and the middleman for ordering major aircraft parts from supply. The truck is constantly on the run, picking up and deliver all the parts ordered on the flightline.

Sierra 19 answers. "Go ahead 9027."

"Can you stop by?"

"What spot?"

"Joker."

Rob stops writing. "You know, after I heard Alpha-2, I put this plane on the flying schedule for tomorrow."

"What time," asked Kyle?

"It has a 10 a.m. takeoff."

"Thanks!" said Kyle.

Rob smiles. "That's what friends are for. Can you make it? Give me a good WAG?"

WAG stands for wild ass guess.

Kyle thinks about it for a few seconds. "Yea, we can make it. Set the ETIC for six a.m. and drop me an extra body out here in a few hours."

Rob is relieved that he made the right call. "You are the best. I'll bring Aaron out in a bit to give you guys a hand."

Kyle laughs. "Yea, he's probably tired of being up your ass all night. A change of scenery might be good for him."

Kyle stands up and slides the butt can back between the seats with his foot. Kyle exits the truck. He hooks the strap back across the door on the way out. He starts walking towards the plane as Sierra 6 pulls away.

It's now one o'clock in the morning. Kyle, Buckner and Boner start to fix and service the plane. Not only do they repair their own jobs, they also help the specialists that come to the plane to repair their discrepancies. A 431XX crew chief has his hands on everything that happens on the plane. Kyle, Buckner and Boner are all over the place. They are up and down the ladder, in the cargo compartment and up inside the plane's tail. They move AGE equipment to the plane, use it and move it back out of the area. They are up and down stands, opening and closing engine cowlings and removing and reinstalling various panels. They roll new tires in, change them and roll the old tires back to the tire trailer. They refuel, LOX and put liquid nitrogen on the plane. They inspect, clean and take care of minor jobs as they move along. They go nonstop for four hours.

It's five-thirty in the morning. The power unit on 90027 is running and is just about the only noise on the flightline. All the other powered and non-powered AGE equipment has been pushed out on both sides of the plane. The lightning that was seen earlier appears to have moved closer. Activity on the flightline has slowed because of the approaching storm.

Kyle, Buckner and Boner have spent the last four hours fixing and servicing the plane. Aaron came upstairs a little while before. They are all sitting at the crew chief table. Kyle is in the forward seat closest to the aisle and Aaron is sitting next to him. Boner is across from Kyle and Buckner is next to him. Boner and Aaron are in their uniforms and Kyle and Buckner are still in their coveralls. They are playing the card game Spades. There are two small white paper spit cups on the table. The radio and the WUC manual are also sitting on the table over by the small window. Aaron is keeping score on a folded piece of paper. Kyle has the aircraft forms on his lap and is writing in them. Boner is shuffling the cards. They have the lights slightly dimmed. All their bags are sitting over on the three-man seat on the other side of the aisle.

"Chief, I have to get a second job," said Buckner. "I have bills out the ass and I'm not getting ahead."

"Doesn't your wife work?" asked Kyle.

Buckner picks up a cup and spits in it. "Yea, but it's still not enough. Car payments, kids and credit cards are killing us."

Kyle looks up from the forms. "Good luck with that. What are you thinking about doing?"

Buckner gets a little excited. "Chief, did you see Men at Work? We could be garbage men. Imagine the stuff we could find and how fun it would be riding on the back of that truck. Let do it!"

Kyle isn't so enthusiastic about Buckner's idea. "I'm not sure being a garbage man in Dover is quite a glamorous as it looks in the movies, and how did I get involved in this?"

Boner laughs. "Yea, I can see you doing that. You'd make a bigger mess spitting dip and sunflower seeds all over the streets. You'd be fired in a week."

"I have to figure out something," said Buckner. "The old lady is on my neck every day."

Kyle passes the forms across the table to Buckner so he can sign off a red X discrepancy. "Bo, catch that X and the forms will be good."

Aaron spits in one of the cups. "You all are taking this ass whooping pretty well."

"What's the score again Aaron?" asked Kyle.

"468 to 401."

Buckner finishes signing the forms and slides them back to Kyle. "That's because you two are sand bagging. Look at those overbooks."

Kyle closes the forms and tosses them across the aisle onto the three-man seat. "All they have to do is go board and slough off."

Boner hands Kyle the cards to cut and gives Kyle and Buckner a few words of wisdom. "Quit your crying and let's finish this. Take it like a man."

Boner starts to deal the cards. As he is dealing you can hear someone coming up the stairs. He finishes dealing. The guys are arranging their cards in their hands.

"Who is it?" asked Kyle.

Boner leans slightly to his right to look down the hallway. "It's Aaron's daddy, Rob."

Rob comes down the hallway and sits on the armrest of the three-man seat. He picks the forms up, throws them on top of the bags and slides down in the seat. He has his clipboard with him. He starts to look at it then throws it on the bags. The card game is more interesting.

"What, you missing your bitch?" asked Boner.

"No, I'll get a little of that before I go home this morning," said Rob.

Kyle, Buckner and Boner smile at Rob's comeback, but Aaron doesn't think it's funny and keeps a straight face.

"My ETIC is almost up," said Rob. "How are things out here?"

Buckner spits in his cup again. "There's a lot of sand bagging going on chief."

Aaron, with his cocky attitude, gives Rob his update. "This is the last hand. We only need board and they are done."

"I meant the airplane." Rob rolls his eyes. "Aaron, did you do anything out here?"

"Yea, I took a nap," said Aaron.

Kyle has his cards arranged in his hand. He looks impressed. "We only needed the extra body for the card game."

Rob rolls his eyes again.

Buckner has the opposite look as Kyle does. He looks worried. "Chief, I don't have squat son. You are going to have to carry us."

Kyle leans over and shows his cards to Rob. It's full of spades and other high cards. Rob likes what he sees in Kyle's hand. Kyle leans back. "What do you think about ten-for-two Buckner?"

"Hell yea! I can hold up my end of that deal."

Aaron looks at Boner. "Board."

Boner gives the same monotone answer as Aaron did. "Board."

Rob is starting to get impatient. He needs a rundown so he can let MOCC and Sierra 4 know the status of the plane. "Someone give me a rundown."

Kyle has his game face on. "Ok, give me a second Rob. Bo, give me a winner."

"I have it right here chief."

Buckner and Kyle slide a card to each other face down. They both pick them up and add them to their hands. Kyle leans back over to show his cards to Rob.

Boner realizes Kyle has a good hand. He is starting to get nervous. "Come on Aaron. Don't let these cock suckers come back on us."

Aaron tries to comfort Boner. "Settle down Boner. We got this."

Buckner sits up in his seat. "I'll drag chief."

Rob picks up his clipboard, sets it on his lap and takes a pencil out of his shirt pocket. The guys start to play. Boner and Aaron throw their cards down on the table normal. As Buckner plays, he slides his cards under the ones that are already on the table. Kyle, using his right hand, makes a clicking sound with his cards and his fingers as he plays them. All the players are silent, as if this is a life or death match. They eye each other's moves and look for any signs that could give them an edge. Buckner and Aaron occasionally spit in one of the white cups. The only conversation throughout the game is Kyle giving a rundown of the plane's condition to Rob.

"Alright Rob…what do you want to know?" asked Kyle.

"Rudder Limiter light intermittent?"

"Adjusted rudder limiter, ops check good."

Ops check means operational check.

"INS number one has a 50-mile drift?" asked Rob.

"R2 number 1 INU, ops check good."

R2 stands for remove and replace.

"Cargo right side interphone cords inop?" asked Rob.

 Inop stands for inoperative.

24

"R2 right forward cargo compartment interphone control box, ops check good."

"After winch inop?"

"R2 winch, ops check good."

"Co-pilots radar will not paint?"

"R2 co-pilots radar scope, ops check good."

"MADAR recorder failure?"

"R2 MADAR tape, fault went way."

"Number one engine channel 8 vibe?"

"R2 SAR 19, performed engine run, ops check good."

"Hydraulic leak number three system?"

"Tightened b-nut in service center, leak check good."

"Forward ramp will not operate in auto?"

"Adjusted ramp lock limit switches, ops check good."

"2A1 and 4C2 tires?"

"Complied with."

"T-tail nav bulbs inop?"

"R2 bulbs."

"Pilot's yoke interphone button sticks?"

"R2 yoke. All the ops checks are complied with."

"Number two engine frequency flux?"

"R2 GCU, engine run ops check good."

"Pilots instrument lights inop?"

"R2 Pilot. Recommend more training."

"Nose landing gear primary strut low?"

"Serviced strut."

"Gas?"

"120,000."

"LOX?"

"25 over 75."

"Nitro?"

"750/750."

"New pre-flight?"

"0500 today."

Now they are all down to the last card of the game. Kyle and Buckner have nine books. Boner and Aaron have three books. The next play will win the match. Boner plays an eight of hearts, Buckner plays a 10 of hearts, and Aaron slides a three of diamonds under the two cards that are already played. Kyle looks disappointed. He holds his card up in the air for a few seconds and then slams it down! It's the three of spades! "BAM bitches!"

Aaron is stunned. "You lucky fucks!"

Buckner can't contain his enthusiasm. "Shut her down Frank, she's smoking!"

Boner is in the same state as Aaron, stunned. "You have to be kidding me."

"What's the score?" Buckner starts in on Aaron. "You see, you mess with the bulls, you get the horns."

Aaron is adding the scores. "428 to 5…oh, whatever!"

Aaron crumples up the paper with the scores on it and stuffs it in his spit cup.

Rob stands up. "Is everything good for this morning?"

I's and E's, DOPP, and pitot covers are already done," said Kyle. "All day shift needs to do is drop in a new set of forms.

"Well, why don't you guys shut this puppy down and let's get the hell out of here," said Rob. "We are in a lightning warning anyway.

Boner gathers the cards and puts them back into the box. Everyone gets up.

"Rob, don't ever put me out here with this crew again," said Aaron. "Boner, you suck!"

"No Aaron, your girlfriend sucks my Johnson!"

Rob starts walking up to the flight deck. "I'll be down stairs in the truck."

Buckner turns the lights back to bright so day shift won't think they were relaxing or sleeping. "Chief, I'll get the visor. Boner, jump on the ground."

Everyone grabs their bags and heads for the flight deck. Aaron, Buckner and Boner head down stairs. Buckner stops in the cargo compartment at the loadmaster's station where the controls to the visor are located. Boner goes all the way down stairs, sets his bag on the ground, pulls out his headset and plugs it into the scanners cord. Aaron goes over and gets in the front passenger's seat of the truck. Kyle stays up stairs and slides into the flight engineer seat. The co-pilots hand microphone is stretched back to the flight engineer's checklist bracket. Kyle uses it to talk to the other guys but it always remains in the bracket. "Boner, is the left APU and systems clear?"

There are two Auxiliary Power Units on the plane. They are used to supply electrical power and air. Systems refer to the hydraulic systems on the plane. There are four separate hydraulic systems on the plane. On C-5s, the left APU is used the most because it is on the left side of the plane and easier to keep an eye on.

Boner answers Kyle. "Clear."

Kyle throws multiple switches and starts the left APU. You can hear it spool up and different lights come on as it starts. Kyle checks the three phases of the volts and frequencies of the APU. He throws more switches and starts the number one and number four hydraulic systems. Number one system is started to replenish the APU start accumulator and number four system is started because it is the system that operates the visor.

"Chief, is number four system up?" asked Buckner.

"You got it."

"Boner, visor clear?" asked Buckner.

"Clear."

Buckner takes the visor switch to close. The visor, which is pointing straight up in the air, starts to move. It shakes the entire plane. It slowly makes it way down until it meets the fuselage. The locks are heard locking and all the visor lights on the panel go out. Buckner releases the switch. "All the lights are out down here. Kill it son."

"Alright, I'm killing everything," said Kyle. "I'll be down in a second."

There are lightning flashes in the distance. Rob pulls away from the plane and heads in. Kyle, Buckner and Boner are in the back of the truck. Kyle is sitting on the igloo cooler next to the door and Buckner and Boner are sitting on the bench. There are several red toolboxes and other pieces of equipment on the floor of the truck next to the side door. The guy's bags are also sitting on the floor. The light is on in the back of the truck. The truck pulls up to the front of building 585. Rob puts the truck in park and turns back to say something to the guys. "You guys turn all your stuff in and go ahead and take off."

Boner is not impressed with Rob's offer. "Wow! Thanks. A whole half hour!"

Buckner is also uncertain about Rob's offer. "Chief, don't count this as a sprout. If you do, it's bull shit."

A sprout means you are released from work early.

"Yea, we want a good sprout like you give your bitch, but we don't want to earn it the same way he does," said Kyle.

Aaron turns and acts like he is in charge. "Just turn your shit in before I change my mind."

Rob turns the truck off and everyone exits. Rob and Aaron walk over and are standing next to the front door. "Aaron, let me get a smoke from you."

"You make twice as much as I do," said Aaron. "I should be bumming cigarettes off of you."

"Come on Aaron. I'll get you back tomorrow."

Kyle, Buckner and Boner have gathered their bags, tools boxes and equipment from the truck. Their hands are full. They walk to the front door of 585. Rob and Aaron are standing there talking and smoking cigarettes. They don't help with the door. Kyle sets his toolbox down, opens the door and holds it with his foot. Buckner goes in first followed by Boner.

Boner lets Rob and Aaron know how he feels. "Thanks you dicks!"

Rob and Aaron keep smoking and ignore the comment made by Boner. Kyle picks up his box and enters as the door closes behind him.

Building 585 is a large single story structure. It is about 100 feet long and 50 feet wide. It is a simple metal-framed building with an aluminum roof and siding. The building is 20 feet tall with a vaulted ceiling.

Inside 585 is CTK. It is a walled off area that takes up about half the building, maybe 40 by 40 feet. There are two, 3' by 3' windows cut out of the wall. They are about 10 feet apart. They are both about chest high. Next to each counters there are conveyer type rollers set up to slide tool boxes and heavy equipment in and out of CTK.

The open area of 585 is pretty basic. The back wall is lined with tall, grey lockers. There is a large set of double doors directly in the middle of the side wall. The front wall looks the same as the back wall. The only exception is a vending machine that sits next to the lockers. Above, there are lights running down the center of the vaulted ceiling. Sitting on the floor, there are four, large, picnic tables lined up end to end in the middle of the room. They are the same type of picnic table that is inside of the debrief truck. Roll call is held three times a day in this open area.

The rest of the shift has been off the line for at least an hour because of the lightning. Most of them are sitting at the picnic tables and playing cards. The others are standing around watching the card games intensely. Half the people are smoking cigarettes and the rest are dipping tobacco or chewing on sunflower seeds. There are a lot of snacks from the vending machine sitting on all of the tables. The snacks are two different types, chips and crackers. There are a lot of soda cans and white paper cups on the tables. Some are actual drinks and others are spit cups and cans. There is a thick cloud of smoke hovering up by the ceiling. The place has the feel of a casino.

Buckner, Boner and Kyle enter through the front door, turn right and head down the short hallway. They emerge into the open area of 585.

They pass by the vending machine. It is about half full. It's odd that entire rows of items are gone and other rows are full.

Buckner, Boner and Kyle are greeted by the rest of the shift. It's as if everyone hasn't seen them in ages. They are the last crew off the line and no one can go home until all the tools and equipment are turned in. The entire place erupts with comments like, "It's about time, and what took you guys so long?"

Buckner and Boner throw the things they are carrying on the rollers and push them through so the guy working inside of CTK can inventory them. They veer off with their bags over their shoulders. They joint the crowd and start talking with the rest of the crews that are sitting at the tables. Kyle sets his toolbox on the rollers and gives it a little push. He waits at the window to make sure everything is checked in and cleared.

"What took you guys so long?" asks the CTK attendant. "I could have been home an hour ago."

"We took a little detour over to your mom's house," answered Kyle.

"You wish."

"The only thing I'm wishing for is that I didn't get her pregnant, because that means we would be related."

"That's real funny."

"Just check the shit in like a good boy and I'll unlock your door and let you out of your cage."

The CTK attendant rolls his eyes and continues checking in the tools. Kyle stands there at the window and watches as if he does not trust him. Kyle turns and looks back at the picnic tables. All the attention of the crowd is back on the card games. There is a lot of chatter back and forth between the people.

Kyle turns back to the CTK attendant. "Hurry the fuck up!"

The CTK attendant closes the last box, turns and throws it on the shelf behind him. He turns back to the window where Kyle is waiting. The CTK attendant picks up Kyle's hand receipt and rips it in two.

A hand receipt is an official form used in the Air Force to sign over tools and equipment and give ownership to various people.

"You guys are clear," said the CTK attendant.

Kyle starts to walk away. "See you tomorrow."

"I'm off of work tomorrow."

"Yea, I know." Kyle stops and turns. "I'm going back to your mom's house tomorrow night. See you there."

Kyle laughs and walks towards the picnic tables where the lively crowd of his coworkers is. Kyle stops for a few seconds to makes some small talk with the guys and then he heads for the doors on the side of CTK.

Kyle comes out the side door of 585 and turns right towards the dorms. He looks to his left. About 50 feet away, Buckner is sitting in his silver two-door Toyota pickup truck. Buckner is slowly moving the truck back and forth, inching it ever so slowly. Kyle walks over to the truck. Buckner has his head down with his attention focused on the center console.

"Bo, what the hell are you doing?"

"Chief-chief, check it out. If I get between that pole behind me and that corner of the old wash rack, I can pick up the Grease Man out of Baltimore."

"Baltimore is 100 miles away...and who is the Grease Man?" asked Kyle.

"Chief, are you shitting me? That's Nino Greasemanelli. He's the craziest ass DJ out there. You've never heard of him?"

"No," said Kyle. "I only listen to Howard Stern."

"Chief, listen to him."

Kyle leans into the window and Buckner turns up the radio a little. A skit call the "Goodship Grease" is playing. Buckner and Kyle laugh off and on. After a minute the radio goes to a commercial.

"We are good on tools," said Kyle. "I'm getting out of here before anyone from day shift sees me."

Buckner shakes his head. "Just take your ass down to the mall and get a haircut son."

Kyle walks away. He pulls his hat out of his helmet bag and puts it on his head. He turns back towards Buckner's truck. "I'll do it when they catch me."

About 15 minutes later Kyle arrives at dorm 408. He lives in room 104. Kyle enters his dorm through the doorway at the other end of a long hallway. The door closes behind him.

There are 18 rooms in the hallway. Sixteen of the 18 rooms have people living in them. In the middle of the hallway are the dayroom on one side and a laundry room on the opposite side. On the laundry room side of the hallway there is a water fountain and a pay phone on the wall. The walls are painted institutional beige. The ceiling is made of white panels and there are lights about every 15 feet. The doors to all the rooms are made of heavy wood and are varnished medium brown. The doors have the room numbers on them as well as a small plaque with the names of the occupants. The carpet is grey with connecting blue squares. There is also a little red mixed in. The carpet is the same in every room except the laundry room. It has dull yellow tile floor.

About 10 feet from the door is Bret Nader.

Bret Nader is a senior airman and is in his early 20s. Nader is from the state of Maine. He is always getting in trouble at work as well as away from work. Somehow he manages to receive a lesser punishment than what fits the crime. He should have been kicked out of the Air Force years earlier, but somehow he's managed to stay in. Nader spends as much time on the flightline as he does doing extra duties because of his troubles.

Nader is dressed in green coveralls that are stained with several different colors of paint. He has several cans of paint, rollers, paint pans and drop clothes at his feet. He is organizing things getting ready to paint the hallway and dayroom. He is moving slow because he just woke up and is pissed off because of the detail he was given. He has been assigned a duty called bay orderly. A bay orderly's main duties are to clean and maintain the dorms. The bay orderly reports directly to the dorm managers, Graywolf and Andy.

Graywolf and Andy are in charge of the four dorms that the crew chiefs live in. The dorms are 408, 409, 410 and 412. The four buildings sit close to each other, about 50 feet apart. They form a cross with a patch of grass in the middle of them. Each dorm is two stories and grey in color. The second floor is accessed by a set of covered stairs on the outside of the building. They are all configured the same inside and out. There are similar dorms in the area but they belong to different squadrons. All the dorms share parking lots located on the sides of them.

Kyle walks up to Nader. "Nader, what's up? What, did you fuck up again?"

"Something like that."

"What did you do this time?"

"I can't say anything right now. They are telling me to keep quiet."

"Come on you pussy, tell me what you did!"

Nader doesn't want to talk about what landed him into bay orderly. He changes the subject. "No, no. I can't. How was work? Busy?"

"No, not too bad. Same ole shit. Your boy Duncan stuck me with a real winner."

Nader knows Duncan's reputation. "Fuck that guy! He's not my boy."

"I thought you two were butt buddies?"

Kyle starts walking down the hall towards his room, which is at the other end of the hallway.

Nader grabs his crotch. "I got your butt buddy right here."

"Look at the sign on my ass faggot." Kyle turns and looks back at Nader. "It says exit only, no entrance."

Nader laughs. "Hey, did you get that problem with your travel voucher straightened out with finance?"

Kyle stops. "No! I got up early yesterday and went over there to talk to them about it. They were supposed to be open until 4 p.m. They closed at one o'clock for training."

"Training! What kind of training?"

"Hell, I don't know. Hopefully they are training on how not to screw up my travel voucher."

"Good luck with that."

Kyle knows he has to take care of his travel voucher and he will get limited sleep today. "Yea, I guess I'll have to get up early again today and go back up there. They'll probably close early today because it's someone's birthday."

Kyle turns and walks on. He walks past the dayroom on his right and looks in.

The dayroom is simple. The television is on the right side facing back into the room. It's an old television and sits on a medal stand. In the middle of the room there are two sofas, one against each wall. There are two chairs at the back of the room by the window. There is also a coffee table in the dayroom. It gets moved around the room, usually where someone is sitting. The furniture is hard and uncomfortable and built to last. If it weren't, it would have been destroyed a long time ago. There are two pictures on each side wall. The pictures are all Air Force scenes and C-5s.

Kyle sees Greg Bailey sitting in his usual chair in the right back corner of the room.

Greg Bailey is a senior airman and in his mid-20s. He is from some backwards ass town in Kentucky. He is a very dirty person. He has a pointy nose and his ears stick out. He is very pale and looks like a rat. He has always worked grave shift and never sees the light of day. It appears that Bailey only goes to work or is in the dorms. Most of his time is spent in the dayroom where he watches television, smokes and eats. He hates Kyle because Kyle is always messing with him.

Bailey is watching TV and eating breakfast out of a white container. Kyle stops and enters the dayroom just inside the doorway. Bailey says nothing, gives Kyle a dirty look and continues watching television.

"Where in the hell were you last night?" asked Kyle. "Why weren't you at work?"

Bailey looks back at Kyle. "I had a CTO."

CTO stands for comp time off. It's a day you are given off of work and not charge leave time.

Kyle acts like he is Bailey's boss. "Who approved that? I sure as hell didn't! Next time you want a day off you better first earn it and second run it though me! Got it?"

Bailey says nothing, looks back at the TV and flips Kyle the bird. Kyle turns and exits the dayroom. He continues down the hallway, opens his door and enters his room. The door closes.

CHAPTER 3

----------August 1989----------

It's half past four on a hot and sunny August afternoon. Kyle walks out the back door of the gym. There is a short sidewalk about and then the road. He is sweaty and tired from playing basketball. He is wearing a t-shirt, shorts and tennis shoes. A small white car approaches from the right. He stops at the street's edge to let the car pass. As the car passes he looks in and sees a beautiful woman behind the wheel. She has black Ray-Bans on, long brown hair and a white top. Kyle is locked onto her as she goes by in what seems to be slow motion. He is memorized. The car passes and he watches it turn the corner. Kyle snaps out of it. He walks across the street.

The dorm Troy Ignacio lives in, 412, sits off to the left, caddy-corner to the gym. Troy lives on the second floor. Kyle walks towards the stairwell. He heads up the stairs and enters the door of the hallway. Troy's door is the second on the left.

Kyle pounds hard on the door in an attempt to startle Troy. "Troy, put it back in your pants and open the door."

Troy opens the door. He is in his work pants and t-shirt. He has taken his boots and socks off.

Troy Ignacio is a senior airman and in his mid-20s. He is from Long Island, about an hour outside of New York City. Troy is one of the nicest guys you'd ever want to meet. He would do anything in the world for you. Troy is very easy going but changes into an aggressive and loud person as the beers go down. He likes bars and drinking with the boys. He is witty and is very good with comebacks. He is a bit of a smart ass at times but also a little gullible. He doesn't chase women like Kyle and Bucky do but if something comes his way he'll take it.

"Calm down boy," said Troy. "I just got home."

Troy turns and walks back in the room to finish changing.

Kyle takes one step into the room. "It's hot as shit in here."

"Yea, I forgot to open the window before I went to work this morning."

"Hurry up and get changed. I'm hungry enough to eat a skunk's ass through a barbed wire fence. I'll be outside waiting."

Kyle starts walking out the door.

"Where's Bucky?" asked Troy.

"He's going to meet us in Graywolf's office."

Kyle closes the door and walks out on the stairwell at the end of 412. He leans against the rail and looks out over a big parking lot. The gym is across the street off to his left and the base swimming pool is 100-yards away off to his right. The pool is fenced in and has an office and locker room on the far side of it. Kyle is killing time waiting for Troy to get changed. He looks over at the pool. It's somewhat crowded yet something catches Kyle's eye. It's the woman that drove past him in the car just minutes before. She is in the pool. He can see her from the chest up. Kyle's heart starts pumping.

All of a sudden Troy walks out the door. He is in shorts, a t-shirt and jogging shoes. His socks are pulled up just below his knees. "Alright boy, let's go."

Kyle informs Troy of the change in plans. "Hold on, we need to go to the pool first."

"What?" asked Troy. "I thought you were starving?"

Kyle and Troy start walking down the stairs and across the parking lot toward the swimming pool.

"When I left the gym, the most beautiful woman drove past me. She was amazing."

Troy is still trying to piece together why Kyle needed to go to the pool. "And?"

"I just spotted her at the pool. I have to go say something to her. I have to meet her."

At this point Troy is just along for the ride. "This should be good. I always like a little entertainment before dinner and I like seeing you get shot down."

Kyle and Troy enter the pool area through the locker room. The pool is standard size with six swimming lanes. The shallow end is on Kyle's left and the deep end is to his right. They turn left and head toward two vacant pool chairs at the shallow end of the pool. Kyle, looking sideways through his sunglasses, spots the woman who is still in the middle of the pool. The pool is crowded with adults and children of various ages.

"So, which one is she?" asked Troy.

"She's the one with the long brown hair in the middle of the pool. She has on a blue bathing suit."

Troy turns to look as they keep walking toward the shallow end of the pool. Kyle doesn't look directly at the woman.

"Are you going in with your gym shorts?" asked Troy.

"Sure, why not?"

Kyle and Troy arrive at the vacant chairs. Troy is ready for the show. "Ok boy. I have a front row seat. Let's see what you got."

The woman once again has Kyle mesmerized. He doesn't respond to Troy. He is discretely watching the woman. Kyle kicks off his shoes and socks and peels off his shirt. He walks over to the edge of the pool. He eases himself in and starts wading towards the woman. At the same time she starts moving towards the shallow end of the pool. As she moves, the water level lowers on her and slowly reveals that she is pregnant. Kyle doesn't break character and acts as if he is heading to the other side of the pool. As they pass, Kyle says, "Hello, how are you?"

The woman smiles at Kyle. "Good, how are you?"

They continue in opposite directions. The woman wades to the end of the pool and starts talking to a young blond haired boy. Kyle veers to the right and gets out of the pool. He walks over to where Troy is sitting. He starts putting his shoes on without his socks. He uses his t-shirt as a towel to dry himself as best as he can.

Troy makes fun of Kyle by stating the obvious. "Hey, she's pregnant. And she has a kid. You sure know how to pick them boy."

Even though the woman is pregnant and has a child, Kyle still realizes her beauty. "Did you see her smile? Great teeth!"

Kyle pauses for a few seconds and then snaps out of it. "Let's go find Bucky."

"You are soaking wet. Are you going to eat like that?" asked Troy.

"No, let's stop by my room real fast and I'll change."

Kyle grabs his socks and continues to dry off with his t-shirt as he and Troy head for the exit.

It's now after five o'clock. Kyle and Troy walk into Graywolf's office which is on the lower floor in building 409. The office is like the dayroom in Kyle's building except the furniture is different. Graywolf's desk is against the window and facing the door. On the left side of the room there is a loveseat and on the right side of the room there is a sofa. There is a hat rack off to the right as you walk in. Graywolf is sitting at his desk. On the front of his desk there is a sign that reads, "My Way or the Highway!"

William Graywolf, the dorm manager, is a technical sergeant in his early 40s. He is from Tennessee. He claims to have American Indian blood in him. He is overweight. He always has a wad of Red Man chewing tobacco in his mouth. His career is going nowhere.

Andy is sitting on the love seat.

Andy McBride is a technical sergeant and also in his early 40s. Andy is Graywolf's assistant. He also will not progress any further in his career. He is less serious than Graywolf and will let a lot of thing slip by if he likes you. His bottom lip has an indentation in it from a fight earlier in his life.

Bucky is sitting on the sofa. He has a cigarette behind his left ear.

Bucky Wirth is a senior airman in his early 20s. He is from Reisterstown, Maryland. Bucky is Kyle's roommate. He is a crew chief but works in the ISO Docks, which is a large aircraft inspection hangar. He is 6'2", weighs 168 pounds and has skin like a baby. His appearance and stature often invites trouble from others thinking he is a pushover, but he is far from it. His passion is boxing. He tried from an early age to become a boxer but broken bones in both of his hands made that impossible. He is a "tell it like he sees it" type of guy and cannot stand posers or fake people. He is into classic rock and rock in general. He smokes. He has a girlfriend back in Reisterstown but their relationship is stormy. He like chasing women with Kyle and is always trying to figure out how Kyle gets so many women.

Graywolf, Andy and Bucky are in their uniforms. They are all laughing at the story Graywolf is telling.

Bucky can't believe what he's hearing. "Get the hell out of here Graywolf!"

Graywolf holds up his right hand. "I swear to God."

Bucky is still amazed at the story. "That's some crazy shit."

Andy chimes in on Graywolf's behalf. "Yea, Graywolf was a bad ass back in his day."

Graywolf continues with his story. "Yea, the cops couldn't find him, so they came and got me and I tracked him down."

Kyle interrupts. "What's up Graywolf, Andy?"

Troy is less vocal than Kyle. "Hey-hey."

"Graywolf, what are you, two-fifths Cherokee?" asked Andy

"It sounds like this story is four-fifths bullshit," said Kyle. "It's getting deep in here."

"What's up fellas?" asked Bucky. "You all ready to eat?"

"Let's do it," said Kyle.

"Yea, I'm starving," said Troy.

Bucky stands up, slaps and rubs his hands together. "Where are we going?"

"I don't care," answered Kyle.

Troy is hungry and just wants to eat. He suggests the easiest option. "What do you guys think about the chow hall?"

Bucky shakes his head. "No way. Reese and Mouse just came from there and said the food sucks today."

Andy adjusts himself on the loveseat and grabs his crotch. "How about some tube steak smothered in sweaty underwear?"

The guys look at him and go back to their conversation.

"How about Wings to Go?" asked Kyle.

Wings to Go is a small takeout only restaurant across the highway from the base. It sits about three 300-yards from the traffic light at the main gate. Wings to Go only sells buffalo style chicken wings in five flavors; mild, medium, hot, extra hot and suicide. Their wings are amazing! All the guys are hooked on them. After having them for the first time, Kyle woke up in the middle of the night sweating and craving for more. At first he was eating them about five times a week. Now he and the rest of the guys eat them on average about three times a week.

Troy likes the idea. "Yea, I could do that."

Bucky likes it even more. "Hell yea, I could rip up some wings right now."

Graywolf leans to his right, spits in the trash can and sits back up. "Ignacio, did you ever clean up that mess in your room?"

Troy disagrees. "That wasn't a mess. There were only a few water stains on the chrome."

Bucky comes to Troy's defense. "Graywolf, why are you such a hard ass when it comes to Troy?"

Andy tries to act responsible but the guys know it's just for show. "We have to keep you boys in line."

"Aren't you all late for your appointment at the VFW?" asked Kyle.

VFW stands for Veterans of Foreign Wars. It's an organization that caters to military personnel and veterans. It's located between the base and the city of Dover, on the right, just before the Blue Hen Mall.

Bucky pulls the cigarette out from his ear. He moves towards Andy and tries to put the cigarette on Andy's lower lip. "Here, let me put this on your ash tray. I'll be back in a bit to get it."

Andy resists as they wrestle around for a few seconds. Everyone is laughing.

"You guys get the hell out of here," said Andy. "It's time for us to go home."

Bucky laughs and is in a good mood. "Alright fellas, we'll talk to you all later."

Graywolf looks at the guys and gives them a few words of wisdom in his southern drawl. "Y'all be good now."

"Later fellas," said Kyle.

Troy just nods his head. They all turn and head toward the door.

"Let me get out of this uniform real fast," said Bucky.

Troy can't believe there is going to be another delay. "Now you have to change! Hurry the fuck up!"

Kyle, Bucky and Troy exit the office and turn right down the hallway.

Forty-five minutes later, Kyle, Bucky and Troy are coming down the hallway of 408. Bucky is now wearing the same thing that Kyle and Troy are wearing, a t-shirt, shorts and tennis shoes. They are all carrying white styrofoam containers. Kyle has a large, green Gatorade, Bucky has a 16-ounce Budweiser in a can and Troy has a 12-ounce Coke in a can, which they bought from the 7-11.

Every time the guys ordered wings, they park at Wings to Go, place their orders and walk down to the 7-11, which is at the traffic light at the main gate. They buy something to drink and walk back to Wings to Go. By that time, their orders are almost ready. In between Wings to Go and the 7-11 are a few small building that were built many years ago. In one of those buildings is a bar called the Brown Fox. A lot of the old timers tell good stories about things that happened in the Brown Fox.

Greg Bailey is sitting in his usual spot in the dayroom watching some stupid movie. Bucky enters first, then Troy, and finally Kyle. Bailey is happy to see Bucky and Troy, but changes his expression when he sees Kyle.

No one notices that the right front picture closest to the TV has been moved.

Bucky greets Bailey. "What's up Bailey?"

"How's it going Bailey?" asked Troy.

Kyle says nothing. Bailey is also silent. They sit down. Bucky sits in the chair next to Bailey and Troy and Kyle sit on the sofa. They slide the coffee table closer so everyone can reach it. They set their containers down and pop open the tops. They are full of chicken wings covered in a red sauce. The smell fills the air.

"Bailey, you want a wing?" asked Bucky.

"No thanks. I just ate."

Troy tries to pressure Bailey into eating a chicken wing. "Come on boy, don't be shy."

Kyle starts in on Bailey and wouldn't mind if he left the room. "Yea, get yourself a wing and take it back to your room and nibble on it."

Kyle stands up and moves towards the TV. "Bailey, are you watching this?"

Kyle knows he was watching the television. Before Bailey is able to answer, Kyle changes the channel to Sports Center. You can tell that Bailey is getting pissed. Kyle sits back down as Bailey lights a cigarette.

Troy protests, "Do you have to smoke that now? Why don't you go outside and smoke it."

"Yea, it looks like you could use a little sun," said Kyle.

Bucky defends Bailey. "You all get off the Bailey."

Bucky stands up and turns towards the window, pulls the curtains aside and slides the window open. As he is opening the window, a nice, older, 1970s model blue Chevy Camaro parks right in front of the window. The car is about 25 feet from the window. Before the driver cuts off the car, he revs it up a few times. It sounds real good.

"Who is making all that noise out there?" asked Troy.

Bucky is still standing at the window. "It's Flores' fat ass."

"I bet he won't turn down a wing if you offer him one," said Kyle.

Flores and his girlfriend Cindy get out of the car.

Roy Flores is a buck sergeant and in his mid-20s. Roy is tall and a little overweight in a baby fat kind of way. He is loud and obnoxious in a big kid sort of way. He has worked hard and has a few things to show for it, such as his nice car. He is a few years ahead of Kyle's era and has a different group of friends. He associates with Kyle because they live in the same dorm and are just a few doors apart. Also, Kyle doesn't take any crap from Flores and vice-versa.

Cindy is Roy's girlfriend. No one knows anything about her. She is a mystery. She appears to be very young.

Bucky gets everyone's attention. "Hey, check out the girl that's with Flores."

All the guys get up and go to the window, including Bailey.

Troy sees Cindy and can't believe his eyes. "Holy shit! How old is she?"

"I'd guess she's 15," said Bucky.

Kyle agrees with Bucky. "Yea, she looks pretty young. I wouldn't even mess with that."

Bailey starts to say something but he is talking too loud. "You know…"

Flores looks in the direction of the window and then looks way. All the guys jump back out of site and shush Bailey. They don't want to be caught looking.

"Bailey, keep it down," said Kyle. "This is some good shit."

Bucky eases back up and slowly slides the window closed so nothing can be heard. The rest of the guys slowly move back and continue looking out the window.

"He was probably cruising the mall and found her at the arcade," said Bucky.

"How does a fat fuck like that guy get a girl like her?" asked Troy.

Kyle has a puzzled look on his face. "It has to be the car."

"Or he's got money," said Bucky.

"Or he's hung like a horse," said Troy.

All the guys start snickering.

Another couple approaches from the left. It's Roy's friend Rex Kellogg and Rex's girlfriend Ann Smits.

Rex Kellogg is a buck sergeant and in his mid-20s. He is a good friend of Roy's. He is a fellow crew chief and lives in building 412. He is a big tall guy and is always in the gym working out.

Ann Smits is Rex's girlfriend. She is in the communications squadron and lives in the dorm across from Kyle and Bucky's room. There are only a handful of women in maintenance and they aren't anything that you'd take home to mom. Ann is the exception. She is hot. Rex and Ann have been dating for a while.

They stop and speak with Flores and Cindy.

"Check it out, it's Ann," said Kyle.

Bucky is all over it. "She's a nice piece of ass."

"Kyle, when you going to hit that?" asked Troy.

"What are you crazy?" said Kyle. "Look at the size of Rex. You think I want that guy on my ass?"

"I bet I could drop him with one punch," said Bucky. "Guys like that are all show and no go."

Rex and Ann wave goodbye to Roy and Cindy. They walk to the left down the sidewalk toward Ann's dorm. Flores and Cindy are getting something out of the trunk of the car. The guys' attention returns back to Cindy.

"Well, you know what I say," said Kyle. "If there's grass on the infield, play ball."

Bucky laughs. "If there's hair, I'm there."

Troy tries to be serious. "You guys are sick. That's someone's daughter."

Everyone pauses for a second and then starts snickering again. They know Troy is being sarcastic.

Bailey adds his two cents into the conversation. "Eighteen to 80, blind, cripple or crazy."

There is a pause. Everyone turns toward Bailey and looks at him in disbelief that he is talking about a woman.

Kyle jumps right on Bailey. "Oh shut the fuck up!"

All the guys return to their seats and start eating again.

"Bailey, I bet you'd tear up that young stuff, wouldn't you?" asked Bucky. "You'd teach her a thing or two."

Bailey grins.

"Bailey, I bet the only time you get ass is when you are wiping yours and have break-through," said Kyle. "I bet if we go in your room right now, the ceiling is covered in stalactites. You should sell tickets to go in there."

Bucky laughs. "Yea, like cavern tours."

Bucky realizes Bailey is starting to get pissed again. "Come on Bailey, you know I'm just messing with you. Have a wing."

Bailey gets up, grabs his cigarettes and starts to walk out. "No thanks man. I'm going to take a nap before work."

Troy prods Bailey. "Bailey, I wouldn't take that shit off Kyle if I were you. Whip his ass."

Bailey exits the room. Kyle stands up, walks over to the window and slides it all the way open. Kyle returns to his seat.

"That guy stinks," said Kyle.

Troy takes a bite from a chicken wing. "Man, you ride that guy hard. One of these days he's going to stab you while you are sleeping. You better watch your back."

Kyle dismisses Troy. "That ugly son of a bitch is the least of my worries. You know, I bet if you put a pair of BCGs on him, his head would explode."

"That is a scientific formula that doesn't need to be explored," said Bucky.

All the guys laugh.

BCGs are birth control glasses. They are military issued prescription glasses with very out of date frames. They look like a smaller version of Buddy Holly glasses. They are called birth control glasses because if you wear them, you will never meet a woman and definitely never have sex with one. Kyle actually wears them all the time but no one realizes it. He replaced the temples on his BCGs with temples from a pair of Ray-Ban sun glasses. He then took the glasses to the store and had the lenses tinted. He also has a regular pair of BCGs that he wears when he goes out to certain places in New York City. In NYC, everything is in fashion.

"What did you get?" asked Kyle.

"A 20 piece, hot," said Troy. "What about you?"

"Twenty hot with extra sauce. That steps it up a little."

"You pussies," said Bucky.

"What did you get?" asked Troy.

"Twenty extra hot. That's a man's order."

"No, a man's order is a 20 piece suicide," said Kyle.

"You're crazy," said Troy. "You'd be shitting fire for a week straight."

Kyle lifts his butt cheek up and farts. "Like that?"

Troy looks disgusted. "You're a pig!"

Bucky laughs. "Speak louder ole toothless one."

They all laugh and continue eating wings.

CHAPTER 4

Later that night, Kyle is at work. He walks to CTK from Joker row to get a tire servicing kit. On his way back to the flightline he runs into two guys from the Red side, Fox and Johnson. They are coming out of building 704. Building 704 is the main office building for crew chiefs. It sits across the street from 585 and behind the giant wash rack hangar. They are carrying two small trash bags full of something.

Kyle approaches them. "Hey! What's going on guys?"

"We are having a little going away party in the wash rack for Grover," said Fox. "Tonight is his last night at work."

"Where is he going?" asked Kyle.

"He has orders to Little Rock," said Fox.

Little Rock Air Force base is home to the much smaller propeller driven C-130's.

Kyle thinks that's funny. "So he's going from being an aircraft mechanic to a lawn mower mechanic."

"Yea," said Johnson. "I told him when he goes out on his first mission, he'll have to fly over my house and trim the hedges."

"What's in the bag?" asked Kyle.

Johnson holds up one bag. It's hard to make out what is exactly inside, but you can see a bottle of ketchup and mustard.

"We cleaned out the refrigerators in 704," said Johnson. "We have a few condiments and some other things that were lying around."

Fox get a big smile on his face. "Grover was a good guy. We have to send him off the right way."

"He'll never forget us or forgive us after tonight," said Johnson.

The three guys turn and walk into the side entrance of the wash rack. There is a Red side plane inside. The Red side has the tow vehicle hooked to the plane and they are getting ready to move it out to the flightline. Almost all of the Red side crew chiefs are in the wash rack. Kyle hangs back by the door as Fox and Johnson join the crowd. They walk to the picnic table and set the two trash bags down. Once they set the bags down the crowd moves over to the table and exposes Grover. He is duck taped to an office chair that has rollers on the bottom of it. His arms are taped to the armrests and his feet are taped to the base of the chair. There is tape all around his body and legs. It is impossible for him to move.

Kyle is surprised at how well Grover is wrapped up. "Holy shit!"

Grover makes a weak attempt in hopes to gain his freedom but the Red side crew chiefs aren't buying it. "Come on guys. I thought we were all friends."

The Red side crew chiefs start to pull items out of the garbage bags that Fox and Johnson brought over. There is ketchup, mayonnaise, mustard, barbeque sauce, pickles and relish. There are also cans of chili, tuna, green beans and corn. Johnson pulls a can opener out of his pocket that he found next door. He hands it to the guys and they start opening the cans. Once they are finished everyone has one or two items in their hands.

Grover issues a stern threat! "The minute you guys cut me loose I'm going to kick everyone's ass!"

Grover is starting to squirm in the chair but there is nothing he can do. The Red side crew chiefs surround him and start pouring the food and condiments all over him. They are all laughing and having a good time. Most everything gets dumped or squirted on Grover's head. The mess that falls in Grover's lap or on the ground is quickly scooped up and strategically reapplied to his face. Grover is trying to fight it but he knows there is nothing he can do. He must sit there and take it.

Kyle sees Fox starting to walk towards the back of the plane. Kyle, with his tire servicing kit under his arm, jogs around the party and catches up with Fox. "That's enough to make you not want to put in for orders."

"Look on the bright side. He gets to go home early tonight." said Fox.

"When are you guys towing this plane out of here?" asked Kyle. "We are supposed to come in here right after you guys leave."

"We'll move it as soon as they get finished with Grover. I'm going to open the doors now. You want to give me a hand?"

"Sure."

"Grab that side."

Fox takes the door on the left and Kyle takes the door on the right. The two doors cover the entire front side of the hangar. They are 250 feet wide and 75 feet tall. The doors sit on railroad type tracks and both sides of the doors have three segments. There is a control panel on each door. On the control panel there is a door opener. The guys both push the buttons and the large doors split at the middle of the hangar and start to open. A loud buzzer sounds as the doors move. They slowly roll and meet the next segments and that part also starts to open. Fox and Kyle slowly walk the doors all the way open. Kyle looks back at Fox, waves and heads out towards the flightline.

Kyle walks over to the entry control point in front of the washer. The cop checks his line badge and lets Kyle pass. As he's walking up to his plane he notices something that doesn't look quite right on the plane next to his. The Calavar is set up behind the left wing and is extended all the way up to the tail. The basket is under the horizontal stabilizer on the left side of the tail.

A Calavar is a mobile boom lift truck. It's used on C-5s to reach anything on the tail. The maintenance platform, or basket, holds two people.

Kyle is standing at the centerline of the taxiway. He is looking up at the Calavar. Then he notices it. The basket, with two people in it, is leaning over at a 45° angle. The two people are 65 feet off the ground. Kyle thinks to himself. "That must suck."

Rob pulls up in the Sierra 6 truck.

"What are you looking at?" asked Rob.

"Check it out!" said Kyle. "The Calavar basket is leaning over."

Rob looks up through the front windshield of the truck and rolls his eyes. "Not again."

"Who is up there?" asked Kyle.

"Caldwell." Rob chuckles. "This always happens to him."

"I'm guessing that's a specialist with him." said Kyle.

"Yea," said Rob. "They are looking at a hydraulic leak up there. Plus, no other crew chief will go up in the Calavar with Caldwell. He gets stuck up there all the time. Last time he was up there for two hours."

"Wonder if this happens to him when he's at Six Flags?" asked Kyle.

Rob laughs. "He's probably not allowed in the park."

Caldwell comes over the radio. Kyle leans in to listen. "MOCC, 173."

MOCC responds. "Go ahead 173"

"MOCC, this is 173 on Lima row," said Caldwell. "Can you give heavy maintenance a call? I'm going to need them out here. I'm up in the Calavar and the basket has drooped and nothing will move."

Heavy maintenance is responsible for maintaining the large specialized flightline vehicles. They are not a part of OMS.

"I'm on the phone with them now." MOCC responds. "I'll get them out there ASAP."

"I bet that hydraulics guy is scared shitless," said Rob. "He didn't know he was going for a white knuckle ride."

Kyle looks back up at the basket. "Caldwell is so use to it he's probably up there just hanging out and smoking a cigarette."

"Do you know why the ground man has to wear a hardhat?" asked Rob.

"Yea, it's because the people in the basket are working above them."

"No. It's to protect them from falling shit after the specialist crap their pants."

They both laugh.

"Are you guys ready to tow?" asked Rob.

"Yea," said Kyle. "We are going to service a few tires and then we will be ready. Once they finish towing they are going to drop the U-30 off here. We've also knocked out most of the wash prep. Once we get in there, all we'll have to do is drop the gear doors."

A U-30 is the tow vehicle used to move C-5s. It's large and weighs 70,000 pounds.

Rob looks at his watch. "Wonder what's taking the Red side so long to get that plane out of there."

Kyle steps aside so Rob can see inside the wash rack. "They are having a going away party for Grover. It's his last night."

The Red side crew chiefs have pulled out several high pressure water hoses and are spraying Grover with them. The force of the water is moving Grover and the chair across the floor of the wash rack. All the guys are laughing and having a good time.

"Looks like they are just about finished," said Rob.

Kyle shakes his head knowing that he'll be in that chair one day. "It was nice of the guys to wash him off before he goes home."

They both laugh.

Rob pulls away and heads next door to Lima row.

CHAPTER 5

----------September 1989----------

It's around eleven o'clock at night. There are about 30 crew chiefs inside of building 585. A few guys are milling around and others are talking in small groups. Some are sitting at the picnic tables. Rob Heidelmann and another technical sergeant walk in. They both have clipboards in their hands. Everyone is in his uniform except for Buckner. He came to work in his coveralls, as usual. Rob walks over to Kyle and Buckner, who are standing next to the vending machine trying to figure out what they want to eat. The other technical sergeant walks over to the back corner of the room. The vending machine only has a few rows of items in it.

"What's up fellas?" asked Rob.

Kyle greets Rob. "Rob, what's up?"

"Chief, you hungry?" asked Buckner.

"Yea, I could use a snack," said Rob. "What's on tonight's menu?"

Kyle sees that there is an entire row of pretzels available. "Looks like it's going to be pretzels."

"Sounds good to me," said Rob.

"Buckner, do you have the money ready?" asked Kyle

"Yea chief. B-6."

Kyle goes to the right side of the vending machine and kneels down by the plug. He wiggles it a few times and positions it so that the power will flicker on and off quickly.

"That's it chief. That's the sweet spot. Ready?" asked Buckner.

Kyle is waiting for Buckner's command. "Yea, go for it."

Buckner drops 50 cents into the machine and selects B-6. The dispenser starts to turn. "Now chief!"

Kyle wiggles the plug constantly. The light inside the vending machines flickers on and off. The machine keeps dispensing bags of pretzels until the row is completely empty.

"That's it," said Buckner.

Kyle puts the plug back in all the way and stands up. Buckner grabs several bags of pretzels from the machine and hands them to Kyle and Rob. There are still 10 bags left in the bottom of the machine.

"So, how are you going to screw us tonight?" asked Kyle.

Rob is a little hesitant. "Well, right off the bat I'm moving Boner off your team."

Buckner protests! "Chief, are you shitting me? Boner is a hard worker. He busts his ass every night."

Rob tries to explain his decision. "I know, but I need to move him over with Billy and Greg Bailey to see if I can get more out of that team."

"Boner is going to eat Bailey alive," said Kyle. "I think you are just doing this for the fireworks."

"So who are we getting?" asked Buckner.

Rob points to a guy sitting at the corner of the picnic table by himself. "That guy over there. His name is Mike Akin."

Mike Akin is an airman first class and in his late teens. He is from Texas. He has been in the Air Force for a year and at Dover for six months. He is a little shy and doesn't look for the spot light. If he can, he will slip away and screw off.

"He is fresh out of QTP," said Rob. "He doesn't know a thing."

QTP stands for Quality Training Program. All crew chiefs new to Dover must attend this four-month course that covers various operations and maintenance procedures on the C-5.

"Chief, can he play spades or hearts?" asked Buckner.

Kyle seems a bit troubled. "He still smells like mothers milk."

Rob fills in Kyle and Buckner on Mike's background. "He was on day shift for a month. After roll call he would walk out to his car and go to sleep. No one ever missed him. Then, one day, the chief walked by his car and spotted him in there sleeping. Now he's on graves."

Kyle feels a little more at ease. "Sounds like a grave shifter to me."

Rob looks at his watch and realizes it's time to start roll call. "Let's get the show on the road."

Rob steps away from Kyle and Buckner. "Alright, form it up Blue side!"

Another technical sergeant joins in. "Let's go Red side."

The crowd slowly separates into two groups on opposite sides of the room. Their backs are to the back wall. The Red side forms up closer to the side door and the Blue side forms up next to the CTK windows. All the guys from both sides look rough. Their uniforms are dirty, most of the guys are pale, some are drinking coffee and a few look half asleep. Both formations are three rows deep and about six people across. Everybody is very relaxed. It's very laid back. Buckner is standing to the right of Kyle and Bailey is standing to his left of him. They are in the middle of the second row. Rob is standing in front of the Blue side formation and the other technical sergeant is standing in front of the Red side formation.

Rob starts roll call. "Ok, looks pretty easy tonight. Barrier, Moyer and Haigh. 467 on Nancy row. It landed an hour ago off of double locals. Inspection is done. Take a tire change kit out with you. 4B1 and 3C2 need changed. It needs 120,000 on gas and it has double locals again tomorrow."

"Russell, Jay, Eric and Emo. 9026 inbound to Papa row. There is no status on it yet. It should be down in 30 minutes."

"Buckner, Kyle, and Akin. 463 On India. 0600 mission launch. They have a ME latrine problem and it has to be fixed before they leave."

ME stands for Mission Essential. The plane must have a ME discrepancy repaired before it's able to fly. There is also the status of MC, for Mission Capable. These type discrepancies are less severe and the plane is allowed to fly without having them repaired.

Rob continues with roll call. "Jackson, Clark, Garcia. 5001. They just got it in the wash rack. Wash prep. It washes in the morning."

Bailey looks over at Kyle and smiles. "Watch out. That will jump up and grab you."

All of a sudden all the people around Bailey smell it. Bailey slipped out a nasty fart, or a SBD, which stands for silent but deadly. They all moan and groan, grab their noses or try and cover their faces with their t-shirts. The whole shift starts to move away from Bailey in all directions. Bailey just stands there and smiles as if he is the proud parent of a new seven-pound, three-ounce baby fart.

"Who did that?" asked Rob.

Jackson waves his hand in front of his face. "Fucking Bailey!"

Russell is shaking his head. "You stinky fucker!"

"What did you eat, rotten cheese?" asked Kyle.

"Oh my God!" cried Barrier.

"Go to the bathroom and wipe your ass," said Jay.

The crowd moves to their right and reforms leaving Bailey on the end. Rob moves with them. The other flight has stopped their roll call and they are all laughing.

Rob tries to finish. "Ok, let's see if we can get through this. Billy, Bailey, Boner…the three Bs. 217…inbound. It's going to the hot spot. It's Alpha 3 for numerous."

Most of the guys chuckle because not only does that team have a crappy airplane, they are over on the hot spot which is on the other side of the runway. The hot spot is large enough to accommodate three planes. It's where planes are parked when they have hazardous cargo or munitions on them. To get to the hot spot you either have to go around the perimeter road or contact the control tower who will grant you access to cross the runway. Either way, it's a pain in the ass being out there because you are so far from CTK and the rest of the flightline support.

Rob wraps up another roll call. "The rest of you head over and help with the wash prep for now and we'll probably tow 217 over from the hot spot later tonight. That's all I got."

The group breaks up. Kyle and Buckner approach the new guy Mike Akin.

"Chief, you are with us tonight," said Buckner. "Grab a tool box and a marshaling kit and jump on the truck."

Kyle takes his first shot at Mike. "And no stopping off at your car."

"Yes sir," answers Mike.

Buckner takes offence to being called sir. "Cut the sir shit. What do I look like, a college boy?"

Kyle and Buckner turn and walk away.

Buckner realizes that he and Kyle have a project on their hands. "He's green chief, green."

Fifteen minutes later the Sierra 6 truck pulls away from 585. Rob is driving the truck and Aaron is riding shotgun in the front passenger seat. The light is off in the back of the truck and it is full of the crew chiefs from the Blue side roll call. One guy is sitting on the butt can facing backwards, another is sitting on the igloo cooler and a third guy is sitting on the right wheel well. The bench is full. Kyle is sitting on the spare tire in the back corner of the truck. A few guys, including Kyle, have changed into coveralls. Next to the side door on the floor are six large toolboxes and other equipment.

The truck pulls up to the cops shack at the entry control point next to the wash rack. A cop comes out of the booth and approaches the driver's side door. He has a belt with a holstered pistol and an M-16 machine gun slung over his left shoulder. He is checking to see that all the people in the truck have restricted area line badges. You must have a line badge to be on the flightline. Rob hands his and Aaron's badge to the cop.

The cop checks the line badges and hands them back to Rob. "Ok."

Rob motions towards the back of the truck. "There are more in the back."

The cop leans in and looks back over Rob's shoulder and sees the rest of the people in the truck. He walks around the front of the truck to get to the side door. The light switch is mounted on the wall just behind the passenger seat headrest. Without looking,

Aaron reaches behind his head with his right hand and turns the lights on.

The cop slightly raises his voice. "Line badges! Pass them up!"

The cop motions to the guys to pass him their badges. Some of the guys have their badges on lanyards around their necks and some have them in their pockets. Everyone pulls them out and starts passing them forward to Haigh, who is sitting on the igloo. He hands them to the cop, one-by-one.

Moyer makes a suggestion to the cop. "Just hand them back to me after you check them and I'll pass them back to the guys."

The cop leisurely agrees. "Yea, yea, ok."

As the cop looks at the badges he hands them back to Moyer who is sitting on the butt can. Kyle motions with his hand to Moyer to keep the badges coming around the truck. Everyone catches on quickly and they pass the badges around in a counterclockwise circle to each other. The cop takes a badge, looks at the front and back of it, and passes it on.

The badges go around the truck at least two times until the cop finally realizes what is going on.

"Wait a minute!" exclaimed the cop. "I've seen this one already."

Everyone in the truck starts laughing loudly. The cop is embarrassed. He steps back away from the truck and waves Rob on. The cop doesn't want to mess with a truck full of crew chiefs. The truck pulls away from the entry control point and onto the flightline.

Kyle shakes his head in disbelief. "You could train a monkey to do that job."

The truck pulls up to India row. Buckner, Kyle and Mike grab their stuff and get out of the truck. They walk over and set their tools and bags in front of the nose landing gear tires. The fleet service truck is parked back by the right side main landing gear.

As Kyle opens the toolbox, Buckner squats down next to him. "I'll head up and get turnover."

Kyle removes a flashlight from the toolbox and then closes it. "Ok. I'll take Mike with me and see what is going on in the troop compartment."

They all head up the ladder. Buckner continues straight up, and Kyle and Mike turn right into the cargo compartment. They snake their way through the cargo and get to the troop compartment ladder. Kyle and Mike walk up the troop compartment ladder. The gate is open and they step right into the troop compartment. Standing up by the latrines is Big Leroy. The first latrine door is open. Kyle and Mike walk up the isle to where Big Leroy is standing.

Big Leroy works for the Air Force as a civilian and in his mid-40s. He is a big, overweight black guy. His appearance is very sloppy. He always wears knee high rubber boots because his job is servicing and de-servicing the latrines and removing the garbage from the planes.

"What the hell is going on back here?" asked Kyle.

Big Leroy nods his hello but doesn't speak.

Slim Sanders sticks his head out from inside the latrine.

Slim Sanders is a buck sergeant and in his early 20s. He is from somewhere in Pennsylvania. He is a hard worker and a very funny guy. He is always telling jokes.

Sanders greets Kyle. "What's up Kyle?"

Kyle looks in the latrine and tries to survey the situation. "Nada. Rob said the latrine was leaking."

"Yea," said Sanders. "They were servicing it, but it won't hold water. The mission is taking 73 passengers, so it has to be fixed."

A smile comes over Kyle's face. "Troubles at the Blue Lagoon."

Sanders also thinks the situation is funny. "Yea right."

"Is SLAW shop on the way out?" asked Kyle.

SLAW stands for Seat, Ladder and Water. The shop, which is located off the flightline, is manned by crew chiefs. They maintain and repair all the passenger seats on the plane. Nine out of ten times, a good crew chief will just fix the seat himself. SLAW is also responsible for the ladders on the plane. Once again, with this system, they are rarely called out to repair a ladder. The water side is a different story. The only operational water system on the plane is the latrines. They are somewhat nasty and crew chiefs will only work on them if it is the last resort. There is a potable water system on the plane that is deactivated because in the wintertime the lines always freeze and crack.

"They are going to be a bit," said Stiffler. "They are in the middle of turnover."

"I'd love to hear that turnover. Wonder if they ever make it through one turnover without saying the word shit?" asked Kyle.

They both laugh.

Sanders gets serious for a moment. "They need to alert this aircrew now. There's no time to wait, so I was going to go deep."

Kyle doesn't argue with Sanders' decision. "Better you than me."

Sanders puts a black rubber glove on his right hand and then slides a large brown trash bag over his arm all the way up to his shoulder. Mike is wide-eyed and speechless. Big Leroy steps back in between the seats.

Sanders is smiling and on the verge of laughing. "I'm going treasure hunting at the Blue Water Spa."

Sanders turns to Big Leroy. "You sure you don't want to do this?"

Big Leroy inches further back between the seats. "Not no, but hell no!"

Kyle doesn't like the security of a single bag. He makes a suggestion to Sanders. "You better double bag that thing."

Sanders starts to put another trash bag over his arm. Once the second bag is up to his shoulder Kyle streamlines it and takes a roll of duct tape and secures the bag around his shoulder and upper arm.

The term double bag reminds Kyle of an old joke. "You know, double bagging is the second stage in the four stages of ugly."

Sanders know the joke and jumps onboard with Kyle. "Big Leroy, have you ever had a chick so ugly you had to double bag it?"

Big Leroy is puzzled. "What the hell are you guys talking about?"

"Sleeping with ugly women," said Sanders. "You can't tell me you've never banged a nasty beast before."

Kyle starts to explain. "You see, there are four stages of ugly. The first stage is you put a bag over her head so you don't have to look at her. The second stage is you put a bag over your head in case hers falls off."

Sanders takes over. "Yea-yea...and the third stage is to drape a flag over her body and do it for your country."

Big Leroy and Mike are starting to chuckle, but Sanders and Kyle are serious as if this is a real science.

Kyle continues. "And the fourth stage is coyote ugly. It's when you were so fucked up the night before that you didn't realize how ugly the chick was. When you wake up in the morning and see how ugly she is, you just want to slip out of bed without waking her so you don't have to face her."

Sanders leans over on the seat and acts like he is sleeping with his arm under his head. "Yea...but the only problem is that she is lying on your arm. So instead of waking her up, you just gnaw your arm off like a coyote caught in a trap and get the fuck out of there."

Sanders bites at his arm as if he is going to gnaw his arm off.

Big Leroy can't believe what he just heard but he knows Kyle and Sanders are messing with him. "Get the fuck out of here. You mother fuckers are crazy."

They all start laughing.

Sanders' attention turns back to the task at hand. "Ok, fuck it. Here I go."

Sanders steps back into the latrine and kneels down on a knee. He slowly sticks his arm down in the latrine. He fishes around a little. All the guys have a disgusted look on their faces.

"Got something!" yelled Sanders.

He slowly pulls it to the edge of the opening. Kyle leans in with a flashlight so they can get a better look at what it is.

Sanders is close to gagging. "It's a fucking diaper."

Kyle slightly panics. "Well don't bring it out. Shove it down the drain."

Sanders works his way back in and stuffs it down the drain.

"I should be getting hazardous duty pay for this."

Kyle jokingly agrees. "Yea, it will be in your next pay check. I promise."

Sanders searches a little more. He figures that since he's in there, why not go ahead and make sure everything is clear. A few seconds go by. "Wait, there's something else in here."

"What is it?" asked Kyle.

Sanders expression is mixed. He doesn't know if he should laugh of throw up. "It feels like a big petrified Lincoln Log."

Kyle is taken back by the find. "Are you serious?"

"Yea and I don't think it'll make it down the drain," said Sanders. "I'm going to try and break it apart."

Sanders hits the massive turd against the inside wall of the toilet. It sounds like a bass drum. He hits it three times. Bom...bom...bom. On the third hit it finally breaks. Sanders and Kyle are snickering. Mike and Big Leroy have a stunned look on their faces.

Sanders stays put. "God damn that was a huge turd. Kyle, see if the drain will close now."

Kyle jumps in the last row of seats on his right. He leans over the folded down seat next to the wall and reaches behind the seat for the latrine drain handle.

"It feels like it is sliding in and out all the way."

Kyle moves back to the edge of the latrine.

Sanders has had enough. He took one for the team. "Fuck it. Ok, I'm coming out."

Sanders slowly pulls his arm out. Once it's out, Kyle undoes the tape and carefully turns the bags inside out and off his arm. Sanders peels the rubber glove off and drops it in the bag. Kyle rolls the bag up.

Despite how nasty the job was, Sanders is still in a jovial mood. "That was some nasty shit...literally."

Kyle turns and tries to blame the huge turd on Big Leroy. "Big Leroy, did you drop that bomb in there?"

Big Leroy defends himself. "Hell no! You think my big ass can fit on that little toilet?"

"As hard as that thing was, it's probably been simmering in there for a while," said Sanders.

"You should drive down to the terminal and see if you can find someone that looks like they just had a baby," said Kyle.

"Let's get the hell out of here," said Sanders. "It's time for me to go home."

"I'll take care of the forms," said Kyle.

Kyle, Mike and Sanders exit the troop compartment. They are talking and laughing as they walk away. Big Leroy stays behind to finish servicing the latrine. He grabs his radio and calls his coworker that is on the ground at the latrine servicing truck.

A few minutes later Kyle, Buckner, and Mike are sitting at the crew chief table. Buckner is in the first seat, Mike is across from him and Kyle is in the first seat of the three-man seat. Buckner and Kyle's seats are reclined and Mike's seat is upright. Kyle's feet are up on the wall.

Buckner has the forms in front of him. "So, I sign it off as cleared drain?"

"Yea, that's fine," said Kyle. "But call it in as, 'removed diaper and Lincoln Log from troop compartment aft latrine'."

"Chief, I'm not going to say that over the radio," said Buckner.

Kyle holds out his hand. "Give it to me. I'll call it in like that."

Buckner hands Kyle the radio.

"MOCC, 463."

"Go ahead 463, this is MOCC."

"I have a job to close when you are ready."

"Go ahead."

Kyle is snickering. "Today's date, 5011. Removed Lincoln Log from troop compartment aft latrine. No leaks noted."

Kyle, Buckner and Mike start to laugh.

Buckner grabs the radio. Now he wants to get in on it. "That's petrified Lincoln Log."

Buckner hands the radio back to Kyle as various comments start to fly. "My butt hurts." "I feel better...any left overs?" "I'm hungry!"

Then you hear the sound of a toilet flushing over the radio.

Kyle, Buckner and Mike are laughing. Big Leroy passes the crew chief table and steps into the flight deck latrine.

Someone else comes over the radio. "Can you come to my plane? I have a latrine write-up."

"Buckner, look through the forms and give me Sanders' man number," asked Kyle

Buckner flips a few pages. "Here it is, 01779."

Kyle gets back on the radio. "MOCC, 463."

"Go ahead 463."

"Man number 01779. And we are fixed. Copy Sierra 6?"

The MOCC controlled can't resist. He has to get in on the action. "Got it, removed Lincoln Log, man number 01779. The aircrew is being alerted now."

"Sierra 6 copies."

Kyle hands the radio back to Buckner. Big Leroy comes out of the bathroom with a large bag of garbage. He starts walking up towards the flight station door. The garbage bag is leaking something.

Mike notices the leak. "Hey mister, that bag is leaking."

Big Leroy stops and lifts the garbage bag up just enough to see the leak. "Oh, yea, I don't have another bag to put it in."

Buckner comes unglued. "Chief! Are you shitting me?"

"Well why didn't you leave it in the can and go get another bag?" asked Kyle.

"I don't know."

"Well don't just stand there!" said Buckner. "Put it back in the can or take it down stairs!"

Big Leroy turns and starts back towards the flight station door and down the ladder. He is dripping what looks like soda all the way from the latrine to the flight station and down the stairs. Kyle gets up and follows him to the top of the stairs. He is careful not to step in any of the liquid that is on the floor. He sees Big Leroy make it to the ground and comes back to the table.

"That fat fuck," says Kyle shaking his head. "Look at the mess he made."

Buckner grabs the radio. "I'll call for a mop and a bucket of hot water. Akin, looks like you have your first job."

It's now half past two in the morning. Buckner, Kyle and Mike are still in the same seats as before. Buckner is asleep, Mike is looking through the forms and Kyle is sitting with a stack of white paper cups that he got from the galley. He has a sewing needle and is poking small holes in the bottom of every third cup and restacking them onto each other.

All of a sudden you can hear voices down stairs and people coming up the ladder. Kyle jumps up and goes to the flight deck. He looks down the stairs and sees the crew. Some are shuttling crew bags and luggage from the bus to the base of the ladder and others have positioned themselves every few steps on the ladder. There are also two guys in the cargo compartment. One-by-one the bags and luggage are handed up and stacked in cargo compartment.

Kyle walks back to the crew chief table and wakes Buckner up. "Bo, the crew is here."

Buckner wakes up and stretches. "Chief, I was out like a light."

"Yea you were."

"How long was I asleep?"

"About two hours."

Buckner grabs the radio and calls. "MOCC, 463."

"Go ahead 463."

"Crew show."

"MOCC copies, crew show."

Kyle grabs the stack of cups that he was poking holes in and takes them back to the galley. He puts them in the cup dispenser and returns to his seat and puts his feet back up on the wall.

Buckner motions to Mike. "Chief, get up so the crew can sit there and look at the forms."

Mike gets up as the crew comes back to the table. There are three of them. Kyle tucks in his feet and Mike slides by and sits in the seat next to the wall. Kyle puts his feet back up on the wall.

"How does she look?" asked one of the crewmembers.

"I'd get on it," said Kyle.

Buckner spins the forms around so the crew can see them. "Cherry. Take a look."

One crewmember sits down where Mike was previously sitting and the other two stand behind him and look over his shoulder. They flip through the forms, page-by-page, looking for vital information and the open discrepancies.

"Looks good to me."

Another Crew Member asked, "Is nitro topped off?"

"Chief, 750/750."

They all head back up front to the flight deck to start their pre-flight inspection.

"So what do we do now?" asked Mike.

Kyle stretches. "Just wait to see if they fuck something up."

It's just after five o'clock in the morning. Kyle, Buckner and Mike are sitting and leaning on the Jersey barrier wall out in front of the plane. The Sierra 6 truck pulls up from the left and swings around so the truck is pointing at the plane on India row. Rob puts the truck in park and turns the headlights off. Kyle, Buckner and Mike walk up to the driver's door.

"Is the ER signed yet?" asked Rob.

ER stands for Exceptional Release. Before any of the planes fly, the forms are reviewed and the plane is deemed safe and ready to go. A qualified and authorized person accomplishes this. The driver of Sierra 4 is the person that grants, or signs, ERs. This position is always held by a master sergeant, or above, or a civilian equivalent.

Buckner spits. "Yea Chief, where have you been? I called it in over the radio."

"Oh, I was taking care of some important business," Rob answers sheepishly. "I must have missed that."

Kyle sees right through Rob. "Who won?"

Rob pauses for a second. He knows that the guys know he has been screwing off. "Eric and Emo."

"Yea, that's what I thought," said Kyle.

Kyle yawns and stretches.

"What, are you tired?" asked Rob.

"Yea, I was woken up this morning for a piss test. I was asleep for about an hour and they came and notified me."

"That sucks," said Rob.

"And that was my third piss test this month!" said Kyle. "But this one was worth it."

"What do you mean," asked Rob.

Kyle starts smiling as he tells his story. "I went up there and checked in. The place was packed. This guy comes in behind me and really has to go but the professional meat gazers tell him he has to wait his turn. The guy can't stand still. He's about to piss himself. So a chief walks up there and convinces them to let him cut the line and go next. So they hustle the guy in the bathroom and let him piss."

"What is so funny about that?" asked Rob.

Kyle starts laughing. "The guy got in there, pissed in the bottle and the bottle had a crack in it."

They all start laughing.

Buckner taps Rob on the shoulder a few times. "Chief, check it out. Kyle just pissed under the power unit. We called Kilo and told them we think it has a fuel leak."

Kilo is the radio call sign for the flightline AGE driver. He delivers and retrieves powered AGE in a bobtail just as Sierra 18 does with non-powered AGE. The difference is Kilo works under the Field Maintenance Squadron, or FMS. All the AGE equipment on the flightline belongs to, and is maintained by AGE.

Rob laughs. "You are pissing everywhere today."

"Yea," said Kyle. Let's see if this AGE driver passes my piss test."

A bobtail pulls up to the plane and backs up to the power unit. The power unit is shut down and the cord is rolled up. The AGE driver gets out of the truck and hooks the power unit to the bobtail's pintle hook. He walks around to where Kyle peed, bends over, drags two fingers through the piss and smells his fingers. He pulls his fingers away from his face when he realizes it's piss. Kyle, Buckner, Mike, and Rob are laughing their asses off. The driver gets in the truck, slams the door and drives straight towards the Sierra 6 truck. All the guys stop laughing and are acting as if they don't know what is going on.

Rob turns off the interior light. "Oh shit, here he comes."

The bobtail, with the power unit in tow, gets about 50 feet away from the Sierra 6 truck and veers to its right. The driver hangs out the window, flips the guys off and drives on. All the guys start laughing again.

Buckner spits. "Chief, he was pissed!"

"Yea, he'll get over it," said Kyle. "That guy is a friend of mine. His name is Stone."

"Is this what you guys do out here every night?" asked Mike.

Kyle shrugs his shoulders. "More or less."

Rob looks at his clipboard and throws it back on the dash. "Never a dull moment."

The plane flashes its landing lights signaling the guys that they are ready to start engines. There are two crewmembers downstairs standing next to the fire bottle.

"Pull up there so we can throw our stuff in the truck," said Buckner.

Rob puts the truck in drive and pulls towards the plane. The three guys follow the truck.

It's just before seven in the morning. Buckner, Kyle and Mike launched the plane and are back in 585. Kyle is back in his uniform. He exits the side door of 585 and runs into Troy.

"Hey, slow down there boy. What's your hurry?" asked Troy.

"Trying to get back to the dorms before the sun comes up. You know how grave shifters are."

"So what's going on this weekend?" asked Troy.

"I'm heading to New York City. I'm going to get a few hours of sleep and head up this afternoon. You should come," suggested Kyle.

Troy shakes his head. "No, I can't. I have to work tomorrow morning. What's Bucky doing?"

"He's heading to Baltimore to pick up a truck his uncle is giving him."

"How is he getting up there?" asked Troy.

"That cop friend of his he grew up with is taking him. They went to the same high school. I think his name is Broderick."

"Alright boy, I guess I'm here solo."

"If you get lonely, go over to the dayroom in my building and hang out with Bailey," said Kyle.

"Yea I'll do that. And bring him some cheese. I have to get in here. Roll call is about to start. I'll see you later."

"Later."

Troy enters the building and Kyle walks away.

CHAPTER 6

Three days have passed. It's half past five in the evening on a Monday. Kyle, Bucky and Troy are sitting at a table in the chow hall. They are all in civilian clothes. The guys all have trays in front of them. On the trays are drinking glasses, plates and silverware. They are finishing dinner. The chow hall is about a half full.

The chow hall, or dining facility, is a large building that can seat over 100 people. There are two entrances on opposite sides of the building. Inside, it is one big room with two separate serving lines. One line serves a variety of dishes on a weekly basis and the other is the snack line. It always serves hamburgers, hot dogs and French fries. The chow hall is open every day of the year serving breakfast, lunch, dinner and a midnight chow.

Kyle is in the middle of a story. "So once I find a good parking spot for my car, I put 20 dollars in the ash tray. It's enough to pay for tolls and gas. That's my insurance policy for getting back here."

"Does your car ever get broken into?" asked Troy.

"No, but they've stolen my Alabama license plate twice." said Kyle.

"Where do you stay?" asked Bucky.

"I stay in Jackson Heights, Queens, but I party mostly in the city. At first I was staying with an ex-girlfriend. She was a flight attendant. But now when I go up, I stay with a bunch of want-to-be actresses from Iowa."

"How is it in Jackson Heights?" asked Troy.

"I don't go to the bars there," said Kyle. "I just sleep and eat there. They have a few good restaurants in the area. The Ranch is the best for a hangover. Good breakfast. I party mostly in the city, down in the Village."

"That's where all the freaks are, right?" asked Bucky.

Troy jumps in. "You mean all the fags."

Kyle wags his finger in disagreement. "No, it's cool."

"How are the bars?" asked Bucky.

Kyle sits up straight. "Good. I usually hit Bleecker Street. I have a few favorites down there like Mondo Cane, The Bitter End, Rock and Roll Café and CBGB if there is a good band. If I feel like a nightclub, I usually hit a place called the Limelight"

"I might have to go up there with you sometime," said Troy.

Kyle laughs. "Troy, it's the city, not Long Island. You'd never make it up there."

Bucky rubs his forehead. "My head still hurts."

"What the hell is wrong with your head?" asked Troy.

"Check it out."

Bucky leans forward and shows Troy the top of his head. There is a half-moon cut in it and it is stitched up.

"Holy shit! What happened?" asked Troy.

Bucky starts to tell the story. "Well, Debra and I are in this bar in Fells Point having a few drinks and watching the O's."

Troy interrupts. "The Orioles right?"

"Yea, the Orioles." said Bucky. "Anyway, the third baseman boots a ground ball. So I start talking about the best third baseman to ever play the game."

Kyle knows what Bucky is going to say. He's heard it 100 times. "Brooks Robinson right?"

"That's right, the human vacuum cleaner." Bucky continues. "So these guys next to me are all drunk and they start talking shit to me about ole Brooksie. And the worst part is, they are Baltimore fans. They know he is the man."

"Did you know them?" asked Troy.

"No, probably white trash from Dunndalk (trashy town near Baltimore). Anyways, I start having words with these guys and before you know it me and one of the guys are going at it. Little did I know the whole bar was full of his friends. One thing leads to another and I'm fighting the entire bar. So Debra jumps in and starts throwing blows."

Troy can't believe what he is hearing. "Are you serious?"

"Yea! They finally held me down and smashed a beer mug over my head. The next thing I remember is coming to out on the street."

"Holy shit!" said Troy. "Even Debra was going at it?"

"Yea! It was like 15 on one, or two."

Kyle laughs. "And how did it come out?"

Bucky smiles and holds his head high. "The O's won that day and Brooks Robinson is still the man."

They all laugh.

A black guy, Lee Booker, is walking towards the table. He has a tray in his hands. He is walking all cool, as if he's some kind of pimp. He is wearing a necklace with a big African medallion on it. Lee sees the guys sitting at the table. He quickly looks for an empty table around him so he doesn't have to walk past them. Lee is out of luck. There are no empty tables. He has to man up and walk past the guys. He knows they are going to mess with him. He continues walking.

Bucky spots Lee. "Look at this shit. Booker, what's up?"

Kyle starts messing with Lee. "Did you hurt yourself? I see you are limping."

Lee rolls his eyes. "No, that's my natural walk."

"What, do you have one leg shorter than the other?" asked Troy.

Everyone laughs except Lee.

Lee has had enough. "Screw you guys."

"Nice necklace. I thought you were an American?" asked Bucky.

"I am. This is where my roots are from." said Lee.

Kyle is all over it. "Roots? Who do you think you are Kunta Kente's great grandson?"

Lee has had enough. "Oh I see how it is."

Bucky keeps it going. "You probably can't even name five countries in Africa."

"Fuck you guys!" said Lee.

All the guys start laughing again. Lee starts walking away.

Kyle yells at him. "Lee!"

Lee stops and turns around.

"See you at the gym Saturday morning." said Kyle.

Lee acknowledges Kyle with a head tilt and continues on his way.

Troy leans in. "We'll all be in Social Actions tomorrow morning."

Social Actions is the office that deals with racial complaints, discrimination and sexual harassment.

"Na," said Kyle. "Lee is cool. He knows we are just fucking with him."

Ross Higa comes and sits at the table with a tray of food.

Ross Higa is a buck sergeant in his mid-20s. He is of Japanese descent. His family is from New Jersey. Bucky likes to mess around with Higa about his Asian roots. He knows Higa is Japanese and that Higa is sensitive about the subject. Higa is very short, maybe 5 feet if he is lucky. His drinking limit is about two beers. When he starts getting a buzz, his face turns red and he smiles constantly.

"Hey, what's up guys?" asks Higa.

Troy greets Higa. "What's up Higa?"

Bucky makes fun of Higa as if he is Korean. "What do you have to eat Higa, Kimchi?"

Everyone starts laughing. Higa rolls his eyes.

"No Bucky," said Higa. "I don't eat Kimchi. I'm Japanese, not Korean."

Bucky doesn't let up. "You all look alike to me."

"Speaking of Social Actions," said Troy.

Higa attempts to straighten out Bucky. "Only Asians can tell other Asians apart. That's a gift we have."

Kyle switches back to Bucky. "Bucky, every time you go home you fuck yourself up."

Troy remembers one of those times. "Yea, like that time you cracked your jaw."

"How'd you crack your jaw?" asked Higa.

Bucky starts to explain. "I was down at the reservoir with the Selmont brothers and Broderick. We were putting away the beers pretty good and it was starting to get dark, so we decided to leave. On the way out, I had to take a piss so I slid the side door of the Red Shed open and let it go. I had my legs spread real wide. I was holding onto the headrest of the passenger seat with my left hand and had my pecker in my right."

The Red Shed is the nickname for Bucky's van. It's about seven-years old and the red paint is faded. The back of the van is completely empty.

"You were in your van?" asked Higa.

"Yea, Eddie Selmont was driving. So anyway, he hit the brakes for some reason and the door comes sliding forward and smashes my head between the door and the frame of the van."

Higa is amazed. "Are you kidding me?"

"No! It knocked me out. I would have fallen out of the van, but Broderick grabbed my belt and pulled me back in."

Higa starts to eat. "That's crazy. That could have killed you."

"It's going to take more than a van door to do that," said Bucky.

Another guy, obviously light in the loafers, comes walking towards the table. Troy is the first one to spot him. "Look at this one."

All the guys look at him and turn back toward each other. The guy passes.

Bucky laughs. "That's On Holiday Harry."

"How'd he get that name?" asked Troy.

"Bucky and I were in line one day and the lady at the cash register says, "Harry, where have you been?" and he replies, "I've been on holiday." said Kyle.

Troy is in agreement with Kyle and Bucky. "Yea, no one straight calls a vacation 'on holiday'."

Higa cuts in. "Speaking of homos, I finally heard how Bret Nader got in trouble."

"This should be good," said Kyle.

Higa stops eating and sets his fork down. "Well, it turns out that Graywolf and Andy walked into Nader's room and he was in there with two women and another guy."

Bucky can't believe it. "Get out of here!"

"Are you serious?" asked Troy.

"Yea, they were all naked and having sex."

"Wait a minute," said Kyle. "Who was having sex with who?"

"I don't know the exact details, but I heard that they were all tied up in a pretty good knot. I heard when Graywolf and Andy walked in it was dark and everyone kind of jumped up before they turned the lights on. So they didn't really get to see exactly what was going on."

Bucky starts to laugh. "If they were doing it doggie style maybe they would have gotten stuck together."

Everyone laughs.

Troy shakes his head. "That Nader is always in trouble."

"Yea, but somehow he always manages not to get kicked out or lose a stripe," said Kyle.

CHAPTER 7

----------October 1989----------

Its eleven thirty at night and Kyle has just finished receiving turnover from swing shift. Kyle is sitting in the first seat at the crew chief table, Buckner is across from him and Mike is sitting across the aisle in the first chair of the three-man seat. Kyle has coveralls and his field jacket on. His field jacket is stained with grease, oil and hydraulic fluid. Kyle washes the jacket every week but the stains will not come out. Buckner is wearing a military issue brown wool sweater with coveralls over it. Mike is in his uniform and is wearing his field jacket. It looks brand new compared to Kyle's.

Mike has been on leave for a few weeks visiting his family in Texas. It's his first night back at work. Kyle has the aircraft forms in front of him and is looking through them. He is formulating a game plan to fix the plane. He has ripped a blank 781A from the forms, folded it in half and is using it to take notes. He is running the show tonight so he has the radio sitting on the table in front of him.

"Chief, you got it figured out?" asked Buckner.

"Yea, give me a second." said Kyle.

"How do I get a pair of coveralls?" asked Mike. "I've already ruined two sets of uniforms out here."

Kyle stops writing. "You have to write up and clear 500 discrepancies before the shift chief will give you a pair."

Mike nods his head not realizing the joke.

"Chief, all you've done so far is mop the floor, check out tools and marshal out a hand-full of planes," said Buckner. "You better get on the ball."

They all start laughing.

Mike really wants to be a part of the team and do his share of the work. He doesn't like being treated like a rookie, even though he is. "Well you guys won't let me do anything."

"That's because you don't know anything," said Buckner. "We do it a different way out here on grave shift."

Kyle sits back. "Yea, this isn't QTP or day shift. This is the working shift."

Buckner gets up, steps into the crew latrine and spits. He comes back out and stands at the table. "Everything you learned in QTP, forget it. Just listen to what we tell you, pay attention and you'll learn fast."

"Ok, I got it," said Kyle. "Let's start with the tire and then we'll let the specialist work. We'll CSS the gas somewhere there in the middle."

CSS stands for Concurrent Servicing Supervisor. A CSS refuel is only granted by Sierra 4 under certain circumstances. It happens mostly during aircraft launches. A CSS refuel allows you to have more activities going on, like loading cargo, fleet service and certain aircrew duties, all while you are pumping gas. The individual that supervises a CSS refuel wears an orange vest with the letters CSS on the front and back of it.

"Who's driving Sierra 4 tonight?" asked Buckner. "You think they'll ok CSS on a non-flyer?"

"Keiderling is driving," said Kyle. "If you have a good reason for doing it and it's totally legal, he's ok with it. We are training Mike.

"Chief, I'm not sure about Keiderling," said Buckner. "He's wrapped a little too tight for me."

"No, he's cool," said Kyle. "He's just a little quiet. You have to understand his humor. One night I was sitting in the break room eating my leftover chicken parmesan sandwich and he came up to me and asked me, 'Do you like chicken?' Of course, I said yes. Then he said, 'Then why don't you choke my chicken?' and walked away laughing."

They all laugh.

"Hold on," said Kyle. "Let me get the ball rolling."

Kyle grabs the radio. "MOCC, 217."

"Go ahead 217, this is MOCC."

"Yea MOCC, can you send Jets out now for the nicked blades? Also send Sheet Metal out for the Abradable write-ups. Give me Hydro in 30 minutes for the filters. In an hour send A/R for the aileron flutter. You can send Comm/Nav out now. GAC can also come out now, but let them know I might not be able to give them systems for a few hours or until A/R and Hydro are finished. Also, can you upgrade the 1C1 tire to a red X?"

MOCC delays for a few seconds. "Got it."

Kyle turns his attention back to Buckner and Mike. "Let's do the tire first and then we'll knock out the rest of this stuff they wrote up."

"Alright, I'll take Mike down, set up for kneeling and start on the tire," said Buckner. "Fire up the APU and let's get this show on the road."

The guys grab their headsets from their bags. Kyle grabs the radio and puts it in his left upper pocket. They all head toward the flight deck.

"Do I really have to sign off 500 write-ups to get a pair of coveralls?" asked Mike.

"No chief, we'll go by the Jet shop or A/R shop tonight and try and steal you some," said Buckner. "You better start realizing that these guys are fucking with you half the time because you're the new kid on the block."

Buckner and Mike head down stairs. Kyle looks over at the pilot's center console to see if the radios are on. He sits at the engineer's station. He starts positioning switches, closing red guarded switches and pulling a few circuit breakers to set up for the tire change. He also grabs the APU checklist, sets it in front of him and opens it to the emergency procedures.

Buckner's voice comes over the interphone. "Chief, you're clear."

"Coming up," said Kyle.

Kyle starts the left APU. You can hear it as it comes on speed. He checks the volts and frequencies and then moves a few more switches. The hydraulic systems start up.

"Are we all set up?" asked Buckner.

"Yea, go ahead," said Kyle. "Four is up and you are set for individual kneel. You have the gear pin in?"

"Yea. Chief, do you have new hardware?" asked Buckner.

"Yea, I have some in my bag," said Kyle. "I'll be down in a second."

Kyle walks back to the crew chief table. He reaches into his bag and pulls out a plastic sandwich bag. Inside the sandwich bag are new nuts, bolts and cotter keys needed for the tire change. Kyle gets two of each out of the bag, closes it and drops it back inside his helmet bag. He turns and heads downstairs.

Kyle comes down the crew entry door ladder and starts walking back to the number one main landing gear. Kyle has his headset on. It's very loud because the power unit, APU and hydraulic system are running. The plane they are working on is 68-217. It still has the white and grey paint job. As Kyle walks up to the gear there is an open toolbox, tire change kit and a large torque wrench in a long black plastic case on the ground. The orange "remove before flight" streamer that is attached to the landing gear pin can be seen blowing around inside the gear. Leaning against the number three landing gear is the new tire. Buckner is kneeling down by the tire that they are going to change. He spins the core out of the tire's valve stem and the air starts to race out.

Mike walks over in front of the gear and opens a small, hinged panel above the refuel receptacles. It swings out about six inches and locks in place. A light attached to the panel comes on. Directly inside the panel is the individual kneel switches for the two left main landing gears. Mike reaches up, holds the switch and looks at Buckner. Buckner gives him the thumbs up. The gear starts to slowly rise. As it does, the counter on the side of the kneel motor moves from 000 and starts to rise. As the gear goes up the other four struts start to take on the weight of the plane. The struts bang and pop as they compress and the entire plane shakes. All the tires on the number one gear finally leave the ground. The tire they are changing gets about three-inches off the ground and Buckner signals Mike to stop. Mike releases the switch.

Mike walks over and kneels down next to the tire. Buckner joins him. Kyle grabs a few rags out of the tire change kit and takes a knee next to the guys. Mike takes a ratchet and removes the four bolts from the tire deflation valve. He slides the valve straight out of the axle, twists off the cannon plug and hands the valve and bolts to Kyle. Kyle takes a rag out of his pocket, lays it on the ground and sets the valve and the bolts on it. Mike peels the large O-ring off the wheel and hands it to Kyle. Kyle takes another rag and starts to clean the O-ring.

Buckner hands Mike the tire change adapter. Mike slides it inside the six-inch castellated nut. Buckner leans over him and inserts a breaker bar into the adapter. Mike leans in and puts all his weight against the adapter as Buckner pushes down on the bar and breaks the torque on the nut. Mike hands the adapter and breaker bar back to Buckner. Mike spins the nut off the axle with his hands and passes it, and the lock ring, to Kyle. Kyle starts to clean them with his rag.

Mike gets in front of the tire and Buckner gets behind it. They grab the wheel with their hands, lift up and slide the wheel and tire off the axle. Mike rolls the tire over to the tire trailer and shoves it into the empty slot. As he is doing that, Buckner takes a hammer and bends back the heat shields on the new tire.

Kyle looks over the brake to make sure it isn't damaged. He aligns the brake discs so the new tire will slide straight on. He then cleans the axle with a rag. He grabs a can of grease out of the tire change kit and lubes the axle. Kyle returns to the pile of parts and starts to put anti-seize on the large nut.

Buckner rolls the new tire up beside the axle. Mike returns and they line up the wheel with the brake slots. They lift the wheel and tire in the same fashion they took it off and slide it over the brake and onto the axle. They are very careful and pay attention, making sure they do not knock the wheel bearing out of the wheel.

Mike kneels down again and Buckner is right over his shoulder making sure he does everything 100 percent right. Kyle hands Mike the retaining ring and Mike fits it to the axle, making sure it is in the groves. Kyle then hands Mike the large nut and Mike starts spinning it onto the axle. He pays special attention not to unseat the retaining ring. Mike tightens it as much as possible with his hands.

Kyle takes the large torque wrench from the case and sets it to 250 foot-pounds. He hands it to Buckner to verify the setting. Mike fits the adapter inside the nut and Buckner attaches the large torque wrench to the adapter. As Mike holds the adapter in place, Kyle spins the tire clockwise. As the tire spins, Buckner slowly tightens the nut until the torque reaches 250 foot-pounds. The torque wrench gives with a click and Buckner removes it quickly from the adapter. They have seated the tire. Buckner hands the torque wrench back to Kyle and he changes the setting to 100 foot-pounds. Buckner grabs the breaker bar, inserts it into the adapter and breaks the torque on the nut. He removes the breaker bar and Kyle hands him the large torque wrench back. Buckner verifies the setting and reattaches the torque wrench again. Kyle spins the tire as Buckner tightens the nut. At 100 foot-pounds, the torque wrench clicks and Buckner removes it from the adapter.

Mike pulls the adapter away to see if the grooves in the castellated nut are aligned with the round holes in the retaining ring. Kyle and Buckner also lean in to see. They all spot one that is a hair off. They all signal to each other that the nut only needs a slight touch. Mike inserts the adapter again and Buckner attaches the breaker bar to it. Buckner slowly starts to pull up and tighten the nut. It moves a hair and Buckner stops. Mike pulls away the adapter and breaker bar and they all lean in again. It appears to be aligned.

Kyle reaches in his pocket, takes out the new hardware and sets it on the inside of the wheel. Mike starts to install the new hardware as Buckner closely watches him. He tightens the nuts and bolts and then cotter pins them. They must be perfectly aligned. Kyle sets the torque wrench to 300 foot-pounds and hands it to Buckner. He verifies the setting again as Mike inserts the adapter again. This time, Mike sits back leaning on his hands and holds the adapter on with his feet. Buckner attaches the torque wrench and pushes down on it, applying a back torque. This is to ensure the nut and ring are secured and locked in place. Click! Buckner removes the torque wrench and Mike sets the adapter aside.

Kyle hands Mike the big O-ring. Mike tries to get it seated on the wheel. It's eight-inches in diameter and will not cooperate with Mike. Buckner shoos away Mike and jumps on the ground. He works the O-rings into the slot, almost like he's working a vase on a clay wheel. He gets it seated and moves out of the way. Mike jumps back in as Kyle hands him the tire deflation valve. Mike attaches the cannon plug and slides the valve into the axle. He carefully lines the tabs on the valve with the groves on the nut and slides it in. It's a miracle. He hits it the first time. He looks up at Buckner and gives him a look of confidence. Kyle hands four bolts to Mike. Mike, pressing the valve tightly into the wheel and axle, installs the bolts with his fingers. After a certain point, he tightens them the rest of the way with the ratchet.

They are done. Kyle walks away and heads upstairs. Buckner plugs his headset into the interphone cord as he and Mike start to clean up all the tools and equipment. Buckner makes sure nothing is under the tires and calls upstairs to Kyle. He lets him know the gear is clear. Kyle rotates the kneel select switch to unkneel and takes the kneel command switch to unkneel. The gear starts to slowly come down. As the tires reach the ground the gear starts to share the weight of the plane and all the struts bang and pop again. The plane shakes until the counter reads 000.

Kyle lets Buckner know the gear is finished unkneeling. He knows from the indicator light on the kneel panel. Buckner checks the counter for 000 ± 1. He walks over, climbs on the gear and pulls the gear pin out. He walks back over to Mike and they carry the tools and equipment back to the front of the plane. As they walk towards the front of the plane, two specialist trucks pull up and park.

A few hours later Kyle and Mike are standing at the wall taking a break. Their hands are dirty and they both have black grease marks on their faces. They, along with Buckner, have changed a tire, updated a preflight, serviced a hand full of tires and accumulators, and fixed a lot of crew chief discrepancies. They've also assisted specialist in all of their jobs.

"In QTP, that tire change took us an hour," said Mike. "We did it in 15 minutes."

"Listen, this is how it is out here, the Reader Digest version," said Kyle. "The only thing day shift does is launch the locals at 10 o'clock and go to appointments."

Locals are training missions for the aircrews. They usually last four hours. The planes fly around the base and practice takeoffs and landings.

Kyle continues. "Day shift does a lot of cleaning, working on forms and occasional changes to the TO file."

TO stands for Technical Orders. TOs tell crew chiefs and maintainers how to work on the plane's various systems. Each TO is the size of several large phone books put together, about five inches thick. There are over fifty TOs on the plane."

"At two o'clock the planes land from their locals," said Kyle. "In day shift's eyes, there's not enough time to do anything, so they leave most of the work for swing shift. LSD or "let swings do-it"."

Mike is all ears. "Ok."

"So the planes land at the end of the day shift and swing shift gets them back up again for their six o'clock locals. After that, swing shift starts trying to fix the planes on the ground and everything day shift blew off. They are not so worried about cleaning and the TOs. Then at 10 o'clock, the locals land again and swing shift does everything they can do prior to us coming on."

"Why does day shift blow off stuff but swing shift busts their asses at the end of their shift?" asked Mike.

"There's different people and a different management style."

"And our shift?" asked Mike.

"The planes have flown most of the day with little time for maintenance. They carry forward a lot of write-ups and they end up in our laps. Grave Shift is the time to fix everything and get it ready for the next day. It's a nonstop 24/7/365 event out here."

"What about weekends and holidays?" asked Mike.

Kyle laughs. "That means nothing out here. There are no locals on the weekends, unless it's a UTA weekend."

UTA weekend is the one weekend a month that Reservists have to work.

Kyle continues his dose of reality. "A weekend means there is more time to fix the planes. It's kind of like the post office. The mail never stops, rain, snow and all that crap. That's funny when you think about it - half the guys out here are postal!"

They both laugh.

"Well, on UTA weekends there are a lot of extra people here, right?" asked Mike.

"They don't work on graves. They are mostly on day shift. All they do is go to appointments. If they do come out on the line, they usually fuck something up and we waste time fixing it. It's a real scam."

Mike has more questions. "What about QA? I was told to watch out for them."

QA stands for Quality Assurance. QA inspectors come around to check people's work and the general safety of the flightline.

"They are mostly on days, just playing the game," said Keith. "You hardly see them out here on graves. If they do drop by, they usually just look at the forms and leave. We always have our forms up tight. It's our methods that are questionable."

"What do you mean?" asked Mike.

"There is so much to do and so little time, you have to cut corners," said Kyle. "That's why QA doesn't come out here often. Everyone from the top down knows if you followed the book, nothing will fly out of here on time. It's like launches. You'll never see QA out on a launch. It's an unwritten rule."

Mike looks a little overwhelmed.

"Don't worry," said Kyle. "You'll catch on. Just pay attention and learn as much as you can. Learn how to do it the right way first and then when the shit hits the fan, you'll know where you can take a short cut or two. Within a year you'll know more than a guy that's been on day shift for three years."

Sierra 6 truck pulls up from the right. Kyle and Mike step toward the truck.

"Hey Akin, have you switched over to separate rats or are you still on a meal card?" asked Rob.

A meal card is issued to all new airmen. It allows them to eat at the chow hall for free. It can also be used to get box lunches from fleet service. Box lunches are simple meals served in a small white box. They usually contain two sandwiches, potato chips, a drink, a piece of candy and a fruit snack.

Separate rats stands for separate rations. It is extra money the Air Force gives you to buy food. All grave shifters are on separate rats because of the hours they work and the odd times they eat.

You can't have a meal card and separate rats at the same time. It's one or the other.

"Yes sir," said Mike. "I still have my meal card."

"Cut the sir shit," said Rob. "Do you see anything on my shoulders?"

"Yea, I still have my meal card. Are you going to get me a box lunch?" asked Mike.

Rob turns on the interior light and grabs his clipboard. "Let me see your meal card."

Mike pulls his card out of his wallet and hands it to Rob.

"We're all getting box lunches tonight," said Kyle.

Rob flips to the back of his clipboard. He adds Mike's name and meal card number to a long list. He then hands Mike his meal card back. "Gotta go! I'll be back shortly."

The guys step away from the truck and Sierra 6 pulls away.

Mike looks like he just got taken by a street hustler playing Three-Card Monte. "So he's going to get me a meal right?" asked Mike.

Kyle laughs. "Yea, the truck keeps a list of meal card numbers. Some nights Sierra 6 will fill out a box lunch request form and get as many lunches as he can."

"What if I'm not at work and I use my meal card at the chow hall on the same night Sierra 6 orders box lunches?" asked Mike.

"Don't worry about it. We've been doing this since I got here and we haven't been caught yet. The fleet kitchen guys graduate from pumping shit to making lunches. You think they are going to rock the boat? And how smart do you think they can be if they chose that career field? Let's head back up."

Kyle and Mike start walking toward the plane.

"Hey, do you have a roommate?" asked Mike.

"Yea. I believe almost everyone does. What dorm are you in?" asked Kyle.

"Building 472, the FMS dorm. I was stuck over there because there were no open rooms in the OMS dorms."

"That sucks," said Kyle.

"Is your roommate cool?"

"Yea," said Kyle. "Why do you ask?"

Mike starts to tell his story. "I think there is something strange about my roommate. The first day I go to my room, the bay orderly takes me there. He has my key but is afraid to go in the room. He knocks a few times and then finally enters with the key. He opens the door slowly and says, 'John, are you in there?' It's dark as shit. Like a bear cave. All of a sudden a boot flies across the room at the door and we hear this deep voice say, 'Who the hell is it?' I'm thinking what the hell!"

"I would be too," said Kyle.

"The bay orderly says, 'John, it's your new roommate. We're coming in.' So, the guy opens the door a little, hands me my key and turns and splits. I walk in a few steps then hear the voice say, 'You can have my food and drinks, just replace them. You can watch my John Wayne movies if you want. But never fuck with my Crown Royal.'"

"Holy shit!" said Kyle.

"Yea, I'm not sure about the guy," said Mike. "He's pretty strange."

"Now I know if you don't show up for work one night, you had a craving for a Crown and Coke."

A few minutes later Kyle and Buckner are sitting at the crew chief table. Mike is in the first chair of the three-man seat. There are two Comm/Nav specialists working up in the flight deck. All three guys are eating their box lunches. Kyle has the radio and the forms in front of him. He is working on the forms and going through his lunch at the same time.

"Did everyone get the same thing?" asked Kyle.

"Sandwiches," said Buckner.

"Yea, sandwiches," said Mike.

"Bo, did you de-service the hydraulic systems?" asked Kyle.

"Yea, I showed Mike how to do it using the alternate method."

Kyle hands Mike the forms. "Here Mike, sign this off then."

Mike signs the write up off. Kyle gets a sandwich out of the box lunch. It is still wrapped in plastic. Mike hands the forms back to Kyle.

"Thanks," said Kyle.

The two Comm/Nav guys walk back to the table. "We are finished."

"What took you so long?" asked Kyle

"I was training my new guy."

"There is a lot of that going around these days," said Buckner.

Kyle leans up so the second specialist can put a TO back in the file behind the seat.

"What did you do?" asked Kyle.

"We changed the ADF controller."

Kyle thinks for a second. "ADF, that's on page 24."

Kyle flips the forms open to page 24 and turns them towards the specialist so he can sign off his write up.

"There you go. You guys didn't make a mess up there, did you?" asked Kyle.

"No."

Kyle takes this sandwich out of the plastic and takes a bite out of it. He sets it back down on the plastic and looks at it. There are greasy fingerprints on the bread from his hand. Kyle looks at his hands and they are half black. Kyle gets pissed. "Shit!"

The two specialists take their eyes off of the forms and look at Kyle's sandwich. They look back at the forms and continue writing.

Kyle is starving. He hasn't had anything to eat in hours. Kyle carefully places his fingers back where the fingerprints are on the sandwich, picks it up, carefully takes a bite and sets the sandwich back down. The two Comm/Nav guys look at Kyle in amazement but are too shocked to say anything about the way he is eating his sandwich.

The specialists finish signing their write up off. "Ok, all finished."

"Hold on," said Kyle.

Kyle swings the forms around and reviews what they signed off. "Ok, good to go. Hey, do me a favor. Show my new guy what you guys did up there, will you?"

"Sure, our truck won't be here for a few minutes anyway."

"Mike, go see what they did," said Kyle.

The specialist and Mike walk up to the flight deck.

"Chief, I found a second job," said Buckner.

"Doing what?" asked Kyle.

"Repossessing cars! Chief, I'm going to be a repo man."

"Get the hell out of here. Are you serious?" asked Kyle.

Buckner is excited. "Hell yea. I talked to the guy today. I'm going to start this weekend. I'm going to ride with another repo man until I get trained up, then I'll be on my own. It sounds like a blast."

"It sounds like it a good way to get shot," said Kyle.

"No Chief. The owner told me most of the time you never see the people. You grab the cars while they are at work or sleeping."

"Who was that crazy guy in Repo Man?" asked Kyle.

"Hopper Chief. Dennis Hopper."

"Yea, that's him. Good movie."

Mike walks back and sits down.

"Did they show you what's up?" asked Kyle.

"Yea. I never knew that radio could pick up radio stations," said Mike.

"That's how you learn," said Kyle. "When those guys come out to fix something, ask them about it. They love to try and show you how smart they are. Also, you have to make sure they didn't fuck up the forms or leave a mess. If you don't make them clean up after themselves, then you'll be doing it yourself."

"Chief, this is like your house," said Buckner. "Don't let them come in and shit on your floor and leave."

"Remember, regardless of rank, you are in charge out here," said Kyle.

"Chief, if a general comes out here and leaves a TO out, get on his ass!" said Buckner.

"Then kick his ass off the plane and tell him don't come back until he learns some manners," said Kyle.

They all laugh.

Day shift has just finished roll call. Its twenty minutes after seven in the morning. Kyle and Buckner are in the computer room in building 704. The computer room is a small, closed in cubical with big glass windows all around it. There is also a door. The windows allow you to see what is going on down the hallway and in the other cubicles. There are three computers on a long table. Kyle and Buckner are looking at their training qualification printouts. Kyle is sitting at a middle computer and Buckner is standing next to the door. Buckner is still in his coveralls but Kyle is in his uniform.

"This training is killing me," said Buckner. "Every time I turn around I have something due."

"Yea, me too," said Kyle. "Remember, just distract Hank when he comes in and I'll try to get his password. He should be in here any minute. He always jumps on the computer before he goes out to the plane. If we can get his info, we'll have God rights to GO81 and never have to do training again."

Not only does GO81 track and record aircraft information, it also tracks and records personnel information. One of the biggest issues crew chiefs have is their training. They are constantly fighting to keep up and stay ahead of it. The GO81 administrator has given access rights for almost every screen to Hank Tomasello, including training. Hank can add, delete or update anything in the system. The guys call this God rights. If Kyle and Bo can figure out Hank's user name and password, they will never have to do any training again.

Someone comes in and tries to sit to Kyle's left.

"Chief, use the other one," said Buckner. "This one has been screwed up all night."

The guy moves over to the other computer to Kyle's right. He realizes something is about to go down, but he knows he's probably better off minding his own business.

Buckner looks back down the hallway. "Chief, here he comes."

Kyle glances down the hallway and then turns back to his computer. "Ok."

Hank comes in and sits down with his coffee. Hank is to Kyle's left. Buckner is still standing and is on the other side of Hank. They have him boxed in.

Hank Tomasello is the top civilian crew chief that works on the flightline. He is in his fifties. Despite his age, Hank still has a lot of fire left in him. He either likes you, or he doesn't. Hank takes good care of his plane, 5003, and the team of guys that are assigned to it.

"Hank, how's it going?" asked Buckner.

Kyle also greets Hank. "What's up Hank?"

"How are you guys doing this morning?" asked Hank.

"Good, good," said Buckner.

"Who was on my jet last night?" asked Hank.

"Don't know," said Buckner. "We were on that shit box 217. Tire change and a bunch of crew chief write ups."

Kyle has his left hand on his head and his elbow is resting on the table. He is acting like he is reading something on the computer screen but he is really watching Hank's fingers on the keyboard. Hank has turned his attention to Buckner.

"Hank look, there's Ben," said Buckner. "Does he ever go out to his jet, or does he just hang out in the break room and drink coffee all day?"

Hank starts to get a little heated. He doesn't like Ben. "That lazy son of a bitch."

Ben has a cup of coffee and is heading into the computer room.

Buckner prods Hank. "I thought you guys were friends?"

Ben enters the room.

Hank looks Ben directly in the eyes. "Hey Ben, how do you take a break when you are always on break?"

Ben doesn't answer. He turns, walks out and heads back down the hallway. Hank is heated.

Buckner knows he's touched a sensitive nerve. He keeps going. "I heard day shift is putting him in for an award."

"Oh, that's not happening!" said Hank. "I'll shut that shit down ASAP."

Hank turns away from Buckner and faces his computer. Hank is a little hot and mumbling something under his breath. He starts typing his info into the computer. Kyle is still looking under his left hand. Hank finishes typing and is waiting for the information to register. Hank takes a drink of coffee.

Kyle stands up and winks at Buckner. "Ok Hank, we're out of here."

"Yea, ok. Good job last night. You guys go home and get some sleep."

Kyle and Buckner walk toward the front door.

"Chief, did you get everything taken care of?" asked Buckner.

"Oh yea."

They walk out the front door and head toward the parking lot across the street.

CHAPTER 8

A few weeks have passed. It's eight o'clock in the evening. Troy enters the door of Kyle and Bucky's dorm. The first thing he hears is the music coming all the way from Kyle's room at the other end of the hallway. Living Colour's *Cult of Personality* is playing.

Troy shakes his head. "What the hell."

Troy continues walking down the hallway. Just as he gets to the dayroom entrance he can hear Greg Bailey talking but he can't make out what he is saying. Troy stops short of the door, acts like he is getting a drink of water from the fountain and listens for a few seconds. Now he can hear Bailey clearly.

"You know Kyle. That guy with the hair," said Bailey.

Troy turns and enters the dayroom. Bailey is in there with another guy that Troy doesn't know. Bailey is surprised that Troy just showed up and is worried that Troy might have heard him talking about Kyle.

"Uh...Uh, what's up Troy?" asked Bailey.

"What's up Bailey?"

"Oh nothing. We're just watching TV."

"Sounds like you were doing more than that," said Troy.

Troy turns and walks out. Bailey has a worried look on his face. He doesn't want Troy to tell Kyle that he was talking about him. He doesn't want Kyle to come down to the dayroom and give him a hard time.

Troy walks down the hallway to Kyle and Bucky's room. The door is slightly open. Troy doesn't knock on the door. He pushes the door open and walks in.

All the rooms in the dorms are very small and have the same floor plan. They are intended to house two people but they are barely big enough for one. Each room has two beds, two nightstands, two wall units and two closets. What makes each room different is how the people that live in them arrange the furniture and what they have hanging on the walls.

Once you walk into Kyle and Bucky's room, the bathroom is immediately on the left. Inside the bathroom there is a full sized bathtub with a shower and a toilet to the right. On the right side of the front door there are two large closets. They are both about four feet wide and extend from the floor to the ceiling. Each closet has two wood veneer covered doors with a light above.

As you step further into the room, it should open up, but the guys have put a wall unit there to try and separate the bathroom section from the living area. To the left, the back of the wall unit forms a small hallway that leads to the bathroom sink. A small wall jets out on the right side of the sink to enclose the area. Below the sink is a cabinet. Above the sink is a small stainless steel shelf. Just above that is a medicine cabinet. The medicine cabinet's doors are mirrors. Above the medicine cabinet there is a light.

Back on the right side of the room, next to where the closets end, sits a small, dark brown half refrigerator. Next to the refrigerator is another wall unit. The wall units are six and a half feet tall and about three feet wide. There are three shelves on them that are two feet deep. The lower shelve is covered with a door that folds down and forms a desk. The bottom of the wall unit has three drawers for clothes. The doors are made of wood and stained medium brown. When you are standing at this wall unit, you have stepped into the living part of the room. Kyle's wall unit is next to the fridge on the right and Bucky's wall unit is facing out into the room on the left.

On the very top of Kyle's wall unit is a large Bose speaker lying on its side. On the top shelf of Kyle's wall unit there are vinyl records and books. The shelf below is filled with cassettes and a few other personal items. The third shelf's door is closed as usual. When it's open, it impedes movement between the two areas.

The top of Bucky's wall unit is filled with hats, both military and civilian. The top shelf of his wall unit is full of his personal items and the second shelf has a stereo receiver and a separate cassette player on top of it. The third shelf's door is also closed because of space.

On the right side of the room is a set of bunk beds. Bucky has the top bunk and Kyle has the bottom. Hanging on the corner of the top bunk is a pair of red Everlast boxing gloves and black boxing headgear. Above Bucky's bed is large poster of a Budweiser can. Next to it is a Grateful Dead poster. It says, "Grateful Dead in Concert '81" with pictures of San Francisco, New York and another city all connected by the famous bridges in those cities.

The back wall of the room has a large window. It's the same window and curtain set up as the dayroom. On the back wall below the window there is a combination heating and air conditioning unit. It sticks out of the wall about eight-inches. On the floor, stretching the remaining length of the back wall, is a long, low and deep couch. It is two-toned tan with a little black in it. It's a dorm couch and was a hand me down from Sal Remis. It's a very comfortable couch and many people come by the room and visit as an excuse to hang out on the couch.

Behind the couch next to the heater is an old C-5 sliding side window. When a window is changed on the plane, the bad one is considered garbage. A lot of the crew chiefs in the dorms take the windows and make tables out of them. The best windows to make tables with are the pilot's and co-pilot's front windows. They are more symmetrically even and are made out of glass. Kyle and Bucky have the side window in their room for one purpose only and that's to play the drinking game quarters. The side window is made out of plastic so a quarter bounces off of it much better than a glass window. Kyle and Bucky never made a permanent table out of it because, in their eyes, there just isn't enough room for it.

The wall on the left side of the room is a collage of professionally framed pictures and posters of women. The entire wall is almost covered. There are three, large, framed black and white pictures. There are also four newspaper-sized advertisements of women that Kyle cut out of large W fashion magazines that an old girlfriend used to subscribe to. The rest of the wall is covered with pictures cut from various magazines. The pictures aren't your typical dorm pictures. They are tasteful and artsy. This is another reason people like to come in and sit on the couch.

On the floor, beneath the pictures, sits a single hard ass dorm chair. Next to it is a small trashcan. There are also two nightstands. They both have three drawers and are about two feet tall. The other Bose speaker sits on one of them. In the corner of the room, where the wall jets out to enclose the sink area, there is a small table with a nineteen-inch television on it. On top of the television is a turntable for playing vinyl records. Above the turntable there is a shelf mounted on the wall with a lamp and a phone sitting on it. Between the lamp and the phone is a thirty-inch tall black wooden carving of an African woman.

The room is lit by three large, white track lights hanging in the center of the ceiling.

Bucky is in the shower. Kyle is at the sink. They are getting ready to go out to Loockerman Exchange. Loockerman Exchange is a nightclub in Dover. It's located on the corner of Loockerman and South States streets. It is one of the most popular nightclubs in the area.

Troy enters the room. "Hey! Hey! Turn that shit down!"

Kyle steps out from behind the wall. He is shirtless. "Troy! What's up?"

Kyle walks around and turns the music down to where you can still hear it playing.

"It's time to rally," said Kyle. "Are you ready for tonight? I hope you took a nap today."

"Don't worry about me boy. Hey, what is this shit? Don't you have any Zeppelin or Beatles?" asked Troy.

"That would be a no. You need to get with the times. This is Living Colour."

Kyle opens the fridge and hands Troy a beer. Kyle already has an open beer sitting on the shelf above the sink."

Troy opens his beer. "You boys sure start early around here don't you?"

"You want me to get a nipple for that?" asked Kyle.

Kyle pauses for a second and looks at what Troy is wearing.

"Hey, are you wearing that out tonight?" asked Kyle.

"Yea, what's wrong with what I have on?"

"Oh nothing."

Troy walks into the room and sits down on the couch. He looks up at the wall of women. Kyle goes back to the sink and comes back around into the living area with a bottle of Kouros cologne.

"What's that you are putting on there, Ode to the Commode?" asked Troy.

Troy laughs at his comment. Kyle sprays five or six shots of the cologne into the palm of his hand and makes a little puddle. He sets the bottle down on the edge of the wall unit, rubs his hands together and applies the cologne to his face and on his ears.

"Why are you putting that around your ears?" asked Troy.

"So when I lean in to whisper a lie to a woman, she can get a good whiff of it. This is the magic potion. It sets off my pheromones. What in the hell are you wearing, Old Spice?" asked Kyle.

A grin comes over Troy's face. "Yea boy. Maybe my ship will come in tonight. I put a little extra on my nuts so when she leans in, she'll get a good whiff of my magic potion."

"A ship full of sailor boys is all you'll get tonight."

They both start laughing.

Bucky comes out from the bathroom with a beer in his hand. He only has a towel around his waist. Kyle disappears back into the sink area.

"Is that Troy I hear?" asked Bucky. "What's up Troy Boy?"

"You guys sure are fired up tonight," said Troy.

"Yea, we've been going at it for a while. You ready for another beer?" asked Bucky.

"Calm down boy. I just opened this one."

Troy stands up and waves Bucky over. He doesn't want Kyle to hear what he is going to say.

"Hey Bucky, you see anything wrong with what I have on? Kyle asked me if I was wearing this out tonight."

Bucky starts to laugh. "No man. He's just fucking with you. You're fine."

Troy looks relieved. "Yea, I didn't think so. You guys have any tissues in here? I need to blow my nose."

Bucky points towards the bathroom. "No man. Just use the toilet paper in the bathroom."

Troy disappears into the bathroom to blows his nose. When he comes back out, Bucky is dressed except for shoes and socks, and Kyle has his shirt on. All three are standing in the middle of the room.

"That's some nice toilet paper you guys have in there," said Troy.

"What!" exclaimed Kyle. "You think I use that John Wayne shit the Air Force gives us?"

"John Wayne?" asked Troy.

Bucky jumps in. "Yea. It's ruff and tuff and doesn't take shit off of anyone."

They all start to laugh. There is a knock at the door. The guys turn and Roy Flores is already in the room.

Flores is a little excited. "Hey guys, come down to my room. I have to show you something."

"What, do you have a crib set up?" asked Troy.

"No! Come on!"

They all grab their beers and walk out of the room.

Roy Flores' room is on the same side of the hallway as Kyle and Bucky's room. It is several doors down and the first room on the other side of the dayroom. The four guys arrive at Flores' door. The door is half way open. Flores pushes the door all the way opens and enters. Flores has a little grin on his face. He steers everyone into his bathroom. Flores has taken a shit and it covers the entire bottom of the commode and comes out of the water. It looks like a volcano.

Kyle enters first and pulls away with his hand over his mouth. "Holy shit!"

"What?" asked Troy.

Troy and Bucky stick their heads into the bathroom together and have the same reaction as Kyle did.

"You sick fuck!" said Troy.

Flores is laughing uncontrollably.

"Did that really come out of your ass?" asked Bucky.

"Yea. I was constipated for a few days and suddenly... That's a good one isn't it? I had to show you guys."

Flores is still laughing.

Troy can't believe what he just saw. "That's not human."

"Flores, only out of your fat ass," said Bucky.

"That's a shit a Sasquatch would take," said Kyle. "Come on. Let's head out."

The three guys start walking down the hallway back to their room. Flores is still laughing. Flores walks over and sticks his head into the dayroom. Bailey is still sitting there watching television with some guy.

"Hey Bailey!" said Flores. "You guys come in here and check this out!"

Kyle, Bucky and Troy enter their room and close the door.

Loockerman Exchange is a large nightclub. The club entrance is on Loockerman Street. Once inside, there are steps directly in front of you. The right side of the club is slightly elevated from the left side. On the elevated side is the main bar. It runs the length of the club and parallels a long set of windows that face State Street. Small tables and chairs line the windows. At the end of the bar is a small room that has a foosball table in it. At the back of the bar there is a ramp that leads down to the bathrooms. A dance floor is centered in the main bar and is on the lower level. There are wide steps that lead down to it.

Directly to the left of the entrance is another small bar about one-third the size of the main bar.

It's after midnight. Kyle, Bucky, and Troy are at the small bar. They are all standing even though they have bar stools. They've been going at it pretty hard for about three hours drinking pitchers of beer and doing shots. They are laughing and joking around mingling with different men and women. Their pitcher of beer is almost empty.

"Ok, who's up in the rotation?" asked Troy.

"I think you are," said Bucky.

Kyle agrees. "Yea, you are."

It doesn't add up in Troy's mind. "I just bought the last one!"

"No, Bucky bought one while you were in the bathroom," said Kyle.

"Well, what happened to the one I bought?" asked Troy.

"I filled up a couple of thirsty gal's glasses but it turned out to be a bad investment," said Kyle.

"So that means it's your turn Kyle," said Troy. "You are a fucking tight wad! Pull that money out of your yamaka and get us another round."

Kyle and Bucky start laughing. Troy realizes they are messing with him. He starts laughing too.

"Get on it boy!" Troy holds up an almost empty pint glass. "If this glass runs dry, you are going to lose your tip and without that tip, no vacation this year to Jerusalem."

"Yea, yea," said Kyle. "I have a trip you can go on."

They all laugh and Kyle turns and motions to the barkeep to come over. He orders another pitcher of beer. The bartender fills it from the tap right in front of them and sets it down. Kyle throws money on the bar, grabs the pitcher and fills everyone's glasses.

"You just might make that trip after all," said Troy.

All the guys are feeling really good. The song *Electric Boogie* by Marcia Griffiths comes on.

Troy starts to get excited. "I know how to do this dance!"

"No you don't," said Bucky.

Troy disagrees with Bucky. "Yea, this is really big up on the Island."

"You are full of shit Troy," said Bucky. "You don't have a hair on your nuts if you don't go out there and show us how it's done."

Bucky elbows Kyle signaling him to play along.

"Well, let's see this shit," said Kyle. "Maybe some young ladies will recognize your talents and snag you."

Troy takes a swig of his beer and sets it on the bar. "After I get done, I'll be beating the bitches off me with a baseball bat."

Troy heads straight for the dance floor as Kyle and Bucky fill up their glasses and head to the upper level. They stand at the edge of the dance floor to get a better view of Troy's performance.

Troy is in the middle of the pack. There are at least 40 people on the dance floor. Troy appears to know the dance but is so drunk that he is always a step behind the rest of the people. Troy is bouncing off the people in front of him behind him and to the sides of him. Troy has a real look of confidence on his face but he is also getting irritated because he thinks all the people around him are messing up. Kyle and Bucky are laughing their asses off. The song finally ends. Troy walks straight back to the bar as Kyle and Bucky walk back down to where they were hanging out. Troy picks up his beer and takes a big drink as if he'd been working out.

"Damn Troy, you tore it up out there," said Bucky.

"Yea boy, I didn't know you had it in you," said Kyle.

Troy has an air of pride about himself. "You'd be surprised at my hidden talents. These Delaware fucks are doing something wrong. Somehow they are a step off."

"Maybe they need to take a trip up to Long Island and learn it the right way," said Kyle.

"Yea Troy," said Bucky. "I think all 50 people out there were off except you."

Troy still has the look of confidence. Kyle and Bucky are snickering.

"Where are all the bitches tonight?" asked Troy.

"After your dance performance, they all sobered up and ran back home," said Bucky.

"What!" exclaimed Troy. "I got some moves, boy!"

"It's almost last call and I've taken too many laps around this place already," said Kyle. "I'm about done."

To their left, is a table with three women sitting at it. One of them gets up and walks outside.

"What about that table?" asked Troy. "Those women have been sitting there all night and it doesn't look like any guys are with them."

"I can't believe Troy is so clueless," said Bucky. "Troy, they are dikes."

"What! They are carpet munchers?" asked Troy.

"Yea," said Kyle. "That's why no guys are hitting on them."

Troy can't believe it. "No way. They are all nice looking."

"They've eaten more pussy than you Troy," said Bucky.

All the guys start laughing.

Troy gets an idea. "Hey Kyle, I'll bet you 20 dollars you can't pick one of them up."

"Let's see the money, yamaka boy," said Kyle.

Troy pulls out his wallet and grabs a 20-dollar bill.

"Here, give it to me," said Bucky.

"What, don't you trust me?" asked Troy.

"No!" said Kyle. "That 20-dollar bill will be in the donation box at your synagogue before I get my hands on it."

Troy hands the money to Bucky.

"Alright boy," said Troy. "Let's see you work."

Bucky sticks the money in his pocket and then rubs his hands together in excitement. "Which one are you going for?"

They all look at the table. Only two girls are there.

Kyle makes his decision. "The one that went outside."

Just then, the woman that went outside walks back through the door and heads back towards her table. Kyle grabs a napkin, tears a piece off, sticks is in his mouth and quickly makes a spitball. He takes it from his mouth with his right hand.

"Watch this."

The woman passes close to the bar on her way to her table. She is about 10 feet from the guys. Kyle throws the spitball in the back of girl's hair and it sticks. She doesn't notice it because of all the hair spray in her curly hair. The girl sits down at her table with her friends.

Troy is blown away. "What the…"

Kyle starts towards the table with his beer in hand.   "Wish me luck."

He walks over to the table and approaches the woman on her left side where there is an empty seat. The other two women give him a dirty look. Kyle leans over to talk. The girl seems surprised at the visit.

"Hey, what's up?" asked Kyle.

The woman is a little hesitant. "Uh…nothing."

"Listen, something has been bothering me all night and I have to say something about it," said Kyle.

"What?"

"There's this piece of paper in your hair."

Kyle reaches and gently removes the spitball from the girl's hair and shows it to her.

"This has been in your hair all night and no one has had the balls to tell you."

"Really!" Well thanks!"

Kyle leans over and extends his hand. "My name's Kyle."

"I'm Shay."

Shay Skolnik turned 21 a few weeks before. She is not in the Air Force. Shay is a lesbian and not afraid to flaunt it. She is from a suburb right outside of Philadelphia and has a real Philly attitude. She is in Dover going to Wesley College. She is having a little trouble in school with her grades because of too much partying. She is tall with long, black, curly hair and has a few extra pounds on her.

Shay and Kyle shake hands. Kyle slides into the empty chair next to Shay. They start talking.

"Look at this son of a bitch," said Troy. "What a set of nuts on this guy."

"I wonder what he is saying to her," said Bucky.

All of a sudden Ross Higa walks up. He is red faced and drunk off his ass.

"Hey, what's up guys?"

"What's up Higa?" asked Bucky.

"Higa," said Troy. "Do you want a beer?"

Higa takes a second to process Troy's question and finally answers, "Sure." He has something else on his mind. "How are you guys getting back to the base?"

Troy pours Higa a beer and hands it to him.

"I'm going to call the upstairs hall phone in 409," said Bucky. "Reese or Mouse are supposed to answer it and come and get us."

"Can I catch a ride back with you guys?" asked Higa.

Bucky takes another jab at Higa with a Chinese joke this time. "Are you too drunk to drive your ox cart?"

Bucky and Troy start laughing. Higa is getting pissed. Higa rolls his eyes at Bucky and takes a drink of beer.

"Alright, let's get out of here, said Troy. "Bucky, go call Mouse."

Bucky sets his beer down and walks towards the door. He exits Loockermans and heads up the street to the right. There is a pay phone on the sidewalk about one 100 feet from the door. Troy and Higa continue to talk.

Terry "Mouse" Statton is a senior airman from Ohio in his early 20s. Most of the time he is really quiet but the more he drinks, the louder and more talkative he becomes. He works with Bucky in the ISO docks.

It's after one in the morning. Mouse is driving everyone home. Troy has raised the armrest and is sitting in the middle of the front seat. Bucky is riding shotgun. Somehow, Kyle has talked Shay into coming back to the dorms with him. Shay is in the back seat behind Mouse, Higa is in the middle and Kyle is behind Bucky. Kyle and Shay are separated by Higa because he fits better in the middle with his short legs on the hump.

"Hey Mouse, thanks for coming out this late and getting us," said Bucky.

"Don't worry about it. I'm sure it will come back around."

"Yea Mouse. You are the best!" said Troy.

Higa tries to speak, but due to the alcohol, his brain and his mouth aren't working together. "Mouse! Mouse!"

"Higa, shut the fuck up," said Kyle. "You can't even complete an entire sentence."

Higa tries to pull himself together and wants to prove it. "I'm perfectly fine. Mouse, pull over! I'll drive. I'll show you."

Higa is starting to get on Bucky's nerves. "Higa, shut up before I reach back there and slap the shit out of you."

Higa burps really loud. The burp has a smell of whatever he had eaten earlier. Everybody is grossed out.

"You sick fuck!" said Kyle.

Troy jokingly wipes the back of his neck with his hand. "I think I got some of that on the back of my neck."

Bucky takes yet another jab at Higa with a Vietnamese joke. "What the hell did you eat today, Pho?"

"Damn it Bucky, I'm not Vietnamese, I'm Japanese!"

"After that, who's hungry?" asked Troy. "Let's stop at the 7-11."

Shay is a little taken back because she knows no one and everyone seems to be drunker than she is, except for Mouse.

"Yea, I could use a free burrito and a few more beers," said Bucky.

Troy tries to be funny and takes a jab at Shay. "Kyle, what are you guys going to get, a can of tuna?"

All the guys start laughing. At the same time Kyle slaps Troy in the back of the head and Bucky elbows him in the ribs.

"What? What?"

"Quit being a dick!" said Kyle.

Troy plays as if he's innocent. "What? That's an honest question."

Shay isn't going to take any shit. She fires right back at Troy. "Hey Red, if you have something you want to say to me, speak up."

"No, no. Why?"

"That's what I thought," said Shay. "Now shut the fuck up before I slap the shit out of you."

Higa's brain has finally processed the thought of getting something to eat. "Yea, food sounds good right now."

Higa leans up towards the front seat. Kyle pushes him forward so he is on the edge of the seat. Higa has his forearms resting over the front seat. Kyle and Shay both lean toward the middle of the car and starts whispering to each other.

"Higa, don't fuck with me," said Troy.

"So Higa, what are you going to get to eat at the 7-11?" asked Bucky.

"I don't know."

Bucky has turned a little sideways now and is facing towards the middle of the car so he can talk to Higa.

Bucky gives Higa another jab with a Filipino joke. "Higa, I bet you are going to get some dog on a stick."

Higa looks disgusted. "That's sick. And Japanese don't eat dogs."

"Isn't that a delicacy in the Philippines?" asked Bucky.

Bucky elbows Troy in the side to play along.

"Yea Higa, I think I'll get a few of them myself," said Troy. "Mmm, nice and juicy."

"Dog on a stick is the best!" said Bucky.

Troy motions with his left hand to Mouse to weave on the road a little bit to mess with Higa.

"Mmm," said Bucky. "I can't wait for some juicy dog on a stick. I'm going to slurp that shit up."

"Yea, with some Tabasco!" said Troy.

Higa is thinking about how nasty the food is. The weaving car is starting to get to him. He suddenly leans back in the seat and parts Kyle and Shay.

"Higa, what the fuck!" yells Kyle.

Kyle takes a hard look at Higa. "Hey man, are you ok?"

Higa is pale. "Na, I don't feel so good."

Bucky keeps working Higa.   "Yea, juicy dog and a big glass of tomato juice! Hell yea!"

Mouse looks through the rear view mirror. "Higa, don't get sick in my car!"

Kyle is getting worried. "Higa, what the fuck!"

"Pull over, pull over!" yells Higa.

Mouse is frantically trying to find a spot to pull over. "Ok, hold on!"

Troy and Bucky have turned around and are watching Higa. Kyle has moved as far as he can into the corner of the back seat. Shay is doing the same thing in her corner. Kyle and Shay both have a look on their faces like Higa is a bomb that is getting ready to explode.

"Mouse, pull this bitch over!" yells Kyle. "He's about to spew!"

Higa starts having convulsions and puts his hand over his mouth.

Mouse is slowing down and trying to pull over as he watches Higa in his rear view mirror. "Don't puke in my car!"

Higa lunges towards the window on Shay's side. Shay is terrified! She lets out a frightening scream as if someone is trying to murder her. Higa is over her lap and trying to roll the window down. She is trying to slide away from him and towards Kyle. She is kicking and pushing Higa off of her. Mouse reaches back with his left hand and rolls the window down quickly. Shay is still screaming wildly.

Kyle can't believe this is happening. "Don't do it dude!"

Bucky and Troy are laughing. Mouse gets the window down just in time. Higa gets his head outside of the car and pukes. The puke sprays all down side the car. Shay is trapped and still pushing Higa away and trying to slide her legs out, but with no luck. Higa finishes puking and pulls his head back in the car. He falls back in the middle of the seat. Shay is now fighting to get back into her corner of the seat. She finally stops screaming. Bucky and Troy are still turned and watching Higa. They are both laughing.

"Ah. That felt good," said Higa.

Mouse is pissed. "You fuck! I just washed this thing today. Now the whole car reeks of puke."

"God damn it Higa," said Bucky.

Bucky and Troy turn and sit back normally. Kyle rolls down his window to get some fresh air. Shay already has her face out her window.

"Anybody still hungry?" asked Troy.

Mouse shakes his head. "Fuck that! I'm not stopping. I want him out of the car before he pukes again."

Bucky agrees with Mouse. "Yea, he's not looking so good. Let's get his little Asian ass back to the dorms."

Kyle and Bucky's room is dark. The curtains are closed and all the lights are off. It's sometime after seven in the morning. Kyle and Shay are asleep in Kyle's bunk. Kyle is on the outside and Shay is on the inside next to the wall. They are spooning facing the wall with a blanket over them. Kyle is in his boxers and Shay is naked. Bucky is on the top bunk. He stayed up partying with some other guys in the dorms to give Kyle and Shay the room to themselves. He came in sometime later that morning. He is out like a light with a blanket over him.

Andy and Graywolf are doing random room inspections and are outside the door. There isn't supposed to be any overnight guests in the dorms between mid-night and eight in the morning. There are three, hard, rapid knocks on the door. Graywolf, using his master key, unlocks and opens the door.

Graywolf yelled, "Room inspection!"

Graywolf enters the room first, followed by Andy. They turn on the hall light. They close the door behind them. Bucky doesn't move. He is not affected by the noise. Kyle jumps and sits up quickly. Shay is startled also. She is half asleep.

"Who the hell is that?" asked Shay.

Kyle whispers to her. "Lie back down and act like you are asleep. If you move an inch it's my ass. Stay still."

Shay lies back down. Kyle flings the covers off of him and halfway off of Shay. He exposes all of Shay's body from her thighs up. He jumps out of bed and heads between the wall units towards the door to stop Graywolf and Andy from entering the room any further.

"What the hell are you guys doing?" asked Kyle.

"Room inspection," said Graywolf.

Graywolf has a serious look on his face and Andy looks like he is having fun.

"We've come to see what you and Bucky are up to," said Andy

Kyle puts his right index finger to his lips and signals Graywolf and Andy to stay quiet. He motions to them to come over and look in his bed and to be quiet again. Kyle goes first followed closely by Graywolf and Andy. Kyle enters the main part of the room and Graywolf and Andy peek around the corner of the bunk bed. They freeze in awe as they see Shay naked in front of them. The hallway light in the room gives off just enough light to see her. Shay doesn't move. Graywolf slowly gets a grin on his faces and Andy has a smile from ear to ear. Kyle lets them look for about five or six seconds and then motions them to back up. Graywolf and Andy are hesitant to move, so Kyle has to push them back. Once Shay is out of their sight, Graywolf and Andy's trance is broken.

Kyle signals them to be quiet again and motions with his hands for them to leave. Graywolf and Andy are smiling and are very satisfied as they move back toward the door. Graywolf ducks into the bathroom and turns the light on. Andy stops at the door and pulls a piece of cloth and a grease pencil from his pocket. Andy cleans the Plexiglas room inspection plaque on the back of the door and writes a grade on it. You can't see what he writes. He then opens the door, turns, winks at Kyle and exits into the hallway.

Graywolf cannot be seen in the bathroom but you can hear him. "Showers dirty."

Graywolf is heard spitting his chewing tabacco into the toilet and not flushing it. That is one of his signature moves. Graywolf exits the bathroom to the hallway. Kyle closes the door behind him and sees a B plus grade on the door. Kyle's expression on his face is of satisfaction. He picked up a nice looking woman and dodged a bullet by showing her naked body to the dorm managers. Kyle reaches in and flushes the toilet and turns off the bathroom light. He turns off the hallway light and walks back to bed with Shay. He pulls the blanket back over them. She is sound asleep already. Bucky hasn't moved an inch.

Out in the hallway, Graywolf and Andy are walking side by side down the hallway toward the dayroom. They are both looking straight ahead and smiling.

"What did you give her?" asked Graywolf.

"B plus."

Graywolf has the exact same expression of satisfaction on his face as Kyle did when he saw the grade.

"Which room do you want to hit next?" asked Andy.

"Bret Nader's room."

It's now ten in the morning. Shay is sitting on the couch. She is wearing a pair of Kyle's sweats and one of his t-shirts. Kyle is still in bed with only his boxers on. He has propped up two pillows against the headboard and is sitting back against them. He and Shay are both a little hung over. Bucky is still knocked out in the top bunk.

"What was all that noise this morning?" asked Shay.

"The dorm managers. They were doing a room inspection."

"So early? And on the weekend? Is that normal?"

"They never miss an opportunity to be pricks," said Kyle. "You really saved my ass this morning. I'll compensate you for that later."

Kyle winks at Shay and she smiles.

"I'd like that," said Shay. "How did I save your ass?"

"Well, you weren't supposed to be here overnight."

"But last night you told me it was ok."

"I'm sure I did," said Kyle. "Anyway, back to the guys knocking on the door. Now and then, they'll do random or unscheduled room inspections. This morning they hit us. When I heard the knock I knew I was busted. So when I got out of bed I flung the covers off of you and let them sneak a peek at you so they wouldn't mess with me."

Shay jumps up. "You asshole! How much did they see?"

Kyle laughs. "All the good stuff."

Shay is trying to keep a serious face. "Will you get in trouble later?"

"No," said Kyle. "Those old farts just looked, got a thrill and graded you on their way out."

"Graded me?"

"Yea, graded you," said Kyle. "Instead of grading the room for the condition it's in, they graded you on how hot they thought you were. Go look on the back of the door and see how you rated in their eyes."

Shay walks over to the door and looks at the grade they gave her. Kyle starts to smile.

"What!" said Shay? "Only a B plus! I'm much hotter than that!"

Shay's voice wakes Bucky as she walks back into the main part of the room. She is a little heated.

Kyle consoles Shay even though he thinks the entire episode was hilarious. "I think so too babe. But I wasn't one of the official judges his morning."

Kyle thinks Shay is sexy when she acts mad.

Shay goes off. "Those assholes! Where are they now?"

"Hey, it'll be ok," said Kyle. "I'm sure if they saw your face, you would have gotten an A plus."

Bucky rolls over and sits up. "What's going on? Sounds like I missed something."

"Two guys came in the room this morning and Kyle showed them my ass while I was sleeping."

Bucky starts laughing.

"Did we pass?" asked Bucky.

"B plus!" said Kyle.

"Thanks Shay for taking one for the team," said Bucky. "I'll buy you a beer next time we are out."

Shay looks pissed, but knows it's funny. Bucky and Kyle are snickering. Bucky lies back down and grabs his head.

"What time is it?" asked Bucky.

"Time for a smoke. Do you have any?" asked Shay.

Bucky, with one hand still on his head, points towards his wall unit with the other. "Is there a pack there, inside the door?"

Shay drops the door down. "No."

"I must have smoked them all last night," said Bucky.

"Babe, go down to the dayroom," said Kyle. "It's in the middle of the hallway on the left. I'm sure there is someone in there who smokes."

"Those guys aren't out there are they?" asked Shay.

Kyle laughs. "No, they are probably home jerking off right now."

Bucky jumps in on Kyle's humor. "Sounds to me like the only way they'd recognized you, is if they saw your ass. I think you're safe."

Shay gives Kyle an evil look but is smiling at the same time. She leaves the room and heads for the dayroom.

Shay walks down the hallway and into the dayroom. It's much cooler in the hallway and the dayroom. Shay's nipples can be seen through the t-shirt. She has her Philly attitude turned on. Greg Bailey is sitting in the dayroom in his usual seat, watching television, drinking a Coke and smoking a cigarette. He has moved the coffee table over in front of him. His pack of cigarettes, lighter and Coke are on the table in front of him. There is also an empty Coke can on the table that Bailey is using for an ashtray. Bailey is surprised and stunned because he is never around women and one just walked in. Shay is even more surprised by Bailey's filthy, rat-like appearance, but it only shows on her face for a second. Shay sits in the chair next to Bailey.

Shay wouldn't know this, but the left front picture closest to the door has been moved slightly. Bailey doesn't realize it either.

"What are you watching?" asks Shay.

"A movie."

"Can I have one of your smokes?" she asks.

"Yea…"

Bailey leans up and grabs his cigarettes and lighter and hands them to Shay. She removes a cigarette, throws the pack back on the table and lights the cigarette. She takes a big drag and exhales. She throws the lighter back on the table. Bailey is watching television and glancing at her nervously. Shay looks at Bailey and can't believe how ugly he is.

"Where'd you get that Coke?" Shay asks.

"There's a soda machine across the hallway in the laundry room."

"How much are they?"

"Fifty cents."

Shay has everything in the room. She doesn't have a dime on her. "Can I borrow 50 cents?"

"Sure!"

Bailey reaches into his front pocket and pulls out some change. He separates two quarters and hands them to Shay. "There you go."

"Thanks!" said Shay.

Shay gets up and walks out of the dayroom in her Philly style. She crosses the hall and goes into the laundry room. Bailey watches her ass shake under the sweat pants and gets a little grin on his face. You can hear the Coke drop from the machine. Shay re-enters the dayroom and Bailey's eyes are quickly shifting back and forth from the television to Shay's breasts. Shay catches Bailey looking, but says nothing. She sits back down in the chair next to him. They are both sharing the ashtray Coke can and drinking their Cokes.

"Where are you from?" asked Shay.

"Kentucky, a small town called..."

Shay puts her hand up and cuts him off. "I'm sure I've never heard of it."

Shay sets her Coke on the table, gets up and walks towards the television. Bailey is watching her ass again.

"Are you watching this?" asked Shay.

She starts to change the channels.

"Well...I...was," said Bailey.

Shay ignores him and keeps flipping through the channels only staying on each one for a few seconds. Shay is standing with one hand on her hip and her cigarette in her mouth. Bailey is really staring at Shay's ass and the corner of his mouth is turned up in agreement with the view. Shay stops at a random channel and turns towards Bailey quickly. She catches him again looking at her, but says nothing. She returns to her seat. She takes a last drag on her cigarette, drops the butt in the Coke can and blows the smoke towards him. Bailey is watching the television again nervously even though Shay has changed the channel to a different program.

"Can I have a couple more of those cigarettes for later?" asked Shay .

She knows Bucky will want one and Bailey would never say no to her. He hands her the pack.

"Sure, take what you need," said Bailey.

Shay takes four cigarettes and throws the pack back on the table. Shay stands up, takes the last drink of her Coke and sets the can on the table.

"Thanks!" says Shay as she walks towards the door.

She shakes her ass a little extra because she knows Bailey is eagerly watching. She exits the dayroom and turns right. Bailey is going crazy. He gives her a few seconds to get down the hallway and rushes quickly to the doorway. He peeks around the corner in the direction that Shay turned. He wants to get a last look. He has the excitement of a little boy at Christmas. He watches her intently as she strolls down the hallway disappearing into Kyle's room.

All of a sudden Bailey's attitude changes from happy to pissed off. He realizes that Shay is with Kyle. He is pissed that he was nice to Shay and she is with the guy he dislikes most in the dorms. He walks back to the television, turns the channel back to what he was watching and returns to his usual seat. He is still pissed off. He takes a drag off his cigarette and exhales. "Fucking Mansfield..."

CHAPTER 9

It's just after eleven o'clock at night. All the guys are lined up for the Blue side roll call. The Red side is in their area doing their own thing. As usual, all the guys look tired and dirty. They are in their field jackets and Buckner is in his coveralls.

Rob is almost finished giving out assignments, except for one. "Buckner, Mansfield, Akin. Inbound, 6013, going to Oscar row. It should be pulling onto the spot any minute now. It's a mission return. It's Alpha-2 for autopilot issues. Ok, you guys be safe out there. That's all I got."

Immediately, three guys break out of the formation and run for the side doors. The rest of the formation slowly scatters. The three guys run between the tables in the middle of the room and Red side roll call. The Red side expediter pauses and then continues. A few guys in the formation laugh. The three guys burst through the side doors, turn right and disappear. Mike turns to Kyle.

"What the hell was that all about?" asked Mike.

"When Rob is finished giving roll call he always says, "That's all I got," said Kyle. "If he didn't call your name, that means he doesn't need you tonight and you are off."

"So why did the guys run out of here like their asses were on fire?" asked Mike.

Kyle and Mike walk out the side doors.

"Two reasons," said Kyle. "First, they are getting out of here before Rob changes his mind. And he's been known to do that. If they are gone, he'll never get ahold of them. Second, they still have time to make it to Tap Works for last call."

Tap Works is a bar located about a mile from the front gate of the base. If you are heading towards the city of Dover from the base, it's on the left hand side of the road. It sits on the end of a little strip mall. It's the closest bar to the base besides the Brown Fox.

Kyle and Mike look across the vast parking lot in front of building 585. The three guys are still running. They jump the Jersey barrier wall at the end of the parking lot. The wall separates the lemon lot from Atlantic Street. The lemon lot is a designated parking area where cars for sale can be displayed.

Mike is getting a kick from watching the guys run. "Look at them son of a bitches run!"

"They must be thirsty," said Kyle. "Hey, let's grab our shit before the line builds up."

Kyle and Mike turn and walk back in and head for the checkout window.

Kyle continues explaining Rob's rule. "So, if your name is never called, you are off for the night."

"How often does that happen?" asked Mike.

"Now and then," said Kyle. "It will never happen to you for a while though."

"Why is that?"

"Because you need to get trained first," said Kyle. "Know your job and bust your ass for Sierra 6 and then he'll start taking care of you."

Kyle and Mike stop and wait at the back of the line for their equipment. Beside them is the vending machine. It is empty.

Kyle continues to give Mike a few words of wisdom. "Not only do you have to impress Rob, you also have to impress all the other higher ranking people out here. They give Rob feedback as well. Don't ever look for the easy way out, especially as a new guy. If you get the reputation as a lazy scumbag, then it will stick with you. My first night out here, before I got out of the truck, tech sergeant Bishop pulled me aside and told me to get in the game or get left behind."

"I believe I understand," said Mike.

Kyle is on his soapbox. "It's like checking out these tools. You do it because you are the lowest guy on the totem pole. No questions asked. I checked them out for a year and a half straight before Boner came along. And it doesn't stop there. If there is a tow, you volunteer for tail walker. If there is a refuel, you volunteer for SPR. If there is an engine run, you volunteer for ground man. It will all come back as a positive for you, like an investment."

"What do you mean?" asked Mike.

"If you get a reputation as a hard worker you'll get rewarded with TDYs and extra time off," said Kyle. "They might even put you in for an award."

"And if I don't?" asked Mike.

Kyle points at the guy behind the counter working in CTK. "Then you'll be back there, handing out tool boxes."

It's just after roll call. The plane, 6013, has just blocked into Oscar row. The Sierra 6 truck pulls into the slightly congested parking area in front of the left wing. Buckner and Kyle jump out with their bags. Buckner has the radio and Kyle has a mat and bunny suit. Akin gets out of the truck last, grabs his bag and the toolbox. They all have their headsets on. They walk under the nose of the plane and put their things in a pile.

Buckner talks to a few swing shift crew chiefs. He takes a short turnover from them and they walk back toward the Sierra 6 truck. Buckner, Kyle and Mike walk over to the base of the ladder and join the crowd of people waiting to go up on the plane.

Kyle turns to Buckner. "Buckner, delay the fleet service guys and I'll run back to the troop compartment and see if there is anything to eat. I'm going to take Mike with me."

Besides servicing the latrines, one of fleet service's jobs is to remove all the trash and left over food from the plane after it returns from a mission. No one is supposed to take the leftover food. If you are caught, it is more than likely fleet service will turn you in and you'll get in trouble.

"Chief, I'm so hungry right now," said Buckner. "Get me two of whatever you find."

Kyle gives Buckner the thumbs up and turns to Mike. "Mike, follow me. I need to train you on a very important aspect of being a crew chief."

"Ok. What is going on?"

"Flight meal raid," said Kyle. "Buckner is going to stall the fleet service guys and we are going to see if there are any passenger meals in the troop compartment."

Buckner walks over to the fleet service guys and starts talking to them. He puts himself between them and the ladder. Customs clears the plane and Kyle shoots up the ladder. Mike is right behind him. They top the ladder and turn right, disappearing into the cargo compartment. A few aircrew members come down the ladder. This delays the people on the ground from going on the plane.

Kyle and Mike run up the troop compartment ladder. They are in a hurry and know they have limited time. Kyle stops near the top step, unlatches the gate and raises it. While holding the gate, Kyle steps up into the troop compartment. Mike climbs the rest of the way up the ladder and turns right towards the galley. Kyle drops the gate back down and it locks in place. They take a few steps and are at the troop compartment galley.

The troop compartment galley sits on the left side of the plane and faces inward. It is eight feet wide. It has a stainless steel counter top that sits about four feet off the ground. Built in above the counter top are two small ovens, a coffee maker and several cabinets and drawers. Below the counter are two refrigerators that are spaced about two feet apart. There is a large door to the right of the refrigerators. Behind the door is a large trashcan.

Kyle goes to the first refrigerator and opens the door. He pulls out a drawer and grabs a box lunch. It's heavy. He opens it up and it's full for food. "Jack pot! We can't let this go to waste."

Mike is still not clear on what is happening. "What the hell!?"

Kyle throws the box lunch on the counter. "Mike, check that other fridge."

Mike opens the door to the second refrigerator and starts pulling out the drawers and looking through them. Kyle is frantically stacking box lunches on the counter. Mike starts pulling out sodas and setting them on the counter. He's caught on and is getting excited over all the free food. Kyle knows their time is almost up.

Kyle turns to his left. Against the back wall of the troop compartment is two thirty-inch in diameter round negative pressure doors. They sit one on top of the other. One is about knee level and the other is chest high. They are both hinged at the top and do not lock. When the plane is in flight, the pressure inside holds the doors closed. There is a flimsy aluminum guard designed to keep people away from the doors. It acts as a buffer zone. It is hinged on one side to a closet that extends out from the back wall. The guard has a fastener on the other side that secures it to the back wall.

Between the two doors and mounted on the side of the closet is a crash axe. Kyle unseats the bottom portion of the crash axe. Kyle pops open the aluminum guard, opens the lower negative pressure door and pins it up with the lip of the crash axe.

"Here, hurry!" said Kyle. "Jump inside and I'll start handing this stuff through to you."

Kyle's intention is to hide the food behind the door in the hayloft area and retrieve it once fleet service has left the plane.

Mike hits the floor like he's doing a football drill and crawls head first through the round opening and disappears back into the hayloft. A second later his arms and head reappear from the opening.

"What do you want me to do with it?" asked Mike.

"Just stash it back there and we'll get it after everyone leaves."

Kyle starts taking box lunches and sodas from the counter and setting them on the floor. Mike is grabbing them and piling them into the hayloft as fast as he can. There is a grated section of floor next to the galley. As Kyle is moving box lunches and sodas from the counter to the floor, he is looking through the grates down into the cargo compartment to see if the fleet service guys are coming. All of a sudden he sees someone.

"Ok, that's it!" said Kyle. "Get out of there! They are coming!"

Mike scurries out of the hayloft. Kyle unpins the door and reattaches the crash axe. He then snaps the guard back in place.

Kyle calms himself down and acts as if nothing has happened. "Ok, let's go."

Kyle and Mike walk over to the top of the troop compartment ladder. Mike opens the gate, latches it up in place and goes down the ladder first. Kyle looks back at the galley and makes sure everything looks normal and then heads down the ladder. Kyle is almost to the bottom as the fleet service guys walk up. Kyle steps off the ladder.

"Hey, are you guys from fleet service?" asked Kyle.

One of the fleet service guys answers, "Yea, why?"

"Did the crew tell you about one of the latrines leaking?" asked Kyle.

"No. No one said anything to us."

"We just went and looked and didn't see anything leaking," said Kyle. "If you guys notice any leaks, let us know. We'll be up front."

The two fleet service guys shake their heads. "Sure, ok."

"Thanks," said Kyle.

Kyle and Mike start walking forward through the cargo compartment. The two fleet service guys head up the ladder. Kyle looks back and the guys are out of site. Kyle holds his hand up and Mike gives him a high five.

"We'll sign you off on that task in your training record," said Kyle.

They both start laughing.

Three hours have pasted. Fleet service has finished all their duties and left the plane hours ago. The plane landed in great shape. The guys have knocked out an inspection, I's and E's, oil, gas, and a few minor things. They still need to LOX the plane, but they'd rather have the specialist fix their autopilot discrepancy first. Buckner is at the crew chief table in the first seat. Mike is in the first chair of the three-man seat. There are several box lunches on the table along with the forms. They hit the jackpot - fried chicken box lunches! Buckner and Mike are eating the chicken, bags of potato chips and drinking sodas.

Kyle is standing at the crew galley. The galley is on the right side of the plane behind the crew latrine. The crew galley is basically the same as the troop galley, only half the size. The galley is about four feet wide and runs from the floor to the ceiling. The counter is stainless steel and almost four feet tall. Below the counter on the left there are three drawers. On the right side there is a small refrigerator. Above the counter there is a small slot where the garbage goes. Above that is the coffee maker. To the right of the coffee maker is an oven. Above the oven is a galley control panel and two storage compartments.

Kyle has taken the top of his coveralls off and tied it around his waist using the sleeves. There are several box lunches sitting on the galley. Kyle rips the top off of a box lunch, puts several more pieces of chicken on it and puts it in the oven. He shuts the door and turns the heat up all the way. He lets Buckner and Mike know what he did.

"Hey, I just put a few more pieces in the oven," said Kyle.

Kyle walks back to the table and sits down across from Buckner. Mike is eating like a pig. There are two specialists moving back and forth from the flight deck to the aft avionics compartment. They are troubleshooting an autopilot problem the plane landed with.

"God damn Mike, slow down on that chicken," said Kyle. "When's the last time you had something to eat?"

"I've been eating Ramen Noodles for the past few days," said Mike. "I had to give up my meal card because they put me on separate rats."

"Separate rats won't kick in until your next payday," said Kyle.

"Yea, until then, I'm broke," said Mike.

Buckner laughs. "Another few inbounds like this and you'll be set for the week."

"Separate rats are a good deal," said Kyle. "You'll eat half your meals out here for free and the other half you'll eat at the chow hall at a discount rate. The rest of your separate rats money can go to beer and partying."

Buckner stands up, takes the top of his coveralls off and ties them around his waist like Kyle. "Chief, it's as hot as a fresh fucked fox in a forest fire up here. When are those pointy heads going to be finished with that autopilot shit?"

Buckner sits back down and Kyle stands up.

"Let me check on them," said Kyle.

"Do you want me to check on them?" asked Mike.

Kyle laughs. "No, you just keep eating."

Kyle walks up front. The specialists are sitting in the pilots and co-pilots seats. They are both facing each other and pushing buttons on the center console.

"How are things going up here?" asked Kyle.

The higher-ranking specialist answers. "We changed a computer and we are running it through now. I'm doing a little training so it's taking longer than usual."

Kyle laughs. "Oh, I thought it was shop clean-up back in your building so you were milking this job to get out of it."

The two specialists smile.

"I'll be back at the table," said Kyle. "Take your time. We're in no rush."

Kyle walks back to the crew chief table. Buckner is writing in the forms. Mike has finished eating, reclined the seat back and has his feet up on the wall. He has the look of a gorged lion after a kill. Kyle disconnects the interphone cord from the wall, pulls the curtain closed and reconnects the interphone cord. He sits down across from Buckner again. He notices Buckner has road rash on his right forearm. Buckner closes the forms and slides them off to the side.

"How do the forms look?" asked Kyle.

"All that's left is their write-up. How are they doing?"

"They are almost finished. They are doing a little training. It's only three o'clock. We still have time to get inside and get a few card games in. What happened to your arm?" asked Kyle.

"Chief, check it out. I was in New Castle today."

"All the way up there?"

"Yea," said Buckner. "So we find this car that we've been looking for. The guy spots us and jumps in the car. So I jump out of the tow truck and run up to the passenger side window. I'm yelling at him to stop the car but he backs out of his driveway."

Mike has started to listen more intently but has little energy after his feast.

"What did you do?" asked Kyle.

"I dove in the passenger side window and tried to turn off the ignition."

"Get the fuck out of here," said Kyle.

"Chief, I was holding on for dear life with one hand and trying to grab the keys with the other. That cocksucker got it backed out onto the street and punched it. He had ahold of my arm and I couldn't get the keys."

Kyle can't believe what happened to Buckner. "No way!"

Buckner continues. "All of a sudden my legs smash into something! The guy lets me go and I go rolling out the car.

"What the fuck! How fast were you going?" asked Kyle.

Buckner stands up, unties his coveralls and pulls them down. He exposes a big bruise on his right leg. "Chief, I have no idea."

"Holy shit! What did you hit?" asked Kyle.

"I hit the mail box in the yard over at the next house."

Kyle shakes his head in disbelief. "Man, you are a crazy son of a bitch."

Buckner slides his coveralls back up, ties them at the waist and sits back down.

"Well, what did you do?" asked Kyle.

"Jerry jumped out of the truck and came running over. I thought I broken my legs, but all I did was knock the mail box over. It was the type of mail box that sit on a skinny metal post."

"You are lucky he didn't run you over. Did you guys go after him?" asked Kyle.

"No, we just let him go."

Kyle doesn't understand. "After all that? Why?"

"Jerry didn't want to go after him. Plus, you don't want to mess with people that will fight for their shit. People with jobs, and those a little down on their luck, will fight for what is theirs. People that don't have a job can care less what happens. They'll just give you the keys."

"You should have stuck with your garbage man idea," said Kyle. "Seems a little safer, but you would have smelled like shit every day."

Mike sits up in his chair. "Speaking of smelling like shit, do you guys smell something burning?"

Buckner, Kyle and Mike pause for a second and smell the air.

"The chicken in the oven!" said Kyle.

Kyle jumps up and runs back to the galley. Buckner and Mike follow him. Smoke is seeping out from behind the oven door. Kyle turns the power off and pulls the circuit breaker. He then opens the door and smoke billows out. The cardboard that the chicken was on is smoking. All the guys are laughing.

"Shut her down Hank, she's smoking!" said Buckner.

"Mike, are you still hungry?" asked Kyle.

Kyle slides a step to his right, unlatches the number two hatch above him, pulls it down, and sets it on the three-man seat behind the galley. Mike and Buckner are waving their hands in front of their faces to clear the smoke.

Mike has had his fill and the burnt chicken doesn't appeal to him. "No, not anymore."

"Chief, you're no Colonel Sanders," said Buckner.

"I don't guess so."

Buckner and Mike walk back and sit down. Buckner reclines his seat and Mike puts his feet back up on the wall. Kyle takes his Leatherman out of his pocket, opens it, grabs the edge of the burnt cardboard and slides it out of the oven. He drops the burnt chicken into the box from which he tore off the top. He pours some soda over the chicken and box top to cool it off and slides the box right into the garbage.

Kyle walks back to the table. "How about a little after dinner mood lighting?"

Kyle reaches to his right and dims the lights.

Buckner starts to get comfortable in his seat. "Chief, you read my mind."

Kyle sits down and reclines his chair. He looks over at Mike. Mike is already asleep. Kyle grabs the radio, adjusts the volume and sets it right in front of him. He slides the forms over onto his lap, opens them and starts reviewing them.

At least two hour have past. All the guys are asleep. The noise of a taxiing plane can be heard. It sound like it has stopped right in front of their plane. Kyle wakes up. Buckner adjusts in his seat and Mike doesn't move.

"Chief, that doesn't sound good," said Buckner.

"Yea, I'm going to check it out."

"What time is it?"

Kyle looks at his watch in disbelief. "Holy shit. Its half past five!"

Kyle stands up, grabs the radio and heads through the curtain. The two specialists are still working. One is in the aft avionics compartment and the other is in the hallway behind him. The specialist in the hallway backs into the aft bunkroom to let Kyle through.

"You guys are still here?" asked Kyle.

Kyle doesn't give them time to answer. He walks up to the flight deck and sits down in the pilot's seat. He looks out the window. A plane has left its parking spot and stopped on the front taxiway just to the right of Kyle's plane. It can't go any further because Sierra 4's pickup truck is parked in the middle of the taxiway to Kyle's left. The pickup truck has its flashers on and its headlights off. It's not moving.

Mike comes walking up from behind and sits in the copilot's seat. "What going on?"

"The plane is stuck on the taxiway because the Sierra 4 truck is in the way and won't move."

All of a sudden the Sierra 6 truck flies up between Kyle's plane and the plane on the taxiway. It drives out to the pickup truck. A guy gets out of the side door of the Sierra 6 truck and tries to open the passenger door of the pickup truck with no luck. It must be locked. The guy runs around to the driver's door and tries to open it but it's also locked. He starts pounding on the glass. This wakes up the person inside. The guy outside the truck steps away and points at the plane on the taxiway with its engines running and all its light on. All of a sudden the pickup truck takes off and moves over to the parking area in front of the plane to Kyle's left. The guy jumps back in the side door of the Sierra 6 truck and pulls over to where Sierra 4 has parked. The plane on the taxiway revs up its engines and continues taxing.

Kyle gets a smirk on his face. "I guess we're not the only ones taking a nap tonight. Hopefully he had a bible with him."

"A bible? Why is that?" asked Mike.

"When you are going to sleep in a truck, you need to lock all the doors, open a bible and set it on your lap. Then put your head down and go to sleep."

"I don't get it," said Mike.

"If someone comes up to the truck, it looks like you are praying." Kyle demonstrates the technique. "All you do is wake up, do the sign of the cross and then lift your head."

Kyle and Mike start laughing.

The two specialists walk back up front to the flight deck. Kyle looks at his watch. "What the hell is taking you guys so long? It's going on six o'clock."

"Well, we had it fixed and then we smelled something burning," said the higher-ranking specialist. "I believe we got a bad computer or we have a wiring problem."

"You dumb ass!" said Kyle. "The burning you smelled was us cooking chicken in the galley."

The specialists get a stupid look on their faces.

Kyle stands up. "Clean your mess up, put everything back together and sign this shit off. It's time to go home."

Kyle walks back towards the crew chief table and disappears behind the curtain. Mike looks at the specialist and shakes his head in disbelief. The specialists just look at each other.

Its half past seven in the morning and the sun is just coming up. Buckner has headed to CTK to turn in the tools and equipment. Kyle is sitting in the pilot's seat and Mike is sitting in the co-pilot's seat. Kyle has dozed off and Mike is awake listening to the radio. The plane next door to the right has its visor open. Mike looks over and sees a guy without a harness climbing out of the pilot's window. He is standing on the windshield wiper fairings and balancing himself with his hands. Another guy hands him a bottle of glass cleaner and a few rags. The guy standing on the fairings cleans the windows fast, hands the cleaner and rags back inside and then climbs back in through the window.

"What the fuck," said Mike.

Seconds later, the same two guys reappear at the crew entry door threshold. One of them heads down the ladder, looks over the visor and the ramp area, looks around to see if anyone is in the vicinity and gives a thumbs-up to the guy upstairs. The guy upstairs nods his head. He steps backwards, into the cargo compartment and disappears from site. All of a sudden the visor starts to move and closes. The guy on the ground walks back up the ladder and steps into the cargo compartment.

Mike looks at his watch and wonders what's taking day shift so long to get out on the flightline. He looks to the left to see if there is any movement. Just then, a truck pulls out from behind the wash rack hangar and up to the entry control point. The cop walks over and starts checking line badges. As he does, two more trucks pull up at the entry control point. The cop waves the first truck on and it pulls onto the flightline. The next truck pulls up.

"Kyle, Kyle, wake up. Here comes day shift."

Kyle stirs, looks at his watch and stretches. "I could have slept another hour."

"Hey, I just saw a guy climb out of the window over there and clean the front windows. Is he crazy?" asked Mike.

"No. Sometimes guys will put the visor up to hide themselves and climb out and clean the windows. They do it mostly when the plane is flying a CAT 2 local. It's a type of takeoff and landing assault training. Pilots like the windows nice and clean for that. Maybe that's what that plane is doing today. Have you ever seen the planes spiraling up and down over the base?

"Yea."

"That's a CAT-2 local."

A truck pulls up at the plane to their left. Three civilians get out of the truck along with one airman. The civilians are all carrying coffee. One of the civilians has papers in his hand. The airman is carrying the toolbox.

"What the fuck!" exclaimed Kyle. "Look at that crew. Whoever put that bunch together needs to be fired."

"What do you mean?"

"You see the three civilians?"

"Yea."

"That's "Take a Break" Debreak, "Take a Shit" Mick and Stevie "The Lock Ness Monster" Brewer."

Mike needs more information. "And?"

"See the guy in the blue t-shirt?" asked Kyle. "That's Phillipe "Take a Break" DeBreak. He gets his nickname because he never misses one single civilian break. It doesn't matter what's going on, hell or high water, he always takes his breaks."

"The older skinny guy is "Take a Shit" Mick. Every day between half past one and two o'clock, Mick has to take a shit. So he calls the truck, goes in and takes a shit. By the time he gets finished, it's too late to come back out to the airplane, so he just stays inside until it's time to go home.

"And the taller guy with the nice shirt on is "The Lock Ness Monster" Stevie Brewer. He is the union steward for the squadron. He always has union business and is rarely out on the plane doing his real job."

"So why do they call him the Lock Ness Monster?" asked Mike.

"Because he's rarely seen, but talked about a lot."

They both laugh.

"That poor airman is screwed," said Kyle. "The only reason they put him on that crew is to check out a box and give turnover."

"That's fucked up."

"No, that's day shift."

The truck that dropped the four guys off has looped out to the centerline and is turning towards the plane Kyle and Mike are on.

"Turnover is here," said Kyle.

Kyle sits up and looks downstairs to see who is getting out of the truck. "Look at this piece of shit."

It's the FCC Duncan.

"Who is it?" asked Mike.

"It's the most worthless piece of shit ever to walk the flightline. Hurry! Help me spin the LOX gauges so they both look like they are full.

Kyle and Mike jump up fast. Kyle sits at the flight engineer's table. Mike is standing behind him. There are two separate LOX gauges, a 25-liter crew LOX gauge and a 75-liter troop LOX gauge. The gauges indicate quantities of 10 and 35. Kyle, using his left hand, pushes the two LOX gauge test buttons that are just under the gauges. As he pushes the buttons, the needles move counterclockwise. He is jockeying the needle on the gauges and trying to get them so they end up together at 25 over 75, which would indicate full. The crew LOX needle moves faster than the troop LOX needle.

Kyle points with his right hand to a circuit breaker on the panel to his right. "See that circuit breaker labeled Liquid Oxygen Indicators? It's in the green shaded area."

Mike moves to his right, leans over the scanners seats and locates the circuit breaker. He puts his finger on it. The circuit breaker controls the power to both the LOX gauges. "Yea got it."

"When I tell you to pull it, do it."

Kyle has it figured out. First he pushes the test button that controls the slower needle giving it a head start. Then he pushes test button on the faster one. The gauges are rotating counterclockwise. It's a controlled race. As the needles pass just before zero, each red LOX Low light comes on. The troop LOX needle is ahead of the crew needle but the crew needle is catching up. Kyle is hoping he has timed it right and the needles meet to indicate 25 and 75 on the respective gauges. The needles are close. The LOX Low lights go out.

"Pull it!" said Kyle.

Mike pulls the circuit breaker. The needles stop at 24 and 72. You can here Duncan coming up the ladder.

"Ok, when this cock sucker gets up here, we'll show him the gas and the LOX reading," said Kyle. "He'll look at them quickly and then I'll take him back to the table where the forms are. Once we get back at the table you push the circuit breaker back in. This idiot won't figure out the plane need LOX until we are long gone. Got it?"

"Got it."

Mike moves and sits in the co-pilots seat and Kyle moves to the navigator's seat. Duncan comes up the ladder and opens the flight station door.

"Morning," said Duncan.

Kyle starts in on him. "I'm surprised to see you out on the plane. Why aren't you off somewhere wasting the government's money?"

Kyle stands up, reaches over and slaps down the four red guarded switches on the flight engineer's circuit breaker panel that control the fuel gauges. He turns back towards the flight engineer's panel. All 12 fuel gauges and the fuel totalizer come to life. The fuel gauges show the quantity of fuel in each tank and the totalizer shows the total quantity of fuel on the plane.

"Check it out," said Kyle. "The gas is 120,000 and the LOX is 24 over 72."

Duncan looks at the panel and verifies the totals.

Kyle points towards the back of the plane. "The forms are back at the table."

Duncan turns and heads back to the table. Kyle turns and winks at Mike. Mike gives Kyle a thumbs-up. Kyle walks back to the table with Duncan. While Kyle is back with Duncan, Mike slides out of the co-pilot's seat and into the engineer's seat. He leans over and coughs loudly as he pushes the circuit breaker back in. The LOX gauges roll back to 10 over 35. Mike slides out of the seat and walks back to the table. Kyle and Duncan are sitting at the table. Duncan has the forms in front of him. He's already breezed through them.

"So, that's it," said Kyle. "I'm handing you a perfect plane. Try to stay out here at least an hour today and don't fuck up anything. Mike, you ready?"

"Yea."

Kyle stands up next to Mike. They walk forward toward the flight deck.

"You both have a nice day," said Duncan.

Kyle doesn't turn around. "Fuck off."

Mike grabs his bag from the navigator's station table and heads down the stairs. Kyle grabs his bag off the same table and looks over at the LOX gauges. They read 10 over 35. Kyle smiles and heads down the stairs.

CHAPTER 10

It's a week later and the guys are in Kyle and Bucky's room. It's after seven o'clock in the evening. Kyle and Troy are sitting on the couch. Kyle is next to the bunk beds and Troy is over next to the wall. Bucky is sitting on the bottom bunk. They are drinking Budweiser out of cans. The radio is on very low. They are dressed and ready to go out to Loockermans later but they have some time to kill. Troy gets up and heads to the fridge to get another beer.

"Hey Troy, are you tired?" asked Kyle.

"No, why?"

"Then grab me another beer since you have all that energy."

"Bastard. Bucky, you need one?" asked Troy.

"Sure, why not."

Bucky guns down the rest of his beer and pitches it across the room into the garbage can. Troy grabs three beers, hands them to the guys and then sits down. They all open them. Kyle opens his and puts a small dent at the top of the can opposite of the opening.

"So anyway, finish your story Troy," said Bucky.

Troy sits back down.

"Ok, hold on," Troy said. "Kyle, why do you always dent your beer can like that?"

Kyle holds up the can. "That's the Alabama drivers dent. You see, when you are driving around in Alabama and drinking beer you always dent the can on the opposite side of the mouth hole."

"Why's that?" asked Troy.

"So when you are driving with the beer between your legs you don't have to look down and make sure that the opening is lined up with your mouth. Have you ever picked up a beer, took a swig of it and the opening was off centered? You spilled the beer all over you."

"You people down there are really fucked up but that kind of makes since," said Troy.

"Yea and you keep your eyes on the road at all times," said Kyle. "It's a safety thing. Plus, you don't want to fuck up your shirt before you go into the bar or before you are going to meet someone."

"What was it you guys said you used to do down there, bar pushups?" asked Bucky.

"Yea, bar pushups," said Kyle. "We use to get to a bar or a club and before going in we'd lean against the car's fender and rip off 20 or 30 pushups."

Kyle sets his beer down on the floor, stands, leans against the top bunk and does a few pushups. "That way, when we went in the bar, our guns were all pumped up."

"Why didn't you just do them on the ground?" asked Troy.

Kyle sits back down.

Kyle looks at Troy like he is crazy. "And what, get all dirty?"

"I still can't figure out how you people lost the war," said Troy.

They all laugh.

"Come on Troy, finish telling that story about that bar," said Bucky.

Troy gathers himself. "Ok, ok. So like I said the place was called the Boardy Barn. It was out in the Hamptons. A bunch of friend and friends of friends would all throw in money to rent a place out in the Hamptons for the summer. A lot of people from the city would come out. You know...Kyle's people."

"New York City?" asked Bucky.

"Yea. So this place was the craziest place I've ever been to. They are only open from four until eight on Sundays. There'd be a line to get in so we'd always get there early. There was a ten dollar cover charge and beers were a dollar. We'd get a good spot at the bar and hunker down. They served warm draft beers in clear plastic cups. The place was so packed you couldn't move."

Troy stands up to demonstrate the next part. "The line to the bathroom was so long we'd just piss right there at the bar."

Bucky laughs. "Get the fuck out of here."

Troy sits back down. "There was so much beer on the floor from people throwing them at each other that you couldn't tell."

"Were you guys throwing beer?" asked Kyle.

"No, there were bouncers everywhere. We didn't want to get kicked out. So, since the beers were so cheap we were ordering 15 or 20 at a time. People were walking by and stealing them right off the bar. So we started pissing in the empty cups and setting them on the bar next to us."

They all start laughing.

"I'm telling you this place was crazy," said Troy. "We should ride up there one weekend."

"Forget about the Island," said Kyle. "The girls up there are too stuck up."

"They're not stuck up. They just see right through your bull shit," said Troy.

"It is tough up there," said Kyle. "You almost have to tell the truth."

"And when they find out you are in the Air Force and not a rich kid they want nothing to do with you," said Bucky.

"It's so much easier in the south," said Kyle. "They are all so gullible."

"What about that time you were TDY down there and you told that girl that you were there to catch the space shuttle when it landed," said Bucky. "That was in Florida right? Not the south."

TDY stands for Temporary Duty. Working at another base or a location other than the base you are assigned to is considered a TDY.

"What?" asked Troy.

"Oh yea," said Kyle. "But it was in the pan handle of Florida. That's the Red Neck Riviera."

Higa enters the room. He looks a little buzzed. He stands in front of Bucky's wall unit. "Hey! What are you guys up to?"

Troy hasn't seen Higa since he threw up in Mouse's car. "Holy shit he's alive!"

Kyle hasn't seen Higa either. "Higa, you almost fucked it up for me a few weeks ago. If you would have barfed on that chick I would have kicked your little ass."

Higa has a shit eating grin on his face. "Yea, I might have had a little bit too much to drink but it was Bucky talking about all that food that got me sick."

"You know Higa, Mouse was weaving the car back and forth also."

"That son of a bitch," said Higa. "I should have puked in his car."

Bucky gets up, walks over to the refrigerator and gets Higa a beer. He hands it to him.

Bucky doesn't miss his opportunity to get under Higa's skin. "Not sure if this is what you guys drink in Thailand, but this is a good American beer."

Everyone starts laughing except Higa. He walks over and sits in the chair. He gets a little heated. "God damn it Bucky. I told you I was Japanese."

Higa takes a big gulp of his beer and sits there. His face is turning red.

Troy gets the previous conversation back on track. "So what about this girl and the space shuttle?"

Kyle continues. "Well I was out at this bar and I met this girl. She asked me what I was doing there and I told her I was there to catch the space shuttle. It was actually landing the next day."

"But you are up in the pan handle and the space shuttle lands down in Cape Canaveral," said Troy.

"That's the beauty of it," said Kyle. "It's that simple."

"So did you get that ass?" asked Troy.

"Of course," said Kyle. "And I had an out because I had to get up early the next morning and block the shuttle in."

Troy shakes his head. "Fucking guy."

They all start laughing.

Bret Nader walks in. He has a cast on his left arm. It runs from his hand all the way to his elbow.

"Hey, what's up guys?"

"What in the hell happened to you?" asked Bucky.

Nader opens the refrigerator, grabs a beer and sits down on the couch between Kyle and Troy. He puts the beer between his legs and opens it with his good hand. "I broke a bone in my hand and messed up some tendons in my wrist playing football last weekend."

"But that was five days ago," said Bucky.

"Yea I know," said Nader. "It's been hurting for a while and I finally went to get it checked out. They said it was bad. I might have this cast on for at least two months."

"Two months!" said Troy. "I think you sat on it to long before you jerked off. Was it worth it?"

"Why do you sit on your hand before you jerk off?" asked Higa.

"So it numbs up and it doesn't feel like it's your hand," said Troy.

Everyone laughs.

"What did work say?" asked Kyle.

"They were pissed at first but I told them I didn't want to miss any work," said Nader. "So they are going to let me drive Sierra 18 until I get this off."

"How in the fuck are you going to load the tire trailer or pull a B-2 stand with a cast on your arm?" asked Kyle.

Nader laughs. "Oh, I'll manage."

Nader burps loudly.

"Do you kiss your mother with that same mouth?" asked Troy.

They all laugh.

All of a sudden the Rolling Stones song *You Can't Always Get What You Want* comes on the radio. Bucky jumps up and turns up the radio. "Shut up everybody! Let me show you guys how Keith Richards does this."

Bucky sits back down on the bed and starts playing the air guitar to the beginning part. He also is acting like he has a cigarette in his mouth. At one point he takes the cigarette out of his mouth and pretends to stick it at the top of the guitar in the strings. Everybody is just enjoying his playing. Higa is even drunker now off the beer he just finished and seems to be turning a deeper shade of red. The song and Bucky's performance goes on for a minute or so and then there is a loud knock at the door. Bucky stops playing.

You can hear a voice from the hallway but no one can see who it is. "What the hell is going on in there? Turn that music down!"

Bucky jumps up and turns the radio volume down. You can barely hear it. He starts walking towards the door. "Who the fuck wants to know?"

Milos comes through the door wearing his service dress uniform.

Pete Milos is a buck sergeant and in his mid-20s. He lives next door to Kyle and Bucky. He is of Greek descent. His family has money but he doesn't like to admit it around the guys. Milos is pulling dorm guard or CQ.

CQ stands for Charge of Quarters and fills the gap when Graywolf or Andy is off duty. The CQ watches over the dorms and the people who live in them. CQs work out of Graywolf's office and are supposed to make rounds through the dorms every hour.

"Calm down," said Milos. "It's just me."

Bucky turns and sits back down. Milos stands at the corner of the bed.

"What the hell are you doing in your blues?" asked Bucky.

"Let me guess, parking cars for extra money," said Kyle.

"No, they started up CQ again," said Milos.

"Why'd they do that?" asked Nader.

Milos starts to laugh. "Someone set the mops and brooms on fire at the chow hall end of 410."

Bucky sets his beer on the floor. "Here's a fire for you!"

He rocks back, takes his lighter and lights it next to his ass. He grunts a little and farts. The fart lights off and shoots a small flame from Bucky's jeans."

"Holy shit!" said Troy.

Kyle can't believe what he just witnessed. "That really works?"

Nader is laughing. "That was cool! Do it again!"

Higa is just smiling.

Bucky jumps up! "God damn! I think I burnt my ass hole."

Bucky is jumping around and waving his hands behind him trying to air his ass out.

Nader, being an expert on the dorms, adds a little history to the conversation. "Last time they had CQ was when that guy did a burnout on this motorcycle all the way down the hallway of 412. That was during the endless summer keg party."

"Yea, that happened below me," said Troy. "I heard it that night and thought it was a little loud. That guy ruined the entire carpet in that hallway."

"Troy, what about that guy that lived in your hallway who kept getting naked, jumping out of his second floor window and sliding down the light poll?" asked Kyle.

Troy laughs. "Yea and then running all the way back across the grass to the stairs and back up to his room."

Bucky picks his beer up and sits back down on the lower bunk. "I never heard about that."

"Yea, that guy. What ever happened to him?" asked Kyle.

"He got out and went to Montana or somewhere out west," said Troy.

"I heard he's a rodeo clown now," said Nader.

"Milos, when do you have to have your dad's car back?" asked Bucky.

Milos goes on the defensive. "That's not my dad's car, that's mine."

"My ass!" said Bucky. "How does anyone living here in the dorms afford a BMW?"

"I just watch my money," said Milos. "I've had a few good TDYs also."

Kyle sees Milos is on his heels and jumps in. "We saw you the other night at Loockerman talking to that girl."

"You had your keys out on the bar so the girl could see your BMW key ring," said Bucky. "What a dick move."

Milos shrugs his shoulders. "It worked."

"Did you tell the girl you were Greek?" asked Troy.

"What's that have to do with anything?" asked Milos.

"You know how Greeks are," said Troy. "You guys are all tail gunners. Butts are for fun and pussies are for babies."

Everybody laughs. The Guns N Roses song *Sweet Child of Mine* comes on the radio. Bucky hears it somehow, jumps up and turns the volume on the radio back up. He starts doing his Axel Rose impression. Milos stands around for a few second, shakes his head and leaves the room. Kyle, not wanting to disturb Bucky's performance, stands up and shakes his empty can at everyone, asking if they need another beer. They all nod yes and take their last swig. They all pass the empty cans to the right, around to Higa, where he drops them into the garbage can.

It's around midnight. Kyle, Bucky and Troy are at Loockerman sitting at the upper bar in the far corner with their backs to the windows. Kyle is to the left, Bucky in the middle and Troy on the right. Bucky and Troy are talking to each other and Kyle is talking to a woman that he doesn't know. They have a pitcher of beer in front of them and are all drinking out of pint glasses.

"Who's this girl Kyle hooked up with?" asked Troy.

"No clue," said Bucky. "She wasn't there a few minutes ago."

"Does Kyle know her?" asked Troy.

Bucky takes a drink of his beer. "Who knows?"

The woman talking to Kyle puts her arm around him.

"Jesus Christ, she's all over him," said Troy.

"I don't know how he does it," said Bucky.

"What the hell does he say to all these women to get them all the time?" asked Troy.

"Whatever it is, its magic," said Bucky.

The woman leaves and Kyle turns to Bucky and Troy.

"Wow!" said Kyle.

"Who the hell is that?" asked Bucky. "She's all over you."

Troy laughs. "What lies did you tell to get this one?"

Kyle is a little stunned. "I don't have a clue who she is or what her name is. I've never seen her before."

"Where did you meet her?" asked Bucky.

"I met her right here, just a few minutes ago," said Kyle. "We haven't gotten up since we've been here. She just came up to me and whispered in my ear that tonight she was going to screw my brains out."

"Oh my God! Are you serious?" asked Troy.

Kyle still can't believe the woman's aggressiveness. "Yea!"

Bucky likes the action. "Hell yea!"

"I'm not so sure about it though," said Kyle.

"What!" said Troy.

Kyle takes a drink of his beer. "She's not really my type. She's way too short."

"She has a nice body," said Bucky.

Kyle is still not impressed. "But did you see her face?"

"No, not really. What's wrong with it?" asked Troy.

"She is wearing a lot of makeup," said Kyle. "I'm trying to figure out what she is covering up. And what it will look like tomorrow morning."

Bucky starts to smile. "Well you know what they say. It's not the face you are fucking, it's the fuck you are facing."

They all laugh.

"Well, what are you going to do boy?" asked Troy.

Kyle pulls his wallet out of his back pocket. "Order another pitcher."

"No, about the woman," said Troy.

"I don't know," said Kyle. "I'm on the fence right now. Maybe a few more beers will help me see clear."

Bucky raises his glass. "Here-here."

Troy just laughs it off. "Oh yea, that always helps."

Kyle flags down the barkeep and orders another pitcher.

Troy thinks for a second and makes a bold statement. "Well if you don't want it I'll take it."

"What! You couldn't handle that shit Troy," said Bucky.

Troy gets a cocky look on his face. "Oh yea! I'd like to show her a thing or two. And when I get done I'll give her some lotion for her face."

All the guys laugh.

Kyle is obviously not interested in the woman. He agrees with Troy's idea. "Ok, I'll try and push her your way if she comes back."

"If he does, don't blow this Troy," said Bucky.

Troy still has his cocky attitude. "Don't worry about me. I know how to treat a woman."

"How is that?" asked Kyle.

"Thanks! See you later and don't worry, I'll call you," said Troy.

They all laugh.

The barkeep drops off the pitcher and Kyle slides a 10 dollar bill towards him. Kyle grabs the pitcher and tops off all the glasses. Kyle sets the pitcher down and they all take a drink. The barkeep returns and drops Kyle's change in front of him. Kyle puts the change in his wallet and returns the wallet to his back pocket.

"Ok, let me figure this out," said Kyle.

About 15 minutes go by. They guys have been drinking beer, talking and having a good time. At the same time Kyle has been trying to figure out how to get Troy and the girl by themselves. The woman walks back up and is all over Kyle again. Bucky and Troy have a "holy shit" look on their faces and turn and talk so they don't mess up anything. Kyle talks to the woman for a bit and then she gets up and leaves again.

Kyle turns to Bucky and Troy. "Ok, here's the story."

"Where did she go?" asked Troy.

"She went to tell her friends that she was leaving," said Kyle. "She's going to tell them to get a cab home."

"How is Troy supposed to hook up with her?" asked Bucky.

Kyle starts to explain his plan. "I told her that we came out here separately and that your car was a fancy two-seater sports car. And, you were too drunk to drive home and you only trusted me to drive your car. So supposedly, you and I are driving home together."

"But we took a cab out here," said Troy.

"She doesn't need to know that," said Kyle. "Try and keep up."

"Ok, I get it. What about me?" asked Troy.

Kyle continues with the plan. "You are going to ride back with her in her car and show her where I live. Once you get her alone in the car you can make your move. You'll have her all to yourself. Bucky and I will find a way back to the base."

"Ok, sounds like a plan. What's her name?" asked Troy.

Kyle is not the least bit interested and he's terrible with names. "She told me but I forgot."

"Don't blow this Troy," said Bucky.

"The only thing I'm going to blow is a load," said Troy.

They all laugh.

"I bet you can't score with her," said Bucky.

"What do you want to bet?" asked Troy.

"It doesn't matter because we won't have any proof," said Bucky.

Kyle laughs. "Yea, what are we supposed to do, smell your fingers in the morning?"

Troy has a plan of his own. "How about this? I'll give you guys the keys to my room. You guys get there before me and hide in the room and I'll show you who the man is."

Bucky doesn't like the plan. "That's fucked up."

"No, come on. This could be pretty funny," said Kyle.

"Where are we going to hide?" asked Bucky.

"There's hardly any clothes in my roommate's locker," said Troy. "He practically lives with his girlfriend off base."

Kyle laughs. "Yea right, Bucky and I stuffed in that locker together."

Troy likes his plans and won't give up on it so easily. "One of you gets under the bed. There's nothing under there except a few pair of shoes. Ok, hold on, here she comes."

Bucky makes a split second decision and decides to go for it. "Give me the key to your room, hurry."

The woman walks up and there is a little small talk between her and Kyle. Troy slips the key to his room to Bucky.

Kyle stands up and introduces the girl to Bucky and Troy. "These are my friends Bucky and Troy."

Bucky and Troy turn on their bar stools so they can meet her. Kyle has forgotten her name so he stays quiet and leaves it up to the guys to ask.

"Hey, I'm Bucky, nice to meet you. What's your name?"

"Wanda."

"High, I'm Troy."

"Wanda. Nice to meet you."

"Ok, let's get out of here," said Kyle.

"Are we square with our drinks?" asked Bucky.

"Yea, we're good," said Kyle.

Bucky and Troy stand up. They all walk along the bar, down the stairs and out the front door. They stop on the street.

Wanda points up Loockerman Street. "I'm parked up the street a few blocks, across from the Old Towne Pub."

Kyle motions down towards State Street. "We are around the corner a few blocks, past Smithers, over by route eight. Ok, I'll see you in a bit."

W.T. Smithers is a restaurant/bar on State Street. It's located about 200 feet or three buildings down from the corner of Loockerman and State Street.

Wanda seems excited. "Yea, see you in a bit."

Troy has a slight smirk on his face. "Ok, I'll see you guys later."

Troy and Wanda turn and head up Loockerman Street. Kyle and Bucky spin around, walk a few steps to the corner and turn left on State Street. They get about 50 feet from the corner and both turn around and look back to make sure that Troy and Wanda are not behind them. They continue walking.

"What do you think?" asked Bucky.

Kyle seems a bit relieved. "I think I just dodged a bullet in some way."

"No, about Troy."

"Maybe he can pull it off," said Kyle. "She seemed a little crazy."

"We should leave Troy be and not mess with him tonight."

Kyle agrees with Bucky. "Yea, maybe you are right."

The guys stop in front of Smithers.

"How about last call?" asked Kyle.

"Sounds good to me."

Kyle and Bucky walk into Smithers for their last beer of the night.

A few blocks down the street, Troy and Wanda are getting into her car. She starts the car and pulls out aggressively onto Loockman Street. She is buzzed and on a mission to see Kyle. Troy is starting to think that maybe this was not a good idea. He is starting to get nervous. He reaches down and checks his seatbelt. They head down Loockman Street until they hit US 13, where she makes a right turn.

"You know where you are going right?" asked Troy.

"Yea!"

They come to the US 13 and US 113 split and she veers left through the intersection.

Troy is thinking to himself, "Please don't get pulled over or into an accident."

They are now on US 113 which is a four lane highway divided by a grass median. They pass the Blue Hen Mall and the VFW on the left. Further down they pass Tap Works on the right. Troy is nervous and is making small talk with Wanda. He hopes that she will forget about Kyle and go for him. Troy doesn't know that Kyle and Bucky have called off the plan. The car passes through the light at the intersection of the north gate and Route 10.

"So, do you live here in Dover?" asked Troy.

She points off to the right. "Yea, right over there in base housing. Are you sure Kyle lives with you?"

"Yea...yea."

Troy starts thinking to himself. "If this girl lives in base housing she has to be married or have kids."

"So are you in the Air Force?" asked Troy.

"No! My husband the asshole is. He's gone TDY all the time and I'm tired of it."

Troy smirks. "So I take it you guys don't get along?"

"Yea, I had him kicked out of the house and into the dorms last week."

"Oh yea, what dorm?" asked Troy.

"It's the dorm right next to the post office. I don't remember the number. What are you writing a book?"

Troy gets a surprised look on his face. That dorm is on the other side of 408, Kyle and Bucky's dorm.

"Oh...ok. Are you sure you can drive through the gate after drinking tonight?" asked Troy.

"Yea, I'm fine. The cops don't give a shit. Plus, if I get in trouble, what are they going to do to me? It will all fall on that asshole husband of mine."

They are approaching the intersection at the base's main gate. Wanda gets in the left turning lane for the base. Ahead, the left turn signal arrow is red. There is also an extra lane on the right side of the highway that allows cars to turn into the 7-11, base housing and billeting. There is a yield sign and a triangle shaped cement traffic island. The island is about six inches high. It forms the turn and helps separates the traffic.

As Wanda is slowing down, for some reason she looks over at the 7-11. There are two guys going in the door. From a distance they resemble Kyle and Bucky.

Wanda screams, "Look, its Kyle!"

Troy is caught off guard. "Huh?"

Wanda jerks the car violently to the right without even looking behind her for oncoming cars. The tires screech. Troy is thrown into the center armrest. He is holding the handle above the window for dear life. "What the fuck!"

She cuts across all four lanes of the highway, misses the turning lane, hits the island and the car goes airborne! Troy is bracing for impact. The car lands and sparks fly everywhere! Wanda regains control of the car, turns right and pulls into the 7-11 parking lot. Troy is holding the handle with his right and has his left hand is on the dash board. He is ready for her to ram into the side of the building. Wanda pulls the car into a parking spot on the side of the 7-11 and slams on the brakes. The car comes to a screeching halt. Wanda throws the car into park, jumps out of the door and runs around the corner into the 7-11.

Troy takes a second to gather himself. He reaches over, cuts the car off and gets out. Troy slams the door behind him. He has just gone for the ride of his life and he is still alive. He walks up on the sidewalk and leans against the wall. He is trying to figure out what has just happened. He wipes his forehead.

"Crazy bitch."

Troy looks over towards the base and sees that one of the guards has walked out from the guard shack and is trying to figure out what was going on. Troy tries to act nonchalant. He looks away and down at the car. The right front rim is bent and the tire is leaking air. The rim is almost on the ground. Troy shakes his head and is still in disbelief. He thinks to himself that he needs to get away from this girl, and quick. His only option is to get inside the gate which is about 150 yards away.

Troy starts walking towards the entrance to the parking lot that they pulled into. He gets down to the side walk, turns left and starts heading towards the intersection. He knows he only has seconds before Wanda realizes that Kyle is not in the 7-11. Troy starts walking faster. He makes it to the corner and looks back.

There is a set of gas pumps in the 7-11 parking lot that Troy is hoping will partially block her view and aid his escape.

Wanda comes out of the 7-11 and turns right towards her car. She is looking around for Troy. Troy doesn't hesitate. He turns and jogs across the street but because of traffic he has to stop on the median. He looks back to see where Wanda is. She is walking around her car, looking it over and looking for Troy.

All of a sudden she sees him and screams! "Troy! Wait for me!"

Troy flips her "the bird" and gives her the "up yours" gesture. The highway is clear and Troy turns and starts jogging towards the gate. He looks ahead and there are two cops standing out in front of the guard shack. The main gate guard shack is more like a small building. Troy slows to a walk and looks back. Wanda is crossing the highway on foot.

Troy approaches the cops and pulls out his wallet to show his military identification card. "How are you guys doing tonight?"

"What the hell is going on over there?" asked one of the cops. "Why are you running?"

"I was in the 7-11 and this crazy bitch came running in and screaming all kinds of shit," said Troy. "I think she's drunk or high on something. So I thought it was best just to get the hell out of there."

Troy holds his ID card up. The cops see it and nod ok. Troy puts his wallet back in his back pocket.

"Do you know her?" asked the cop.

Troy keeps his cool. "No, I've never seen her before in my life. I think the manager of the 7-11 called the cops."

"Well get going." said the cop. "We'll handle this."

"Yea, yea, thanks," said Troy.

Troy starts walking fast again. He crosses the small parking lot behind the guard shack. His only thought is to make it to the post office and then he can disappear into the maze of buildings. But that is at least 100 yards away. The cops didn't get a good look at his ID and all Wanda knows is Troy's first name. He looks back and the cops are both facing the 7-11. Wanda is getting closer to the gate.

Troy says to himself, "Fuck it!"

Troy takes off running. He passes under the big tree that sits next to the parking lot and crosses the main road. He sprints through a grass field and into the parking lot of the post office. He passes the post office on his left and is back in the grass running towards the Linen Exchange building. He's almost home free. He slows a bit and turns to look back. As he does he trips over his own feet and wipes out in the grass.

"Son of a bitch!"

Troy gets up and looks back at the gate. He can't see what is going on because the cops are out in front of the guard shack. Off to Troy's right in the distance he sees a blue flashing light from a cop car. He steps closer to the building, next to the bushes and freezes. The cop car doesn't turn towards him. It stays straight on the main road and heads for the front gate.

Troy takes off running again, crosses the street and passes the dorm where Wanda's husband lives. He runs through a small patch of grass and into the bottom floor of Kyle and Bucky's dorm, 408. He walks quickly through the dorm and out the other side. He cuts across the grass area that separates the dorms and starts up the stairs of his dorm, 412. He enters his hallway at the opposite end of his room. He finally slows down and feels like he made it. He is breathing hard and sweating. He can't wait to tell Kyle and Bucky what just happened. He gets to his door and it's locked.

"What the hell!"

Troy knocks on the door and no one answers.

"Where the hell are these guys?"

Troy pounds on the door hard! There is still no answer. It turns out Kyle and Bucky forgot about Troy's key. Just then, Milos comes through the hallway door next to Troy's room. He is still on CQ duty.

"Troy, what's up?" asked Milos.

Troy tries to act nonchalant. "Oh nothing."

Milos is looking at Troy's pants and jacket. "What the hell happened to you?"

Troy looks down at himself. His jeans have grass stains on the knees and one of them is ripped. He has bits of grass all over him from when fell.

"Oh, I thought I'd jog from the gate to here and try and get a little of this beer out of my system. I tripped over something in the grass next to Linen Exchange.

"Yea, looks like you took a spill."

"I think I lost my keys when I fell. Do you have the master key on you?" asked Troy.

"Yea."

Milos pulls some keys out of his pocket and opens Troy's door.

"Thanks Milos. I'm going to hit the sack. I have to get up early and go over there and see if I can find my keys."

"Alright Troy. Take it easy."

Troy shuts the door. He has no interest in finding Kyle and Bucky tonight. He's already been through enough. All he wants to do is go to bed.

CHAPTER 11

The next day, Kyle and Bucky are sitting in the dayroom. It's around ten o'clock in the morning. Kyle is sitting in the chair on the left side of the room and Bucky is sitting on the sofa which is on the same side of the room. Bucky is smoking a cigarette. His smokes and lighter are sitting on the table in front of him. There is also an empty Coke can on the table. Kyle is slowly drinking a Coke and eating some crackers that he got out of the vending machine in the laundry room. They are both nursing hangovers. The TV is off because the noise would just make their hangovers worse. Bucky has a few loads of laundry going next door. Troy enters the dayroom. Under his arm, rolled up, is the pair of jeans he had on last night.

The left back picture is moved but neither Kyle nor Bucky have noticed it. Troy does not notice it either.

"Hey, what's up with you guys? Where the hell were you last night?" asked Troy.

"What's up Troy?" I didn't think I'd see you up this early." said Kyle.

Bucky laughs. "When did your girlfriend leave?"

"Oh, wait until I tell you guys what happened last night," said Troy.

"Let me guess, you guys hit it off so well last night that you are meeting today to pick out rings," said Kyle.

They all start laughing. Troy sits down on the sofa next to Bucky.

Bucky rags on Troy a little more. "Ha! We'll help you pick out a ring today and then stop at the Bull on the Beach to celebrate with some beers."

"Oh stop it," said Troy.

Kyle and Bucky start laughing.

"Not even close," said Troy. "You guys are never going to believe this."

Troy stands up and unrolls the pants he had on last night. He shows Kyle and Bucky the grass stains and the tear in one of the knees.

"Holy shit Troy!" said Bucky. "What, did you do her in the grass?"

Troy sits back down and throws the jeans on the sofa between him and Bucky. "Oh my God! Where do I start? I knew the minute we got in her car something wasn't right."

"I kind of had that feeling when I met her," said Kyle. "I'm glad I let you figure it out. Let's hear it."

"Well I guess I had to learn the hard way. This crazy bitch was out of her mind."

Across the hallway Bryan's voice is heard. It interrupts Troy's story. "Are these clothes still in the dryer?

Bucky yells across the hallway into the laundry room. "That my shit and don't fuck with it."

Bryan leaves the laundry room and steps into the dayroom. Bryan is six feet tall and well built. It's obvious that he goes to the gym and works out all the time.

"Your shit has been in there forever," said Bryan. "Hurry up and get it out."

"You don't need to worry about my shit," said Bucky. I'll take it out when it's ready. By the way, who the fuck do you think you're talking to?"

"I'm Bryan. I just PCS'd in from Travis."

PCS stands for Permanent Change of Station. Someone PCSing is permanently transferred from one base to another.

"Well I'm Bucky Wirth and as long as my shit is in that dryer, that dryer is mine."

Troy looks over at Kyle. "Who the hell does this guy think he is?"

Kyle does everything he can to avoid confrontation but in his current state, Brian has pissed him off. Kyle sarcastically enters the conversation. "Hey Brian, shouldn't you be at the gym lifting weights and looking at yourself in the mirror?"

Troy is also pissed. He turns and stares at Bryan. Bryan looks over at Kyle for a second. Kyle stares right back at him. Bryan turns his attention back to Bucky. "So you are Bucky Wirth. The dorm managers were telling me about you. They said you were a boxer."

"That's right," said Bucky. What's it to you?"

"I was a golden gloves boxer in Chicago," said Bryan. "I fought in a lot of fights there. I've been training for years."

"Really?" asked Bucky.

Bucky takes the last drag of his cigarette, drops it into the empty Coke can and stands up. Kyle and Troy look at each other and have that "here we go again" look on their faces.

"Well let's do a little shadow boxing and see what you got," said Bucky.

Bucky steps out into the middle of the floor. Bryan takes a few more steps into the dayroom. Kyle and Troy pull back the table to give them a little more room. Bucky gets in his classic boxers stance and rocks a little. Bryan dances around a little in front of him. Bucky throws a few quick slaps that are way too fast for Bryan to defend. Bucky sees that he is superior to Bryan. He starts moving more and working Bryan over with slap after slap. Bryan is trying his best to stop Bucky but he can't keep up or even think of mounting an offensive attack. Finally Bucky throws a light punch and Bryan falls back on the floor next to the TV.

"Ok, ok!" said Bryan.

"Golden gloves boxer my ass!" said Bucky. "I'll hit you with so many rights you'll be begging me for a left."

Kyle laughs at Bryan. "Looks like you need a little more training. You better hit the gym a little harder."

Bryan gets up slowly. "Whoa, whoa! Sorry man."

Bucky sits back down. Troy pushes the table back in place with his feet.

"The dorm managers were right, said Bryan. "You are good."

"I should have wiped the floor with you," said Bucky. "Don't fuck with my laundry and don't come in here talking shit."

"Bryan, you are one crazy son of a bitch," said Troy.

"I said I was sorry," said Bryan.

Bryan extends his hand to Bucky. Bucky stands up and shakes it.

"Next time Graywolf and Andy tells you something you better listen," said Bucky.

"Yea-yea, no kidding," said Bryan.

Bryan turns and leaves the dayroom. Bucky sits back down and shakes his head. "I can't believe that squirrel tried me."

"Speaking of little fury animals, where in the hell is Bailey?" asked Kyle.

"Oh my God, I can't wait until he goes off on you," said Troy.

"Maybe Graywolf and Andy set traps last night," said Kyle.

They all start laughing.

"Ok Troy, finish your story and we'll go get some lunch," said Bucky.

CHAPTER 12

----------December 1989----------

Its 15 minutes before grave shift roll call. Rob is smoking a cigarette next to the side door of CTK. He has his clipboard in his hand. Kyle walks up with his bag in his hand. He is in uniform and has his field jacket on. On his head is a green helmet liner. It rolled up nicely and only covers his head above his ears.

"Rob!" said Kyle. "How are things looking tonight? Slow I hope."

"Not good," said Rob. "The new section OIC is here to meet all you guys and hand out some letters of appreciation."

OIC stand for Officer in Charge. This position is usually held by a lieutenant or a captain.

"New OIC! What happened to the shit for brains Captain Willie Stedmond?" asked Kyle. "Or as he likes to be called, Captain Stud-man."

"You aren't going to believe this if I tell you," said Rob. "But first, you have to promise not to say anything to anybody."

"Yea ok, sure. Come on, get on with it," said Kyle.

"Well you know how the Captain is big into weight lifting? He goes to competitions and all that shit," said Rob.

Kyle laughs. "Yea, he's the greatest thing in his own mind. I don't see how he puts up with himself."

Rob also laughs. "Yea right, God's gift to the Air Force."

"You know he was getting a few of the younger guys on day shift into lifting and competitions, one of them being Jimmy Newman," said Rob.

"Yea, I know Jimmy. He's a good guy," said Kyle.

Rob continues. "Well, Jimmy overhears his wife on the phone saying, "Oil you up" and "I'll be there in 30 minutes." When he asked her where she was going, she said nowhere and took off. So Jimmy star 69s the call and it was Captain Stedmond."

Kyle is blown away. "Get the fuck out of here!"

"It only gets better," said Rob. "So Jimmy takes a while to put it all together and finally drives over to Stedmond's house and there's his wife's car in the driveway. He parks and goes up to the door and Stedmond answers the door. He is in his speedo and he's all covered in baby oil like he's doing a body building competition."

"No way! You are fucking with me. What's the joke?" asked Kyle.

Rob is not smiling a bit. "No joke. I'm serious as a heart attack. Anyway, they start arguing and finally his wife comes to the door and she also has baby oil all over her."

"That dick. Did Jimmy beat his ass?" asked Kyle.

"No," said Rob. "He kept his cool and drove right back into work and told Chief Hammond what happen. The Chief had Stedmond fired, so he's no longer with us. That's why we have this new Lt."

"Did they bust Stedmond down to Lt?" asked Kyle.

Rob starts to smile. "Here's the kicker. Stedmond got a better job. He's working for the base commander now."

Kyle can't believe it. "What! That cock sucker! What a double standard! If it would have been an enlisted guy he would have lost a stripe, lost some of his pay and been given 30 days of extra duty."

Rob is in agreement. "Tell me about it."

Kyle and Rob stand there in disbelief for a few seconds.

"So who is this new Lt?" asked Kyle.

"I'm not sure but he looks like he is about 18 years old," said Rob.

"Who's getting recognized?" asked Kyle.

"Your team," said Rob. "The lieutenant was so impressed with the way you straightened out the training on the shift…and the work you guys do of course."

Kyle is shocked. "I didn't straighten out shit! I stole Hank Tomasello's password and fudged all the training."

Rob laughs. "He doesn't know that. By the way, where is Buckner?"

Kyle is still a little dazed. "Who knows? Probably out on a repo job. Last night he was talking about a hot lead he had on a car down in Rehoboth. Is Mike here?"

"Yea, he's in there," said Rob. "Let's get inside and line up before the Lt gets here."

Rob drops his cigarette on the ground and puts it out with his foot.

"You know there's a butt can right there," said Kyle.

Rob laughs. "Yea I know. I'm just giving day shift something to do tomorrow."

They open the side door and enter 585.

Both the Blue and the Red side have lined up together in formation. As usual the guys look tired and dirty. Everybody is in their uniform and a few guys have their field jackets on. Rob and the new Lt are up in front of the formation. The Red side expediter is standing off to the side of the formation. The only one missing from both sides is Buckner.

Rob stands at attention and calls the formation to attention. "Flight, attention!"

The entire flight comes to attention.

Rob issues his next command. "At ease."

All the guys in the formation slump back to less than an at ease position. They aren't very military and do not like to see day shift management on the shift.

Rob continues. "Before we get started I'd like to introduce the new section OIC…"

As Rob is speaking, you can hear a truck rev up and tires sliding sideways. Loose rocks and gravel from the worn cement outside of 585 sprays the side of the metal building. Everybody freezes and looks over at the side doors where the noise is coming from. The engine cuts off and you hear a car door open and slam closed. Buckner rips the door open and walks in quickly. He is in his coveralls. Some of the guys on the shift are snickering and others are smiling. They have their heads down trying to hide their expressions. Rob has an "oh-shit" look on his face. Buckner realizes something out of the norm is going on and hustles to the back of the formation and lines up. All the guys in the formation turn their attention back to Rob and the Lt.

Rob is a little red faced and has a slight smirk. He's not quite sure how to handle the situation so he just continues. "As I was saying, this is our new section OIC Lt Michael Harris. He'll be taking Captain Stedmond's position. Captain Stedmond moved up to work with the base commander.

All the guys show total disrespect. They come alive and applaud and whistle loudly for the departure of the hated Captain Stedmond.

Rob holds his hands up and steps forward. "Ok, ok, that's enough. Lt, they are all yours."

Rob moves over next to the other expediter.

"Thanks Sergeant Heidelmann. I'm Lt Mike Harris. I thought I'd come around and introduce myself and let you guys lay eyes on me. I'll be bouncing around to all the shifts and try to get to know you guys. If you guys have any issue please come and see me. My door is always open."

There is not much reaction from the guys. They've hear this speech before. They know nothing good comes from a new and inexperienced OIC. What is ahead are rookie mistakes and bad changes.

The Lt continues. "I'd like to recognize a few guys on the Blue side. From what I was told there was a huge training issue on the shift but this team took it under their wing and straightened it out. Also, I'd like to recognize their hard work on the flightline. So can I have Sergeant Buckner, Senior Airman Mansfield, and Airman First Class Akin up here?"

Buckner, Kyle and Mike break from the ranks. The other guys say things to them as they press through the formation. They know how Kyle and the team fudged all the training. "Brown nosers. Suck ups. You fags. Wipe your knees off."

Buckner, Kyle and Mike line up side by side and the Lt presents each of them a letter of appreciation. One by one they take the letter, shake the Lt's hand and salute him. The Lt returns each of their salutes. The Lt says something to them but it can't be heard.

The Lt steps to the side of the guys. "Ok, how about a round of applause."

The formation comes alive again, applauds and says a few other things jokingly. "Yea! You guys are the best! I want to be just like you when I grow up."

Rob and the Red side expediter are laughing and rolling their eyes.

The Lt raises his hand and the formation quiets down again. "I hope the rest of you strive to be your best. You all are doing a great job out there. Keep up the hard work."

The Lt turns to Rob and motions that he is finished.

Rob comes to attention. "Flight, attention!"

The formation comes to attention.

"Carry on, carry on, thanks," said Lt Harris.

All the guys slump back to their normal less than military stances as the Lt walks towards the front door. As he does, he walks past the vending machine. The vending machine is almost empty except for a few rows.

Everyone takes a few second to give the Lt enough time to get out of the building then they start talking and laughing amongst themselves.

Rob steps up front with one more thing. "I'd also like to give an award tonight for the best entrance at an awards ceremony. And the award goes to Bo Buckner!"

Everyone applauds, whistles and laughs as Buckner jokingly holds up his hand to be recognized for the award. "Chief, that's how Earnhardt brings her into victory lane!"

"Ok, let's get on with this shit," said Rob.

The formation slowly separates and the guys divide back into the Blue side and the Red side.

It's midnight. Kyle is sitting in the first chair of the three man seat. He has his coveralls and his field jacket on. Buckner is sitting at the crew chief table facing forward. Mike is down stairs. Kyle has the forms on his lap and is looking through them. The radio is on the table.

"Chief, how do the forms look?" asked Buckner.

"Looks like we didn't get screwed for once," said Kyle. "Rob was right, we only need to LOX and that's it. There's a write-up in here for screws missing on a panel but that's an easy fix. Mike is looking around down stairs. Hopefully he doesn't find anything major."

"Chief, I need a nap really bad," said Buckner.

Kyle laughs because he knows Buckner has too many irons in the fire. "What, is the repo job getting to you?"

"Kind of. I'm tired as a one legged man in an ass kicking contest," said Buckner.

"Well shit Buckner. You repo during swings, work on planes on graves and watch your kid during the day. When are you supposed to sleep?"

Buckner starts to tell what happened to him earlier. "Chief, the wife came home today and went off on me."

"Why'd she do that? What happened?" asked Kyle.

"I guess I fell asleep sometime during the day. I'm really not sure when. The wife comes home from work and wakes me up. She is madder than hell. The kid got into the fridge and ate all kind of junk…and left the door open."

"Yea, I guess that's a good enough reason," said Kyle.

"That's not the worst," said Buckner. "The kid had food all over his shirt and a diaper full of shit."

"That's what diapers are for," said Kyle.

Buckner laughs. "Not this one. Shit was running down his leg."

Kyle snickers.

Mike walks up. He sides into the seat at the Crew Chief table across from Buckner. "Everything looks good down stairs. There is a tire with a cut though. It's close. One of you needs to look at it."

"You mean those cock suckers even nitro'ed?" asked Buckner.

"750/750," said Mike. "I have a question about tonight. I met Captain Stedmond a while back. He seems ok. Why does everyone hate him so much?"

Kyle yields. "Buckner has been here longer than me. You tell him."

Buckner gets a little passionate. "Chief, if that cock sucker was on fire I wouldn't waste my piss on him to put out the fire. He uses people like you would not believe. Like you said, he seems to be a nice person. But if he needs to use you or to sacrifice you to advance his career he will do it in a heartbeat and not think twice about it. All he's focused on is number one. You are just a pawn out here."

"He must be good at his job," said Mike. "Since I've been here he's won several awards."

"That's just it," said Buckner. "All his awards are written off of what you, me, and everyone else does out here every single day. All he does is take credit for it. But, when you do something wrong or get in trouble he is the first one that wants to burn you at the stake."

Kyle jumps in. "Yea, no heart at all. He'll smile in your face one minute and stick a knife in your back the next. Don't let his friendly facade fool you. Keep your guard up around him. If he comes around you and is joking and trying to be one of the boys…watch out. He is more than likely testing you. A lot of new guys fall for his bull shit."

"So what should I do if I run into him?" asked Mike.

"We don't have to worry about that anymore," said Buckner. "That cock sucker is gone. But keep in mind what we said if he comes up to you at the BX or somewhere. He is a snake in the grass."

Kyle makes a suggestion. "Let's grab a cup of coffee and then Mike can service the LOX."

"You guys go grab a coffee by yourselves," said Buckner. "I'm going to go to take a nap."

"There won't be anyone here to watch out for you. What if you get caught?" asked Kyle.

Buckner grins. "Chief, I have that figured out."

Buckner gets up and goes into the aft bunk room. Mike follows and stands in the hallway. Kyle gets up, throws the forms on the table, grabs the radio and steps over next to Mike.

Both bunk rooms have two bunks that are about 15 inches off the floor and run from the doorway out toward the side of the plane. They are separated by a 30 inch walking space. The bunks double as storage compartments and have hinged covers on top. Between the two bunks there is a storage area. There is a third bunk above the lower two. This bunk is against the wall and runs forward to aft. All three bunks have thin, three inch blue mattresses on them and they all have seatbelts that run across the middle of the bunks.

Buckner lifts the cover on the lower aft bunk. There's nothing inside. "Chief, I'll sleep under here."

"What! Are you crazy?" asked Kyle.

Buckner crawls in the storage area under the bunk and starts to close the cover.

Kyle grabs ahold of the cover. "Hold on. You'll smother in there. Here, stick this in there so you can breathe."

Kyle takes the buckle of the seat belt and sticks it in between the cover and the side of the bunk, creating a one inch space. Kyle and Mike step back to see how it looks.

"How does it look from out there?" asked Buckner.

"Not bad," said Kyle. "You'd never figure anyone was in there."

Bo lifts the bunk cover up with one hand and holds the buckle with the other. "Ok, wake me up after a few hours."

Bo closes the cover and carefully puts the buckle in place. It's like he's in a coffin and closes his own lid.

"Ok, we're killing power and going to get coffee," said Kyle. "We'll be back in a little bit to LOX."

Kyle and Mike walk up front to the flight deck. Kyle gets ready to kill power. He has his hand on the switch.

"That's one crazy son-of-a-bitch," said Mike.

Kyle just shrugs his shoulders as if to say, What do you want me to do about it?

Kyle kills power and the lights go out. They head downstairs to look at the questionable tire. They walk over to the 3A2 tire on number three main landing gear. Mike turns on his flashlight and points out the cut to Kyle.

"There it is, right on top of the tire. How could they miss it?"

"Let me see the tire depth gage," said Kyle.

Mike pulls the gage out of his pocket and hands it to Kyle. Kyle measures the depth of the cut several times and then measures the depth of the closest tread groove several times.

"What is the cut limit on the tire?" asked Kyle.

Mike kneels down, finds the cut limit on the side of the tire and then stands back up.

"It's 11/32nds," said Mike.

"Yea, it's bad. There are three things we can do at this point."

"What are they?" asked Mike.

Kyle hands the depth gage back to Mike. "Well, the first option is to change it. The second option is to kneel the gear and spin the tire so that the cut is on the bottom."

"And the third option?" asked Mike.

"The third option is to plug it and cover it up," said Kyle.

"What do you mean?" asked Mike.

"Here, let me show you," said Kyle.

Kyle walks over to where two slabs of concrete meet on the ramp, pulls out his Leatherman and kneels down. Mike is right there with Kyle providing light and watching what he is doing. Kyle opens his Leatherman and pulls out the knife. He slices away a small piece of the rubber-like material that is in between the concrete slabs. They both walk back over to the tire. Kyle starts to measure the piece of rubber with the cut in the tire. He tears away little pieces and shapes the rubber so it will fit perfectly inside the cut. He gets it shaped as close as possible and sticks it in the cut.

"There you go. A perfect fit. Now the cut is plugged," said Kyle.

Mike shakes his head. "But you can see that there is a piece of rubber stuffed in the cut. It looks like crap. No one will buy that"

"I'm not finished yet," said Kyle. "There's one more step. Let me see that light."

Mike hands the flashlight to Kyle. Kyle shines it up in the gear and looks around. He finds a blob of grease and scoops it up with his finger tip.

"Watch this," said Kyle. "It's the finishing touch."

Kyle takes his finger and rubs the grease across the top of the cut. He fills in the voids and smooths out the grease. They both step back and take a look at it.

"Look at it now," said Kyle. "It looks like a grease spot on the tire. No one will think twice about it. Engineers won't touch it because they don't want to get their hands dirty."

"Let me see that light," said Mike.

Kyle hands the flashlight to Mike. Mike walks around the tire and looks at the grease spot from various angles then he walks back over to Kyle.

"Not bad," said Mike. "I would never notice it or think twice about it."

"It looks like we are going with option three. Come on, let's go get some coffee," said Kyle.

It's a half hour later. Kyle and Mike are in the terminal.

The terminal is a small version of an airport. It has a large lobby, a check-in counter, a gate or holding area and a place to eat. There is also an arrivals section with a baggage claim area. Dover's terminal processes thousands of military and space available passengers every year and is never empty.

Space available passengers or space A's consist of military retirees and their immediate families members. Space A flights are free if there is space available, hence the name space available.

Kyle and Mike have just come from the cafeteria and both have a cup of coffee in their hand. They are walking through the terminal toward the back exit, which leads to the flightline. They run into the Sierra 4 driver, Senior Master Sergeant Robert Leo. He is talking with some old military retirees and is drinking coffee.

Robert Leo is a senior master sergeant in his mid-40s. Robert has a medium build and is black. He is a character similar to George Jefferson in the TV show Good Times. He's done it all. He talks fast and is always right. Robert has spent his entire career on the flightline. He is calm at first but always gets excited over anything or anybody that pushes his buttons. All in all he is a good guy.

"How's it going Sergeant Leo?" asked Kyle.

"Good," said Robert. "You boys have that jet tuned up yet?"

"Yea, we are almost there" said Kyle. "All that's left is LOX. We are waiting on the cart. Buckner is doing the forms now."

"Alright. Sounds good to me," said Robert.

Kyle and Mike start to walk away.

"Talk to you later," said Kyle.

Mike just nods his head.

"Yea, yea, keep up the good work boys," said Robert.

Robert Leo turns back towards the retirees and keeps talking. Kyle and Mike continue to walk through the terminal toward the exit. There are a bunch of older men and women in the terminal. Some are asleep, some are talking to each other and some are just milling around trying to kill time. Some have just arrived at the terminal and others have been there for days. Space A flights are free but they are also a gamble. It's never a certain thing.

"Look at all these retirees," said Kyle. How do they do it?"

"Do what?" asked Mike.

"Sit in this terminal all day and all night waiting on a flight that's not even a guarantee."

"What else do they have to do?" asked Mike.

"Good point," said Kyle. "I just can't see myself doing that when I retire. Seems like such a waste of time. Those poor bastards are suffering I'm sure."

Kyle and Mike exit the back door of the terminal. They see Rex Kellogg and Roy Flores at Robert Leo's Sierra 4 pick-up truck. Rex and Roy have the passenger door open. They are startled and think they are caught until they see it's not Robert Leo. Kyle and Mike walk over to the driver's side door and open it so they can see what's going on.

"What's up guys?" asked Kyle.

Rex and Flores are laughing.

"Did you see Robert Leo in there?" asked Rex.

"Yea, he's talking to some old farts and drinking coffee," said Kyle.

Mike can't believe what he is seeing. "What the fuck!"

Rex and Flores have a large, dead rabbit propped up in the passenger seat of the Sierra 4 truck. It's strapped in with the seat belt. The rabbit is stiff and has its two front paws sticking straight out. They are adjusting the rabbit and the seat belt, trying to get it to sit straight.

Flores can hardly speak because he's laughing so hard. "Check this out. We found this guy on the way back from the hot spot. Isn't he cute?"

"Robert Leo needs someone to talk to while he rides around so this little guy will be riding shotgun with him tonight," said Rex.

Kyle shakes his head. "Robert Leo is going to go ape shit when he sees it. He might have a heart attack."

Rex and Flores are still laughing. They shut the door of the truck and walk toward the back door of the terminal. Kyle and Mike shut the driver's door, turn and walk away from the truck. They are also snickering.

"Never a dull moment," said Kyle.

Kyle and Mike are standing at the fire bottle in front of their plane on Hotel row. Kyle has the radio sitting on the fire bottle. Mike is in LOX gear which consists of a bunny suit, a long plastic dark green apron and a thick pair of leather gloves. There is also a white construction worker helmet with a face shield. Mike is holding the helmet in his hand. There is a LOX cart just behind the number one main landing gear. Mike pushed in the fire bottle from the left wing for safety. Kyle and Mike still haven't disturbed Buckner who is still under the bunk sleeping.

"Make sure you purge the cart real good," said Kyle. "If not, it will take forever."

Robert Leo comes on over the radio in a panic! "God damn it!"

Kyle points at the radio. "Listen!"

Robert Leo is yelling. "Who in the hell put this rabbit in my truck?! Funny thing happened to me this morning! I woke up and had this many mother fucking stripes! So someone get their ass down here and get this rabbit out of my mother fucking truck!"

Kyle and Mike start laughing.

"I told those guys he was going to go ape shit when he found that rabbit," said Kyle.

"I thought you weren't supposed to curse over the radio," said Mike.

Kyle laughs. "You're not."

"So you're sure it's ok to LOX with Buckner upstairs asleep?" asked Mike.

"Yea, he's under the bunk," said Kyle. "If QA comes snooping around they'll never find him."

"What if something happens and he can't get down the ladder?" asked Mike.

Kyle doesn't think it is a big deal. "He'll throw an escape rope out and shimmy down the side of the plane or go out the hatch, down the wing and jump off the wing tip."

"That's 10 or 12 feet," said Mike. "He'll kill himself."

Kyle laughs. "Buckner fell out of the number seven door before, got up and walked away. He'll be ok."

Mike turns and walks back to the LOX cart. Kyle picks up the radio from the fire bottle. He makes sure it's turned up so he doesn't miss anything. He sets the radio back down and leans against the fire bottle. He pulls out his pencil and starts drawing on the top of the fire bottle.

A few minutes later the Sierra 4 truck drives up to the plane on the left. Rex is in the front seat and Flores is sitting in the bed of the truck. The truck stops in front of the plane. Flores jumps over the tailgate, stays low and ties something onto the bumper of the truck. Rex gets out slowly, talks for a few seconds and when he sees Flores stand up he closes the door and waves. The truck pulls away as Rex and Flores walk up to their plane. They stop, turn around and look at the Sierra 4 truck as it heads down the flightline. The truck passes in front of Kyle's plane and continues on. The truck is dragging the rabbit down the flightline. The rabbit is tied onto the truck with a rope from a chock. Kyle chuckles and goes back to his drawing. It's a man screwing a rabbit from behind. Above the drawing it says "Robert Leo" and below it says "Humps Rabbits".

After Kyle gets finished with his drawing he walks over to the right side of the plane. In front of the number two main landing gear he finds the panel that is missing screws. He pulls a hand full of screws out of his pocket and picks the correct screws that are supposed to go in the panel. He sticks the screw in the hole and it goes completely in and sits flush in the panel. He pulls it out and tests the second hole. It does the same thing. The nut plates are missing. Kyle pulls a small bottle of super glue out of his pocket and glues the screw in place. He steps back and looks at the panel.

"Perfect."

Kyle walks back to the fire bottle to wait on Mike.

CHAPTER 13

A week has past. It's now five o'clock in the morning. Kyle, Buckner and Mike are sitting in the crew rest area. Mike is looking through the forms at the crew chief table. The radio is in front of him. Kyle is sitting in the three man seat against the wall and Buckner is sitting next to the aisle. They both have their feet up on the wall in front of them. The plane that they are on flew two locals the day before. The guys have spent the entire night getting it ready for another day of locals. Everything is good. They are only waiting to hear from Rob. There is a truck horn blowing downstairs.

"Hey! Do you guys hear a horn?" asked Mike.

Kyle listens for a second. "I don't."

"Is the radio on the right channel?" asked Buckner.

Mike picks up the radio and checks it. "Yea, it's on the right channel and it's turned up."

"Mike, walk up front and see if there is anyone downstairs," said Buckner.

Mike closes the forms and walks up to the flight deck. He leans on the pilot's seat and looks down in front of the plane. The Sierra 6 truck is down there.

From the truck, Rob sees someone looking through the pilot's side window. Rob rolls down his window, blows his horn a few times and motions to the person to come down.

Mike turns and walks back to the crew rest area. "I knew I wasn't hearing things. Sierra 6 is downstairs."

"Let's go see what he wants," said Buckner.

All the guys get up and go downstairs. They walk around the back of the truck and get into the side door. Mike sits on the bench, Kyle pulls the butt can out and sits on it and Buckner sits on the igloo cooler.

"Ok, are all you guys in?" asked Rob.

"Why didn't you call us on the radio?" asked Kyle.

"My battery is dead," said Rob. "I think this radio is a piece of shit. I've already gone through four batteries tonight."

"Chief, we are all in," said Buckner.

Rob picks up his clipboard. "Ok, that makes the total 16. Pay me the money now."

All the guys pull out their wallets and hand Rob five dollars each. Rob pulls a stack of money out of his pocket and adds the fifteen dollars to it. He also has a list of names on a piece of paper.

"You aren't starting leave tomorrow I hope?" asked Buckner.

Rob laughs. "No, I wouldn't do that to you guys. Trust me."

Kyle isn't sold on it. "You really didn't sound convincing."

"No, this is all on the up and up," said Rob. "Do you think I want 15 people after me? Here's the deal. We've decided to use your plane. It's the only one flying locals today."

Rob grabs a piece of chalk from the center console and hands it to Kyle. "Sixteen even blocks."

"Make sure you mix up the names and I want to know what number I get before I leave here tonight," said Buckner.

"You guys divide up the names now and me and Mike will go over and mark the tire," said Kyle.

"Ok," said Rob.

Buckner gets up and slides into the front seat. Kyle and Mike leave the truck and walk over to the nose landing gear. They kneel down at the outermost tire. Kyle starts to draw straight lines on the sidewall of the tire with the chalk. He draws sixteen of them from the wheel to the tread. They are all evenly spaced. Then he writes the numbers one through 16 in between each line. They both stand up and look. The tire looks like a Las Vegas roulette wheel.

"So tell me how this works again?" asked Mike.

Kyle explains. "We all pitched in five dollars. Sixteen guys on the shift. That's why there are 16 equal pieces of the pie. When we get back in the truck Rob will give you a number. The plane will fly two locals tomorrow. So after flying around all day the plane will end up back here before we start our shift. We'll come out and whoever's number is pointing at the ground will win all the money."

"I like that," said Mike. "The odds aren't that bad."

"Yours are better than mine," said Kyle. "I never have any luck. Let's go see what our numbers are."

Kyle and Mike walk back to the truck and get in.

CHAPTER 14

----------January 1990----------

It's particularly cold outside tonight and snowing. It's after eleven o'clock. Roll call has just finished inside of 585. There are people walking back and forth. Mike is wearing a military issued Parka. It's bulky, olive green and has a hood on it with fake white fur around the edges. Everyone is issued a parka when they arrive at Dover. No one wears them though.

Kyle walks over to Mike. "Nice parka."

"You know, you are the fifth or sixth guy that's made a comment about my coat tonight. Why is everyone making fun of me or giving me dirty looks?" asked Mike.

"We were all issued a parka but they are too bulky to work in," said Kyle. "And look at that hood. All it's going to do is get in the way or get caught on something. It's an unwritten rule on the flightline. No one wears a parka out here."

"But it is cold as shit out there tonight. You don't get cold?" asked Mike.

"You have to learn to layer and still be able to move," said Kyle. "Like on the bottoms; thermals, uniform, coveralls and raingear. The rain gear works great in the cold. It keeps the wind from cutting through you. On the top; t-shirt, thermals, uniform, coveralls, field jacket with liner."

Across the room is another guy with a parka on. He works on the Red side. Mike spots him and points him out. "Well what about him? He always wears a parka."

Kyle laughs. "That's Simon "Riceman" Wong. He's from Kona on the Big Island of Hawaii. Hell, he never owned a pair of shoes until he came into the Air Force. He only wore flip-flops. He's not use to this shit. He gets a pass."

Mike thinks for a few seconds. "Well what about Fukumoto on day shift? He's from Hawaii and he doesn't wear a parka."

"Fukumoto is from Wahiawa on Oahu," said Kyle. "It gets cold up there."

Mike is puzzled. "Cold? How cold does it get there?"

Kyle looks at his watch. "Sometimes in the upper 50s. Let's head out."

Mike looks at Kyle like he is crazy. Upper 50's does not seem that cold to Mike, but for a native Hawaiian it can be quite drastic. Kyle and Mike turn and walk toward the front door. People are turning and looking at Mike as if he is an alien. They walk past the vending machine where two guys are finagling it for an entire row of potato chips. The bags drop one-by-one until there are no more. There is nothing left inside. The vending machine is completely empty.

Its four hours after roll call. Kyle and Mike are on 465 on Oscar row. They are both stuffed in the crew galley area and it's very cold. The forms, radio and the -06 WUC manual are on the galley counter. The door that separates the crew rest area from the latrine and galley is closed. This door is normally open and held in place with a door stop. The oven door is open and the oven is turned up as high as it will go. The plane has a fuel issue and they are not allowed to have the APUs on or an external heater running. Kyle is trying to use the galley oven to warm up the area that he and Mike are standing in. The oven is humming and it is still snowing outside.

"So when are the fuel cell guys coming out?" asked Mike.

Fuel Cell is a separate shop. Their specialty is the plane's fuel systems. They are dispatched out to the planes when needed.

"They are down there now," said Kyle. "All they are doing is cure checking the valve they put in yesterday and then they'll leak check it."

"Then we can turn the APU's on, right?" asked Mike.

"Yea," said Kyle. "We'll get it nice and toasty up here. We'll be able to catch a short nap."

"I thought the flightline was going to be shut down tonight?" asked Mike.

Kyle laughs. "They always say that to get everyone's hopes up and then they crush them. It's the flightline way."

Someone comes up the ladder. Kyle cracks the door open and sees it's the fuel cell guys. They are coming down the hallway. Kyle opens the door all the way and drops the door stop with his foot.

"About time! Are you guys finished?" asked Kyle.

"We've been sitting in the truck watching the snow fall for the last 30 minutes," said the fuels tech sergeant.

The tech sergeant looks at Mike's parka. "Nice jacket."

Kyle can't believe it. "That's real fucking romantic. We've been up here freezing our asses off waiting on you."

"The cure looks good," said the tech sergeant. "We are going to move a little gas around now and see if it leaks."

The tech sergeant turns to his coworker. "Go up front and start transferring gas into that tank."

The coworker walks up towards the flight deck.

"Mike, go with him and watch what he does," said Kyle. "He'll explain to you what he's doing."

Mike squeezes through and walks up to the flight deck. Kyle spins the forms towards the fuels guy. "Here, sign that shit off. The cure check is on the next page."

The tech sergeant starts to write in the forms.

Kyle sticks his hands next to the oven to warm them. "Did you hear the one about Santa running into the woman while he was delivering presents?"

The tech sergeant is still signing off the cure check. "No."

Kyle starts to tell his one and only Christmas joke. "So, Santa comes down the chimney and starts throwing presents under the tree. A woman comes down the stairs in a robe and walks up behind him. She says, 'Santa, stay with me tonight and make love to me.' Santa turns around and looks at her and says, 'Gotta go-gotta go-gotta go. Gotta get the presents to the children don't you know.' He turns back and starts pitching presents under the tree again. So she takes off her robe and she is now in her sexy underwear. She says it again, 'Santa, stay with me tonight and make love to me.' Santa turns around and looks at her and says, 'Gotta go-gotta go-gotta go. Gotta get the presents to the children don't you know.' He turns back and starts pitching presents under the tree again.'"

"Yea..." said the tech sergeant.

Kyle finishes his joke. "So the woman gets naked and says, 'Santa, please, stay with me and make love to me all night.' Santa turns around and looks at the woman and says, 'Gotta stay-gotta stay- gotta stay. Can't get up the chimney with my dick this way.'"

The two start to laugh.

"That's pretty good," said the tech sergeant. I'll use it when I get back to the shop."

He finishes signing the forms. "There you go. We'll walk down and take a look at it on our way out. If it's good we'll jump in the truck and pull away."

"Ok," said Kyle. "Just leave the stand there. We'll get Sierra 18 to pull it out with his truck."

The fuels cell tech sergeant is happy. This is his last job on the flightline tonight. "Sounds good to me."

Kyle takes one more shot at him. "Where are you and your partner headed now? Back to the shop to hold hands in front of the fireplace?"

He just laughs and walks up front. Kyle turns the forms back to him and makes sure that the write-ups are signed off the correctly.

It's six in the morning and the sun has not come up yet. There is a peaceful feel to the flightline. Kyle and Mike are reclined back in the pilot and co-pilot seats. The APUs are running and the heat is on. They have stripped off their warm jackets and coveralls. It's stopped snowing. There are four or five inches of snow on the ground. There is a large, dark green snow plow with a yellow flashing light on top of it running from right to left on the front taxiway. The plow has started clearing snow from the taxiway. It has been running for hours. Over time, it's slowly pushing the snow towards the wall, clearing over half the front taxiway. There are also snow plows running on the back taxiway and on both runways.

Kyle and Mike thought they could take a nap but they are too excited about the snow. On average, it only snows about three times a year in Dover, so this is a special occasion. Also, they both grew up in areas where it never snowed so this doubles their excitement.

"Where the fuck is Sierra 18?" asked Kyle.

"They've been calling for him on the radio for the past hour," said Mike. "Is that normal? Who's driving 18 tonight?"

"Nader," said Kyle.

Someone comes over the radio. "I found Sierra 18. He was in the terminal. His radio was on the wrong channel. He's on his way out."

Nader's voice comes over the radio. "This is Sierra 18. MOCC, how do you copy me?"

MOCC replies, "Loud and clear."

"About time," said Kyle. "Now we can move this B-2 stand and start making our way inside."

Mike is watching something out the window to his left. He sits up and points his finger at something at the other end the flightline. "Look!"

Kyle sits up and looks out the window to his left. The Sierra 18 bobtail is coming down the flightline and doing donuts in the unplowed portion or the snow. Kyle and Mike are stunned.

"Holy shit!" said Kyle. "What the fuck is Nader doing?"

Mike laughs. "He's going buck!"

Sierra 6 approaches Sierra 18 and they stop side by side. They sit there for about twenty seconds and then Nader gets out of the bobtail and gets in the Sierra 6 truck. Someone else gets out of the Sierra 6 truck and into the Sierra 18 bobtail. Both trucks pull off in different directions. The Sierra 6 truck heads off the flightline towards 585 and the Sierra 18 bobtail starts down the flightline.

Kyle and Mike sit back in their chairs.

"You think he just lost control?" asked Mike.

"No," said Kyle. "With Nader, it can't be that simple. Let's shut this shit down, move the stand out and fuck with the guy driving the plow."

"Ok," said Mike.

Kyle and Mike get up and start putting their coveralls and jackets back on. Kyle grabs the radio and they both head back to the galley to see if the can find any trash bags.

A minute later Kyle and Mike head downstairs into the cargo compartment. Kyle gets to the bottom of the ladder and turns on the curb, side and overhead cargo compartment lights. Over on the right side of the forward ramp there are three cases of oil and three cases of hydraulic fluid stacked neatly on top of each other. There are also four chocks stacked next to the oil and hydraulic fluid. The cases of oil, hydraulic fluid and chocks are secured with a cargo strap.

Kyle and Mike walk over, loosen the cargo strap and toss it to the side. Kyle opens one of the hydraulic fluid cases and pulls out two one gallon red cans. He kneels down and sets the cans on the floor. Mike kneels next to him. Kyle reaches in his coat pocket, pulls out a can opener and starts to open the cans. He punches holes in the cans. At the same time Mike pulls two small clear garbage bags out of his pocket. Mike whips one bag open and holds it so Kyle can pour the hydraulic fluid in. Kyle carefully lifts a can and pours the bright red fluid into the bag. He empties the first can and starts on the second.

"So once he passes we'll walk out and bury it in the edge of the snow bank," said Kyle. "When he makes his next pass, as fast as he is going, the bag should explode when he hits it."

"Can we get in trouble for this?" asked Mike.

"Who cares," said Kyle. "It'll be funny. I bet the guy shits his pants. If something happens just act like you don't know anything."

Kyle finishes pouring the second can and sets it on the floor. "Tie it up real tight so nothing leaks out."

Mike ties the top of the bag together in several knots. Kyle whips the second bag open and Mike sets the bag of hydraulic fluid inside it.

"We'll double bag it to make sure it doesn't break while we are carrying it out there," said Kyle. "Once we get out to the snow bank, we'll take this outer bag off."

"So this is opposite of the ugly theory?" asked Mike.

"Yea, single bag it and hope it breaks," said Kyle.

They both laugh. Kyle ties one knot in the outer bag and they lower it to the floor. Kyle and Mike stand up.

"So you say you are a soccer player?" asked Kyle.

"Yea, my high school had a pretty big program," said Mike. "I was also the place kicker on the football team."

Kyle picks up the two empty cans and starts walking back into the cargo compartment. "Let's see what you got. Turn on the loading lights."

Mike walks over to the loadmaster's control panel and turns on the forward ramp loading lights. Three larger flood lights come on. The ramp area is lit up even more now.

Mike walks back to where Kyle is. They are about 25 feet from where the ramp meets the ramp extension.

The ramp extension attaches to the ramp and when opened they both form the forward loading complex. The ramp can be opened into two configurations, either drive in or truck bed. The ramp extension when closed stows vertically. It's about 10 feet tall. Between the ramp extension and the ceiling there is a four-foot gap.

Kyle sets one empty can down on the floor. He kneels down on one knee and places the empty can on the tip of his boot. He tees it up like a football.

"Ok superstar," said Kyle. "The gap above the ramp extension is the goal post. You get one shot. Don't choke Pele."

Mike moves behind Kyle, lines up and eyes the kick. He makes his three step approach, kicks the can and they both watch as it flies towards the opening. It easily makes it over the ramp and falls out of sight. Mike holds both his arms up like a referee to indicate a field goal.

"I think I could back it up five yards and still make it," said Mike.

Kyle stands up. "Here, hold one for me."

They switch positions. Mike is now the holder and Kyle is the kicker. Kyle has more of a routine. He grabs his right foot, pulls it behind him and stretches his leg. He drops his foot and does the same thing with his other leg.

"Watch and learn rookie," said Kyle.

Kyle approaches and kicks the can over the ramp. Kyle does a fist pump. "Yes!"

Mike stands up and they give each other a high five. They both start walking toward the ramp. Kyle goes to the very center of the ramp extension where the A-frame is. Kyle flips up the two locks on the A-frame, pulls it off the ramp extension and sets it off to the side.

"Let me grab these cans," said Kyle.

Kyle bends and slides sideways, stepping into the open gap in the ramp extension. He disappears through the small opening. Mike stands next to the opening. Kyle hands Mike the empty hydraulic cans one at a time. Both cans are dented from being kicked. Kyle steps out from behind the opening and slithers out sideways.

"Go shut down power and I'll straighten up down here," said Kyle. "Then we'll walk out and plant the hydraulic fluid in the snow."

Kyle turns and puts the two empty cans back in the case as Mike heads upstairs to turn off the APUs and power on the plane.

Ten minutes later Kyle and Mike are kneeling down next to the snow bank that the plow has created. Each time the plow passes the snow bank grows a little and it's pushed out closer to the wall. The sun has started to rise. The plow has just past and can be seen in the distance moving away from Kyle and Mike. Mike digs a hole into the snow bank about two feet off the ground.

"Ok, that looks big enough," said Kyle.

Kyle slowly removes the inner bag that is filled with two gallons of hydraulic fluid and places it gently into the hole. They both pack snow around the opening to hide the bag. They stand up to look and see if you can tell that something is buried inside.

"Ok, put a little extra on top and smooth it out," said Kyle.

Mike leans down and adds a little more snow. "How's that look?"

The bag of hydraulic fluid is completely covered.

Kyle gives Mike a thumbs-up. "Looks good."

Mike stands back up and they both look around to see if anyone is watching them.

"He'll be back by in five or ten minutes," said Kyle. "Let's get out of here."

Kyle and Mike start walking back toward the plane. They get up to the centerline on the taxiway and Sierra 18 pulls up.

"What happened to Nader?" asked Kyle. "I thought he was driving tonight?"

"That dumb ass," said the driver. "Remember at roll call they said they were going to shut down the line?"

"Yea," said Kyle.

The driver continues. "Well Nader figured he didn't have to work anymore so he headed down to the terminal, started bull shitting with some people and ended up drinking a shit load of beer. By the time they found him it was too late. He had at least a six pack in him…maybe a 12 pack."

They all start to laugh.

"I told you something was up," said Kyle. "Nader is always getting in trouble. Hey, grab this B-2 stand will you?"

The driver nods his head. "Yea, hook me up real quick then I need to go give turn over."

The driver pulls up in front of the plane. Kyle and Mike walk up behind him. Earlier, before they walked out to bury the hydraulic fluid, they pulled the B-2 stand out from under the right wing. Kyle walks to the front of the stand and releases both front brakes by kicking them with his boot. He guides Sierra 18 back and hooks the B-2 stand's tow bar to the pintle hook. Mike releases the back breaks. Kyle steps out of the way and waves Sierra 18 on. Sierra 18 takes off quickly down the ramp towards stand land.

Stand land is where all the stands are kept when they are not in use. It is located in front of Wiskey row.

The bobtail's transmission is geared low so it shifts fast as Sierra 18 pulls away. The front right wheel on the B-2 stand starts shimmying violently and making the entire stand rattle even more than it already is. Sierra 18 taps the brake on the bobtail, slowing it a bit and stopping the B-2's tire from shimmying.

Mike and Kyle walk over to the fire bottle in front of the plane. Both their bags are sitting on top of the fire bottle. The Sierra 6 truck pulls up and stops. Art Humm, the day shift expediter, is driving. He's in the truck alone. Art rolls down the window.

Art Humm is a technical sergeant and in his early 30s. He is the day shift expediter for Sierra 6. He is from somewhere in Montana. Art loves porn. Anytime he is away from the building he is looking at porn magazines. He has a filthy mind and always wants to know about Kyle's exploitations with women. Every morning on the way to work Art always looks for Kyle's car parked somewhere outside the main gate. If he sees it he knows Kyle was out the night before. Art makes it a point to ask Kyle what he did. Art always writes FTW (Fuck The World) on everything he can.

"Hey man, what the fuck is going on out here?" asked Art.

"Oh nothing," said Kyle. "The plane is good to go. We left the guy in the snow plow a little gift."

"You guys want a ride in?" asked Art.

"Yea," said Kyle.

"Jump in," said Art. "I have to stop and pick up another guy on Uniform row. I want to know about this gift you guys left."

Kyle and Mike pick up their bags, walk around the front of the truck and get in the side door. Kyle closes the door and the truck pulls away. On their way down to Uniform row Kyle tells Art about the bag of hydraulic fluid in the snow.

Five minutes later Art pulls away from Uniform row. He is going to drop off Kyle, Mike and a crew chief named Briggs at 585. Kyle is sitting on the igloo cooler, Mike and Briggs are sitting on the bench. Briggs is right behind Art and Mike is a few feet further down the bench. Kyle doesn't know Briggs but he has seen him around 585 in the morning during roll call. He seems like a nice, quiet, likable guy. Briggs is returning from a long TDY. On the floor of the truck is his large green duffle bag.

Kyle decides to make small talk with Briggs. "So, how long have you been gone?"

"Two months. I was in Sigonella, Italy," said Briggs.

"That's not bad at all," said Kyle. "You probably made some extra cash. Are you married?"

"Yea," said Briggs.

Art butts in on the conversation. "Hey man, did you set a PCD?"

"What's a PCD?" asked Briggs.

Art laughs. "Pussy cut-off day."

Briggs looks puzzled. Mike leans in so he can hear Art better. He's never heard the acronym PCD. As Kyle talks, Art is glancing back in the rear view mirror as he drives.

"Yea, PCD," said Kyle. "It's when you have to stop screwing the girl you are messing around with while you are TDY. You have to do it several days before you get home so your nuts have time to build back up."

Briggs looks a little shocked. He's never heard this before.

Kyle continues. "Yea, and when you get home don't let your old lady talk you into a bubble bath."

"Why's that?" asked Briggs.

Kyle starts laughing. "All she's doing is trying to get you in water deep enough to see if your nuts float or sink."

Art jumps back in. "If they sink like steel ball bearings you are ok, but if they float like buoys you are fucked!"

Everybody starts laughing. Briggs is kind of chuckling along. He doesn't know Kyle at all but he's figuring out that Art and Kyle are messing with him.

Art looks over where Kyle and Mike left the bag of hydraulic fluid. "What the fuck is this?"

Art slows down in front of Oscar row. The snow plow is stopped and a pickup truck is beside it. The side of the snow bank is sprayed in red hydraulic fluid. There are two people standing by the snow bank looking around. Art loops around to where the pickup truck and snow plow are parked, stops and rolls down his window.

Kyle motions to Mike to look out the side window of the truck. "Mike, check it out."

Two guys walk over to the Sierra 6 truck. The older guy seems nervous and the younger guy is scared to death.

173

Art has a serious look on his face. "What the hell is going on out here?"

The older of the two guys answers. "Not quite sure. Looks like my driver hit something or someone, or maybe an animal? Who knows? That looks like blood to me."

"You sure your truck isn't leaking something?" asked Art.

"Yea, we checked it out. The truck isn't leaking a thing."

The younger of the two steps in. "I'm really tired but I'm sure there was nothing in front of me."

Art remains serious. "Well, let me get these guys inside and I'll come back and help you look around and try to figure out what you hit."

The two guys step away from the truck. "Thanks! We'll keep looking around."

Art rolls up the window and pulls away. He loops back around and starts back towards 585. The two guys turn and go back toward the snow bank. Kyle, Mike and Briggs are looking through the back windows at the mess. The Sierra 6 truck gets about 100 yards away and everyone starts laughing except for Briggs.

"What's so funny?" asked Briggs.

"Oh nothing," said Kyle.

"I hope they don't call Wing Safety out," said Art.

Wing Safety is the overall safety office for Dover Air Force Base. They are called out to all major accidents that happen on the flightline.

Kyle could care less about Wing Safety. He turns back to Briggs. "Hey, here's one more thing to do when you get home."

Everyones attention goes back to Kyle.

"Yea, what's that?" asked Briggs.

"When you get home drop your bags before you get to the door," said Kyle. "Pick up a brick, ring the doorbell, and yell honey I'm home. Then step back away from the door, count to ten and throw the brick over the roof."

"And then what?" asked Briggs.

Art can't resist. "Listen to see if the brick hits a guy running out the back door."

Everyone starts to laugh, even Briggs.

"You guys are fucked up," said Briggs. "I think you are sleep deprived."

The truck pulls up and stops in front of 585. Everyone gets out. Right before Kyle walks away Art stops him. "Hey man, you need to go over and see management."

"Why?" asked Kyle.

"They are moving you to day shift," said Art.

Kyle is stunned. "Are you serious?"

"Yea man," said Art. "The new Lt likes you a lot. He says you are sharp. Said you turned around the training issue on your shift. Rob Heidelmann has been over there all morning fighting it but I think it's a done deal."

Kyle gets pissed. "I knew stealing Hank Tomasello's GO81 password was going to bite me in the ass."

Art gets a little excited. "You have Hank's password?"

"Yea, I have God rights to GO81 now," said Kyle.

Art smiles. "Good, you can fix my training when you get here. And listen to this little piece of gossip. They are putting Nader into permanent bay orderly."

"Again!" said Kyle.

"Yea, it's something to do with drinking," said Art. "I didn't get the entire story."

Kyle laughs. "Drinking! He was wasted last night. He was doing donuts on the flightline in the Sierra 18 bobtail."

"Are you shitting me?" asked Art.

Kyle takes a deep breath and exhales. "No. Ok, let me go in here and slick my hair back before I go next door."

CHAPTER 15

A few days have passed. All the snow has melted but it's still cold outside. Bret Nader is once again working as the bay orderly. He's in a good mood because he knows he's dodged another bullet. He still has all his stripes and he is still in the Air Force. Nadar, Graywolf and Andy are sitting in the dorm manager's office. Graywolf is at his desk and Andy and Nader are sitting across from each other on the furniture. They are all in their uniforms. Nader still has his cast on his arm. It's lunch time.

"So, did you get that mess cleaned up out there?" asked Graywolf.

"Yea it's all cleaned up," said Nader.

Graywolf spits in his trash can. "If I find out who did that I'm going have their asses."

Andy laughs. "What, your Indian tracking skills don't work on beer cans and cigarette butts?"

Graywolf gives Andy a dirty look.

"When are you supposed to get that cast off?" asked Graywolf.

Nader raises his cast and looks at it. It's all ratty. "Tomorrow morning."

"About time," said Andy. "Maybe we'll get more work out of you then."

"Andy, I'm the best bay orderly you ever had," said Nader.

Graywolf gets a smirk on his face. "I don't know about the best but you've definitely worked here longer than anyone else."

"Graywolf, I'm getting a little hungry. Can I run over to the chow hall and grab some lunch?" asked Nader.

"Yea, go ahead," said Graywolf.

Nader gets up and grabs his hat off the coat rack. "I'm just going to grab some takeout so I'll be back in a few minutes."

Nader exits Graywolf's office and turns right. He walks down the hallway and out the door of building 409. He hustles across the small grass area and into building 410. He doesn't have his jacket on so he's cutting through the dorms to stay warm. He gets to the end of building 410 and walks out the door. He jogs across the street and into the chow hall. He tucks the bill of his hat down into the back of his pants and heads over to the snack line. He's decided on fast food for lunch today. He walks up to the servers.

"Can I have two burgers and some fries please?" asked Nadar. "And that will be to go. Thanks!"

The guy behind the counter puts two burgers and some French fries in a white styrofoam container and hands it to Nader.

"Thanks again," said Nader.

Nader moves over to the drink dispenser and sets his food container down. He fills two paper cups with ice and then fills them with soda. He puts lids on the cups and sets the cups on top of the container. He pulls his hat out of his pants and holds it with his fingers that are sticking out from the cast on his left arm. He picks up the container with his right hand and uses his cast to help steady the drinks. Nader starts walking towards the door he entered from.

Both entrances to the chow hall have a set of double glass doors with a small area between them. Each door swings in and out. There is a guy just in front of Nader that notices he has a cast on. The guy goes ahead of Nader, pushes the door open and holds it for him. Nader walks through the door. Once Nader passes through the first door the guy releases it. The guy pushes through the next door and holds it for Nader. Nader starts to walk out. He is trying to put his hat on with his left hand while balancing his lunch in his right hand. The guy holding the door is distracted and lets go of it before Nader clears. The door swings back quickly at Nader. Before he can react, it slams into him. His food and drinks explode out of his hand covering him and the area around him. Nader is stunned and takes a step back from the door. He pauses for a second and looks down at the mess and his uniform. He is steaming and the pressure is building inside of him. Without thinking of the consequences, Nader rears back with his cast and punches the glass door. The glass shatters and falls to the floor. He stands there shaking his head in disbelief.

CHAPTER 16

----------February 1990----------

It's ten o'clock in the morning. Kyle is dead asleep on the sofa on the left side of the dayroom. He is still in his clothes from the night before. Greg Bailey is in his usual spot, the chair on the right side of the room. The TV is on and the volume is low. Kyle, Bucky and Troy went out last night. The right back picture closest to Bailey's favorite chair has been moved. No one notices it. Bucky enters the dayroom and tries to wake up Kyle.

"Kyle, Kyle, get up man," said Bucky.

Kyle wakes up. For a second he doesn't know where he is at.

"What the hell are you doing sleeping out here?" asked Bucky. "I was wondering what happened to you last night."

Kyle moves around a little bit. "Oh, my neck. This furniture is the most uncomfortable shit I've ever slept on."

"Come on man, wake up!" said Bucky.

"I need something to drink," said Kyle. "I feel like a cat slept in my mouth last night."

Bucky starts laughing. "Maybe Bailey was tea bagging you this morning."

Kyle looks across the room. Bailey looks at Kyle and gets a shit eating grin on his face.

Kyle shakes his head. "I said cat not rat. I need something to drink."

Kyle sits up and grabs his head. "My head is killing me. How many shots did we do last night?"

179

"At least one too many," said Bucky.

Kyle reaches into the right front pocket of his jeans and there is nothing. He reaches into the left front pocket and pulls out a wrinkled up one dollar bill. "Yes!"

"Come on!" said Bucky. "Get your ass up and let's go smoke a cigarette."

Kyle stands up. "Ok, let me grab a Coke."

Bucky walks out of the dayroom, turns right and heads down the hallway. Kyle walks across the hallway into the laundry room to get a Coke out of the vending machine. He straightens the dollar out as best as he can and puts it in the machine. The machine sucks it in half way and then rejects it.

"Come on, don't do this to me," said Kyle.

Kyle straightens the dollar a little more and tries it again. This time it works. As the Coke falls from inside the machine Kyle sees the stamp on his left hand from Loockerman. He licks his fingers on his right hand and tries to clean off the stamp, but only smears it a bit. He gets the Coke, his change and heads out of the laundry room. He opens the can and takes a big drink. Bucky comes out of their room with a cigarette and a beer.

"Are you serious?" asked Kyle.

"Hair of the dog," said Bucky. "Want me to grab you one?"

Kyle holds up his Coke. "Not yet. Let me see how this works."

They both walk out the exit and onto the steps right outside the door. It's a bright sunny day but not too cold for February. Kyle squints at the light. He walks a few steps out onto the sidewalk and turns back towards Bucky. Bucky sits down on the steps and lights a cigarette. He sets his lighter on the steps.

"You didn't have to sleep in the dayroom last night," said Bucky.

"No worries," said Kyle. "You had that chick in there and I didn't want to cock block you."

"What happened to your girl?" asked Bucky.

Kyle is slowly starting to recall the events from the night before. "Oh my God. What a mess that turned out to be."

Bucky sets his cigarette down on the step and takes his keys out of his front pocket. He starts to punch a hole in the side of his beer can.

"What are you doing?" asked Kyle.

"I'm going to shotgun this beer," said Bucky.

"I've never seen it done like that before," said Kyle.

Bucky starts to give Kyle blow by blow instructions on the way he knows how to shotgun a beer. "Yea, see, you get a small hole in it like this."

Bucky punches a one inch diameter hole on the lower side of the can. He drops his keys between his legs on the steps. "Get your mouth over the hole and suck on it to create a pressure. Then lean back a little and pop the top. It shoots in your mouth. Here, watch this."

Bucky follows his directions to a tee and the beer is downed in seconds! Bucky takes the can away from his mouth and smashes it in his hand. Bucky shakes his head. "Wow! That was ice cold!"

Kyle is amazed. "Are you shitting me?"

Bucky drops the can on the steps. "I'm already feeling better. You've never seen that before?"

"No, really," said Kyle. "That's some crazy shit."

"How do you guys do it down in the south?" asked Bucky.

Kyle takes a drink of his Coke. "By drinking it the normal way or with a funnel."

"So anyway, what happened last night?" asked Bucky.

Kyle starts to tell his story. "So, we are in the front seat of her car and making out. Right out here in the parking lot where you guys got out. Things are getting hot and heavy..."

All of a sudden Bucky's stomach starts to go haywire. He starts having convulsions. Bucky gets a little pale. Kyle steps over to Bucky's right.

"Hey, are you ok?" asked Kyle.

Bucky throws up the beer. It comes out in a perfect stream just like water from a garden hose. It shoots out three or four feet straight in front of Bucky.

Kyle jumps back! "What the fuck!"

Bucky regains his composure. "I believe that beer was too cold. Did you see my stomach going crazy?"

"Yea!" said Kyle. "Did you see how perfect the stream of beer was that came out?"

They both start to laugh. Bucky picks up his cigarette and takes a big drag.

A few seconds later Troy comes out the door. "Hey! There you guys are."

Kyle greets Troy. "What's up Troy?"

Bucky does the same. "What's up Troy Boy?"

"Bailey said you guys were out here," said Troy. "Kyle, he said to ask you how his balls taste."

Kyle takes a swig of Coke, rinses his mouth and spits it out on the grass. Bucky and Kyle start laughing.

"What's so funny?" asked Troy.

"Bailey tea bagged Kyle while he was sleeping in the dayroom last night." said Bucky.

Kyle blows off Bucky. "Yea right."

"You slept in the dayroom last night?" asked Troy. "You should have come over to my room. My roommate is never there."

"I couldn't have found your room last night," said Kyle.

"So what happened with those girls? Did you guys get lucky?" asked Troy.

"I had a crazy dream last night that a dog was licking my fingers," said Kyle.

Bucky laughs. "That wasn't a dream...that was probably Bailey."

All the guys get grossed out. Kyle takes another drink but doesn't spit it out this time.

"You guys are some sick basters," said Troy. "So come on, tell me what happened last night."

"Fuck last night!" said Kyle. "You should have seen Bucky a minute ago shotgun this beer and then throw it right back up."

Bucky shivers. "That shit was ice cold."

"Oh my God, are you guys drinking already?" asked Troy.

"You finished with that cigarette yet?" asked Kyle.

Bucky flicks his cigarette butt into the grass. "Yea, let's go in."

Bucky picks up his keys, lighter and empty beer can off the steps. They all go back inside 408 and walk down the hallway toward the dayroom. They enter the dayroom. Bucky pitches his beer can into the garbage. Bailey is sitting in his normal spot. He's pulled the table over next to him and is eating a microwaved burrito and drinking a Coke. Kyle and Troy sit on the sofa and Bucky sits in the chair next to Bailey.

Troy is in the middle of a story. "That was the craziest thing I've ever seen last night. I can't believe we made it through the gate."

"Yea, did you see the cop's face?" asked Kyle. "He knew she was fucked up but with her being an officer he didn't want to press it."

"Yea, and then the guy gave her a salute," said Troy. "That's when I knew we were home free."

"So what happened in the car?" asked Bucky.

"So you stayed in the car with your girl, and…" asked Troy.

"And I brought mine back into the room," said Bucky.

"So, we are in the car," said Kyle. "We start making out and one thing leads to another and…"

Troy interrupts. "You did her right out there in the parking lot?"

"Yea," said Kyle. "She wanted it bad. Where else was I supposed to do her, in the bushes? Let me finish."

"Yea Troy, shut the fuck up," said Bucky.

Bailey starts to pay more attention.

Kyle continues. "Anyway, I get off of her and her mood starts to change instantly. All of a sudden she gets all sad and starts crying."

Troy can't believe what Kyle is saying. "Really? Oh my God."

Bucky thinks it's funny. "Get the hell out of here."

Kyle takes the last drink of his Coke. "Yea, she starts telling me that it's been a year since she's been with a guy and how overwhelming all this is to her. I was like…are you serious?"

"So did you stay and comfort her?" asked Troy.

Kyle starts to laugh. "Hell no! I told her that I needed to use the bathroom and I'd be back in a second. She asked what room I was in and I told her."

"You never came in and took a piss," asked Bucky.

"I know," said Kyle. "I walked into the dorm, right past the room and came in and laid down right here."

Kyle points at the sofa.

"So you just left her out in the car?" asked Troy.

"Yea, it appears that's what happened," said Kyle

Troy shakes his head in disbelief. "What a set of nuts you have."

"I guess that's when she came to the room and got her friend," said Bucky.

"Bucky, what were you guys doing?" asked Troy.

Bucky sits up. "I was on the couch and we were both naked. I was trying to bang her but I couldn't get it up."

"Was she that bad?" asked Troy.

Bucky laughs. "No, she was nice but I had too many shots. I was too drunk. I had my thumbs like this trying to stuff it in her."

Bucky demonstrates his technique from the night before.

Troy rolls his eyes. "Oh my God."

Bucky continues. "And then there was a knock at the door. I throw on my boxers and go to the door. It's Kyle's girl. She had eye makeup running all down her face. She says, 'Is Kyle in here?' I told her no and she started crying. Then, her friend gets dressed real fast and they split."

"So you never ended up screwing her?" asked Troy.

Bucky sits back. "No."

Troy turns to Kyle. "And the whole time this was going on you were right here in the dayroom?"

Kyle gets a smile on his face. "I guess so."

"That's unbelievable," said Troy.

"So I guess I ended up cock blocking you in the long run," said Kyle.

"I don't think I was going to do too much anyway," said Bucky.

Troy laughs. "So Bucky got a little last night and Kyle had sex twice."

"Twice?" asked Kyle.

"Yea, once with the officer and once with Bailey," said Troy.

They all start laughing.

Flores enters the dayroom. "What's so funny? I can hear you guys talking and laughing from my room."

"Bailey tea bagged Kyle last night," said Bucky.

"That's sick!" said Flores. "Hey, come and look at what someone left in my room."

Troy smirks. "What is it, a registered letter from Child Protective Services?"

Flores shakes his head. "No really, come and look."

All the guys get up and leave the dayroom. On the way out Bailey throws his empty burrito wrapper in the garbage. They turn left toward Flores' room. Flores enters his door first followed by Troy and Bailey. Kyle and Bucky are right behind them. Right away they notice the stench. Flores flings open the bathroom door! There is a huge turd in the bowl! It is shaped like a boomerang and is at least a foot long and three inches in diameter. One end of the turd is sticking down in the drain of the toilet. The other end is sticking out of the water a few inches and straight up in the air. All the guys are shocked.

"You sick fuck," said Troy.

"That's disgusting man," said Bailey.

Bucky and Kyle just turn and walk out.

Flores starts to laugh. "I've already tried to flush it but it won't go down."

"What are you going to do?" asked Troy.

Flores starts to laugh louder. "I guess I'll hack it up with a coat hanger."

Troy and Bailey turn and walk out of the room.

Flores grabs a coat hanger off the door handle of his closet. "Come on, one of you guys stick around and help me!"

Flores is laughing uncontrollably like a little kid. Troy and Bailey enter the dayroom. Kyle and Bucky are sitting where they were before.

"That guy is not right," said Troy.

"Anybody hungry?" asked Bucky.

"After seeing that, not me," said Kyle.

"I'm starving. What about subs?" asked Troy.

"I have a taste for a McDonald's Quarter Pounder," said Kyle.

"What about wings?" asked Bucky.

"I'm not sure I can handle wings right now," said Kyle.

Troy likes the idea. "Yea, I could do wings."

"Troy how is it that you feel so good?" asked Kyle.

Bucky notices the same thing. "Yea, you were right there with us all night."

"No way!" said Troy. "When you guys started doing shots I was just dumping mine in a glass of water or on the floor."

"Get the hell out of here!" said Bucky.

"Yea, I didn't want to feel like shit today," said Troy. "Shots always do that to me."

"You pussy!" said Bucky.

Kyle grabs his head. "So I guess its wings."

Troy stands up. "I'll order them from the pay phone here and we can go pick them up."

"I need to tap MAC," said Kyle.

"Me too," said Bucky.

"We can do that on the way," said Troy. "I'll drive. Bailey, you want some?"

"No thanks," said Bailey. "I just ate a burrito."

Bucky jumps up. "Come on Bailey, eat some wings with us."

"No, that's ok, said Bailey. "I'm full."

Troy smirks. "You probably don't eat wings because it reminds you of red wings."

"You ever had red wings before Bailey?" asked Bucky.

Bailey doesn't answer.

Kyle throws his hands up in the air. "Hell, he's never had pussy before."

Troy laughs. "You know when you get your red wings that string isn't for flossing your teeth."

Kyle shakes his head. "Great! Bailey's balls, Flores' shit and now red wings! Maybe I'll just go throw up instead of eating."

"Ok, so what do you guys want?" asked Troy. "I'm going to call it in."

"Twenty extra hot," said Bucky.

"Twenty hot with extra sauce," said Kyle. We also need to stop at the 7-11. I need a few green Gatorades."

Flores enters the room. "She put up a good fight but in the end she sank to the bottom."

"Hey Flores, we are ordering wings. Do you want some?" asked Troy.

"No, I've already eaten," said Flores. "Plus I have to start getting ready for my TDY."

"Where are you going?" asked Bucky.

Flores gets a smile on his face. "Rota, Spain for 90 days."

"Are you shitting me?" asked Troy. "I've had my name on the list for that TDY for years."

"How'd you pull that off?" asked Kyle.

"Well, remember when Rex and I were at the mall and we saw that seagull eating a piece of pizza crust and Rex bet me I wouldn't eat it?" asked Flores.

"Yea, you shooed away the seagull and ate the piece of crust," said Kyle.

Flores starts to laugh. "Yea and that lady came up to us and asked us if we were in the military. I answered back with a yes ma'am and burped right in her face. Remember it turned out that she was a Chief in the supply squadron."

Kyle needs more information. He knows there must be more. "And?"

Flores continues. "Well, the other morning Rex and I are leaving work and I don't have my hat on. The new Lt comes up and we salute him and he asks me where my hat is. I told him it was in my pocket. Then he asked me why it wasn't on my head and I said because my head won't fit in my pocket."

Everybody starts to laugh.

"Are you serious?" asked Troy.

"Yea," said Flores. "He got so pissed. I guess he also heard about the rabbit deal with Robert Leo. He was going to fry me but Robert Leo stood up for me. They made a deal with him to get me out of his site for a while."

"So you fucked up and your punishment is 90 days in Spain?" asked Kyle.

Flores has a shit eating grin on his face. "Yea! Can you believe it?"

"Looks like you'll miss the junior prom," said Troy.

Bucky is envious. "You lucky son of a bitch. You'll have Senoritas and Sangria for three months."

"So when do you leave?" asked Kyle.

"In a few days," said Flores.

Bucky laughs. "Then we still have time to hand receipt your girl over."

"I wonder what grade Graywolf and Andy would give her?" asked Kyle.

Troy smiles sarcastically. "G!"

They all start laughing.

Flores goes into a defensive mode. "Come on now, she's 18."

Kyle stands up. "The only 18 I see there is 18 years in jail."

"Ok, enough of this shit!" said Troy. "I'm starving! I'm making the call."

CHAPTER 17

A few weeks have past and Kyle is settled into days shift. He enters 585 through the front door. It is just before the seven AM day shift roll call. There are a lot of people coming and going. Day shift has twice the amount of people that grave shift has. There are also a few grave shift guys still turning in tools.

Kyle goes straight for the vending machine. It is almost empty but it still shows it has chewing gum in it.

Kyle puts 50 cents in the machine, presses the buttons for a pack of gum, and nothing comes out. "Pay back is a bitch."

He turns and heads to where Sierra 6 forms up for roll call.

On day shift, Sierra 6 lines up in their normal spot. Sierra 7 lines up beside them. So the two Blue side teams have their backs to the back wall of 585. The two Red side teams, Sierra 8 and 9, line up on the other side of the building with their backs to the front wall. Management stands with their backs to CTK. Every morning they brief all the crew chiefs on important issues. Most of the crew chiefs joke amongst themselves that the briefing is nothing more than their daily dose of brain washing propaganda. Once management is finished giving their briefing the old burly senior master sergeant always says, "Alright, let's do it safe, by the book and then on-time."

Kyle sees Troy over where Sierra 6 forms up. He walks over and stands next to Troy.

"Troy, you have any gum on you?"

"Damn boy, you do smell like a brewery," said Troy.

"Yea, I had a few too many last night," said Kyle.

Troy reaches in his front pants pocket, pulls out a pack of gum and hands a stick to Kyle.   "I always bring my own from home," said Troy. "I don't understand it but that vending machine is always empty. If they would fill it more often they could make a killing here."

Kyle is being sarcastic but Troy does not realize it. Kyle knows why the vending machine is always empty. "Yea, I wonder why they never stock it. I don't get it either. Hey, are we slow today?"

"Must be," said Troy. "There were four grave shift card games going on when I walked in this morning."

The management staff walks into 585. Art and the other three Expediters veer off toward their teams.

"Alright! Form it up! Let's go!"

All the guys in the building start to divide into sections. Kyle looks around the room at all the people. Day shift has three times the amount of crew chiefs that grave shift does. Most everybody's uniforms are clean and laundered and their boots are polished as if they worked in an office. Kyle, in his far from perfect state, has a moment of extrasensory perception. He can hear the ass kissing and smell the stench of politics in the air.

Roll call ended about 30 minutes ago. Kyle is standing outside, next to the front entrance to 585. He is talking to a few grave shift crew chiefs while he waits on the Sierra 6 truck to swing back in. The Sierra 6 truck finally pulls up and parks. Kyle says bye to the guys that he was talking to and they start walking toward the parking lot. Kyle walks around, opens the side door and gets in the back of the truck. Art turns around.

"What's up Art?" asked Kyle. "You didn't put me on anything today. Does that mean I can go home?"

"Fuck no," said Art. "Hey man, I saw your car behind the 7-11 when I was coming in so I figured you were out late last night."

"That would be correct," said Kyle.

"So tell me what you did last night?" asked Art.

Kyle sits down on top of the igloo cooler. "Come on...can it wait?"

"No man," said Art. "Every time I see your car there I get excited. Remember, I'm married."

"This is some funny shit. Are you sure you are ready for it this early in the morning?" asked Kyle.

Art laughs. "If it's that good I'll give you the truck, run home, roll my old lady over and take care of business."

Kyle starts to tell Art what he did last night. "Ok, I was downtown last night, sitting at the bar drinking a beer and eating some peanuts. I've been craving peanuts for a while and had to get it out of my system."

Art is impatient. "Yea, get to the good stuff."

Kyle continues. "So I feel someone staring at me on my right side. I turn and it's the girl right next to me at the bar. I was so focused on these peanuts that I didn't even notice her."

Art interrupts. "Hey grab the cooler so I can make some Gatorade. Do you want green or orange?"

"Green. Hey wait, it's winter!" said Kyle. "What are you making Gatorade for?"

"It's a new policy," said Art. "Lt Harris wants all the guys to have something to drink regardless of the time of year. So I'm making it the same way I do in the summer...lots of ice."

"Who would want to drink warm Gatorade anyway?" asked Kyle. "Maybe he's realized there are a lot of crew chiefs at work with hangovers and he's trying to sober them up quicker."

"Yea man. Maybe he's trying to increase production," said Art.

They both laugh.

Kyle steps out of the truck, turns and grabs the igloo cooler and heads for the front door of 585. Art grabs two cans of Gatorade mix from the floor between the seats and gets out of the truck. They meet at the front door of 585, open it and enter. They turn left and head back to the ice machine.

"So was this chick hot?" asked Art.

"Yea, pretty hot," said Kyle. "I don't even remember if she was sitting there when I arrived or she came up after. Anyway, we get to talking and hit it off. Next thing I know she is inviting me back to her place."

"Should I start my boner now?" asked Art.

"Yea, maybe you can spice up the Gatorade," said Kyle.

They both laugh.

They arrive at the ice machine. Kyle spins off the top of the cooler and sets it on top of the ice machine.

Kyle returns to his story. "So, apparently this chick is from out of town and is house sitting. The place was right around the corner from the bar. We have a few more drinks and a shot and we start at it."

Kyle takes the cooler to the large sink next to the ice machine and rinses it out.

"Where are you guys at?" asked Art.

"The kitchen," said Kyle.

Art's getting eager. "Ok, go on."

Kyle comes back over, sets the cooler on the floor and starts shoveling ice in it with a stainless steel scooper that was in the ice machine. "So we are undressing each other as we make out and we are down to our underwear. I pick her up and she wraps her legs around me and I carry her to the couch and sit down with her on top of me. I pop her bra off and..."

"Were they nice?" asked Art.

Kyle nods his head. "Oh yea. Anyway, it's time for my new move."

"New move?" asked Art.

"Yea," said Kyle. "I like clearing off a table or counter with one arm as I hold the girl in the other arm. Then throw her on top of whatever it was I cleared and go at it. It adds excitement to the moment."

Kyle has finished filling the cooler with ice. He pitches the scooper back in the ice machine and closes the door. Art starts to open the cans of Gatorade and pour the powder on top of the ice.

"Who cleans up the mess?" asked Art.

Kyle shrugs his shoulders. "Who cares? So I stand back up with her still wrapped around me, kneel down beside this huge coffee table, clear it with one arm and throw her on it."

"What was on the table?" asked Art.

Kyle is getting annoyed at Art for asking so many questions. "Beer bottles, an ash tray, a few more things. Who give a shit?

She is all into it. I slide my boxers off and then slide her panties off and I head south. I get down there and it's a jungle."

"Bush?" asked Art.

Art finishes pouring the Gatorade powder in the cooler. Art and Kyle lift the cooler and set it inside the sink. Kyle turns the water on and the cooler starts to fill.

"Yea, like I've never seen before," said Kyle. "I was waiting for a tribe of pygmies to walk out. It was like something from the 60's or 70's. So I get an idea. I tell her to hold on and I go into the kitchen. I am rummaging through the drawers looking for some scissors."

"You are going to trim her bush?" asked Art.

"Yea," said Kyle. "If you saw this thing you'd want to do the same. So finally I find some scissors. I come running around the corner with the scissors in my hand like this. I have this crazy look on my face because I'm on a mission."

Kyle demonstrates how he was running with the scissors in his hand. Art is not really paying attention to the water level in the cooler as it's almost overflowing. When Kyle returns he quickly cuts the water off.

"She sees me and starts to scream!" said Kyle. "She jumps up and is scrambling to get away from me, backing up over the couch and knocking over a lamp!"

Art doesn't get it. "Just because she didn't want her bush cut?"

"No," said Kyle. "From her perspective, picture a guy she just met. I come running around the corner all excited with a pair of scissors in his hand. She thought I was going to kill her!"

They both start laughing.

"Holy shit!" said Art. "Well then what happened?"

Kyle is relieved that he is at the end of his story. He hopes Art is satisfied. "I finally got her calmed down and explained what I wanted to do. We had another drink, she got some free yard work and we both got laid."

Art looks happy. "That's some crazy shit man."

Kyle looks around for something to stir the Gatorade with. There is a broom in the corner next to the sink. Kyle grabs the broom and uses the handle to stir the Gatorade. Kyle and Art aren't fazed by this at all. As Kyle stirs the Gatorade they continue talking.

Kyle laughs. "Yea, I'll never forget the look on her face. It was pure horror."

"Are you going to see her again?" asked Art.

"Who knows?" said Kyle. "She is going back to WVU today. She gave me her number. Maybe I'll drive over there one day."

Kyle finishes stirring the Gatorade and tosses the broom back in the corner by the sink. Art grabs the lid from on top of the ice machine and spins it back on tight. They each pick up one side of the cooler and walk out of the room. As they are walking out they continue to talk to each other.

"Are you heading home now to knock off a piece of ass?" asked Kyle.

"Can you pass a sobriety test if the cops stop you?" asked Art.

Kyle shakes his head. "I doubt it."

Three hours later Art is sitting in front of Tango row. The truck is positioned between the centerline of the taxiway and the wall. It's facing directly at the plane on Tango row. Art is looking though a porn magazine. Art looks at the magazine for a little while then looks around the area to makes sure no one is sneaking up on him. He doesn't want to get caught with a porn magazine at work. The plane on Tango row has a lot of activity going on around it. It's getting ready to launch on a mission. Kyle is in the back of the truck. He is lying on the bench taking a nap and using his bag as a pillow.

The radio sounds. "Sierra 6, MOCC."

Art answers. "Go ahead MOCC."

"6013 is going to need to add 160,000 pounds of gas," said MOCC. "280,000 is their final fuel."

"MOCC I copy. "280,000 on gas. 6013, do you copy?" asked Art.

6013 comes over the radio. "6013 copies. MOCC this is 6013. Can you send us gas?"

"On the phone now," said MOCC.

6013 is heard calling Sierra 4. "Sierra 4, 6013."

Sierra 4 answers. "Go ahead 6013."

"We need CSS permission. We are putting on an additional 160,000 pounds," said 6013.

"You got it 6013. Copy MOCC? Give 6013 CSS," said Sierra 4.

"MOCC copies and gas is on the way out."

About 10 minutes later Art watches fuels pull a pit cart into the plane with their bobtail and drop it off about 25 feet in front of number three engine. The bobtail pulls away and leaves. A crew chief and a fuels guy position the pit cart and start to unroll the two hoses on it.

There is one short thick hose that attaches to the fuel pit on the ground. This hose is 10 inches in diameter and 10 feet long. The fuel will be pumped from the ground, through this thick hose and into the pit cart. The other hose is thin and long and attaches to the plane. This hose is five inches in diameter and 60 feet long. It will move the fuel from the pit cart to the plane. The crew chief and the fuels guy almost have everything set up.

Art tries to wake up Kyle. "Hey man."

Kyle is dead asleep and doesn't answer.

Art tries again. "Hey man."

Kyle is not fazed at all. Art raises his voice. "Hey Man! Wake the fuck up!"

Kyle jumps up. He is trying to look like he wasn't sleeping. He thinks someone is coming up to the truck. "What's up?"

"I need you to help these guys refuel this plane," said Art.

"Are you kidding me?" asked Kyle. "You woke me up for this shit? I've already LOX'd a plane, helped change a tire and did a set of I's and E's and DOPP for you."

Art looks in the rear view mirror. "Come on fucker. All you've been doing all morning is sleeping."

Kyle stretches and yawns. "How long was I out for?"

"Maybe 15 minutes," said Art.

"Ok, take me up there," said Kyle.

Art laughs. "Walk up there you lazy fuck. A little fresh air might do you good." Art holds up his porn magazine. "Plus, I'm studying for my next stripe."

"Yea, it looks like it," said Kyle. "I'll leave you out here by yourself so you can twist one off."

Kyle stands, grabs his bag and heads out the side door of the truck. He walks towards the plane. He gets to the fire bottle, pulls his headset out of his bag and puts it on. He drops his bag at the fire bottle and heads back towards the right side SPR.

SPR stands for Single Point Refuel. This is where the hose from the fuel pit will attach to the plane. The C-5 has four SPRs located in front of the main landing gears. Two of them are on the left side of the plane and two of them are on the right. There is also a connection for an interphone cord a few feet in front of the SPRs.

Kyle surveys the situation and realizes they need a fire bottle at the SPR. He walks out to the wing tip, leans the fire bottle back on its tires and pushes it towards the pit cart. He stops about 15 feet from the pit cart and sets the bottle upright on its stand.

Kyle walks over and plugs his headset into the SPR interphone cord. He walks back and leans against the 2A2 tire. His arms are crossed. The fuel pit cart's long hose is stretched all the way out and is lying at Kyle's feet. The cap that covers the SPR is off and is hanging from its chain. Kyle is watching the refuel supervisor who has been in the Air Force at least three years longer than he has. He is standing at the front of the plane by the fire bottle. The fuels guy is at the fuel pit cart waiting to send gas to the plane. He is also watching the refuel supervisor.

The refuel supervisor is in charge of the refuel as well as the plane. His headset is plugged into the long scanners cord. He is nervously flipping through his refuel checklist and pacing a bit. He walks over to a tool box, pulls out an orange CSS vest and puts it on. He is now the CSS. He walks back to the fire bottle. He finally says something over the interphone. "Uh-ok, panel. Have you reviewed your emergency procedures and how many people are up there?"

The guy sitting panel is upstairs at the engineer's station. He is controlling the refuel panel.

The guy sitting panel comes over the interphone. "Uh, hold on."

"SPR, uh, are the chocks set?" asked the CSS.

"Yea, I checked them when I walked up," said Kyle.

The CSS is flipping around the checklist even more. Kyle is realizing that he doesn't have a clue about what he is doing.

"Panel, have you figured out what tanks the gas needs to go in?" asked the CSS.

"I'm doing that now. Give me a minute," said the panel.

The CSS doesn't sound confident. "Ok, while you are doing that I'll figure out what I'm going to say in my safety briefing."

At this point Kyle has seen enough. He unplugs the interphone cord and clips it on the base of the cord where it attaches to the aircraft. He walks up to the CSS. "Give me that checklist, vest and the cord and get your ass back on the SPR!"

The CSS is shocked but also relieved. He hands over the checklist, vest and the cord without a fight. He walks back to the SPR, grabs the cord and plugs his headset into it. He has just been demoted to SPR. Kyle flips open the checklist to the applicable page and sets it on top of the fire bottle. He puts the CSS vest on and plugs into the scanners cord.

Kyle starts talking over the interphone. "SPR, hook up the hose and make sure it's locked."

The SPR guy hooks up the hose to the plane and lock checks it.

Kyle continues. "Panel, open the right side."

The right side is the right SPR valve.

Panel answers sheepishly. "I'm still figuring out the balance of the tanks."

Kyle repeats his first request but in a stronger manner. "Shut the hell up and open the right side. And open all the auxiliary and extended range tanks! I'm guessing all the mains are full?"

Kyle has gotten the attention of the guy at the panel. "They are. Right side is open...and the tanks are open."

Kyle points at the fuels guy. "SPR, tell the fuels guy to send it."

The SPR guy makes a motion with his hand for the fuel guy to send the fuel to the plane. The fuels guy starts pumping fuel to the plane. The hoses on the fuel cart start jumping as the fuel is initially forced through them.

"Panel, let me know when you get pressure and flow. How far off are the tanks from the totalizer?" asked Kyle.

"They are about even," said the panel. "We have pressure."

Kyle walks to his right and scans the plane's wing and the area. "Ok, listen up. Go off of the totalizer and put 283,000 on the plane. As far as the tanks go, you can distribute the gas evenly when we are finished or as they reach their limit."

"What if we are off?" asked the panel.

"If we are off we want to be off on the high side," said Kyle. "The crew will always take a little extra. It's factored in to burn off 3,000 pounds of fuel on taxi anyway."

"What about wing balance?" asked the panel. "We have flow."

Kyle walks to the other side of the plane and scans the wing and the area. "The most you should have to close is a tank or two. If one tank starts to run away from its opposite just shut it down. Once the opposite one catches up, open it up again. And when you are adding up the wing difference, just add the numbers and not the tenths. It's easier that way. At this load, when we finish you'll probably only have to transfer fuel around in a hand full of tanks. Just let me know when you start closing tanks so I can have the fuels guy tweak down the pressure."

Panel seems excited. "Got it."

Kyle walks over and leans against the fire bottle. "Now watch how fast this goes on."

"Where did you learn all this?" asked the panel.

"Grave shift," said Kyle.

"How long have you been in?" asked the SPR.

"Two years," said Kyle.

It's less than an hour later. The refuel is completed and everything is ready to go on the plane. Kyle walks back to the Sierra 6 truck which hasn't moved the entire time. He gets in the passenger seat. Art is still looking at his porn magazine.

"How did it go?" asked Art.

"Those guys are idiots," said Kyle.

Art starts laughing. "That's my dream team man. I was wondering how long it would take you to kick that guy off the cord. Did he say anything to you?"

"What could he say?" asked Kyle.

"Now you know what I deal with every day," said Art. "These guys have two speeds, slow and stop."

Kyle shakes his head. "And now I know why grave shift has so much work every night."

Art reaches into his bag which is between the seats and hands Kyle a porn magazine. "Here, study some technical data. Maybe you'll learn something new."

Kyle looks at the cover. "I've seen this already. You showed it to me last week."

Kyle stuffs the magazine back in Art's bag and looks up at the plane. Two large buses and a large stair truck pull up behind the plane and park. The buses are full of passengers waiting to board the aircraft.

Kyle points at the buses. "Check it out. Let's do a PAX review."

PAX is short for passengers.

Art looks up from the magazine and smiles. He puts the magazine in his bag and starts the truck. They pull off to the right toward an empty parking spot where they can cut behind the row of planes.

A few minutes later Sierra 6 pulls up to the back of the plane. Art positions the truck about 100 feet away. He is lined up so he and Kyle can see in between the stair truck and the buses. The stair truck has pulled up to the left side of the plane and raised its staircase so it is in line with the number six service door in the troop compartment.

A voice comes over the radio. "MOCC, 6013."

MOCC answers. "Go ahead 6013."

"MOCC, close out the #1 HF radio job," said 6013. "Serviced coupler, ops check good."

"MOCC copies."

Art picks up his clipboard, finds the HF radio job for 6013 and lines through it. "About fucking time. Those Comm specialists are slow as shit."

Two people come walking down the crew entry door ladder. It's the Comm specialists. They have a small red tool box and a regular bicycle pump. The pump is used to service the HF radio coupler. They set everything on the ground and wait for their ride.

Kyle spots the bicycle pump. "Art, check this out. I'm going to fuck with everyone on the buses."

Kyle jumps out of the truck and walks hurriedly to the front of the plane.

"What the fuck is he up to?" asked Art.

Kyle walks up to the two Comm specialists and talks to them for a few seconds. He grabs their bicycle pump and heads back to the #3 landing gear on the left side of the plane. He sticks the hose of the pump into the outer most wheel on the gear. He wedges it in under the valve stem. Kyle stands with a foot on each side of the pump and starts pumping up and down.

"What the fuck?" said Art.

The people on the buses are all looking at Kyle and starting to stir. He appears to be pumping the massive plane tire with a bicycle pump. Kyle is doing everything he can to keep from laughing. He pumps a few more times, bends down and pulls the hose from the wheel. He then kicks the tire a few times as if to check the pressure in it. He then turns and gives a thumbs up to Art in the truck. Art has his hand over his mouth to cover his laugh.

Kyle walks the pump back to the Comm guys at the front of the plane and then returns to the Sierra 6 truck. The people on the bus are still in a stir about the bicycle pump and the tire. Kyle holds a straight face until he gets in the truck, then he bursts out laughing with Art.

"You crazy fuck!" said Art.

"Did you see the look on their faces?" asked Kyle. "They were shitting their pants. I can't believe I didn't lose it."

The passengers start to get off the buses and head toward the staircase. Two lines form and merge into one as they reach the bottom of the stairs.

"Here they go," said Art.

Kyle chuckles. "Let's see what we have today!"

All different types of people are mixed in the line. A hot woman gets off the bus with two kids.

"Check that one out," said Kyle.

"Mother-want-another," said Art.

"She still looks good even though she has two trophies," said Kyle.

After a few more people come off the buses a fat woman appears.

"Look at that pig," said Art.

Kyle looks at Art. "You'd hit it."

"How would you even find the hole?" asked Art.

"Roll her in flour and look for the wet spot," said Kyle.

Kyle and Art start laughing.

Some old people come off the bus. They are having trouble walking.

"Retirees...how do they do it?" asked Kyle.

"They've probably been sitting in the terminal for a week," said Art.

Kyle shakes his head. "When I retire I'll never Space A."

"What else do they have to do?" asked Art.

A hot woman in an Air Force uniform gets off the bus.

"Holly shit!" said Kyle. "Check her out. Why can't we have people like her working out here?"

"You think we'd ever get anything done if she worked with us?" asked Art.

"Good point," said Kyle. "The whole shift would be trying to service her."

"No, I'd keep her in the truck with me all day," said Art.

"And do what with her, read porn magazines and dip snuff you dirty old man?" asked Kyle.

Art points at his nose. "I have a seat ready for her right here."

Art and Kyle start laughing.

CHAPTER 18

----------March 1990----------

It's a Saturday in March. At the far end of building 409 there is a pavilion. It has a 20-by-20-foot cement floor. Four large square supports hold a vaulted roof. The roof has a slight overhand that provides more cover. It's painted the same color as the dorms and the shingles match the shingles on the dorms.

There are four guys under the pavilion. One of them is Bret Nader. They have set up a full drum kit and three large speakers for the instruments which include two guitars and a bass. There is also one microphone on a stand. The four guys are adjusting and tuning their instruments and have started doing sound checks. Each guy is in his own world. They have never played together and are not very organized but they are determined to rock out. The picnic table that usually sits under the pavilion has been moved out in the grass. A hand full of people have gathered around it. On the table is a large cooler full of beer. Kyle, Bucky and Troy walk up to the corner of the pavilion where Nader is standing.

"Look at this shit," said Bucky.

Troy smirks. "Hopefully they play music better than they fix planes."

"Nader, what the hell are you guys doing?" asked Kyle.

"We are going to have a little concert," said Nader. "It's warming up and spring is about here so we decided to celebrate. We've invited everyone in the dorms to come out."

"Well when is the event going to kick off?" asked Kyle.

"We're getting everything together now," said Nader. "It shouldn't be long."

"Have you guys ever played together?" asked Troy.

"No, this is the first time," said Nader.

"I hope there's no cover charge," said Troy.

"Did you invite any chicks out?" asked Kyle.

"There's none that live in the dorms," said Nader. "The last two moved out last year."

Troy laughs. "Weren't those the two you got caught with?"

"Yea," said Nader.

"What is the name of this show, Sausage Fest?" asked Bucky.

Troy gets Nader's attention. "Hey, I play an instrument. Can I jump in with you guys?"

"Sure, what do you play?" asked Nader.

Troy answers with a serious face. "The skin flute."

They all laugh. Nader turns his attention back to his guitar. Kyle, Bucky and Troy walk out to the parking lot to get away from the noise. The band keeps tuning their instruments, all focused on their own sound.

"So, what are you guys going to do?" asked Kyle.

"I think I'm going to go back to my room and take a nap," said Troy. "I've got a little headache."

"I'm going to just chill out in the room," said Bucky. "Maybe do some laundry."

"I'm going to hit the gym," said Kyle. "Troy, when I finish I'll swing by and get you. Then we'll grab Bucky and come back over and check this shit out."

Bucky spots the cooler of beer. "If I'm not in the room I'll be out here."

Kyle and Troy turn and walk back toward building 408. Bucky makes a bee-line for the cooler.

An hour later the crowd around the pavilion has grown to over 50 people. They are all drinking beer and talking among themselves. The guys in the band have huddled around the drums and are talking amongst themselves. Bucky is standing at the edge of the crowd drinking a beer. Kyle and Troy walk up.

"Bucky, what's up?" asked Kyle.

"They are getting ready to play," said Bucky.

Troy looks at his watch. "Jesus, it's been at least an hour or so. They haven't played yet?"

Bucky thinks it's funny. "No! First they blew a fuse for the outlet so they had to find a bunch of extension cords and run them from the closest rooms. Then Zack broke a string. Then more sound checks."

"What's next, one of them is going to get his period?" asked Troy.

Finally Nader comes over the microphone. "Ok, sorry for the delays."

The crowd is yelling things back at him. "You guys suck! Play Free Bird! Don't eat the brown acid!"

Nader continues. "Yea, we had a few technical problems but…are you guys ready to rock?"

The crowd goes a little crazy. They hold their beers up in the air and scream.

Nader comes over the microphone. "A one-two-one-two-three-four."

The guys start playing the ACDC song Back in Black.

Zack steps up to the microphone and starts singing. "Back in black, I hit the sack, I've been to long, I'm glad to be back!…

They are 30 seconds into the song. The crowd erupts! All of a sudden a cop car comes around the corner and blasts its siren. The band stops playing. Everybody turns toward the cop car. The crowd starts booing. They stop booing when the car doors open. Two cops get out of the car and walk through the crowd to the pavilion.

"Officers, what can I do for you today?" asked Nader.

"We've had several complaints from people in the area about the noise," said one of the cops. "You guys are going to have to wrap it up and shut this down."

Nader can't believe it. "Are you kidding me?"

"No, I'm not kidding you," said the cop. "If we hear one more note or get one more call about loud music then someone's first sergeant is going to get a call. Is that clear?"

"Yea, sure," said Nader.

The cops start to walk away and make it back to their car. The crowd is starting to talk amongst themselves. They are starting to boo again. Nader gets energy from the crowd. He looks at all the other band members and they have disappointed looks on their faces. Nader walks up to the microphone and yells. "Rock and Roll baby!"

Nader hits a few notes on his guitar! The other guys in the band are shocked. They want to join in but they know better.

The cops turn around, walk back through the crowd and head straight for Nader. "Ok, let's go!"

Nader knows the drill. He takes off his guitar and sets it down. "Hey Zack, take care of my stuff for me."

The cops take Nader by each arm and walk him through the crowd to their car. The crowd starts chanting. "Nader, Nader, Nader!"

The cops put Nader in the back seat of the police car. As they pull away the crowd starts chanting, "Attica-Attica-Attica!"

The cop car turns the corner and disappears. Just like that it's over. The crowd slowly starts to disperse. After hours of preparation and sound checks Nader's group played for less than a minute.

"Well, I guess that a wrap," said Kyle. "They were actually sounding pretty good."

"Yea they were," said Troy. "I can't believe Nader. What a set of nuts on that guy. Where do I get my refund at?"

"Nader will get out of this somehow...he always does," said Bucky.

"Isn't that the truth," said Kyle. "He's done enough shit to get six people kicked out of the Air Force but somehow he slides by."

Troy laughs. "No shit, right?"

"So what now?" asked Kyle.

"I'm going to do some laundry," said Bucky.

"I need to go to the mall," said Kyle. "Troy, you want to ride with me?"

"Yea ok," said Troy.

The guys start walking toward 408. Half the crowd has already left and the other half have gathered around the picnic table to finish the rest of the beer. The three remaining band members have joined the crowd and are drinking with them.

Two hours later Kyle and Troy return from the Dover Mall. Kyle parks his car and they both get out. Troy heads back to his room in building 412. Kyle heads into building 408. He comes down the hallway and enters his room. He shuts the door behind him. He passes the bathroom, the sink area and steps into the main part of the room. He stops dead in his tracks when he sees a beautiful blonde girl sitting on the couch. The girl looks like Kelly Bundy from the TV show *Married with Children*. She has on blue jeans that are ripped at the knees and what appears to be a men's blue dress shirt. The shirt is way too big for her so she has rolled up the sleeves. She has also rolled up the lower part of the shirt and tied it around her waist. Bucky is sitting at the opposite end of the couch. Bucky's laundry is folded neatly and is on top of his bed. Bucky and the stunning blonde are drinking a beer.

"Hey, what up?" asked Kyle.

Bucky didn't hear Kyle come in. He jumps up when he sees Kyle. "Hey Kyle! What's going on?"

Kyle turns his attention to the female. "How are you?"

She answers. "Fine thanks."

"Kyle, I have to talk to you for a second," said Bucky.

Bucky turns to the female. "Will you excuse us for a second?"

"Sure," said the female.

Bucky forces Kyle out through the room and into the hallway. Kyle is facing Bucky and giving him a "holy shit" look. They go into the hallway and Bucky pulls the door closed but doesn't shut it. They both try to keep their voices down.

"Holy shit! Who is that? Where did you meet her?" asked Kyle.

"That's Cindy," said Bucky.

It doesn't register with Kyle. "Cindy?"

"Yea Cindy, Flores' girl," said Bucky.

Kyle is blown away. "Are you shitting me? What happened to her? Last time I saw her she looked like a high school freshman."

"I know, right," said Bucky. "I couldn't believe my eyes either."

"How did you hook up with her?" asked Kyle.

"I went to get my clothes out of the dryer," said Bucky. "When I turned the corner into the laundry room I saw her sitting by herself in the dayroom. I said hi to her, went into the laundry room and started getting my clothes out of the dryer. She came in and started asking me if I knew when Flores was getting back. I guess she heard from someone that he was coming back early from his TDY. She has been hanging out in the dayroom waiting for him. I hold her I didn't have a clue about Flores and the next thing I know she is helping me fold my laundry."

Kyle looks puzzled. "Flores has only been gone a month. Why would he come back early? Anyway, I still can't believe it's her."

"Yea I know," said Bucky. "So she follows me back here and we start shooting the shit and drinking beers."

"Are you going to try and hit it?" asked Kyle.

Bucky hesitates for a second. The thought did cross his mind. "Come on man, I can't do that to Flores."

"Fuck that fat bastard," said Kyle. "She's bad ass! Go for it. He doesn't deserve anything that looks like that."

"Maybe you're right," said Bucky.

"Hell yea!" said Kyle. "Let me grab a quick shower and I'll get out of your hair. I'm going to meet that artist chick from the other night."

"The crazy one?" asked Bucky.

Kyle chuckles. "They're all crazy. That's what I like about them. It keeps it interesting."

"Ok, I'll take Cindy down to the dayroom and smoke a cigarette and give you time to get ready," said Bucky.

"I'll be fast and hopefully I'll be gone for most of the night," said Kyle.

"Cool," said Bucky. "Oh, one more thing."

"What?" asked Kyle.

Bucky's expression changes a bit. "I gave the Red Shed to Darrell Evans today."

"What!" said Kyle. "Gave it? The Red Shed is you. That think has so much history. Why the hell did you give it to him?"

"Darrell's a good guy," said Bucky. "He's having problems with his old lady and he had to move out of his house. They only have one car and she kept it. He needed a way to get back and forth to work. I have the pickup truck my uncle gave me so I'm good."

Kyle shakes his head. "Oh man. I'm going to miss that thing."

They both start to walk back in the room but stop in the doorway.

"Remember that time in Ocean City when we were all drunk in the Red Shed and the cops stopped us?" asked Kyle.

"And we had the shopping cart in the back?" asked Bucky.

They both laugh.

Kyle realizes he doesn't want to waste Bucky's time reminiscing about the van. Kyle pats him on the back. "Get in there and take care of business."

They walk into the room and close the door.

It's three o'clock in the morning. Kyle is back at the room and doesn't know what to expect. Kyle has been out all night drinking. After the bar closed he ended up over at the artist chick's house. He is a little wobbly. He enters the room quietly so he doesn't disturb Bucky. He turns on the bathroom light and looks in the room. Bucky is not in the top bunk. Kyle looks a little relieved that Bucky isn't there.

He walks over and picks up his alarm clock off of the air conditioner. It reads three AM. The alarm is set for five forty five AM. Kyle rolls the alarm forward to six forty AM. He has to be at work by seven. He sets the alarm down and undresses. Instead of getting into bed he starts to puts his uniform on. He gets fully dressed, including his boots. He puts his wallet and keys in his pants pockets. He picks up the clock one more time, checks the alarm and sets it back on the air conditioner. He gets in bed and falls asleep instantly.

It is now six forty AM. Kyle's alarm goes off. Like a Jack-in-the-Box, Kyle springs up quickly and slams his hand on the top of the clock to silence the alarm. He rolls out of bed and hurries to the sink. He splashes water on his face and hair and then dries off quickly with a towel. He grabs his tooth brush, puts paste on it and starts brushing his teeth. At the same time he squeezes some hair gel into his hand and rubs it in his hair. He combs his hair quickly, rinses his mouth and spins away from the sink. He grabs his bag and hat off the top of the refrigerator and runs out of the room.

The door at the end of 408 bursts open and Kyle runs out. He knows he must run all the way to work to get there on time. He runs across the dorm parking lot and past the pavilion. The pavilion area is a mess from Bret Nader's almost famous rock concert. The table is still in the grass and there are beer cans everywhere.

Kyle thinks to himself. "Graywolf and Andy are going to have fun with this mess."

Kyle then cuts across the grass and in between the bowling alley and the recreation center. He gets in front of the recreation center and can see 585 in the distance. He is winded from his hasty departure and from the alcohol he drank the night before.

As he starts through the dimly lit parking lot of the recreation center he kicks a bottle across the pavement. It bounces a few times then shatters. All of a sudden he notices that the entire parking lot is full of Old English 800 and Schlitz Malt Liquor bottles and cans. Every week the recreation center hosts a party called "The All-Nighter" that features soul, R&B and rap music. Kyle is running through a mine field of 40 ounce bottles and 16 ounce cans. Kyle weaves and hurtles his way through the mess. He's not doing bad considering the state he is in. He ends up kicking a can at the edge of the parking lot.

Kyle thinks to himself. "What the fuck!"

Kyle makes it through the parking lot, crosses Atlantic Street and jumps the Jersey barrier wall. He is in the Lemon Lot. There are at least 15 cars for sale, plus a boat. He notices Buckner's repo tow truck backed up to one of the cars. Kyle slows down a bit. Buckner emerges from behind the car. Buckner just left work and is still in his coveralls.

"Buckner, what time is it?" asked Kyle.

Buckner looks at his watch. "Chief, slow the hell down son. You still have 10 minutes. Chief, check it out. They don't get any easier than this."

Kyle slows to a walk and approaches Buckner.

"Chief, you are sweating like a hooker in church," said Buckner.

Kyle laughs. "A hooker in church after payday. Yea, I woke up a little late. I have to keep moving."

Kyle takes off jogging across the parking lot towards 585.

It's shortly after roll call. Art is sitting in the truck by himself. He has already taken all the crew chiefs to their planes. Kyle comes out the front door of 585 with a tool box and throws it through the side door of the truck. He gets in the truck, sits on the igloo cooler and puts the straps across the door.

Art turns back towards Kyle. "Hey man, you look pretty rough this morning. What did you do last night? I saw your car parked at billeting so don't try and bull shit me.

Billeting is an on base hotel for military personnel. Dover's billeting is beside the 7-11 and just across the street from the main gate.

"I had a date last night and only intended to drink a few beers," said Kyle. "We ended up doing a few shots and went back to her place."

"Did you do her in the butt?" asked Art.

Kyle laughs. He knows Art wants to hear something good. "I might have but I went for a rodeo fuck instead."

"Rodeo fuck?" asked Art.

"Yea, I was doing her from behind," said Kyle. "I reached up, grabbed a hand full of hair with my left hand and held my right hand in the air. Then I told her she was the worst piece of ass I'd ever had and tried to stay inside her for eight seconds."

Kyle and Art start to laugh loudly. Art turns back forward. Art is looking out the front windshield staring at someone. "This son of a bitch is going to make my day miserable."

"Who?" asked Kyle.

Kyle leans down so he can see out the front windshield. In front of them is the Sierra 4 pickup truck. Outside the truck is Kurt "Ricochet" Rubler.

Kurt "Ricochet" Rubler is a Master Sergeant and in his early 40s. He looks more like he is in his 50s. He is one of the Production Superintendents or Pro Supers. He always has a cup of coffee in one hand and a cigarette in the other. He moves quickly because of the amount of caffeine he takes in every day. He is often backtracking because he gets to ahead of himself and his mind is moving a mile a minute.

Ricochet has his clip board on the front hood of the Sierra 4 pickup truck. He is smoking a cigarette, drinking a cup of coffee and talking on the radio. He is juggling everything in a nervous combination. He is pacing a little and then turning back to his clipboard.

Art shakes his head. "He's probably already had six cups of coffee and a half a pack of cigarettes, and it's not even eight o'clock yet."

"That fuck is going to have a heart attack by the time he's 50," said Kyle.

Art laughs. "The way he's already going at it today, I bet he has one by lunch time."

"Art, I need a nap," said Kyle. "Is there a Hotel Galaxy out there with reservations for one?"

"What, are you hung over?" asked Art.

"I don't believe I'm to that stage yet," said Kyle.

Art turns back towards Kyle. "Yea man...if you let me smell your fingers."

"You are one sick pervert," said Kyle.

Art smirks, puts the truck in gear and pulls away.

Several minutes later Sierra 6 pulls up and parks in front of a plane on India row. Kyle unhooks the strap and steps out from the side door. He turns and hooks the strap across the side door, reaches under it and grabs his tool box and bag. He walks over to the ladder and sets the tool box and bag down on the ground. He unlocks the tool box, removes several tools and sets them on the ground. He locks the tool box and stands up. He walks over and starts the power unit. He throws the power unit's cord to the ground, picks up the end of it and drags it to the external power connection point on the side of the plane. He pops the small hinged door open and connects the cord to the plane. He walks back to the power unit, throttles it up and sends power to the plane.

Kyle walks back to the ladder. He kneels down and adjusts the two ladder extensions so they are about an inch off the ground. He stands and steps on the lowest step to test the ladder to make sure it hits the ground if someone steps on it. This will make a noise and send a vibration through the plane that will alert him that someone is coming up the stairs. Kyle picks up his tools and bag and heads up the ladder.

Kyle enters the flight station, closes the door behind him and sets his bag on the scanners seat. He goes to the flight engineer panel, checks power to make sure the volts and the frequencies are ok and turns the plane's power on. He goes to the pilot's seat and pushes the master caution buttons, stopping the warning lights. He steps over to the navigator's station, takes the seat cushion off and throws it under the table. He reaches over and removes the radio from his bag and sets it on the navigator's station seat. He grabs the tools and crawls under the navigator station table. He lies on his back and sticks his legs out from under the table and in front of the flight station door. If the flight station door is opened it will hit his legs and wake him up. It will also prevent someone from being able to come in through the door until Kyle moves his legs. Kyle takes the tools, places them next to him and puts a screw driver on his chest. He can easily reach the rest of the tools to pretend he's fixing something. He does this as a precaution in case someone comes up. Kyle adjusts the seat cushion under his head and uses it as a pillow. He closes his eyes and falls asleep.

Three hours later Kyle is still sound asleep under the table. You can hear someone coming up the ladder but it doesn't wake up Kyle. Suddenly the door pops open and hits Kyle in the legs. He is startled and grabs the tool on his chest. "Hey-hey, hold up. Let me get out of the way."

Kyle slides his legs towards him so the door can open. "Who is there?"

Two guys come up on the flight deck. They work for life support. "It's life support. We need to check the date on our form."

"Yea, yea, go ahead," said Kyle.

The life support guys walk back to the crew rest area. Kyle looks at his watch and realizes he's been asleep for three hours. He drops his head back on the seat cushion in disbelief. He reaches up and sets the tools on the table. He slides out from under the table, stands up and stretches. The life support guys come back to the flight deck. Kyle has moved the radio and is reattaching the seat cushion to the chair. "Is it good?"

"Yea, we are all good," said the life support guy.

The two guys head down the stairs. Kyle looks out the flight station windows and sees Sierra 6 driving down the centerline. Kyle grabs the radio. "Sierra 6! Hold up, you're dragging something."

The Sierra 6 truck stops fast and Art jumps out. Art walks to the back of the truck, gets on his hands and knees and looks under the truck. Kyle grabs his bag, tools and radio. He turns power off of the plane and heads down the stairs.

Art realizes someone is messing with him and he looks around suspiciously. He sees Kyle coming down the stairs and walking over to the power unit. Art gets back in the truck and pulls in front of the plane that Kyle is on. Kyle, with his tool box and bag in hand, walks towards the truck. Kyle throws his tool box in side door and gets in front with Art.

"Hey man, did you get your beauty rest?" asked Art.

"Yea, I'd still be asleep if those life support guys hadn't come in," said Kyle.

"You feel any better?" asked Art.

Kyle stretches. "This morning I swore I'd never go out again on a school night. But after that nap...I'm thinking about going out again tonight."

Art smirks and starts to pull away.

Kyle looks out the window to his right. "Clear. Where are we heading?"

"Down to 463," said Art. "They've been a pain in my balls all morning."

Sierra 6 pulls up to 463 on Mary row. There are two bicycles parked under the nose of the plane. The bikes belong to QA. Two crew chiefs walk up to the truck at the driver's door. They look frustrated.

"What the fuck is going on out here?" asked Art. "Is QA still out here?"

"Yea, these guys have a hard on for us," said one of the crew chiefs.

"You guys want me to go into CTK and sign out a few more buckets for you?" asked Kyle. "How much longer are you going to milk this shit out?"

The Other crew chief looks over at Kyle. "You can jump your ass out and help if you want. We have an extra stool upstairs."

Art continues talking to the crew chiefs. Kyle gets out of the truck and reaches into the side door. He unlocks his tool box and removes a six inch crescent wrench. He walks over to the bikes. He loosens bolts on the handle bars and the seats of both bikes. He turns and walks back to the truck. He puts the wrench back in the tool box, locks it and gets back in the truck. Neither of the crew chiefs or Art noticed what Kyle did.

Art finishes his conversation. "All right, just get the shit knocked out. I'll bump the ETIC up an hour."

The crew chiefs walk away as Art pulls away from the plane.

Kyle looks out the window to the right. "Clear."

"Where'd you go?" asked Art.

Kyle laughs. "I left QA a little present."

Ten minutes later Art and Kyle are sitting in the Sierra 6 truck. The truck is out by the wall in front of India row and is facing towards the planes. Art is looking at a porn magazine and Kyle is day dreaming.

Art shows Kyle a picture from the magazine. "Hey man, take a look at those tits. She could feed an entire village in Africa."

Kyle frowns. "They are nasty…and look at those nipples."

Art smirks. "I think she's hot. I'd put my face in between them and go brrrrrrrrrrrr."

"I have to disagree with you there Art," said Kyle. "I'm a lower half guy. Give me a nice pair of legs and a great ass and I'm happy."

"What about tits?" asked Art.

"I can do without them," said Kyle. "Tits are just a rest stop on a trip to the ultimate destination."

Art shakes his head. "You are crazy man. I love a good pair of fun bags."

Art closes the magazine and puts it in his bag. He leans over to his left, pulls the mirror in and looks at himself. He takes his right hand and strokes his mustache several times with his fingers. "Hey man, are you participating in Mustache March?"

Mustache March is a contest. Whoever wants to participate throws in a set amount of money at the beginning of the month. At the end of the month, whoever has grown the best mustache wins the pot. There is always an argument between a few guys but an impartial judge makes the final decision.

"No way!" said Kyle. "I've tried to grow a mustache five or six years ago and it just wasn't me. I had verification on it also."

"What do you mean verification?" asked Art.

"Well, I was seeing this girl named Heidi," said Kyle. "She lived about two and a half hours from my house so I'd only go up about every week or two. I use to go up there with my friend Rick the Dick."

"Rick the Dick?" asked Art.

"Whole other story," said Kyle. "Anyway, I decided to grow a mustache and after about two weeks it had come in pretty good. I thought my face was a little too crowded but what the hell. So I drove up on a Friday to see Heidi. I got to her house, rang the doorbell and she opened the door."

"And?" asked Art.

"She was shocked," said Kyle. "I walked right in, she gave me a razor and I shaved it off just like that. The look on her face was worth a thousand words and the first five words were, 'Shave that shit right now!' Since then, I've never even thought about giving it a second chance."

"She sounded pretty traumatized," said Art.

"Traumatized!" said Kyle. "I was traumatized. It was a life changing moment for me. I'll never have a flavor savor."

Art puckers, raises his upper lip and smells his mustache. "Mmm. That was some good shit."

"Don't you take a shower?" asked Kyle.

They both start laughing.

"I bet you wake up in the morning and your face looks like a glazed donut," said Kyle.

"Yea," said Art. "I wake up every morning and peel that shit off like a mask. It's good for the skin."

MOCC comes over the radio. "Sierra 6, MOCC."

Art is talking to himself. "What's this fuck want now?"

Art replies to MOCC over the radio. "Go ahead MOCC."

"The Red side needs a plane," said MOCC. "Their local is crapping out and they want to go to the spare. Is it ready?"

Art shakes his head. "Yea, it's ready."

Art slams the truck into drive and starts to move off to the right. He is talking to himself again. "Shit!"

MOCC comes over the radio again. "Ok, I'll send the crew your way."

"What's wrong?" asked Kyle.

"The Spare is kneeled and I need to get it up off the ground before the crew shows up," said Art. "QTP was out there earlier and decided to go to lunch."

Kyle pushes Art's buttons a little more. "Speaking of lunch, I haven't eaten yet."

Art is looking at his clip board while he is driving. "I knew I shouldn't have let those two guys go to CBPO."

CBPO stands for Consolidated Base Personnel Office. It's the base's personnel center. It's also were all crew chief's important paperwork goes to be lost.

Kyle laughs. "Yea, more like Commissary, BX, Post Office and out around the base."

Art agrees. "More than likely."

"Quit pinging," said Kyle. "It's embarrassing. You are acting like Kurt 'Ricochet' Rubler. Take me by there and I'll do it myself."

Art looks at Kyle. "But you need two more guys."

"Not on grave shift," said Kyle.

"Well you aren't on graves," said Art.

Kyle cracks his knuckles. "Take me there and I'll have it done in 10 minutes."

"No way," said Art.

"If I get it up in 10 minutes, let me go home," said Kyle. "You can get those fucks that went to CBPO to launch it."

The Sierra 6 truck pulls up in front of the plane on Fox row. The guys notice that the back doors are also open.

"Ah great!" said Art. "The back doors are open."

"So what do you say? Do we have a deal?" asked Kyle.

"Ok, deal," said Art. "I want to see this anyway."

Kyle grabs his radio from his bag and jumps out of the truck. He runs around the front of the truck to Art's window. "Put your radio on tow net. If you see QA give me heads up."

They both switch their radios to the tow net.

"Start the clock!" said Kyle.

Kyle takes off running towards the plane without giving Art a chance to respond. Art notes the time on his watch.

Kyle is at the front of the plane. He scans the left and right wings making sure there is nothing around the plane. He goes to the crew entry door ladder which is retracted and throws the nose landing gear pin on the ground. He changes the ladder select switch and then runs up the stairs.

Kyle comes running into the flight deck. He sets his radio down on the engineer's table. With his right hand he immediately slaps down all the red guarded switches on the engineer's circuit breaker panel. He grabs the APU and kneeling checklists and throws them on the table in front of him. He then turns the battery switch on and with both hands he starts the two APUs. They slowly start winding up.

Down at the Sierra 6 truck, Art is looking at plane and looking around for QA.

Kyle puts the APU select switch to left APU. He then reaches down and pushes in all the circuit breakers at the engineers station. He takes a second to locate and pull out one circuit breaker. Next, he goes up to the kneel panel and turns the mode select switch from forward to unkneel. Then he unhooks the map light and wraps it once around the bar above the engineer's seat. At this point both APUs have come online. Kyle checks the volts and frequencies for one, then the other. He then moves the APU/Off/External Power switch to APU. Power comes on the plane.

He goes forward to the copilot's seat and pushes in the master caution button. He looks to his right and makes sure the aft doors are armed. He switches a radio on and tests it with Dover's Ground Control.

"Dover Ground this is Reach 5003 on Fox row, UHF radio check, how copy?"

Before Dover Ground answers him, he is back at the engineer table with the microphone. He places the microphone in the engineer's checklist bracket and starts throwing switches on the environmental, hydraulic and ATM control panels. The hydraulic systems come up.

Down stairs Art is still looking around.

Dover Ground calls back over the radio. "Reach 5003 this is Dover ground. I copy you loud and clear, how me?"

Kyle grabs the microphone. "Loud and clear, thanks!"

Kyle positions the kneel command switch to unkneel. The plane starts to slowly rise. He takes the cord from the map light and uses it to hold the switch up in place. He grabs the radio and takes off down the stairs.

Kyle runs back through the cargo compartment to the aft ramp. He looks at both hinges on the pressure door and then comes back and adjusts the aft leg on the troop compartment ladder. Next he goes to the control panel and moves the guarded switch to operate. A loud thump is heard. The aft loading complex has hydraulic pressure. He moves the ramp control switch to close. The ramp and pressure door starts to close. Kyle patiently watches for all the not locked light to go out. They finally do. He lets go of the ramp switch and moves the mode switch from truck bed to off.

Art is watching the plane slowly rise and the aft ramp close at the same time. "Holy shit!"

Next Kyle moves the cargo doors switch to close. He looks through the gap between the pressure door and the fuselage and can see the side door moving. The side doors completely close then the massive center door starts to move. It drops down, closes and locks as Kyle watches the not locked lights go out. Kyle releases the switch and moves the guarded switch back to complete. A thump is heard indicating hydraulic pressure is off of the aft loading complex. Kyle takes off running for the flight deck.

Kyle comes running up the stairs to the flight deck. He sets the radio on the engineer's table. Just as he gets there the kneeled lights go off one by one. After the last light goes out Kyle counts with his fingers to five. He releases the kneel command switch from the cord. Kyle shuts down the hydraulic systems and sets the environmental panels back to the way it was before he started.

In the truck, Art seems somewhat relieved but is still looking around.

Kyle steps up and cuts off the radio and hits the master caution buttons one more time. He reaches over and flips a switch to de-energize the back doors. Then he moves back to the circuit breaker panel. He pulls the circuit breakers for the ones he pushed in, pushes another one back in and flips up five red guarded switches. He turns off power to the plane. Everything goes silent. You can hear the APUs running. Kyle turns off both APUs at the same time. He listens to them wind down as he waits for the APU door open lights to go off. He turns the battery switch off, grabs his radio and runs down stairs into the cargo compartment to the crew entry door.

The retracted ladder is now five feet off the ground. Kyle opens a small panel to his left, reaches in and holds down the lever that controls the ladder. The ladder slides down into its normal position. Kyle hustles down the ladder and grabs the nose landing gear pin. He walks over, crawls up in the front of the nose gear and inserts the pins.

He steps behind the nose landing gear, pulls the safety pin out of the kneel pad and tosses it by the ladder. He then pulls the kneel pad t-handle and repositions the pad. He reaches up and repositions the folding bulkhead. He steps to the left side of the gear, locks and pins the folding bulkhead. Kyle steps to the nose landing gear scissors on the back of the gear and unpins the strut limiter. He pitches it over by the ladder with the kneel pad safety pin.

Kyle takes off running back to the number four main landing gear. At the base of the strut he pulls off the kneel collar. He runs around to the number three main landing gear and does the same thing. With the two collars in his hands Kyle runs up to the ladder and drops the collars next to the kneel pad safety pin. Kyle jogs over to the truck and gets in the passenger side. He is a little winded.

"How did I do?" asked Kyle.

"You were close," said Art. "That was worth the price of admission. I believe you just won a free trip back to the dorms."

"Screw the dorms," said Kyle. "I'm going to your house for a facial."

They both start laughing.

"Let's do this," said Kyle. "I'll save this sprout for another day. Go find me something to eat and I'll stay out here and launch his thing. Hell, all I've done today is sleep."

Art acts disappointed. "Shit man. I was hoping you would go to my house and knock some chores out after your facial."

They both laugh.

"Maybe next time," said Kyle. "Let me get this thing ready."

Kyle gets out of the truck and grabs his bag and his tool box. The truck pulls away and Kyle walks over and sets his things down under the nose of the plane.

CHAPTER 19

Several days have passed. Kyle, Bucky, and Nader are sitting in the room drinking beer. Kyle is sitting on his bed, Bucky is next to him on the couch and Nader is at the other end of the couch. They came back from eating at the chow hall about an hour ago.

Bucky is telling the story about Cindy. "So I hung out with her for a few beers."

Troy walks in. "So who are we talking about?"

"Flores' girl Cindy," said Bucky. "So I was with her here in the room. Kyle saw me. We were drinking beers and she was folding my laundry."

Troy grabs a beer from the fridge and sits down in the chair.

"I still can't believe how she looked," said Kyle. "I didn't even recognize her."

Bucky continues. "We hung out in here for a while and then we went up to Nader's room and started drinking. I was going to try and hit it but there were too many people all over her."

"Yea I know," said Nader. "At a certain point I had to run all those guys out of my room. They were like vultures."

"So you had her all to yourself. What did you do?" asked Troy.

Nader shakes his head. "Nothing. My roommate Brad was there. Cindy was all drunk. She passed out and Brad was able to get her undressed and get her in bed."

Troy catches the undressed part. "What?"

"Was she that fucked up?" asked Kyle.

"She was pretty gone," said Nader. "I didn't want to touch her and neither did he. So Brad put her in bed and took all her clothes off."

Troy is on the edge of his chair. "All of them?"

"Yea, she was so out of it that we knew in the morning she wouldn't remember what happened," said Nader. "Listen to this. Here is the best part. Brad took pictures of her!"

"Where are they at?" asked Troy.

Nader takes a drink of beer. "Brad is afraid to get them developed. He's looking for a place that won't ask any questions."

"How did she look?" asked Kyle.

"Shaved clean," said Nader.

Bucky sits up. "That's what she was talking about when we were together here in the room. She said she had everything set just the way Flores liked it. That dirty old man."

Troy sits back and takes a drink of his beer. "Oh my God. What did she do the next morning?"

"She got up, went down stairs and checked to see if Roy was back. And then she split," said Nader.

"Did she say anything about waking up naked?" asked Kyle.

"Not a thing," said Nader.

Bucky is relieved. "I'm glad I got out of there."

"Where did you go?" asked Nader.

"I went over to my buddy Broderick's room," said Bucky. "He's a cop. I ended up crashing over there."

"You know I'm dating a cop now?" asked Nader. "We've been going out for a while."

Troy snickers. "There aren't too many brains in that relationship."

"What do you mean?" asked Nader.

"A crew chief and a cop," said Troy. "The only career fields that work 24-7 and are on 12 hour shifts all the time."

Kyle points at Troy. "Good point. You're on top of it. What, did you get a nap today?"

"I think I'm serious about her," said Nader. "That's why I didn't mess with Cindy. I'm trying to figure out how to tell her."

Bucky starts to laugh. "Why don't you just have one of your orgies and break it to her in the middle of a four way?"

Everybody laughs.

"No. Come on guys, I'm serious, said Nader. "This one is special."

"Go paint it on her door," said Troy. "You are pretty good with a paint brush."

Everybody laughs again.

Kyle gets serious. "I'll tell you the best way. I do this all the time. It never fails. Go to the commissary and buy an onion."

"An onion?" asked Nader

"Yea an onion. Do you need to take notes?" asked Kyle.

"No, go on," said Nader.

Kyle continues. "Take the onion and cut it in pieces and place it around your room where you might possibly be with her. Behind the head board, at the sofa, places like that. Wherever you make love to her. I take it that you are at that stage now?"

Nader responds in a convincing manner. "Right, not just banging her."

"Right," said Kyle. "Reach over and get a little onion on your fingers. Rub your eyes and tell her she is the nicest girl you've ever met. Your eyes will start tearing up from the onion. She'll think you are in deep and she'll love it."

Troy interrupts. "That's the stupidest thing I've ever heard."

Nader thinks for a second. He's tried crazier things. "Maybe I'll try it."

"Yea, then jump up and go to the sink as if you are trying to pull yourself together. Then wash the onion off your fingers and out of your eyes," said Kyle.

Bucky knows Kyle is making this up but he plays along. "Yea, Kyle usually keeps an onion in the fridge all the time. There's one in there now."

Kyle wags his finger at Bucky. "No, I had to throw it out. It was getting old."

"What, no winners lately?" asked Troy.

"None worthy of an onion," said Kyle.

They all laugh and take a drink of beer.

"Hey, I don't have to work tomorrow," said Kyle.

"Why not?" asked Troy.

"I have to do a bug spray respirator test in the morning. Art gave me the whole day off," said Kyle. He owed me a sprout anyway."

Troy shakes his head. "I've never had to do that."

Kyle's expression has changed to worried. "It has to be bad for you. You totally seal the plane and spray two cans of that insecticide inside."

"And stay in there for 30 minutes while it takes effect," said Troy.

"You know its nerve gas in those cans," said Nader. "It's Vietnam error shit."

"I don't know what but it's some bad shit," said Kyle.

"What do they do it for?" asked Bucky.

"Japanese Beatles," said Kyle. "You've seen the cans on the plane before. They are usually in the cubby hole by the galley. The cans are green."

"Oh yea, is that what that shit is?" asked Bucky.

Troy is serious. "You are fucked. You'll have to do it."

"Not if I fail the breathing test," said Kyle.

"How are you going to do that?" asked Troy.

Kyle holds up his beer can. "A lot of these!"

They all toast.

"Where'd you go today?" asked Troy. "You missed all the fireworks."

"I had to go to CBPO," said Kyle.

Troy sits up. "Well listen to this. Boner is on a refuel with two other guys."

Nader interrupts. "Boner is on days now? I didn't see him at roll call."

"He's just there for a week to take care of a few things," said Troy. "He's in and out. Anyway, Boner is supervising and that new black kid is on SPR. Boner is asking him things and the kid is not answering. So Boner thinks the kid's headset doesn't work. Boner tells a racial joke to the guy upstairs at the panel."

Nader isn't surprised. "Boner is a little rough. So the kid never heard it."

"No!" said Troy. "It turns out that the kid's interphone cord was fucked up and he couldn't talk but he could hear. The kid said nothing about it and went straight in and told management. Boner was this close to going to social actions. Art and Boner spent the whole afternoon in the office. In the end, Boner apologized and it was all dropped."

"That lucky son of a bitch," said Nader.

"He sounds like he has some of your luck Nader," said Bucky.

"I'm not lucky, I'm smart," said Nader.

Kyle laughs. "Is that what it's called these days?"

Nader changes the subject. "Hey, I have this shit upstairs called Soju. It's from Korea. One of the FCCs brought it back from a trip. You guys want to try it?"

"Sure, go grab it," said Bucky. That's some powerful shit."

"Can't hurt tomorrow's test," said Kyle.

CHAPTER 20

The next morning Kyle enters the hospital. He is in his uniform. He is looking for the room where they administer the respirator tests. He is hung over and his attitude is less than cheerful. He needs to pull this off or he's stuck with the crappy job of spraying the planes for Japanese Beatles. He passes several people but doesn't ask anyone for directions.

Finally he spots a very attractive female nurse. His attitude changes for the better. He approaches her. "Morning."

The nurse turns. "Morning!"

"How are you today?" asked Kyle.

The nurse smiles. "I'm great! How are you?"

"Oh...I've been better," said Kyle. "Hey, I'm supposed to get a respirator test this morning. They said it was somewhere on the first floor. Do you know where it's at?"

"Yes," said the nurse. "You are close. It's just around the corner and the first door on the right."

"Not bad," said Kyle. "I got within a few feet and without a map."

"Yes...pretty impressive," said the nurse.

A male nurse walks close to Kyle and the nurse. He stops at a counter next to them and appears to be ease dropping.

Kyle is rarely in this Air Force "9 to 5" setting. It's a whole different world with entirely different people. The nurse has Kyle's attention. "I've never seen you around before. Did you just arrive?"

"Yea, I got here a few weeks ago," said the nurse.

"From where?" asked Kyle.

"Andrews," said the nurse.

Andrews is an Air Force base in Maryland. It's located just outside Washington, DC.

"Really!" said Kyle. "I love Old Town Alexandria."

The nurse agrees. "That was one on my hangouts."

"Ever eat at the Fish Market?" asked Kyle.

"Yea!" said the nurse.

"And what about that piano player they have upstairs? Isn't he the best?" asked Kyle.

"Yea," said the nurse. "He's really great. I love how he gets the crowd going."

Kyle can't believe this is happening. A good looking woman that is in the Air Force…and she is cool. "So, what's your name?"

"Patricia, and yours?"

"Kyle. Nice to meet you."

Kyle and Patricia shake hands. Kyle is just about to ask Patricia out on a date but he is uncharacteristically nervous. He looks to one side and then to the other. Patricia likes the fact that Kyle is friendly and picks up on his moment of hesitation. She thinks it's cute. She wants to meet new people. Patricia knows what is coming and is waiting for it to happen.

Kyle goes for it. "So, maybe…"

Just then the male nurse turns. He gives Kyle a dirty look and then turns towards Patricia. Kyle has a "what the hell" look on his face.

"Patricia, I need your help right away over in the conference room," said the male nurse. "They are having a briefing in a few minutes and we're not ready."

Patricia is caught in the middle. "Oh, ok. Kyle, I have to run. I'll see you around."

Kyle is caught off guard. In his current state he is a few steps behind. "Yea, yea…see you around."

Patricia and the Male nurse walk away. He is saying something to her but Kyle can't hear it. As he talks to Patricia he looks back at Kyle and gives him another dirty look. Kyle returns the look and the male nurse spins his head around quickly.

Kyle says to himself. "Cock blocking faggot. Oh well…"

Kyle's attitude changes back to less than cheerful. He has his game face on. He turns and heads down the hall. At the corner he turns left and enters the first room on the right. There is a male pulmonary technician sitting at a desk. "Morning. I'm here for the respirator test."

"Mansfield?" asked the technician.

Kyle shakes his head. "Yea."

"Have a seat. How are things today?" asked the technician.

Kyle sits down. "They could have been better."

"What do you mean?" asked the technician.

"Oh nothing," said Kyle. "So how long will this take? I have to get back to work as soon as possible."

"Not long," said the technician. "I already have all your information loaded. Here, take this."

The technician hands Kyle a device to measure lung capacity. "Ok, take a death breath and blow as hard as you can."

Kyle inhales, holds it for a second and blows. He blows as hard as he can. He is hung over and gets a little dizzy. The technician takes the device and looks at it. The result is very poor.

"Oh come on...you can do better than that," said the technician.

The technician resets the device and hands it back to Kyle.

Kyle plays along and looks determined to do better. "Ok. I'll try harder."

Kyle inhales again, holds his breath for a second and blows a little harder. He starts coughing and is seeing stars.

"Hey, are you ok?" asked the technician.

Kyle hands the device back to the technician. "Yea, I'm fine."

The technician looks at the device. Kyle registered about the same result. It might be a hair better but still poor.

"That's about the same as your last one. Let's try one more time," said the technician.

"Ok, whatever you say," said Kyle.

The technician hands the device back to Kyle. Kyle takes a deep breath, holds it for a second and blows into the tester. He starts to cough violently, over and over. Kyle is dizzy and can feel himself starting to sweat from a combination of his coughing and his hangover. He hands the device to the technician.

"Are you sure you are ok?" asked the technician.

Kyle pulls himself together. "Yea. I've never felt better in my life. Why?"

The technician looks at the device. The score is about the same. "Well, your scores are very low."

Kyle looks concerned. "Low? What does that mean?"

"For now, I'm going to have to prohibit you from the respirator program and refer you to a doctor so he can check you out," said the technician.

Kyle keeps the act going. "Really? Are you sure? This could affect my job."

"There is no way I can pass you with these scores," said the technician. "I'll make an appointment with the doctor for you."

"I need to talk to the desk and get a few other appointments straightened out," said Kyle. "I'm going on a TDY in a few days. Can I make this appointment myself when I stop by and talk to them?"

"Sure, why not," said the technician.

Kyle stands up. "Thanks! I'll head down to the appointment desk now."

Kyle looks at his watch. "I need to hurry. I told my boss I'd be back by now. He's going to have my ass."

Kyle turns and hurries out the door.

"Have a good day!" said the technician.

Kyle pulled it off! He'll bypass the appointment desk on his way out of the hospital and not make a follow up appointment. More importantly, he will not have to spray the planes for Japanese Beatles. He's ecstatic!

Kyle turns back and sticks his head in the door. "You too!"

Kyle hurries to the exit with no delays. As he does, he looks around for the nurse. She is nowhere in sight. Kyle thinks to himself, "Oh well Patricia, I guess it wasn't meant to be."

CHAPTER 21

----------April 1990----------

It's six o'clock in the evening. Kyle and Troy are sitting on the couch in Kyle's room drinking beer. Kyle is sitting closest to the beds and Troy is sitting at the opposite end. They are dressed and ready to go out for the night. Kyle and Troy are waiting for Bucky. He hasn't been seen by anyone since earlier in the day.

Troy is in the middle of a story. "I'm in the back seat. Brian Kelly and Dwayne Johnson are in the front. Brian is driving and Dwayne has one of those fire extinguishers, you know the big ones about like this."

Troy holds his hands out to show the size. "The kind you can pump up the pressure. It's filled with water. So, Brian pulls up to where you order the food."

"At McDonald's right?" asked Kyle.

"Yea, McDonalds," said Troy. "Anyway, Brian orders enough food to feed ten people. The woman takes his order and says pull on around to the next window. Dwayne places the fire extinguisher right next to Brian so the hose will reach out the window. Brian pulls up and the woman opens the window to take his money. Before she knows it, Brian is spraying her right in the face with water. She takes off running! I'm in the back going 'holy shit!' Dwayne is egging him on. Brian starts spraying the other employees and the customers at the counter."

"No way," said Kyle.

Troy starts laughing. "Yea, the people inside are scrambling for cover. You know those things have some good pressure at first. So I'm yelling to get the hell out of there and those two knuckle heads are laughing their asses off. Finally Brian pulls away and we drive off. I was shitting my pants."

"And this is the night before you were supposed to show up to MEPS?" asked Kyle.

MEPS stands for Military Entrance Processing Station. It is the second step in becoming a member of the Air Force. The first would be signing up.

"Yea," said Troy. "If something would have happened and we would have gotten busted my old man would have cut my balls off and made spaghetti sauce with them."

Kyle laughs. "That's some crazy shit."

Troy starts to tell another story. "That's nothing. Listen to this shit my brother Dave did."

All of a sudden Bucky enters the room. He has his lacrosse stick and ball with him. He looks tired, pissed and sweaty.

"Bucky, where the hell have you been?" asked Kyle.

Bucky sets his stuff down in the corner next to the refrigerator and grabs a beer. "Blowing off some steam. I've been over at the tennis courts bouncing the ball off the wall since I got off work. You aren't going to believe this shit when I tell you."

"Well come on, get on with it," said Troy.

Bucky cracks his beer, takes a big drink and sits down on Kyle's bed. "You know I gave Darrell Evans my van a few weeks ago?"

"Yea, he's having troubles with his wife," said Troy.

Bucky continues. "I guess later on that day another guy offered to let Darrell use one of his cars free of charge. Well Darrell said ok and took the car. Then that bastard turned right around, went downtown and sold my van and pocketed the cash."

Kyle is stunned. "You are right, I don't believe that."

Troy shakes his head. "That fucking scum bag."

Bucky takes another drink. "I was this close to beating his ass but Kenny Merchant and Mark Bush held me back."

"So what are you going to do?" asked Kyle.

Bucky throws his hands in the air. "I can't do shit. I legally signed the registration over to him that day."

"He didn't even offer you some of the money?" asked Troy.

"Not a penny!" said Bucky. "He said he is hurting financially and needs the money."

"That's bull shit," said Kyle. "He's at Tap Works or the VFW every day after work drinking beer with the guys."

"You'll catch him out one of these days and then you can get your money back in a different way," said Troy.

Bucky looks disappointed. "No. Chief Pirez has already warned me. The last time I got in a fight he told me...you know how Pirez talks. He always has that cigarette dangling from the corner of his mouth and the ash on it an inch long. How it never falls off is a mystery to me. Anyway, he said, 'Bucky Wirth, I don't know whether to manage you or kick your ass out of the Air Force.' So he's waiting for me to fuck up."

"Yea, you don't want to get kicked out over a guy like Evans," said Kyle. "He's not worth it."

Troy smirks. "You know they name streets after guys like that...one way."

Kyle stands up. "I guess there's only one thing to do then boys."

"What's that?" asked Bucky.

"Let's go out!" said Kyle.

Bucky's attitude changes for the better. "I'm down with that."

"Well hurry up and get ready," said Troy. "Mouse is giving us a ride in a few minutes. We're going to start out at that preppy college bar Smithers."

"I still have to scrub my ass, go get money and pick up my laundry," said Bucky.

"Get your laundry tomorrow," said Kyle.

"No, you guys go ahead and I'll meet you there in an hour," said Bucky.

Mouse walks in. "Hey, you guys have any beer?"

He reaches into the fridge and grabs one before anyone can answer.

"I thought you were driving?" asked Troy.

Mouse looks happy. "Reese is going to take us down and drop us off. I'm going out with the boys tonight!"

Troy and Bucky stand up.

"Ok, let's roll," said Kyle. "Bucky, we'll see you down there in a bit."

"Alright, I'm right behind you guys."

They all start to walk out except for Bucky. Kyle stops and grabs three more beers out of the fridge.

"Damn boy, you thirsty?" asked Troy.

"Just a few for the road," said Kyle.

Smithers is an old, large, two story house that has been converted into a restaurant and bar. Both the upstairs and downstairs are used. When you walk in the front door there is a room on each side. The rooms are full of tables and chairs. Immediately in front of you is a staircase that leads upstairs. To the right of the staircase is a hallway that leads into the downstairs bar. This area opens up. On the left is the bar. It is about 25 feet long. At the end of the bar is an open space that leads to the back door. There is another section on the right with even more tables and chairs. The two sections are separated by a railing that doubles as a counter top.

Two hours have passed since the guys left the room. Kyle, Troy and Mouse are sitting at the downstairs bar. They are drinking long neck bottles and each has a small pile of money on the bar in front of them. The place is about half full. In the corner by the back door is Glenn Govot.

Glenn Govot is in his mid-20s. He is a very talented local musician and a friend of Kyle's. Glenn plays the piano and guitar as a solo act. He performs a lot in the Dover area and throughout the mid-Atlantic.

Glenn has his piano set up but his playing acoustic guitar. He is playing and singing the song *Jane Says* by the group Jane's Addiction.

"Where the hell is Bucky?" asked Troy. "He said he'd be right behind us and it's been almost two hours."

"Maybe he said fuck it," said Mouse.

"Na...he'll be here," said Kyle. "Let's order another round."

Kyle waves the barkeep over. "Can we get another round?"

The barkeep nods. "Sure."

Mouse pulls a 10 dollar bill from his pile of money. "Here, I'm up. I'm going to take a piss."

Mouse gets up and walks towards the front door. He turns and heads upstairs to the bathroom.

"You know the bars down here are fucked up," said Troy.

"What do you mean?" asked Kyle.

"We've been sitting here for a while and we're on our what, fourth or fifth beer," said Troy.

Kyle takes a drink. "Who's counting?"

"That's not the point," said Troy. "The guy hasn't even offered us one on the house. Up at the Long Island bars I use to go to, if you had one or two they'd always give you the next one on the house. That's good for business."

Kyle laughs. "What do you know about business? Oh wait…that's right…"

Troy shakes his head and laughs. The barkeep puts three beers on the bar and grabs the 10 dollars. He turns to the cash register and returns with change in a few seconds. Troy points to Mouse's money pile and the barkeep puts the change down there.

All of a sudden Bucky walks up. He is in a different mood than before. He is happy, excited and pumped up. "Fellas, what's up?"

Kyle and Troy spin around on their stools.

"What in the hell happened to you?" asked Troy. "I've had to drink your share of beers."

"Yea right," said Kyle. "I should have a six pack in me already but I'm waiting on him to nurse his down."

"Is there a beer in here with my name on it?" asked Bucky.

"Yea, here's one," said Kyle.

Kyle hands Bucky Mouse's new beer. Bucky takes a big drink. Kyle motions to the barkeep to bring one more beer.

"Sorry I'm late but I ran into a little situation," said Bucky.

Kyle rolls this eyes. "What now?"

"No, this is all good," said Bucky.

The barkeep brings the additional beer and sets it next to Kyle's beer. Kyle pulls a five dollar bill off his money pile and throws it on the bar.

"You aren't going to believe this shit," said Bucky.

"I still don't believe the last thing you told me," said Kyle.

Bucky starts telling what happened. "I get finished with all my shit and I'm walking out of the BX. Guess who I run into?"

"Evans?" asked Troy.

Bucky smiles. "No, even better...Evans' wife. We're shooting the shit and I ask her if she's seen Darrell lately. She says no. Then I tell her about the whole van deal and she gets even more pissed than I was. At this point I guess she can't stand the guy. I tell her I have to go and that I'll see her later. She grabs my arm and says wait. Then she says let's go to your room."

Troy is wide eyed. "Oh my God, are you serious?"

"Be quiet Troy!" said Kyle. "Bucky, keep going."

Bucky continues. "So she follows me back to the dorms and we go into the room. I don't even get five feet in the door and she already has my pants down and is blowing me."

"Holy shit!" said Troy.

"She got me so excited that within a minute I was done," said Bucky.

"Are you serious?" asked Troy.

"Did she take it all?" asked Kyle.

"Like a champ!" said Bucky. "Then she tells me that she's had a crush on me for years and that she was the one that was leaving notes on my van last year."

"I love a good mystery," said Kyle.

"So, she gets me right back up again and I bang the shit out of her," said Bucky. "We get finished, she says we should do this again real soon and walks out."

Kyle holds up his beer. Bucky and Troy follow suit. They toast and tap their bottle together.

Mouse walks up and grabs his beer. "Hold on! What did I miss?"

"Here's to the Red Shed! May she rest in peace!" said Kyle.

They all tap their bottles together again and drink.

"Where did you get that van from anyway?" asked Troy.

"I traded Remis my jeep for it," said Bucky. "He was getting out of the Air Force and wanted a jeep so I traded him one for one."

Glenn starts playing the song *Free Falling* by Tom Petty.

"Why did Remis get out?" asked Troy.

"Now this is crazy," said Bucky. "Remis gets a call on the hall phone from a bunch of drunks. They are stuck at the 7-11 because it's raining like crazy. They don't want to walk back to the dorms in the rain."

"Sounds familiar," said Kyle.

Bucky takes a drink of his beer. "So he jumps in the van with his boxers on and goes and gets them. You know how boxers look like shorts? Well, he's coming back through the gate and they stop him because it's after midnight. He's cool because he hasn't been drinking. He shows his ID. The cop leans in to smell if he's been drinking."

Troy jumps in. "Which he wasn't."

"Right," said Bucky. "But they always do that. So the cop looks at his ID and then notices Remis' pecker hanging out of his boxers."

Troy shakes his head in disbelief. "No way."

"Yea, you know how sometime you are sitting there and your shit just flops out," said Bucky.

"So what did they do?" asked Troy.

"The cops wrote him up for indecent exposure and the squadron gave him a Letter of Reprimand," said Bucky. "After that Remis said fuck it."

"What do you mean fuck it?" asked Troy.

"He was ready to sign his reenlistment papers that week," said Bucky. "He changed his mind really quick."

"Oh my God," said Troy. "And all he was doing was trying to help out a few guys."

"That is fucked," said Kyle. "Remis was a good guy. That's who gave us the couch."

"Troy, if we ever get out of the Air Force the couch is yours," said Bucky.

All the guys knock bottles together and drink up.

"You guys ready to hit Loockerman and see if there are any bitches there?" asked Mouse.

All the guys are in agreement. Kyle, Troy and Mouse grab their money off the bar. They each throw a few bucks back on the bar for a tip. They put the rest in their pockets. The group starts walking toward the front door. Kyle is the last one in the group. Kyle turns and gives Glenn a head nod as if to say see you later.

Glenn, still playing and singing, nods back.

CHAPTER 22

A few days have passed and Kyle is back at work. He is on a plane on George row. He only has one more discrepancy to fix. He walks back to the crew galley. On the opposite side of the aisle, about head high, is a small cabinet. It's referred to as the cubby hole. Kyle opens the door and pulls out a large, heavy coffee can. He sets it on the galley. The can does not have a lid. All you can see is a dirty white rag that is bundled up at the top. He grabs the bundled rag and pulls it out of the can. It is loaded with an array of hardware and looks like a lumpy ball. He moves the can, sets the rag down and opens it. There are thousands of pieces with a variety of shapes and sizes. Kyle is looking for one special bolt. Kyle sifts through the hardware. He brushes it with his hand one way and then the other. He picks up various bolts and then throws them back into the pile. Finally he finds the one he is looking for.

"Bingo!" said Kyle.

Kyle walks up to the number one hatch. He pulls the hinged ladder away from the wall. It comes out about six inches and drops to the floor. The bolt that secures the ladder to the left upper hinge is missing. He replaces the bolt and tightens it with a ratchet. He stows the ladder and walks back to the galley.

Kyle lifts the corners of the rag and works all the hardware toward the middle. He puts the corners together, lifts the rag up and makes the ball of hardware. He sets it on top of the can but it will not fit inside. While holding the rag with one hand he lifts the can with the other and drops it on the galley counter. The weight of the hardware forces it down into the can. Kyle puts the can in the cubby hole and closes the door. Kyle walks over to the crew chief table, opens the forms and signs the discrepancy off. He grabs the radio off the table and heads downstairs.

A few minutes later Kyle is sitting on the wall taking a break. Sierra 6 pulls up beside him. "Hey man, what's going on out here?"

"Not much," said Kyle. "I'm knocking out a lot of little things."

Sierra 10 calls Art over the radio. "Sierra 6, Sierra 10."

Sierra 10 is the OMS control center. It is located in building 704.

Art answers. "Go ahead Sierra 10."

"Security Police just gave us a call," said Sierra 10. "Your dog is running wild in base housing and they need you to go catch him."

Kyle and Art start laughing.

Art replies to Sierra 10's message. "Roger that Sierra 10."

Art sets his radio down on the center console and turns towards Kyle. "That God damn dog! I got him a year ago and all of a sudden he's become a terror."

"What do you mean?" asked Kyle.

"Every chance he gets he jets out of the house and we spend hours chasing him down," said Art. "If we leave him in the back yard he either jumps the fence or digs under it."

"Is your wife at work?" asked Kyle.

"Yea," said Art. "She's tired of the shit and refuses to case after him anymore. That's why they are calling me. They probably called her first and she hung up on them or told them to just shoot him."

Kyle and Art laugh.

"He's probably old enough now to where he's getting horny," said Kyle. "That's probably why he's trying to escape all the time. I do the same thing but in a more civilized manner."

"Well I'm getting tired of this shit," said Art. "Astro is about to lose his balls! Let me go so I can take care of this."

Art pulls away and heads for building 585. A few second after Art pulls away a C-5 comes across the airfield from Kyle's right. It is flying very low and slow. The plane has its landing gear down and its flaps and slats are fully extended. It looks like it is going to land but it isn't lined up with one of the runways. This is not normal. Kyle grabs his radio off the wall and makes sure it is turned up. The plane flies past the control tower, power up its engines and starts to climb. It raises its flap from 100% to 40% but it leaves its landing gear down.

MOCC comes over the radio. "Sierra 6, MOCC.

Art answers the radio. "Go ahead MOCC."

"The tower called down," said MOCC. "They are having 7043 fly by the tower. They think the plane is missing several of its nose tires."

Art is supposed to be going home to catch his dog but now one of Sierra 6's planes has a potential emergency.

"Are they sure about that?" asked Art.

"The plane just did a fly by," said MOCC. "They are coming around to do another one."

Kyle looks out at the plane in the distance. It's circling around to fly by the tower again.

Art comes over the radio and sounds frustrated. "MOCC, that plane has been flying touch-and-go's all morning."

"Yea, we are listening to the conversation on the radio between the pilots and the tower," said MOCC. "The plane has already done 10 touch-and-go's. Also, we checked GO81. The nose tires were just changed in ISO."

"Roger that," said Art.

Kyle walks up and turns off the power to his plane. He knows if the plane has lost its tires Art will need him on the tow team. Kyle walks to the back of his plane and waits for 7043 to fly by again. He looks back down the line and a lot of people have stopped working and walked out to watch the plane come by.

The plane approaches again. The landing gear is still down and its flaps and slat are fully extended. The plane is flying very slowly about 300 feet off of the ground. It passes the tower, powers up its engines again and starts to climb out. The number one and number two nose landing gear tires are missing! The axle is completely red. It's covered in a fresh coat of grease. There is way more grease on the axle than needs to be.

MOCC comes over the radio again. "Sierra 6, MOCC."

"Go ahead MOCC," said Art.

"The tower called down and said the two nose tires on the left side of the nose landing gear are missing," said MOCC. "They also said it looks like the axle is glowing red hot."

Art just goes with it. He knows the axle is coated with a new layer of red grease but doesn't want to waste any more time explaining. "Copy MOCC. Two tires are missing and the axle is smoking red hot."

Kyle starts to laugh. "Sounds like Astro is going to have a little more time to play."

He turns and walks up to the front of the plane to wait on Sierra 6.

CHAPTER 23

---------May 1990----------

It's a nice sunny day. It's around four o'clock in the afternoon. Kyle, Bucky and Troy are out at the base's track for their annual physical fitness test. There are also about 100 fellow squadron members at the track. They are all standing around stretching at the start/finish line. Most are talking amongst themselves while they wait for the test to start. Everyone is in gym clothes or some sort of shorts. A few guys are wearing cut off blue jeans. Kyle is talking to a woman from another squadron that just finished jogging. Bucky and Troy are standing close to him. Bucky is smoking a cigarette. Troy is stretching.

"Bucky, are you sure smoking will help you make this run?" asked Troy.

"Can't hurt," said Bucky.

Troy points at Kyle. "Look at this guy. He'd try and pick up ass at a funeral."

Kyle finishes talking to the woman and walks over to Bucky and Troy.

The woman walks by the guys. Troy tries to be nice and speaks to her. "Hey, how are you doing?"

The female looks Troy up and down. "Roll your socks down before your head explodes."

All the guys start laughing as the woman walks away.

"What's her problem?" asked Troy. "What's wrong with my socks?"

"Look at them," said Bucky.

Troy's socks are white with red stripes at the top. They are pulled all the way up to his knees.

"They are all the way up to your knees," said Bucky.

"And they have stripes," said Kyle.

Troy looks pissed. "So! What's wrong with that? This is the way we wear them out on the island."

"Well, you all are fucked up out on the island," said Bucky. "That style went out in the late 70s."

"How can you be so close to New York City and so far behind the times?" asked Kyle.

"I don't like going into the city," said Troy. "Those people are animals."

"Well, maybe you should ride in there and look around once in a while," said Kyle. "It wouldn't hurt."

A guy in uniform, holding a bullhorn, starts to talk. He is at the start/finish line. "Ok, can I have everyone's attention please? Gather around here. We are ready to get started."

Everyone starts to move toward the guy with the bullhorn. They form a semicircle around him.

He continues. "Ok, this is your annual physical training test. You are expected to do six laps, or a mile and a half. You all have to complete this in 15 minutes or less. I'll keep the time on my stop watch. Everybody line up behind the line and good luck."

Everyone lines up on the track behind the start/finish line.

"On your mark, get set, go!"

Everybody takes off running. The younger people take off like rabbits and the older people begin at a more leisurely pace. Lap after lap the people are circling the track. They are all spread out after a few laps. After their sixth lap the fastest people begin to finish the test. One by one they turn off into the grass on the inside of the track.

At the finish line Kyle, Bucky and Troy come across together. They didn't try to set a record or impress anyone. They turn left into the grass in the middle of the track. All their keys and Bucky's smokes are on a bench just off the track. Bucky grabs his cigarettes and lights one up. They stand around, stretch and talk to each other for a few minutes.

"That wasn't too bad," said Troy.

"Piece of cake," said Bucky.

"I hate running for any distance," said Kyle.

"I thought you were in shape?" asked Bucky.

"Yea, for basketball or baseball or volleyball," said Kyle. "But those are stop and go sports. I can do them for hours. This distance thing is for the birds."

Bucky laughs. "I'm only use to running from the cops. That's how I stay in shape."

"Troy, speaking of running, you should to run to the mall and get you some new socks," said Kyle.

They all start laughing.

"Oh stop it," said Troy. "Listen to this. You have to hear what this guy at work did today."

"What?" said Kyle.

"Dan Wright was on a plane today. He was launching it out on a special mission going to the Middle East or somewhere," said Troy.

"Yea, we got that plane ready yesterday," said Kyle. "It was 217."

"That's one of the planes that are still grey and white right?" asked Bucky.

"Yea," said Troy. "I guess this female engineer was breaking his balls and writing up all kinds of stupid shit that really wasn't anything."

"Yea, that plane was good to go," said Kyle.

"So they finally get the plane taken care of," said Troy. "At this point Dan is pissed. He takes a can of tuna that was in his lunch, barley opens it and sticks it under the bunk in the second bunkroom."

"Are you serious?" asked Kyle.

Troy laughs. "Yea!"

"Wonder how long it will take them to figure out it's under there?" asked Bucky.

"Nice!" said Kyle. "The entire crew is going to think she stinks like fish."

"Once they land at their first destination the crew will run to the store and buy her a douche," said Troy.

Troy acts as if he is sticking a bottle up to his crotch and douching. They all laugh.

Troy points at a group of six guys walking up the track toward the finish line. "Holy shit, look at this!"

In the group are Graywolf and Andy. The group is all old timers, all over weight and all smoking cigarettes except for Graywolf. Graywolf has a big chew of tobacco in his mouth. They are all walking and talking to each other.

The guy with the bullhorn has been giving the current time of the test for the last minute, "14:59...14:59...14:59."

The six guys cross the finish line and stop.

"How'd we do?" asked Graywolf.

"Looks like 14:59 this year," said the test administrator. "You guys are good until next year."

Graywolf leans over and spits tobacco juice in the grass. "Outstanding!"

The six guys are happy. They walk away and continue to talk to each other.

"Those fat fucks have it made," said Bucky. "They never have to exercise and will always pass."

Troy laughs. "That will be you one day Bucky...you, Andy and Graywolf strolling around the track smoking cigarettes and chewing tobacco."

"The only place they'll be strolling together is to Tap Works for happy hour," said Kyle.

"You can't beat the four for one beer special they have," said Bucky.

Kyle, Bucky and Troy start walking toward the parking lot where Troy's car is parked.

"What are we eating tonight?" asked Bucky. "We deserve something special after passing this test."

"How about wings?" asked Troy.

CHAPTER 24

A few days later Kyle is headed into 585 for roll call. Art is walking across the street from building 704. He waves his hand to flag down Kyle. Kyle walks over and meets Art at the corner of building 585.

"How's it going man?" asked Art.

Kyle tries to head Art off before he gets started. "No, I didn't go out last night."

"I know," said Art. "I didn't see your car this morning."

"Am I in trouble or something?" asked Kyle.

"No man," said Art. "I need you to skip roll call and do me a favor."

"Sure, what's up?" asked Kyle.

"They just did a schedule change and an ASAP mission dropped down," said Art. "I've been trying to call the plane but they aren't answering. Jump in the truck and ride out there and see what is going on."

"What plane?" asked Kyle.

"6025 on Victor row," said Art. "Buckner and Boner are out there. Who knows what those guys are up to."

"Ok. Do you want me to stay out there and launch it?" asked Kyle.

"Yea," said Art. "I'll have Charlie and his team grab everything you guys need. Charlie already has a set of flying forms printed out. You can start pulling the sticks and looking the plane over. Have Buckner drive the truck back in."

"Got it," said Kyle.

"Ok, let me get in here and start roll call," said Art.

Art turns and heads into 585. Kyle walks over and gets into the Sierra 6 truck. He starts it, puts it in gear and starts to pull out. All of a sudden he stops. He remembers that he is on day shift and there is a large QA presence. All the flightline vehicles are supposed to be inspected at the beginning of each shift. Kyle opens the small drawer at the base of the center console and removes the trucks forms. The forms are kept in a small black folder. He opens the folder, initials and dates the Air Force Form 1800. The inspection is completed. He throws the folder back in the drawer and pulls away.

Three minutes later Kyle pulls up to Victor row. The power unit is running and everything looks normal.

Kyle says to himself. "I bet these guys are sound asleep."

Kyle cuts the truck off and slowly opens the door. He gets out and leaves the door slightly open. The noise made from closing it might alert Buckner and Boner. Kyle walks over to the stairs. The leg extensions on the ladder are slightly raised off of the ground. Kyle kneels down and quietly readjusts them so they are touching the ground. Kyle starts up the ladder step by step like a cat. In spite of the plane's size, noises and vibrations travel through it very well. Kyle makes it to the flight station door which is closed. With one hand on the door handle he uses the other hand to slowly push the door open. As the door folds open he steps into the flight deck. There is no one there. He stops for a second. He smells cigarette smoke.

Kyle walks quietly back towards the crew rest area. As he approaches he can see someone's boots. Their feet are propped up on the wall in front of the three man seat. He can also see legs under the crew chief table. He makes it all the way back to the crew rest area. Buckner is reclined in the three man seat. Boner is hunched over on the crew chief table. They are both asleep. Boner's head is lying on his left arm. In the fingers of his left hand is a lit cigarette. The cigarette has burned down about half way and has a long ash on the end of it. There are also four large TOs stacked on the table. Under them is a uniform shirt. Kyle slowly picks up one of the TOs. He holds it out in from of him about chest high and then drops it. It hits the floor with a bang! Buckner and Boner jump up. They are trying to figure out what is going on. Buckner sees Kyle standing there but he can't quite put it together yet. Boner is in the same state but he's trying to deal with the cigarette in his hand.

Kyle thinks it's funny. "What the fuck is going on out here boys?"

Buckner does not see the humor in it. "Chief, you scared the shit out of me!"

"You asshole!" said Boner. "What the fuck!"

"You are lucky I came up here first," said Kyle. "They've been trying to call you on the radio. This plane picked up a mission and a crew is on the way out."

Kyle walks back to the number two hatch, pulls it down and sets it on the three man seat in the courier compartment. He's trying to let the plane air out from all the cigarette smoke. He walks back to the table.

"Chief, the radio is right here," said Buckner. "I never heard them call."

Kyle is laughing. "You guys were out. You didn't even here me come up the ladder. And what is with the cigarette?"

"A guy showed me this trick the other day," said Boner. "You light a cigarette and put it deep in your fingers. Then you go to sleep. It takes about 20 minutes or so to burn down. When it starts to burn your fingers it wakes you up. It's like an alarm."

Kyle shakes his head. "Get the fuck out of here."

"According to the cigarette we were only asleep for 10 minutes," said Buckner.

Boner takes the TOs off of the shirt. The shirt is his. He holds it up and looks at the stripes on one sleeve and a squadron patch on a pocket. "Check it out. Good as new."

"Yea, that looks like a fine job," said Buckner.

"What did you do?" asked Kyle.

"I have to go see the Lt this morning," said Boner. "One of my stripes and a patch had come undone and was hanging off. I glued them back on with RTV and was using the TOs as a weight and an iron."

RTV is a multipurpose silicone use to repair and seal things on the plane.

"Looks good," said Kyle. "Maybe you should start a sweat shop in your dorm room. What do you have to see the Lt for?"

"I believe the Lt is getting promoted to Captain next month," said Buckner. "He wants Boner to RTV his bars on."

They all laugh.

"I think they need a body in CTK and he is going to ask me if I want to go there," said Boner.

"Chief, getting moved off the line is a disgrace," said Buckner. "Go into the office and tell the Lt hell no!"

"Yea, only fuck ups have those jobs," said Kyle. "You don't want that. All the action is out here on the line."

"Chief, I'm going in with you," said Buckner. "Rob is supposed to be waiting in there for us. He's going in also."

"You are lucky you are not in trouble and you don't have to be in your Blues," said Kyle.

"If that was the case I'd be screwed," said Boner. "Hell, I don't even know where they are."

"My Blues still have mosquito wings on them," said Buckner. "I haven't worn them since basic training and tech school."

"You could go room to room through the dorms and put together a decent set," said Kyle. "Your biggest worry would be the ribbons. Some guys stack their ribbon racks so they can take pictures of themselves and send them home to their moms and girlfriends."

"Yea chief, they might call you out on that Air Force Cross or Medal of Honor ribbon," said Buckner. "A crew chief only has two rows. Three if they're lucky."

"Doesn't it piss you off when you go into one of the offices around base and there is a desk jockey sitting there with four or five rows of ribbons and he's the same rank as you?" said Kyle.

"No shit," said Boner.

"Chief, you could save the world out here and the most they'd offer you would be a CTO…and you'd probably get called in for a piss test or something stupid on that day," said Buckner.

"No shit. Well grab your stuff," said Kyle. "The Sierra 6 truck is down stairs. Drive it in and give it to Art. He's waiting on it. I'm going to start pulling the fan sticks."

Buckner and Boner grab their bags and head for the flight deck. Kyle follows them. They turn and head down the ladder.

A few hours have passed. Charlie and his crew along with Kyle have gotten 6025 ready to fly its mission. Kyle is standing out at the centerline waiting for the aircrew to start engines.

Art drives up in the Sierra 6 truck. "Hey man, what was Buckner and Boner doing out here this morning?"

Kyle steps over next to the window. "Sleeping."

"I knew it," said Art. "Those fuckers are going to get caught one of these days."

Kyle shakes his head. "I don't think so. They had three modes of security set up. There was the ladder, the flight station door and a cigarette."

"Cigarette?" asked Art.

Kyle starts to laugh. "Yea, I've never seen this before. Boner had a lit cigarette between his fingers and was using it as a timer to wake him up."

"Get the hell out of here!" said Art.

"I'm serious," said Kyle. "He said it took 20 minutes to burn down and when he started feeling his fingers burn it would wake him up."

"There's something wrong with those grave shift guys," said Art.

Kyle agrees. "I know. I was on there for three years. I think the sleeping schedule has something to do with it. I don't think I ever got eight straight hours of sleep in all those years."

"I've been lucky and dodged grave shift my entire career," said Art.

"You are a perfect day shift tech sergeant," said Kyle. "You are a yes-man and you've already lost your spine. Sew on master sergeant, lose your brain and you'll be set."

Art laughs. "Screw you man. You know I can't take this shit. I'm going to get out the first chance I get. I'm going to move back to Montana, roll a big fat joint and fuck the world."

"Yea right," said Kyle. "Anyway, I like day shift. My body feels so much better and I can get more work done. I think when you are on graves for so long your body starts to deteriorate so slowly that you never notice it."

"Could be," said Art.

"Plus, I don't miss getting woken up in the middle of the day for all the stupid shit like room inspections and piss tests," said Kyle. "And if it's not that, I have Nader mowing grass outside my window and banging the lawn mower into the air conditioner."

"Hey man, did you hear what Caldwell did on grave shift last night?" asked Art.

"Let me guess…he got stuck up in the Calavar," said Kyle.

"No man," said Art. "He sent Bailey home last night to take a shower. I guess he smelled so bad at roll call it was making some of the guys gag. No one would stand by him."

"I don't doubt that. He lives in my hallway. Half the time he smells like a filthy bum. Hey, so how is Astro?" asked Kyle.

"Well you know I had his nuts cut off last week," said Art. "Now he won't even look at me when I walk into the room. He's lost all his spunk."

"Did your wife have the vet put his balls in a jar so she could set them next to yours on the mantle?" asked Kyle.

They both laugh.

"I run the show at my place," said Art.

"Yea right," said Kyle. "I bet when she goes to work you and Astro sit there and stare at your balls in those jars."

Art and Kyle both laugh.

"Hey man, speaking of my balls, my old lady is breaking them about me getting rid of some old furniture on our back porch," said Art. "Do you think Troy will let me use his pickup truck to haul some stuff to the dump?"

Kyle looks at Art like he's crazy. "Pickup truck…are you serious? Troy got rid of that thing a year ago. Where in the hell have you been?"

"I don't know man," said Art. "I'm not out in the parking lot every morning and every afternoon."

"You never heard what happened to Troy's pickup truck," asked Kyle.

"No," said Art.

"You can't be serious," said Kyle. "I thought everyone heard about that."

"No," said Art. "What's the big deal? What happened to his truck?"

Kyle pauses for a second to compose himself. He's nearly at the point of laughing. "Ok. So Troy was out behind the base four wheeling on the beach."

"Out on Route 9?" asked Art.

"Yea, somewhere out there," said Kyle. "He's with John out on the beach and they were ripping it up. At some point they get stuck and there is no one around. So they have to walk back to the base and get someone to drive out there and pull them out. They walk back to the base and it takes them over an hour. On top of that, by the time they find someone with a four wheel drive truck another hour has past."

"Who'd they find to pull them out?" asked Art.

"Billy McCoy," said Kyle. "So they get back out to the beach and the truck is nowhere to be found. They are scratching their heads but are fairly certain that they are in the right place. They are just about to head back to the base and call the police when Billy spots it."

"Where was it?" asked Art.

Kyle starts laughing. "It was right in front of them! The tide had come in and the truck was underwater! The nasty ass Delaware Bay swallowed it. All that was showing was the top of the cab."

"Are you shitting me?" asked Art.

"No!" said Kyle. "So Troy finds a little rinky-dink row boat and heads out there with Billy's winch cable. He has to jump in the water, go under and hook the cable to the bumper.

Art wants to laugh but he is too stunned. "Did they get it out?"

"Yea," said Kyle. "It took them about an hour but they managed to get it to dry land. Then they got it back to the base and Troy spent the next few days cleaning it up and getting it running.

"What did he do with it?" asked Art.

"He got rid of it, said Kyle. "He took it down to Winter Ford in town and traded it in."

"They took it?" asked Art.

"Yea," said Kyle. "They didn't know or couldn't tell that it was underwater. He didn't get the best deal but all he wanted to do was to get rid of it. And you want to hear the best part. We ran into the salesman a few weeks later at Loockman's. He recognized Troy and was bragging about the money the dealership made from the trade. He told us that the truck was such a steal that he turned around and bought it himself the next day. That's when Troy let him know that the truck had been submerged in saltwater for at least three hours. Some deal right?"

"Holy shit man!" said Art. "I can't believe I never heard about that. That's some crazy shit."

Art is stunned. There's a long pause while he digests the story. Then he changes gears. "Hey man, there's a rumor floating around the office that we are going on 12 hour shifts again."

Kyle pauses and looks at his watch to check the date. "That's odd. We are weeks away from Memorial Day. Usually they spring 12 hour shifts on us during the holidays."

They both laugh.

CHAPTER 25

----------June 1990----------

It's Saturday night. Kyle, Bucky and Troy are at Loockerman. The place is packed. They have found a spot at the upper bar, back in the corner by the windows. There are no bar stools but they are ok with standing. They have been there for three hours. They have been having their usual good time. Several women have stopped by. They've tried to get a phone number or two but haven't had any luck. Throughout the night several co-workers have stopped by to socialize and have a few drinks. They are in a festive mood and feeling no pain. They laugh at the good jokes and strongly criticize the bad ones.

They spot a group of friends that have left Loockerman and are out on State Street. Kyle climbs on to a chair next to the window and presses his butt against it, as if to tell the guys good night. He loses his balance and starts to fall. To his left is a table with two women. Kyle grabs the corner of the table to steady himself. As he lands on both feet he jars the table and knocks the women's drinks over. The women slide back quickly in their chairs and avoid getting any of the spilled drinks on their clothes. The two women get mad but Kyle quickly calms them down with another round of drinks.

Bucky and Troy are talking to each other. They are still drinking, laughing, and having a good time. Kyle eventually sits at the table where he knocked the drinks over and is talking to one of the women that is interested in him. Her friend doesn't like Kyle and is ready to leave. Kyle is trying to hook up but it is difficult due to the friend's disapproval. Kyle eventually gets the woman's phone number and the two leave. Kyle steps back over to the bar where Bucky and Troy are.

"Fill me up will you?" asked Kyle.

Bucky grabs the pitcher. "Sure."

He tops off Kyle's mug.

Troy watched the two women walk away. "Looks like you are going home solo tonight."

"I think I could have pulled that but her friend was cock blocking me," said Kyle.

"Yea, what was her problem?" asked Bucky. "I tried to talk to her earlier but she was acting like her pussy was lined with gold."

Troy smirks. "She probably keeps it in Fort Knox."

"Maybe that's where it's at right now and she didn't feel like driving down to get it tonight," said Kyle.

They all laugh.

"Who gives a fuck!" said Bucky. "We had a good night. Here's to the boys!"

They tap their mugs together.

Kyle looks at his watch. "It's about that time. I'm going to do a final lap and hit the bathroom."

Kyle takes a drink and sets his beer on the bar. Bucky and Troy turn and start talking to each other. Kyle turns left and heads off into the crowd. Kyle walks towards the front door. He gets to the opposite end of the bar and spots the woman that he saw at the swimming pool almost a year earlier. His heart starts racing. It's beating like a drum inside his chest. The woman is close to the front door and is talking to a group of her friends. Kyle freezes. He watches her for a few seconds then turns and hurries back to the guys.

"Holy shit!" said Kyle. "You aren't going to believe this!"

"What?" asked Bucky.

"Remember last summer when I saw that woman at the pool and went over to check her out?" asked Kyle.

"No," said Bucky.

Troy looks away and then it comes to him. "You mean the pregnant one?"

"Yea!" said Kyle.

"No, I don't remember," said Bucky.

"That's because you weren't there to see him get shot down," said Troy.

"I didn't get shot down," said Kyle. "Anyway, she's here!"

"Where?" asked Bucky.

"Over by the front door," said Kyle.

"Calm down boy," said Troy. "I've never seen you this nervous."

"Yea, I know," said Kyle. "What the fuck is going on?"

"Did you say something to her?" asked Bucky.

Kyle holds his hand out to see if it's shaking. "Not yet."

"You better hurry up before she splits," said Bucky. "It's almost closing time."

Troy laughs. "And try not to get shot down this time."

Kyle takes a big swig of his beer and sets it on the bar. He is unexpectedly rattled. "Alright, I'm going in."

Kyle takes off again towards the front door. Bucky and Troy start to talk again.

"Hope he does ok," said Bucky.

"He'll get shot down and be back here in no time. How are we getting home?" asked Troy.

"We'll call the hall phone," said Bucky. "Someone will answer."

Kyle is making his way through the crowd to where the woman is standing. She is talking with her friends and drinking a glass of red wine. Kyle waits until she stops talking and approaches her. It's loud, so when they talk they have to both lean in really close to hear each other.

"Hey…how are you?" asked Kyle.

The woman turns. "Good, how about you?"

"Not too bad," said Kyle. "I'm not sure if you remember me but we kind of met at the pool last summer. Well, at least we said hello to each other."

The woman pauses for a second and then it comes to her. She smiles. "Yea, I remember you."

Kyle extends his hand. "My name is Kyle."

She shakes it. "I'm Rylee."

Rylee Davenport is in her mid-20s. Rylee is from Virginia. She is tall, has long dark hair and is beautiful. She is in amazing shape for having two kids. She married at an early age and is now having issues. She is a free spirit knowing there is more out there and wanting to find it. She lacks adventure in her life. She loves music, art, and photography.

"I can't believe you remember me," said Kyle.

"Well you made it quite obvious that you were there to see me," said Rylee.

"Was it that bad?" asked Kyle.

"No, actually it was nice," said Rylee.

"I'm so surprised to see you tonight," said Kyle.

"Why's that?" asked Rylee.

"I thought I'd never see you again after that day at the pool," said Kyle.

Rylee is a little taken back by Kyle's interest in her. Kyle and Rylee keep talking as the lights slightly brighten, letting everybody know that Loockerman is closing soon. They are hitting it off really well. Bucky and Troy pass behind Rylee on their way out the door. Kyle spots them. They signal that they are going to call for a ride and pass on. Rylee notices Kyle looking at them.

"Are those your friends?" asked Rylee.

"Yea," said Kyle. "That's Bucky and Troy."

"Do you need to go? They aren't leaving you are they?" asked Rylee.

"No, they'll wait on me," said Kyle. "They saw me talking to you."

Kyle and Rylee continue talking. Their interest in each other is seemingly growing by the minute. People are exiting Loockerman but that doesn't break the connection that has started between Kyle and Rylee.

Bucky and Troy are standing at a pay phone about a half block from the front door of Loockerman. Bucky is using the phone and Troy is standing next to him. People who were in Loockerman are walking down the street. Some are in small groups and others are by themselves.

"Is there an answer?" asked Troy.

"If there was I'd be talking," said Bucky.

"Well hang up and try the upstairs phone in my dorm," said Troy. "There's always someone there in the dayroom."

Bucky hangs up the phone with his finger, gets the money out of the change slot and puts it in again. "What's the number?"

"2752," said Troy.

Bucky dials it. He waits and there is no answer again. He hangs up the phone.

"What!" said Troy. "No answer? Where the fuck is everyone at?"

"Who the hell knows? What's another number?" asked Bucky.

"Hold on…I believe 2750 is down stairs in 409," said Troy.

Bucky puts the money in and starts to dial. A total stranger walks up and wants to use the phone.

"How much longer are you guys going to be on the phone?" asked the stranger.

"Just a few more minutes," said Troy.

"Well hurry the fuck up!" said the stranger.

Bucky takes offense to what the stranger said and turns while still listening for someone to pick up on the other end. "Hey man, who do you think you are talking to?"

"Hey buddy, settle down," said Troy. "We'll be off here in a minute."

The stranger directs his attention towards Bucky. "I'm talking to you, you skinny fuck! Now get off the phone!"

"And what if I don't?" asked Bucky.

"Then we might have a problem," said the stranger.

Bucky hangs up the phone. "Might have a problem?! I believe we already do."

Bucky looks around and sees he is right next to an alley.

Troy tries to defuse the situation before it gets out of hand. "Hang on guys, what's the big deal?"

Bucky walks over towards the alley and the stranger follows him.

"Step over here and lets settle this," said Bucky.

They all move off the main sidewalk on Loockerman Street and into the alley. The stranger tries to put his hands on Bucky. Bucky slaps the stranger's hand down and slaps him across the face! The stranger is stunned. He steps back and regains his composure.

"Holy shit!" said Troy.

"That's your ass!" said the stranger.

The stranger comes at Bucky swinging wildly. Bucky remains in his boxer's stance and blocks a few attempt to hit him. Then he throws a straight right and knocks the stranger on his ass. Troy is nervously looking around to see if there are any cops or other people approaching. The stranger gets up and Bucky is right on him. Bucky throws a few more punches and knocks him back on his ass again.

Troy steps forward. "That's enough Bucky! He's had it!"

From the ground, the stranger picks up a trash can lid and throws it at Bucky. Bucky tries to move out of the way but it hits him on the leg. Though a little wobbly, the stranger jumps back to his feet.

"You fucking bitch!" said Bucky.

Bucky grabs the trash can lid and hits the stranger with it. The stranger blocks it with his arm. Bucky rears back again. "You're not man enough to use your hands! Here's you lid back!"

Bucky hits the stranger again with the lid. The stranger has had enough and takes off running down the alley towards the back of Smithers. Bucky starts chasing him with the lid in his hand. Every chance he gets, Bucky hits him on the back, shoulders and head.

Troy is stunned. "Holy shit!"

Troy pauses for a second. He doesn't know whether to stay with Bucky or go back for Kyle. Troy takes off running behind Bucky. He is watching Bucky and the stranger and looking around for cops. Bucky is relentlessly chasing the stranger and hitting him with the trash can lid. All of a sudden Troy changes his mind, stops and turns. Troy takes off running back towards Loockerman.

Inside Loockerman Kyle and Rylee are still talking to each other. They are still standing in the exact same place. They are having a great conversation and really enjoying each other's company. Troy comes down the street and enters Loockerman. He is in a hurry and in a bit of a panic. "Kyle, come on! We have to go!"

Kyle doesn't realize what is going on. "Hold on, give me a second."

"No really!" said Troy. "We need to go right now!"

"Is our ride here?" asked Kyle.

"No!" said Troy. "Bucky is at it again!"

Troy turns and walks out in a hurry. He heads back up the street. Kyle knows exactly what is going on outside. He turns back to Rylee.

"Shit! Listen, I have to go," said Kyle.

"What's going on?" asked Rylee.

"Oh nothing," said Kyle. "It was nice meeting you but I have to run."

Rylee doesn't know what to think. "Yes, nice to meet you also."

"Sorry..." said Kyle.

Kyle starts for the door. He is out on the street in a flash. He heads up the street in the direction Troy went. He has a bad feeling that he will never see Rylee again. Their second meeting was pure luck and now it's gone just like that. Rylee watches Kyle go out the door and disappear out of site. Surprisingly, she has the same feeling that Kyle did. Rylee turns and starts talking to her friends again.

Kyle walks up the street fast to get out of sight of the doorman. He sees Troy at the corner of the alley. Troy is waving him on. Kyle runs up to Troy. Now they are walking hurriedly down the alley.

"What the hell is going on?" asked Kyle.

"We were using the phone and this guy comes up and started shit with Bucky. So Bucky clocked him." Said Troy.

"Where the hell is Bucky now?" asked Kyle.

"The last time I saw him he was chasing the guy down the alley here and beating him across the head with a trash can lid," said Troy.

"What!" said Kyle. "Let's go find him!"

Kyle and Troy take off running. They must find Bucky. They get about 100 feet down the alley and they spot Bucky. He is walking back towards them smoking a cigarette. They run up to him."

"Are you ok?" asked Troy.

Bucky acts as if it's just another day at the office. "Yea, of course."

"What the hell happened?" asked Kyle.

"This guy was talking shit to me and Troy so I put him in his place," said Bucky.

Kyle looks around to see if anyone has caught on to what just happened. "Let's get out of here. Maybe someone called the cops."

The three cut through the bank parking lot behind Smithers. They pop out on Bradford Street. They look to their right and there's a taxi coming down the street. They flag it down and jump in. Kyle is in the front and Bucky and Troy are in the back.

"Where to?" asked the driver.

"The 7-11 across from the base," said Kyle.

Kyle turns and looks back at Bucky. They are all relieved that they are in the taxi and moving away from the area.

"So what happened?" asked Kyle.

"Like I said, the guy came up and started running his mouth and I slapped the shit out of him," said Bucky.

Troy is relieved and can laugh about the situation now. "You should have seen this shit. Bucky was chasing him down the alley bashing in his head with this garbage can lid. Bam-bam-bam! It was the funniest shit."

"What happened to the guy?" asked Kyle.

Bucky laughs. "He's probably still running."

"I was sure the cops were going to show up," said Troy. "We dodge a bullet there."

The taxi takes a left and heads down the street in front of Loockerman. It stops for the traffic light. There are a few cars ahead of it. Kyle spots Rylee walking out of Loockerman with her girlfriend. Kyle rolls the window down, climbs up and sits on the door. His feet are now on the seat. Bucky and Troy are trying to figure out what he is doing. Kyle knows the odds of another chance meeting are slim. He has to go for it and make it happen if he ever wants to see Rylee again. Kyle yells from the top of the cab. "Rylee, I want to see you again!"

Rylee is a little stunned, but in a good way. Kyle has reappeared and is yelling at her from a taxi. She's not quite sure how to explain Kyle to her girlfriend or what she will say. "Well I'm not sure about that."

The traffic light turns green and he cab starts to move. "Come on! I really want to see you again! Meet me at Tap Works next weekend. DMZ is playing!"

The cab pulls away and Rylee waves goodbye. Kyle waves back and slides into the cab. He is in a trance.

"You are one crazy bastard," said Troy.

CHAPTER 26

Its three days later and everybody is back at work. Kyle is on a plane by himself on Sierra row. He is in his coveralls as usual. Kyle is standing under the number one engine with a fan stick. He has taken a white oil absorbent pad, folded it and tied it on the end of a fan stick to create a giant "Q-tip". He is wiping down the oil and hydraulic fluid from the bottom of the engine cowlings. Art pulls up in the Sierra 6 truck and blows the horn. Kyle turns around, drops the stick and walks over to the truck.

"Hey man, can you walk over next door and see why these dumb asses can't get that cowling closed?" asked Art.

Art points next door to Romeo row. Kyle sees two crew chiefs on a B-5 stand. They are under number three engine.

"Sure," said Kyle.

"How's the jet look?" asked Art.

"Great now," said Kyle. "I've spent the last five hours tuning her up. I'm wiping down the last of the leaks. Hopefully this no-go 9th crew doesn't live up to their reputation. If they find something out here they've created it themselves. Let me check out this cowling."

Kyle walks over to the jet next door. There are two guys on top of the B-5 stand. The front rail and one of the side rails have been removed. The stand is centered perfectly under the engine with its ladder facing aft. The guys are trying to close the engine cowling but their technique is wrong. They are trying to use their arms only. Kyle also notices that they aren't putting too much effort into it. Kyle yells to get their attention and waves them down. When they get off the stand Kyle spots the patches on their uniforms. They are reservists. They are there because they missed a drill weekend and are making up the time.

"What seems to be the problem?" asked Kyle.

"It won't close," said one of the reservists.

"You guys are going at this all wrong," said Kyle. "With these older planes, the cowlings can be a little stubborn. Give me that breaker bar."

The reservist hands the breaker bar to Kyle. Kyle starts climbing up the B-5 stand.

"Do you need a hand?" asked the other reservist.

Kyle looks down. "No, I got it."

Prior to getting to the top of the ladder Kyle stops and throws the breaker bar on the platform of the stand. While balancing himself he aligns both sides of the aft cowling with his hands and gives them a good hit with his palms. They don't move much but they are straight. He then crawls up, lies on his back and pulls his knees to his chest. With his feet up above him Kyle kicks each side of the cowlings with the soles of his boots. The cowling closes a little. He then gives the cowlings a second kick and the cowlings close a little more. With the soles of his boots pressing against the cowling he grabs the breaker bar. He reaches up and inserts the breaker bar into the lock, turns it 180° and locks the aft lock. He sits up, hangs his legs over the side of the stand and starts to lock the remaining five locks. While he's doing this, he slides sideways to get to each of the locks. Once all six locks are locked he takes the breaker bar and slaps the two cowling latches closed. He slides sideways back to the ladder and climbs down. Kyle hands the breaker bar to the reservist that gave it to him.

"You just needed to put a little ass behind it," said Kyle. "On the tougher one that you can't close with your legs, turn the B-5 sideways and bang the side of the cowling with a chalk. It works every time."

"Thanks!" said the reservist.

Kyle spots a fleet service truck pulling up to the plane. He sees Big Leroy inside it. Kyle's first thought is to get back at him for messing up the plane's flight deck months ago. Kyle walks quickly over to the crew entry door ladder and heads up stairs. He runs up the ladder all the way to the flight station and runs back to the crew latrine. He pops open a panel at the base of the latrine which exposes the latrine drain handle. He pulls the handle out, counts to five and pushes it back in. This fills the latrine drain tube with several gallons of nasty waste water.

Kyle says to himself. "That will teach you a lesson."

Kyle closes the panel, runs back to the flight deck and heads down the stairs. He hustles down the ladder, hits the last few steps and jumps to the ground. He turns and calmly walks towards the Sierra 6 truck which is still parked in front of his plane. As he is walking back, Big Leroy is marshaling the fleet service truck backwards between the nose of the plane and the power unit. Big Leroy is positioning the truck at the plane's forward latrine servicing port. Kyle jumps in the passenger seat of the Sierra 6 truck.

"Did you get it closed?" asked Art.

"Yea, it just needed a little kick," said Kyle. "Hey, pull out in front of that plane. This fat son of a bitch dripped shit all over my flight deck one night and didn't give a shit about it. Now, it's payback time."

Kyle looks to his right. "You're clear."

Art pulls out in front of the plane on Romeo row and swings the truck around. They are parked between the centerline and the wall, giving them a good view of the plane, the fleet servicing truck and Big Leroy.

"What did you do?" asked Art.

"Watch this shit!" said Kyle.

The fleet service truck is parked right next to the plane. Big Leroy takes the hose off of the fleet service truck and pulls it back to the latrine servicing port. He sets it on the ground. He opens the panel and then unlatches the cover to the servicing tube. There are at least five gallons of waste water in the tube. It blasts out like a fire hose. He has no time to react. The waste water douses Big Leroy from his waist down and a lot of it ends up inside his knee high rubber boots. Big Leroy stands there in disbelief as the blue colored water spreads across the ground.

Kyle points! Kyle and Art are both laughing.

"Holy shit!" said Art.

"Yea! Take that you fat sack of shit! Fuck with me again!" said Kyle.

Art shakes his head. "That poor bastard is going to stink for a week."

"I'm guessing he smells like that every day," said Kyle. "Get out of here before he realizes we did it."

"We?" asked Art.

"Yea we," said Kyle. "I thought we were a team. Drop me off so I can finish wiping down those cowlings."

Art throws the truck in drive and they pull away slowly. The truck pulls down the centerline and heads towards Kyle's plane.

About 30 minutes later Kyle is leaning on the fire bottle at the nose of his plane. He has readied the plane for launch and is waiting for a crew. His radio is propped up on the fire bottle so he can hear it. Next door on Romeo row the fire department has brought one of their trucks to wash away the waste water that spilled on the ground. Sierra 6 pulls up and parks next to the fire bottle. Troy is in the passenger seat.

"Hey man, anything going on yet?" asked Art.

"Nope," said Kyle. "I'm still waiting on this crew. They're late aren't they?"

Art looks at his watch. "Yea, looks like it. Did you get something to eat?"

"Yea, I went to your house for brunch," said Kyle.

"Did you mow the grass?" asked Art.

"No but I washed the dishes you left in the sink this morning," said Kyle.

They all laugh.

"Art, Troy, check this out," said Kyle. "Look at what someone wrote about Art on the fire bottle."

Art puts the truck in park and gets out. Troy gets out of the other side and comes around. Art shakes his legs around and readjusts himself.

"I'm sweating my nuts off in there," said Art.

"That's because you sit on your ass all day," said Troy.

"You have a case of relative humidity," said Kyle.

"Relative humidity?" asked Art.

Kyle starts to laugh. "Yea. That's the sweat that forms on your balls while you are having sex with your cousin."

They all laugh. Art and Troy look at the fire bottle. There is a picture of a man having sex with a goat. The caption under it reads Art Humm Blows Goats!"

"Did you do that?" asked Art.

"No! I'm no artist," said Kyle.

"It bears a striking resemblance," said Troy.

"To me?" asked Art.

"No! That old goat I saw you with at the Brown Fox the other night," said Troy.

They all laugh.

Art pulls out his pencil and above the drawing writes the letters FTW.

"I'll call MOCC and see if I can find out anything about the crew," said Art.

"Ok," said Kyle.

"Troy, are you going to stay out here and give Kyle a hand?" asked Art.

"Yea, yea," said Troy.

Art gets back in the truck and pulls away.

"Anything happening?" asked Kyle.

"No," said Troy. "I was sitting on my ass in the break room and I heard someone say clean up so I jumped in the truck with Art. He said you were out here on your own so I told him I'd keep you company."

"Good," said Kyle. "You can help me chase this crew around and keep them from breaking the plane."

Kyle pulls a pencil out of his pocket. He puts the finishing touches on the picture on top of the fire bottle. Troy walks into the nose gear and starts looking at the plane. Sierra 4 pulls up and stops in the parking area on the left side of the plane. Robert Leo is driving. He has the FCC for the mission in the truck with him. It's Russ Hamlet. Kyle's first roommate at Dover was Russ. Kyle walks up to the driver's side window of the Sierra 4 truck.

"Sergeant Leo, how's things today? Russ, I haven't seen you in a while," said Kyle.

Robert Leo is looking over at the plane on Romeo row. The fire truck is still spraying down the mess that Big Leroy made.

"What the hell is going on over there?" asked Robert Leo. "There's a fire truck on my flightline and I don't know about it!"

"It's nothing," said Kyle. "The fleet service guy dumped the latrine on the ground and the fire department is wrangling turds."

"Those stupid son of a bitches!" said Robert Leo. "Give Russ a hand unloading his stuff."

Russ gets out of the truck and walks to the back. Kyle meets him at the tailgate of the truck and they shake hands. Russ drops the tailgate and they start unloading Russ' luggage and tool box.

"Kyle, how have you been?" asked Russ.

"Not bad," said Kyle. "How long has it been since we've seen each other?"

"Since you moved over into 408," said Russ.

"Yea, that's been a while," said Kyle.

"I've been flying my ass off," said Russ. "Hey, what ever happened to that girl you was seeing? She was beautiful."

"You mean the one from Alabama?" asked Kyle.

"Yea, the Miss Alabama contestant," said Russ. "She was hot!"

They unload everything. Kyle closes the tailgate and slaps the side of the truck a few times to let Robert Leo know they are unloaded. Robert Leo looks in the rear view mirror and pulls away towards the fire truck.

"Well you knew she was living in DC," said Kyle.

"Yea, with some guy that had a lot of money right?" asked Russ.

"Yea, I think he had a pretty good job," said Kyle. "Well, she calls me one day and asks if I'll come over to DC to see her. I said sure. So I drove over to Georgetown to meet her one night. It turns out that the guy asked her to marry him and the wedding was the next day."

"No way," said Russ.

"Yea. So, he was at his bachelor party that night and she was out with me," said Kyle.

"Did you know she was getting married before you went over there?" asked Russ.

"No," said Kyle. "It only gets better. They both had all their families up there. His people were in from wherever and hers were in from Alabama. Then she tells me that she'll call the whole thing off if I'll take her back."

"What?" said Russ.

"Yea. I thought about it for a while and couldn't do it," said Kyle.

"So what did you do?" asked Russ.

Kyle shrugs his shoulders. "I wished her good luck and she left. I walked over to the Paul Mall and had a beer. After that I drove back here."

"So did everything work out?" asked Russ.

"Yea. I met this waitress in the Paul Mall," said Kyle.

Russ laughs. "No, the marriage."

"I heard he got tangled up in cocaine and lost everything," said Kyle. "Not sure what happened to her."

"How's the plane look?" asked Russ.

"Great! I've been out here all morning on it," said Kyle.

"Give me a hand with this stuff ok?" asked Russ.

"Sure," said Kyle.

Kyle and Russ grab Russ' bags and tool box and head to the ladder. Troy sees them and heads over to lend a hand. They meet at the ladder and start carrying Russ' things into the cargo compartment. The aircrew bus finally pulls up. The crew gets off the bus and starts unloading their luggage. They take it from the back of the bus towards the plane leaving it in a pile at the base of the ladder. Kyle, Troy and Russ get all of Russ' things into the cargo compartment. Kyle and Troy come back down and walk out to the fire bottle. Russ continues up to the flight deck to look at the aircraft forms. The crew finishes getting their stuff off the bus and over to the ladder.

The senior pilot comes over to the fire bottle where Kyle and Troy are standing. "How does it look?"

"Like a champ!" said Kyle. "I'd get on it. The forms are upstairs. Let me know if you need anything."

The pilot gives the guys a thumbs-up. "Thanks!"

The pilot walks over to the ladder and heads upstairs with the rest of the crew.

Kyle and Troy are kneeling at their tool box. They inventory their tools, lock the box and walk over to the fire bottle. For the past two hours they've been running around fixing the most insignificant things the aircrew could ever find.

"Can you believe all the piddly shit these guys write up?" asked Troy.

"Yea, some aircrews never want to fly," said Kyle. "If they are flying to a location where the per diem is low it's almost impossible to get them off the ground. I hope they leave though. That means all their wives will be out partying tonight."

Troy starts to laugh. "Yea, they are probably all lined up behind the BX at the end of the runway looking for the tail number and wheels up."

They both laugh.

"So you really filled the shitter tube next door and all that piss water dumped on the fleet service guy?" asked Troy.

Kyle smiles. "Yea, Art saw the whole thing."

Kyle and Troy are interrupted by a very young pilot from the crew. "Excuse me. I was wondering if you can give me a hand loading our bags?"

"I don't think so," said Troy.

Kyle agrees with Troy. "Yea, we are a little busy."

"We are running late and I need you to help me!" said the young pilot.

Kyle senses a confrontation but keeps his cool. "That's not our fault and those aren't our bags, sir."

The young pilot starts to get heated. "Well I'm an officer and I'm telling you to help me!"

Troy gets pissed and is about to lose it. "Is that so?"

Kyle steps in. "Well sir, my commander is a full bird colonel and he doesn't want us doing your job for you."

"Who's in charge out here?" asked the young pilot. "I want to speak with him right now!"

Kyle picks the radio up from the fire bottle. "As you wish...sir."

The young pilot walks back to the ladder and starts to carry the bags up one by one.

Kyle looks around and sees that Sierra 4 is sitting out in front of his plane. "Sierra 4, can you swing up to the plane in front of you? One of the crew members would like to have a word with you."

"On the way," said Sierra 4.

The Sierra 4 truck pulls up immediately and parks. Kyle walks over and meets the truck.

"What going on?" asked Robert Leo.

Kyle points. "The young pilot over there wanted us to help him load his crew's bags. I told him no."

Robert Leo looks over. Now there are three crew members handing bags up the ladder to each other.

"That's not your God damn job!" said Robert Leo. "Did you ask him to help you fix the God damn plane? Hell no! Which one is he?"

"The guy at the bottom of the ladder," said Kyle.

Kyle steps back as Robert Leo gets out of the truck and walks over to the young pilot. Kyle walks back over to Troy who is still at the fire bottle.

"This should be good," said Kyle. "Robert Leo is fired up."

Kyle and Troy position themselves on the fire bottle so they can watch the show. Robert Leo gets the young pilot's attention and they step away from the bottom of the ladder. Kyle and Troy are trying to hear what they are saying but there is too much outside noise. The conversation seems to getting heated. Robert Leo takes over the conversation and is pointing at the young pilot, the crew bags, the plane, his watch, his stripes and Kyle and Troy. He is really in the young pilot's face. Finally Robert Leo walks away and the young pilot grabs the last bag off the ground and heads upstairs. Robert Leo walks over to Kyle and Troy.

"Fucking college boy!" said Robert Leo.

"What did you say to him?" asked Kyle.

"I told him to get his bags and his ass on my plane and fly it the fuck out of here," said Robert Leo.

"You are the man sergeant Leo!" said Troy.

Robert Leo winks at Kyle and Troy. "You God damn straight. I eat a lieutenant for breakfast every morning."

Robert Leo walks back to his truck.

Kyle thinks for a second. "Fuck that pilot. Let's get his ass."

"What do you want to do?" asked Troy.

"Did you catch the name on his patch?" asked Kyle.

"Yea, something Ski," said Troy.

Kyle and Troy walk over to the tool box. Kyle opens the box and removes a spool of safety wire and the safety wire pliers. Kyle closes the box and they head upstairs.

The plane is almost completely full. The crew has stacked their bags in a row and tied them down with a cargo strap. Kyle and Troy start looking at the name tags on the bags. They are searching for a last name that ends with Ski.

"Here it is!" said Troy. "Lt Kopchenski."

"Loosen the strap and pull it out…and hurry!" said Kyle.

Kyle walks over and removes three large chains from the side wall. Each chain weighs around 15 pounds. He carries the chains over to the row of bags. Troy loosens the cargo strap and pulls out Lt Kopchencki's bag. He drops it on the floor, unzips and opens the bag. They are both nervous and looking around. Kyle drops the three heavy chains inside the bag and Troy quickly closes it and zips it back up. Kyle takes the safety wire and cuts a piece. Kyle safety wires the two zippers together. He does it again in another place where two zippers meet. He flips the bag and looks for more places where the bag can be opened. All of a sudden someone comes down the stairs from the flight deck. Kyle and Troy are busted. They look up and it's Russ. They are relieved. He comes down to where they are.

"Holy shit!" said Troy. "You scared the crap out of us."

"What are you guys doing?" asked Russ.

Kyle looks up from safety wiring zippers. "We are leaving that young pilot a gift."

"What did you put in there?" asked Russ.

"Three large tie-down chains," said Troy. "Kyle, hurry the fuck up!"

Russ gets a smile on his face. "Nice. He won't figure this out until he is at billeting in Germany."

Kyle finishes and stands. Troy grabs the bag, returns it to its place in the row and straps it down.

"Don't bring anything to billeting with you to help him out," said Kyle.

"Oh I won't," said Russ. "That guy is a prick. I've flown with him before. He thinks he's Top Gun or something to that effect."

Kyle laughs. "Did you tell him to come down here in the cargo compartment and look around? All he's doing is delivering toilet paper."

"Did you safety wire them nice and tight?" asked Russ.

"Oh yea!" said Kyle. "I bet 100 QA inspectors couldn't find any wrong with this work. He'll have to cut into the bag to get to his clothes."

"That's if he can even carry it to his room," said Troy. "That thing weighs 70 or 80 pounds now."

"They are getting ready to start engines in a few minutes. Let's get downstairs," said Russ.

They all take off down the ladder.

CHAPTER 27

A few days have passed and it's the weekend again. Kyle, Bucky and Troy are standing in front of the liquor store a few doors down from Tap Works. They all have a 16 ounce beer can in their hands. The beer cans are in small paper bags. They are having one before going into Tap Works. They are also waiting for Mouse, Higa and Nader. Tonight is the night that DMZ is playing and also the night that Kyle is supposed to meet Rylee, if she shows up.

"This reminds me of New York City," said Kyle.

"How is that?" asked Troy.

Kyle holds up his beer. "You can stand around and drink on the streets as long as it is covered up."

"Has anyone seen Nader today?" asked Troy.

"No," said Kyle.

"He's been hanging out in the cop's dorm a lot," said Bucky.

"I saw him yesterday and he said he would be out here," said Troy.

"Reese is supposed to bring Mouse and Higa out," said Bucky.

"Yea, when are they showing up?" asked Troy.

Bucky takes a drink of his beer. "They'll be here."

"Why doesn't Reese ever come out?" asked Kyle.

"He doesn't drink," said Bucky.

"Every time he comes in the room you offer him a beer and he takes it," said Kyle.

"Yea, but have you ever noticed that he doesn't drink it," said Bucky. "He just holds it."

Kyle shakes his head in disbelief. "No way. I'll have to check it out next time he comes by."

"I bet that guy has a ton of money saved," said Troy. "He doesn't even own a car."

"No, since he's the only one in the dorms that doesn't drink, everyone lets him use their car in exchange for rides to and from the bars," said Bucky.

"Does he have a girl friend?" asked Kyle.

"Not that I know of," said Bucky.

Kyle laughs. "Troy, maybe you should marry him. You can get all of his money."

"Oh stop it," said Troy.

A few women walk by. They are heading for Tap Works. They are dressed kind of freaky.

Bucky greets them. "Ladies, good evening."

They say hello back. Kyle and one of the women make eye contact.

"Hey Mansfield, how's your sister?" asked one of the girls.

"Hey Martha!" said Kyle. "She's getting bigger."

The girl winks at Kyle and the group keeps moving toward Tap Works.

"Holy shit boy, who is that?" asked Troy. "And what's this about your sister? You don't have a sister!"

"She's the lead singer's sister." said Kyle. "And my sister refers to my dick. We used to go out a while back."

"She's hot! What happened?" asked Troy.

"She'd never let me stay at her place when we woke up the next morning," said Kyle. "She'd always kick me out. I'd have to drive back to the base all hung over and early in the morning."

"That must have sucked," said Bucky.

"Like you couldn't believe," said Kyle. "And I never had my sunglasses with me. Are you guys about ready to walk over?"

Bucky and Troy shake their beers.

"Yea, just a few more swigs," said Troy. "Those guys can meet us inside."

"I'll be done by the time we get to the door," said Bucky.

Kyle, Bucky and Troy walk over to the front door of Tap Works. There are a few people in line ahead of them.

"So you found out about this band from the lead singer's sister?" asked Troy.

"That and the fact that DMZ is spray painted all over Dover," said Kyle.

"You've never seen it anywhere?" asked Bucky.

Troy thinks for a second. "Yea! This is those guys?"

Kyle nods. "Yea. It should be real good."

"So boy, do you think Rylee is going to show up?" asked Troy.

"Who knows?" said Kyle.

"What's this girl look like?" asked Bucky. "I've never really gotten a good look at her."

Kyle starts to drift off as he explains her. "Tall, long black hair, bangs, and beautiful."

"I hope she shows," said Bucky.

"I hope she guns you down like all the other bitches do," said Troy.

They all laugh.

They all pay a cover charge to the doorman and enter the bar.

Once you enter the front door of Tap Works the bar is directly in front of you. It's rectangular in shape and runs almost all the way to the back wall. It's completely circled with bar stools. To the left of the bar there is a small area with tables and chairs. This area and the bar take up half the space. To the right of the bar is a larger seating area. In front of this area and against the back wall is the stage. In the back of the bar there is a wide hallway. It's about 12 feet long. The door to the men's bathroom is on left and the door for the women's bathroom is on the right. There is an emergency exit at the end of the hallway. Also, there is a pay phone on the right wall next to the exit. Usually it's too loud inside of Tap Works to use it.

Kyle, Bucky and Troy enter and head for the right side of the bar. Bucky and Troy look around to see who they know. Kyle keeps looking straight ahead so it doesn't seem like he is looking for Rylee...if she is even there. They spot Nader midway down the bar. They all walk toward him. Little by little Kyle starts scanning the crowd.

"Nader, what's happening?" asked Bucky.

"Where have you been all day?" asked Troy. "I went by your room at least three times."

"After work I came straight here," said Nader. "I got some bad news today."

"You've been drinking since three o'clock?" asked Troy.

"Well more like five," said Nader.

"You are probably shit faced by now, especially after the four for one happy hour," said Kyle.

Nader smiles. "Yea, I'm feeling pretty good. But who cares. Fuck it!"

"What happened?" asked Troy.

"Don't tell me you tried the onion thing and it backfired," said Kyle.

"No. I'm back on bay orderly for a month with no days off," said Nader.

"What did you do this time?" asked Bucky.

Nader starts to explain. "Well I was getting pissed off at work and pissed off at Graywolf for fucking with me so much. So I started punching holes in the walls of the dayrooms."

"What? I never saw any holes in the walls," said Troy.

"In which dorm?" asked Bucky.

Nader continues. "Mostly in our building. The first time I did it I panicked and didn't know what to do so I just moved a picture to cover the hole. No one noticed so I said what the hell. After that, I would punch the wall whenever I got pissed off."

"Holy shit!" said Troy.

Nader has more to add. "Yea, remember when I broke my hand?"

"Yea, you were playing football." said Troy.

"No, I did it punching a wall," said Nader.

Troy is blown away. "You've got to be shitting me."

"Who caught you?" asked Bucky.

"Graywolf!" said Nader. "That fat son of a bitch! When he retires next year he better get the hell out of town."

"How did he know it was you?" asked Kyle.

"Who else would it have been?" asked Nader. "Here, let me buy you guys a beer."

Troy laughs. "Yea, we'll toast to the squadron having the best looking dorms thanks to you Nader."

"Yea I know. I've painted them enough," said Nader.

Nader buys everyone a round of drinks. The barkeep brings a pitcher and three mugs. Bucky and Troy continue to talk to Nader. Kyle scouts around a little more to see if he can spot Rylee. The beers show up. Nader fills the mugs and hands them to the guys.

"Here you go guys," said Nader.

"Thanks Nader!" said Bucky.

"Yea, thanks!" said Troy.

Kyle holds up his mug. "Here's to you fucking up Graywolf in a year."

They all toast and drink.

Troy also isn't fond of Graywolf. "I'd like to get in on some of that action."

Just then Mouse and Higa show up. They've already been drinking in the dorms and are feeling pretty good.

"You guys started drinking without us?" asked Mouse.

Kyle, Bucky, Troy and Nader all greet Mouse and Higa.

"Mouse, Higa, what do you want to drink? I'm buying!" said Nader.

"A beer is good." said Mouse.

Bucky offers Higa a drink. "Higa, what do you want, some Sake?"

Higa is wide eyed. "Holy shit Bucky! I can't believe it. You finally got it right."

Nader orders another pitcher and tells the barkeep to give him a few more glasses.

"Got what right?" asked Bucky.

"That I'm Japanese," said Higa.

"I know man," said Bucky. "You know I've been fucking with you all this time."

"Yea I know," said Higa.

"But I'm still pissed at you for Pearl Harbor," said Bucky.

"Ok, I'll take that," said Higa.

Kyle, still scanning the crowd, sees Rylee. She is at a table on the right side of the bar. The table sits back away from the stage and closer to the front side of Tap Works. She is with two other women. Kyle turns before she sees him looking.

Kyle leans into the group of guys. "It's going to be a good night boys!"

"What, is she here?" asked Troy.

Kyle has a new burst of energy. "Yea."

Troy starts to look around. "Where?"

Kyle smacks Troy on the arm. "Don't be so obvious. She's at a table towards the back of the crowd. See her?"

"Oh…yea. Well boy, what are you going to do?" asked Troy.

"I'm going in. Who wants to do a shot?" asked Kyle.

All the guys agree.

Kyle leans in to the bar and signals to the barkeep. "Six shots of tequila!"

Bucky heard what Kyle ordered. "That's what I'm talking about!"

Troy also heard. "Oh my God!"

Mouse pats Troy on his back. "Come on Troy, you only live once."

"Make it five shots of tequilas and one shot of Sake," said Bucky.

They all laugh.

"If I do this you guys are going to be carrying me home," said Higa.

Mouse agrees. "Yea, just get five. Higa is already at his two beer limit."

"Don't worry, the base is right there," said Nader. "We'll walk to the north gate and jump the fence there."

Kyle still doesn't understand Nader. "Nader, you are fucked up."

"No, it's cool," said Nader. "I do it all the time."

"I'm not walking back," said Mouse. "Reese will give us a ride."

"All of us?" asked Nader.

"Yea, what else does he have to do? He'll make two trips," said Mouse.

The barkeep pours the shots. Kyle signals for only five and the barkeep doesn't fill the last glass. The barkeep also puts down salt and lime. Everyone preps their shot.

Bucky mimics Mickey Rourke giving a toast in the movie *Barfly*. "To all my friends!"

All the guys bang glasses together and do their shot, except for Higa, who is pretty much gone. They all slam their glasses down and have different reactions to the shots.

"That shit is nasty," said Troy. "We should have done a lemon drop."

"Come on boy," said Kyle. "That will grow some hair on your nuts."

Troy laughs. "And take it off my head."

"Troy, let's see who can bag the fattest chick tonight," said Mouse. "I feel like hogging."

"Not yet boy," said Troy. "Let me get my beer goggles going."

The band starts into their first song. All the guys turn to watch. Kyle turns slowly and looks over at the table where Rylee is sitting. At the same time, Rylee has spotted Kyle and is looking over at him. They both see each other. Rylee smiles and Kyle smiles back. Bucky was watching the whole thing. Kyle turns back nonchalantly.

"Is that her?" asked Bucky.

"Yea," said Kyle.

"She's bad ass," said Bucky.

"I know," said Kyle. "I've been thinking about her all week."

Kyle, with his beer in his hand, walks around back of the crowd and approaches Rylee's table from behind. He pulls up an empty chair from another table and sits down next to Rylee. Rylee turns and they greet each other. They are talking into each other's ears because the music is so loud. When Kyle leans in to talk he looks as if he is going to kiss Rylee and at the last second he veers away to her ear. They are both happy to be together. It appears that Kyle wasn't the only one with something on his mine all week.

One of Rylee's friends across the table from her turns and sees Kyle and Rylee talking. She gives Rylee a look as if to say "who the hell is this guy." Her other friend doesn't notice because she is facing the band. Rylee gives her friend an "it's all good" look and the friend turns her attention back to the band. Kyle and Rylee continue talking as the band plays.

The band plays amazing combinations of rock and punk songs throughout the night. All the guys talk, joke around and drink.

Sometimes Kyle is with them and other times he is with Rylee. Friends from work stop by and join the party. Occasionally a woman stops by but she is quickly offended by one of the drunken guys and leaves. Kyle and Rylee continue to visit. As the night goes on they appear to be getting closer and closer.

Later in the night Kyle gets up from the table and returns to the bar with the guys. They are all having a great time and are much drunker than before.

"Troy, what's going on over here?" asked Kyle. "Looks like Mouse found a big one."

Mouse has moved to the other side of the bar. He is talking to a really fat woman.

Troy laughs. "Yea, two tons of fun!"

"He better tie a two by four across his ass if he takes her home," said Kyle.

"And maybe carry a flare pistol in case the two by four snaps and he falls in," said Troy.

They both laugh.

"Where is your girl?" asked Kyle.

Troy snickers. "I sent her home early to take a shower. She smelled like oats and sour milk."

They start laughing. A guy behind Bucky bumps into him.

"This asshole behind me," said Bucky.

"What, the guy with the hat?" asked Kyle.

"Yea," said Bucky. "Earlier he wouldn't leave me alone. He wanted to talk to me as if we were best buddies but he's just some fucked up local drunk. So I warned him to leave me alone and told him to fuck off and now he keeps bumping into me."

Kyle blows it off as nothing. "He's probably so drunk he doesn't realize what he's doing."

"One more time and I'm going to slap his ass off that bar stool," said Bucky.

"Be cool man," said Kyle. "We don't need to get kicked out of here tonight."

Rylee, on her way to the bathroom, walks past the group. She makes eye contact with Kyle. It's a few seconds frozen in time.

Bucky and Troy catch the look. Rylee passes and continues to the bathroom.

"Holy shit! Did you see that look?" asked Bucky.

Kyle is off in another world. "Yea."

Troy also saw it. "Damn boy! I think you might be in."

"Yea...I'll be back in a minute," said Kyle. "I'm going to take a piss."

Kyle walks off towards the bathrooms. Bucky and Troy turn back to the guys and continue talking as the band plays and the beers flow. Kyle walks into the small back hallway of the building where the bathrooms are. He is standing against the wall next to the men's bathroom. He is scoping out the situation and waiting for Rylee to come out of the bathroom.

Back at the bar the local guy sitting behind Bucky elbows him in the back. It is so obvious that Troy and Nader notice it.

"What the hell?" asked Troy.

"Did you see that?" asked Nader.

Bucky turns to the guy. "What's your problem asshole?"

"What are you talking about?" said the local guy.

"You've been bumping into me and elbowing me all night," said Bucky. "If you have a problem we can solve this real quick."

"I don't like you fly boys," said the local guy. "You better watch yourself son or I'll teach you a lesson."

Bucky steps closer. The guy has two friends and now they are paying attention.

"Son?" asked Bucky. "Let's step outside."

Bucky steps back and gives the guy room to get up. The guy heads for the door with his two friends.

"What the hell is going on?" asked Troy.

Bucky takes a drink of his beer. "I'm heading outside to whip this guy's ass."

"Holy shit!" said Troy.

"Let's go!" said Nader.

Bucky heads towards the door with Nader right behind him. Higa is in a daze and too drunk to realize what is going on. He is way past his limit. Troy looks around for Kyle and doesn't see him. He takes off back towards the bathrooms to see if he can locate him.

Kyle is still back by the bathrooms. He's been waiting for Rylee. Two girls come out of the bathroom and are talking to each other. Kyle slips in behind them and he is in the woman's bathroom.

Troy comes back to the area that Kyle was standing at and Kyle is not there. Troy quickly sticks his head in the men's bathroom and doesn't see Kyle. He turns and heads towards the front door to help Bucky if needed.

The women's bathroom is simple. There is a large mirror with two sinks on the left and two enclosed stalls on the right.

Rylee is standing at the mirror refreshing her makeup. She sees Kyle in the mirror and turns. "Oh my God, what are you doing?"

Kyle walks up to her, takes her face in his hands and kisses her romantically. She kisses him back and wraps her arms around him.

Kyle pulls away. "I've wanted to do that all night."

Rylee smiles. "I'm glad you did."

They kiss again. Then Rylee pulls away. "My friends! What if they come in here?"

Kyle looks around quickly. He sees the stalls are empty. He grabs Rylee's hand. "Come on."

They go into a stall and lock the door behind them.

Kyle looks deep into Rylee's eyes. "Kiss me."

Kyle and Rylee kiss very passionately.

Outside Tap Works the two groups of guys have gathered. The local guy is on one side with his two friends behind him and Bucky is on the other with Nader and Troy behind him. They are in the field next to Tap Works. The field is a combination of grass, weeds and dirt. You can see where cars have been driving through making somewhat of a path.

"Anytime you are ready flyboy," said the local guy.

"Let's go faggot," said Bucky."

They dance around a bit while Bucky sizes up the guy. He throws a few jabs hitting the guy around the eyes. It makes his eyes start watering. Bucky sees the guy is in trouble and throws a haymaker that lands squarely on the guy's nose. Blood goes flying and the guy is knocked back on his ass. His buddies help him up.

"You want more?" asked Bucky.

The local guy's buddies start to cheer him on. "Kick his ass!"
Bucky invites him. "Well come on!"

The local guy comes at Bucky and swings. Bucky throws quick combinations of lefts and rights and the guy is back on his ass. His buddies start to move towards Bucky but they see Bucky is ready for them. Troy and Nader have also stepped up at this point.

"You guys don't want any of this," said Bucky. "Take that old fart out of here and if I see him again tonight, I'm going to finish him, and the rest of you!"

The local's friends don't want anything to do with Bucky. "Ok-ok."

They lean down to see if their friend is ok. He has blood running out of his nose and mouth.

"Help me up!" said the local guy.

His buddies help him up. It looks like he is not finished.

"Come on, I'm not finished with you," said the local guy.

Bucky shakes his head. "I warned you."

The local guy comes at Bucky. He is unsteady on his feet. Bucky flicks a jab at the guy and follows it with a devastating body bunch. The local guy has the wind knocked out of him and is bent over in pain. Bucky cocks up a right to finish him off but that is too easy. He wants to teach this guy a lesson. To Bucky's left is a small mud puddle from yesterday's rain storm. Bucky picks the local guy up and slams him on his back in the mud puddle.

"Take that you stupid son of a bitch," said Bucky.

Now it's turned comical. Troy and Nader start laughing.

"I should go in there and get him a bar of soap," said Troy.

"How about a beer Bucky?" asked Nader.

Bucky turns to Troy and Nader. "Sounds good to me."

"What was that guy's problem?" asked Troy. "I can't believe he just elbowed you like that."

Bucky laughs. "Whatever it was, I just fixed it."

The guys turn and walk around the corner. Nader and Troy are patting Bucky on the back. The two local guys are trying to help their buddy up. He is having trouble standing.

Back in the woman's bathroom Kyle and Rylee are still kissing in the stall. They separate and Rylee seems worried.

"God you smell good," said Kyle

"My friends, they are probably looking for me," said Rylee.

"I want to see you again," said Kyle.

"When?" asked Rylee.

"It doesn't matter," said Kyle.

Rylee pulls a pen and piece of paper from her purse and hands it to Kyle. "Here, give me your number."

Kyle writes his phone number down. He hands it to Rylee. She puts it in her purse. "I'll call you soon."

"You are so beautiful," said Kyle.

Rylee grabs Kyle, gives him a kiss and then pulls away. She holds his face with her hands and stares at him as if to get a visual memory that will last until they meet again.

"Go!" said Kyle. "I'll wait in here for a minute so we don't go out together."

"Bye," said Rylee.

She kisses Kyle again and leaves. Kyle leans back against the stall wall and is totally in dreamland. Rylee walks out of the bathroom door and her two friends are right there.

"There you are. Are you ready to go?" asked her friends.

Rylee tries to act casual. Her heart is still racing. "Yea, sure."

They turn and are talking as they walk toward the front door. They disappear into the crowd.

Kyle finishes taking a piss. Two girls walk in and go to the mirror. They start talking. Kyle flushes, puts the seat down and comes out of the stall as if it is no big deal. Many of the clubs that Kyle frequents in New York City have co-ed bathrooms. He walks over to the sink. The girls are shocked and speechless.

"Ladies, how are you tonight?" asked Kyle.

Kyle turns on the water and rinses his hands. The girls don't know what to say. They are giggling and still taken aback that Kyle is in there. Kyle grabs a paper towel and dries his hands.

"Have a good one!" said Kyle.

Kyle walks to the door, throws the paper towel in the garbage and exits the bathroom. He walks through the crowd. Once he gets to where he can see the band he stops and watches them for a few seconds. Kyle walks back over to where the guys are sitting at the bar. Bucky, Troy, Nader, Mouse and Higa are still there. They are all drinking beer. Higa still seems to be in a trance but has a big smile on his face.

"Is there any beer left?" asked Kyle.

Nader pours him a beer from the pitcher.

"Where the hell have you been?" asked Troy.

"In the bathroom," said Kyle.

"I looked in there a few minutes ago and you weren't in there," said Troy.

Kyle takes a drink of his beer. "You looked in the wrong one."

It takes a second to register with Troy. "You were in the woman's bathroom…with her? Oh my God! Are you crazy?"

Kyle plays it off. "Yea. It's a lot nicer in there. They actually have doors on the stalls unlike the men's room."

The men's bathroom is much smaller. It only has one stall, one urinal and one small sink.

Troy laughs. "They still haven't fixed that door in the men's room since I ripped it off the hinges a few months ago."

"You just missed Bucky wax this guy's ass outside," said Nader.

"Who?" asked Kyle.

Bucky points to the empty stool next to him. "The asshole that was sitting here next to me."

"Are you serious?" asked Kyle.

Bucky smiles. "You don't see him sitting here anymore do you?"

"Are you good?" asked Kyle.

"It wasn't anything," said Bucky. "I tapped him around his eyes a few times and after that I knew he was all mine. I don't know why these guys always want to fuck with me."

"Stupid I guess," said Kyle. "Mouse, what happened to your girl?"

Mouse and the rest of the guys start to laugh. The band stops playing. They are finished for the night.

"What's so funny?" asked Kyle.

"She wanted him to take her to Denny's and eat," said Troy.

"But I didn't want to be seen in public with her," said Mouse.

"She wouldn't settle for a burrito or a hand full of Slim Jims from the 7-11?" asked Bucky.

They all laugh. The lights start to come on.

"Speaking of 7-11, I'm hungry," said Bucky.

"Anyone called Reese yet?" asked Kyle.

"Let's go outside. I'll do it from there," said Mouse. "It's still too noisy in here."

They all take a final drink, set their glasses on the bar and walk toward the front door.

CHAPTER 28

It's Monday morning and everyone survived the weekend. Kyle exits his room and heads for the door at the far end of the hallway. He passes the dayroom and sees Nader inside. He is getting ready to paint. He has his usual supplies with him. He also has a few things for repairing holes in the walls.

Kyle walks into the dayroom. "Back at it again I see."

Nader rolls his eyes. "Yea."

"Lucky you are in here," said Kyle. "It's raining like cats and dogs out there."

Kyle walks over to the window and opens the curtains. It is pouring. He turns back to Nader.

"Yea, I just talked to Bailey," said Nader. "He's back already. He said it rained all night and it was busy. He didn't get a lunch so they let him go a little early."

"Did he say what kind of work is out there?" asked Kyle.

Nader chuckles. "Yea, they left an engine change, a jack job, double locals of course and a few mission launch and recoveries."

"What's new? It sounds like another day at the office," said Kyle.

Nader picks up a paint brush. "Yea right...another day at the office."

"A least you have a roof over your head," said Kyle.

"I'm about tired of this bay orderly shit," said Nader.

"I wouldn't worry Nader," said Kyle. "Somewhere out there, there's gotta be a crew chief more fucked up than you are. Hell, look at CTK. They manage to stay fully staffed. Maybe one of those guys is a young Nader in training."

They both laugh.

"See you later," said Kyle.

"Yea. See you later," said Nader.

Kyle walks over to the door and leaves the dayroom. He walks down to the end of the hallway and opens the door. He looks out at the rain which seems to be coming down in buckets. He pulls the hood to his rain jacket over his head and takes off running for his car. The door closes behind him.

CHAPTER 29

It's Thursday. Kyle, Bucky and Troy are sitting in the dayroom. They have finished eating dinner and are having a few beers. It's not the normal party beers. It's more like the end of hard work week beers. They are drinking a six pack of long neck bottles. There are a few empty bottles on the table. The dayroom has been freshly painted, holes repaired and all of the pictures are back in their original places. Kyle's boots are sitting upside down on top of the air conditioner. He is trying to dry them out. Troy smells something funny but he can't put his finger on it.

"What a day huh?" asked Kyle.

"No shit," said Troy. "And that rain didn't help anything yesterday."

"Yea, my boots are still wet," said Kyle. "I've been trying to dry them out since I got home."

"Who sprung for the bottles?" asked Troy.

"Bucky did," said Kyle.

Bucky takes a big swig of beer. "There's nothing better than a beer in a long neck bottle."

"What Bucky," said Troy. "Was it a tough week in the ISO hangar? Did the popcorn machine go out in the break room or something like that?"

Bucky sits up. "Funny thing you mentioned the break room and the popcorn machine. They had an awards ceremony today and this chick Cooper received a Commendation Medal."

"I remember her," said Troy. "They kicked her off the flightline because she was worthless."

"Well she found her calling in the ISO dock," said Bucky.

Kyle is curious. "What does she do there?"

Bucky starts to laugh. "As far as I can tell she bangs one of the dock chiefs and runs the snack bar."

Troy can't believe what he's hearing. "Oh my God. Are you serious?"

"Serious as a heart attack," said Bucky. "I wouldn't bull shit you guys."

"I don't know her. Is she hot?" asked Kyle.

"She's ok," said Bucky.

"On a scale from one to ten?" asked Kyle.

"I'd say a five or six," said Bucky.

"Yea, that sounds about right," said Troy.

"Yea, that's bull shit," said Kyle. "I can see her deserving the medal if she was a nine or a ten, but a five or a six, no way."

They all laugh.

Kyle continues. "Now if she was TDY that would add three points onto her status and make her and eight or a nine."

"What is it about a deployment or a tent that makes a female look so much better?" asked Troy.

All the guys sit quietly for a few seconds and think to themselves.

Bucky breaks the silence. "What are we going to do this weekend?"

"I'm working tomorrow morning but I'm off Saturday and Sunday," said Kyle. "I'm up for anything."

"There is a softball tournament on Saturday here on base," said Bucky. "The squadron is entering a team. You want to play in that?"

"Hell no!" said Kyle. "I'm tired of busting my ass out there. No one can catch a ball, and if he does, he can't throw it to the next guy. Why waste a weekend on that?"

"The weather has cleared up, how about the beach? Hey, do you guys smell something odd?" asked Troy.

"My boots?" asked Kyle.

"Nader just painted this room this week," said Bucky.

Troy can't figure it out. "No, neither one of those."

"The beach sounds good," said Kyle. "Where do you guys want to go?"

"Ocean City!" said Bucky.

Kyle starts to laugh. "The last time we were down there you shit yourself."

"What?" said Troy. "You really shit yourself?"

"His fart-shit separator was inoperative," said Kyle.

"Yea, remember last year we were in that bar and I disappeared for a bit," said Bucky. "I came back and you guys were all on my ass about where I'd been."

"Yea," said Troy.

"Well I was laughing so hard I shit myself," said Bucky. "I went out into the parking lot and took my skivvies off, wiped my ass with them and chucked them right there."

"Why didn't you go into the bathroom?" asked Troy.

Bucky starts to laugh. "It was too crowded. I had to take my shoes and my pants off."

They all laugh.

"You never heard about that?" asked Kyle. "That was some funny shit. I don't like Ocean City. It's too big and to spread out for a beach town."

"Well then what about Rehoboth?" asked Bucky.

"Too many fags," said Troy.

Kyle starts to laugh at Troy. "You mean you are offended when you are walking down the boardwalk with a family on one side of you and a guy wearing daisy dukes and combat boots on the other?"

Bucky joins in. "He's offended by the family."

They all laugh.

"Oh stop it," said Troy. "What about Dewey?"

Bucky points at Troy. "Good call there! There are five or six bars all within walking distance."

"There's Chicken Ed's and Grotto's Pizza if we get hungry," said Kyle.

Troy smirks. "And no guys are wearing daisy dukes."

They all laugh.

Kyle starts to tell a story. "I remember the last time I was down there. It was last year at the end of summer. I got all drunk and couldn't drive back. So I remembered this woman I had met at the beginning of the summer. She had a house there. It wasn't all hers, there were like 50 of them from the DC area that were renting it for the summer. All the bedroom floors were covered with mattresses."

"Where were we?" asked Troy.

"I don't know," said Kyle. "I was there by myself for some reason."

"So was she there?" asked Bucky.

Kyle takes a drink of beer and continues. "I went to the house and it looked pretty quiet. I didn't want to wake anyone up so I just crashed on a lawn chair on the front porch. In the morning this guy wakes me up. We start talking and he informs me that he has been renting the house for the past week and it's only him and his family staying there."

"Are you serious?" asked Troy.

"Yea," said Kyle. "What really convinced me was his wife and young kids standing at the door looking at me like I was crazy."

"Oh my God!" said Troy.

"So what did you do?" asked Bucky.

"I got up, apologized, walked to my car and drove back to the base," said Kyle.

"Holy shit," said Troy.

They all start laughing. Kyle finishes his beer and sets the empty bottle on the table. He gets up to check his boots and see if they are dry. He passes by Troy. Troy gets a whiff of that smell that's been bugging him.

"There it is again," said Troy.

"What?" asked Bucky.

"That smell," said Troy. "It's like…woman's perfume?"

Kyle picks up a boot and sticks his hand in it. It is still damp. He puts it back on the air conditioner. "Oh, that's my watch."

"Your watch?" asked Troy.

Kyle walks back and sits down. "Yea, the perfume that Rylee wears drives me crazy. It's Lancome Magie Noire. She told me the name and I went down to the mall, found a sampler and sprayed it on my watch band."

"What for?" asked Troy.

"So every now and then I get a whiff of it and I think of her," said Kyle.

Troy shakes his head. "You crazy son of a bitch."

"So what's the verdict my friends?" asked Bucky. "Is it Dewey on Saturday?"

"Let's do it," said Kyle.

"Kyle, will you need of a kitchen pass to go?" asked Troy.

Kyle smiles. "Not yet, but hopefully in the near future."

Bucky sits up, slaps his hands together and rubs them. "Dewey it is!"

Bucky sticks his fingers in three of the empty bottles on the table. He picks them up and starts tapping them together. The bottles make a clinking noise. He is imitating the scene from *The Warriors*. Bucky keeps playing the part but modifies the words. "Beautiful ladies, come out to play-ay. Beautiful ladies, come out to play-ay!"

They all laugh.

----------The End----------

Kyle Mansfield

Keith Myers

ABOUT THE AUTHOR

Keith Myers started his career as a "431XX" crew chief at Dover Air Force Base. The majority of his career was spent working on or in conjunction with C-5s. He was also a crew chief on C-141s and C-17s. Twenty of his twenty four years were spent on the flightline. He deployed to over 120 locations around the world. He retired from the Air Force in 2011 from Rota Naval Station, Spain.

Keith currently splits most of his time between Hawaii and Spain (ironically using space-A). You may find him surfing the waves in Waikiki or possibly spot him at Duke's Barefoot Bar. His time in Spain is spent with his son. The two like to follow their favorite soccer team FC Barcelona or attend an occasional bullfight.

Keith is currently working on his second book.

Made in the USA
San Bernardino, CA
12 March 2014